THE DANGEROUS BILLIONAIRE

JACKIE ASHENDEN

St. Martin's Paperbacks

This is a work of fiction. All of the characters, organizations, and events protrayed in this novel are either products of the author's imagination or are used fictitiously.

THE DANGEROUS BILLIONAIRE

Copyright © 2017 by Jackie Ashenden.
Excerpt from *The Wicked Billionaire* Copyright © 2017 by Jackie Ashenden.

For information address St. Martin's Press, 175 Fifth Avenue, New York, NY 10010.

ISBN: 978-1-250-12279-7

Our books may be purchased in bulk for promotional, educational, or business use. Please contact your local bookseller or the Macmillan Corporate and Premium Sales Department at 1-800-221-7945, ext. 5442, or by e-mail at MacmillanSpecialMarkets@macmillan.com.

Printed in the United States of America

St. Martin's Paperbacks edition / May 2017

St. Martin's Paperbacks are published by St. Martin's Press, 175 Fifth Avenue, New York, NY 10010.

10 9 8 7 6 5 4 3 2

To the person who picked this up and thought:
Billionaire Navy SEAL? HELL YEAH.
You're my people.

ACKNOWLEDGMENTS

To all the usual suspects – my editor, my agent, my family and my ladies. You guys rock.

CHAPTER ONE

Commander Sullivan "Van" Tate hated a lot of things about New York, but Leo's Alehouse in the East Village was not one of them. Most especially not after an afternoon spent scattering all that remained of his father from the Brooklyn Bridge.

Leo's had been serving military men for over a century and a half, and from the dark, smoke-stained, low-hanging ceiling to the walls covered in military photographs to the dusty, grimy wooden floor, it reeked of stale beer, sweat, decades-old cigarette smoke, and long nights spent getting absolutely shit-faced.

No, Van might have hated New York, but he fucking loved Leo's.

His father would have approved too. Noah Tate had never despised his Wyoming roots, no matter how rich an oil tycoon he'd become in the end, and his three foster sons holding a wake in his honor in a military dive bar would have appealed to the rebel in him.

Besides, where else were three Navy SEALs supposed to go to raise a glass to their father in this shitty city?

"Cocksuckers," Wolf muttered, glowering at the bunch of drunken marines currently propping up the bar. Van's youngest brother was built like a tank and moved like one too—he just rolled right over people who got in his way and if you were one of those people, then too bad. Wolf had had a boilermaker or four and was spoiling for a fight. Then again, Wolf was always spoiling for a fight. Drinking, fucking, and fighting were Wolf's three favorite pastimes and if he could combine all three, then he was in heaven.

Sadly for Wolf, the bar was full of men, which left him with only drinking and fighting, and since he'd taken their father's death pretty hard, he was jonesing for both.

Also sadly for him, Van wasn't having any of that shit, not when the media had been hounding them pretty solidly for the past week. The unexpected death of an oil billionaire was big news however you looked at it, especially when that death had occurred in "mysterious circumstances" if the press could be believed. Which they couldn't.

Van wasn't having any of that particular shit either. Their father's body had been found way up on the side of Shadow Peak, the mountain behind the Tate family's Wyoming ranch, with a broken neck. His horse had also been found nearby, which made it pretty clear to Van at least, and the local coroner, that the whole thing had been an accident. Nothing mysterious about it.

Still, the press loved a story and they loved the Tate brothers' story in particular. Van could see why: three orphaned boys adopted by an oil tycoon was the stuff of Hallmark fantasies, especially when all three boys were promptly sent into the military at the age of eighteen. And now their father had died? Well, interest was at an all-time high and, quite frankly, Wolf getting into a bar-room brawl and bringing down that media on their heads was the last thing Van wanted.

Van was the head of the Tate family now and getting all that shit on lockdown until the situation had been handled was his job.

"No," he said flatly to Wolf, meeting his little brother's gaze, making it clear he knew exactly what Wolf was thinking. "We're not here to fight. We're here to give Dad a send-off."

Wolf scowled. "Don't recall you being my commanding officer, bro."

Van gave him a grin that had only a little bit of teeth in it. "No, but I'm head of the goddamn family now and that makes me the next best thing."

"Here's what I think of that." Wolf tipped his chair back and raised his hand as if to run it through his dark Mohawk only to fold down all his fingers except the middle one.

"Expressive as always," Lucas murmured dryly. "You have such a way with words, Wolf. I'm impressed."

Lucas, Van's middle brother, was a sniper and one of the most controlled people Van had ever met—which, considering he included himself in that statement, was saying something. Lucas was the very definition of patience, but even he didn't have much of it when it came to Wolf's particular method of dealing with his emotions, not when Lucas preferred to have no emotions at all—which was okay with Van because it meant he had one less person to worry about.

"Yeah and fuck you too." Wolf gave Lucas a belligerent look, baring his teeth in a grin that was just a hair short of feral.

"Lock it down," Van said flatly, injecting all his authority—which was considerable—into the order. "Or do you really want the world's media watching you beat up a couple of jarheads?"

Wolf glowered at him for a long moment, his weird eyes—one blue, one green—full of banked aggression. Then he glanced sourly back at the Marines for another moment before letting out an explosive breath, his chair landing on all four legs with a thump. "Fuck it. I'll go get laid instead."

Thank Christ for that. The last thing they all needed

was Wolf going apeshit in a bar. Especially after a mother of a day like today.

Standing on the Brooklyn Bridge in the rain, emptying Noah Tate's ashes into the East River, the icy rain soaking their dress blues, hadn't been physically demanding—that shit they all had no problem with. It was the emotional toll that was the issue—especially for Wolf, who'd been closest of all to their dad.

Noah Tate had been the man who'd given them a proper home, the first that any of them had ever had. He hadn't been a particularly loving father, at least not to Van, but he *had* been a father to them. And even if what he'd wanted from Van had been more than Van had ever been able to give, his death had been a blow that none of them had seen coming.

Wolf's expression cleared and he grinned in one of his usual quicksilver changes of mood. "Hey, we could take the jet to Vegas. Go play some poker, spend a little quality time with the ladies. Shit like that." He raised his beer and took a swallow. "Fuck knows I could do with some shore leave before I go back to Virginia."

Lucas shook his head. "I'll pass. I've got a few things I need to do in New York."

Wolf raised his eyebrows in sudden interest. "What things?"

"None of your damn business, asshole," Lucas said pleasantly.

Van eyed him. His middle brother had been a cagey bastard since they'd all arrived back at the Tate ranch two weeks ago to prepare for their father's funeral. Van had tried to find out what was going on with him, but it had been like trying to open an oyster with a piece of wet spaghetti—pointless.

Then again, maybe it was the falling back into his old role as big brother and protector that was the pointless thing. None of them were boys anymore. They were fucking SEALs and each had been in the military for over ten years. No one needed protecting, not these days.

Still, Van had always been the one who'd looked out for the other two ever since they'd all been in the St. Mary's Home for Boys together, and old habits died hard.

"Got anything you want to tell us?" Van gave Lucas a meaningful look. "Or rather *me*. Ignore the little bastard in the corner."

"Fuck you," Wolf muttered, offended.

"No." Lucas's silver-blue eyes gave Van back absolutely nothing.

Irritated, Van put his beer on the table with a thump. He couldn't make his brother tell him anything if the guy didn't want to, but that didn't make Van any less pissed. Especially not with that damn envelope burning a hole in the pocket of his jacket.

His father's lawyer had handed it to him just before he'd stepped on the plane to New York, after the funeral, and then turned around and walked away without any kind of explanation. It was only when Van had opened it as the plane climbed into the sky that he'd realized what it was.

The last will and testament of Noah Tate.

And that wasn't all. There were three more envelopes inside, each one addressed to one of Noah's sons.

Van hadn't given those envelopes out yet and he hadn't read the one addressed to him either. He was still trying to get his head around the fact that his father had left the entirety of his massive fortune to Van, including the huge oil and gas empire he'd founded.

He'd had to read the damn thing three times before it sunk in and then, once it had, he'd spent the remainder of the flight trying to master his towering rage, because yet again—as he always seemed to do—his goddamn father had managed to get in the last word.

Ever since his father had adopted him at the age of eight, Noah had been very clear what Van's purpose was, what the purpose of *all* the boys were: they were to protect the Tate legacy.

Van, as the oldest, had been earmarked as Noah's heir, and for years, that's all Van wanted to be. He wanted to work hard, show the old man how grateful he was for everything Noah had given him. Be the kind of son Noah would be proud of.

Then Columbia had happened. On a mission to smash a sex-trafficking ring, he'd fucked up, lost a woman he was supposed to protect, and suddenly being Noah's heir hadn't looked so shit hot after all. What was money compared to woman's life? Compared to *all* the lives he could save as a SEAL that he couldn't save as some dick in a suit?

So he'd stayed with the SEALs instead of joining Noah at the helm of Tate Oil, something that had pissed Noah off no end, and something they'd argued endlessly and bitterly about.

Now, though, it was Noah getting his own back and Van's turn to be pissed off. And the worst part was, there was nothing he could do about it.

He hated the damn city. Hated the suits and the fucking skyscrapers. And he hated being stuck behind a desk, no matter that said desk was in a corner office in a historic old building that housed Tate Oil and Gas in Downtown Manhattan.

He preferred the military. Loved the danger and the thrill of armed service, the comradeship and the loyalty of his team. He was a protector at heart, and protecting people in general and his country in particular were more important to him than protecting the Tate bank account.

Apparently his father hadn't agreed.

Yeah, even though a day had passed since Jeffrey Taylor, the lawyer, had handed Van the will, Van was still as furious about it as he had been on the plane. So furious in fact that he'd been tempted to drop-kick Noah Tate's urn into the East River instead of reverently scattering the ashes.

"Problem?" One of Lucas's dark blond brows rose.

Shit. Van was pretty good at keeping his emotions hidden—as a commander he had to—but the fact that Lucas had picked up on his anger meant he wasn't keeping it quite as under control as he thought. Always a worry.

Then again, being almost preternaturally observant was what made Lucas one of the best snipers in the forces, so maybe it was just his brother being a giant pain in the ass.

"No," Van said, mimicking Lucas's earlier flat denial. "But no one's going anywhere or making decisions about anything until we finish dealing with stuff in New York."

"Seriously?" Wolf was back to glowering. "You two can do whatever the hell you want with the rest of your leave, but if we're not going to Vegas then I'm catching the next flight back to base."

This was unsurprising. Joining the Navy had been all Wolf had wanted to do since he'd watched his older brothers enlist and he didn't have many interests outside it. Unfortunately for him, now that their father was dead, things had changed.

Van gave Wolf a hard look, the look that had always had the men of his team shitting themselves whenever it was directed at them. "You're not going anywhere. Not today." Van shifted his gaze to Lucas. "That includes you too."

Wolf gave a short laugh. "Christ, you're so fucking full of it. Who died and made you God?"

"Dad, apparently," Van said, deadpan.

Lucas ignored this, his icy gaze focused and intent as a laser. "For once I agree with the little bastard. We're not your men, Van. We're your brothers. Which means, with respect, that you can go to hell."

Van didn't even flinch. He stared down harder men than Lucas every damn day and he wasn't about to put up with insubordination. Especially given that they now had other responsibilities. Because it wasn't only him who'd been named in their father's will.

"Yeah," Van said, staring hard at both Wolf and Lucas. "You *are* my brothers. And just because Dad's dead, it doesn't mean we stop being Tates. We're a team, and you know what that means."

"Jesus," Wolf muttered. "Next you'll be telling us we even have a mission."

"We do." Van reached into the pocket of his jacket, brought out the envelope and slapped it down on the table in front of them.

He'd debated about when was the best time to deliver the happy news to his brothers. Looked like that time was now.

"What the fuck is that?" Wolf demanded. "A lottery ticket? Hate to break it to you, Van, but we kind of don't need lottery tickets."

Lucas narrowed his gaze at Van for a long moment. Then he glanced down at the envelope. "Quiet, Wolf," he murmured, reaching out to pick it up and open it. "Little boys should be seen and not heard."

Wolf muttered something incomprehensible and very rude, but Lucas ignored him, sliding out the paper inside the envelope and unfolding it.

Van said nothing. The shit was about to hit the fan any second . . . *now*.

"Jesus Christ." Lucas looked up abruptly from the letter and met Van's gaze. "That old prick."

"Yeah," Van agreed. "That was pretty much my response too."

"What?" Wolf snapped.

Lucas handed him the paper. "Dad's will. Looks like no one is going to Vegas any time soon."

Wolf scowled and took the letter. As he began to read, his rough-hewn features hardened. "This is bullshit," he said eventually, looking up from the letter, his unusual eyes glittering. "This is just fucking bullshit."

Not an unexpected response from his brother, it had to be said.

Van lifted a shoulder. "It is what it is."

"No, *fuck* that." Wolf slapped the letter down on the table. "I mean, is it even legal?"

"Of course. Jeffrey Taylor gave it to me."

Wolf glowered. "Who the fuck is Jeffrey Taylor?"

"Dad's lawyer." Van tightened his grip on his patience. "Old-school New York firm, the best of the best. Jeffrey drew up the will himself, so it's as watertight as they come." Of course, Van *could* get it checked out by another firm, which he'd considered on the flight to New York but then discarded the idea. Noah had been very particular about his legal dealings, and since Taylor and Associates had been handling his business since he'd first started in the oil industry, Van was pretty certain it would all be totally legit.

"I don't care how watertight it is." Wolf sat back in his chair and folded his arms across his massively muscled chest, dark eyebrows pulling down. "I'm not sitting on any board of fucking directors."

Van knew how Wolf felt. He didn't want to sit on the board of fucking directors either. He didn't want to be his old man's heir. What he wanted was to lead his team in defense of his country, to protect civilians caught in the line of fire, something a thousand times more important than the petty concerns of the goddamn oil industry.

However, the will was clear. Noah wanted his three sons on the board to look after the Tate legacy, and Van found he couldn't dismiss that however much it interfered with his own interests. This was their purpose. The whole reason Noah had adopted them in the first place, and they

owed him. He'd brought them all up to put family first, and
no matter how distant and fraught Van's relationship with
Noah had become, Van had always been the example the
others had followed. He'd always been the leader. He
couldn't shirk that responsibility now, no matter his personal opinions.

"Yeah, well, I don't want to be on the board of fucking
directors either," he said flatly, giving voice to his thoughts.
"But like it or not, that's the situation. We're Tates and we
stick together."

Wolf's jaw was tight with denial. He glanced at Lucas.
"What about you? You okay with this shit?"

Lucas leaned forward, his elbows on the table. "No," he
said slowly, his unsettlingly intense gaze focusing on Van.
"No, I am not okay with it."

So they wanted to get into a pissing contest? Fine. He'd
play. He'd always been better at it than these two cocksuckers.

He stared back at Lucas, hard. "I'm sorry," he murmured, before switching to stare at Wolf, "I thought you
guys were supposed to be SEALs. Guess not."

"You prick—" Wolf began hotly.

But Van didn't let him finish. "Our father is dead. The
man who took us from that shitty boys home and gave us
the lives we have now. The man who gave us everything."
He kept his voice quiet but with enough of an edge to show
the other two he meant business. "And now he's asking for
something from us, you're whining about it?"

Wolf's mouth went tight again, a muscle leaping in the
side of his jaw, while Lucas's pretty-boy features were absolutely expressionless. Neither spoke, which was good. It
meant they got what Van was saying.

"So," he went on, "here's what we're going to do. No, we
don't like it, but we're fucking SEALs and so we're going

to step up. We're going to do what Dad has asked us to do and we're going to do it with maximum effort. Got it?"

Silence.

Van gave a curt nod as he reached into the pocket of his jacket and extracted the three individually addressed envelopes that had accompanied the will.

As good a time as any to see what other bombshells their father had in store for them.

He put them down on the table so the others could see their names written on the fronts.

"What the hell are these?" Wolf growled.

"These were with the will," Van explained, picking up the envelope addressed to him. "I don't know what's inside. I haven't looked at mine yet. I figured we should all do this together." And part of him still didn't want to, if he was honest with himself.

Christ, if that will had been a grenade, he was certain these envelopes contained enough plastic explosive to level a city.

For a second none of them said anything, all of them looking at the envelopes as if they were IEDs ready to go off at the slightest touch.

"Fuck this," Wolf muttered, grabbing his, ripping it open, unfolding the paper inside. Then he went absolutely white.

Van frowned, unease turning over inside him. "What's up?"

His brother looked up, glancing first at him then Lucas, his eyes brilliant spots of sapphire and emerald. Then quite suddenly he stood, shoving his chair back so hard it hit the wall behind him, the expression on his face full of savagely suppressed emotion.

"Wolf?" Van's unease tightened further. "What the fuck is the problem?"

But Wolf didn't answer. Instead he turned without a word and shouldered his way out of the bar.

Van half-rose to go after him, but Lucas said quietly, "Let him go."

Cursing under his breath, yet knowing his brother was right, Van sat back down in his seat. Wolf had always needed time to cool off when he was pissed, except Van didn't think Wolf had been angry. More like . . . shocked or even devastated.

"You have any idea what that was about?" he asked, looking at Lucas.

His brother shrugged. "No. Doesn't make me want to open *my* fucking envelope though."

No shit.

Van shoved the envelope addressed to Lucas in his brother's direction. "You first."

Lucas eyed him. "Who was talking about us being SEALs again? Oh yes, that was you."

Ah, Christ.

"Then I guess *I'll* fucking open it," Van growled, reaching for his own envelope.

But Lucas had already picked his up and had torn it open, sliding out the piece of paper and looking down at it. There was no discernible change in his expression. A moment later, he folded up the paper into small squares and then, in a series of small, precise movements, he calmly ripped those squares into tiny little pieces.

Holy shit.

Van stared at him. "Good news then?"

Lucas's eyes had gone very gray, the blue leeched from them and glittering with ice. "You can count me in as a director. And if Wolf's letter was along the same lines as mine, you can count him in too."

The unease already churning in Van's gut got deeper, wider. "You going to tell me what Dad wrote?"

"Open your envelope, then ask me that question again."

"That good, huh?"

Lucas said nothing, just stared at him. There was a tension around his brother now, a tension that hadn't been there before, a kind of brittle edge. As if all it would take was a tap and he'd shatter.

Van gritted his teeth and looked down at the letter in his hands for a long moment. Finally, he ripped it open.

Sullivan, his father had written, *I don't trust anyone with this information but you. There's something I want you to do for me, something you must not tell anyone else about. It's about Chloe . . .*

CHAPTER TWO

Chloe Tate peered out the window of the jet as it slowly came to a stop, but since it was nighttime and raining, all she could make out were the blurry lights of the hangar they were drawing up to.

She hadn't seen much as they'd come in to land either, which was a bit of a disappointment. She'd been hoping for at least a glimpse of the famous Manhattan skyline, but there had been too much low cloud cover, so she'd seen absolutely nothing.

It didn't matter. It wasn't as if she was here for sightseeing.

She was here to meet with her oldest foster brother, Sullivan Tate.

His email demanding her presence couldn't have come at a worse time, not with the new stable complex in the process of being constructed and needing her direct oversight. And definitely *not* while she was still trying to deal with her grief at her father's untimely and sudden death.

Chloe swallowed past the sudden thickness in her throat. No, she couldn't allow herself to think about her father. The grief was still too raw and she wasn't ready to face that, not now, not when she had so many other things she had to handle.

Such as finding out, in the funeral's numb aftermath,

And if he didn't give it to her? Well then. She'd have no choice but to start legal proceedings to contest the will.

It wasn't a path she wanted to take, but she would if she had to. Her father had given her total control of the ranch, had made it her responsibility, and she was used to managing it on her own, answerable to no one. It was hers. And she wasn't going to stand for anyone else telling her what to do with it.

A gust of frigid swirled suddenly around her.

Okay, looked like it was time to go.

Chloe got to her feet, slinging her bag over her shoulder and gritting her teeth against a sudden wave of unexpected reluctance to leave the warm cocoon of the Tate corporate jet.

Making herself move over to the door of the plane, she stood there a moment, checking the darkness outside, the wind catching her hair and blowing it around her face, icy pellets of rain striking her skin.

There was a gigantic man standing on the tarmac waiting for her.

Chloe swallowed, shoving down another sudden spike of nervousness so it wouldn't show.

The lights from the hangar were behind him, shadowing his face, his hands buried in the pockets of the long black coat he wore. He was motionless, in stark contrast to the way the wind took the hem of his coat, making it billow out behind him then wrap around his calves.

There was something dangerous about his stillness. Something menacing. And it wasn't just the fact that he seemed to be about seven feet tall and built like Superman. It was the kind of stillness that reminded her of the cougars she'd seen sometimes in the hills behind the ranch. The kind of stillness before they pounced.

Don't be stupid. You know who this is.

Of course she did. It was the man she'd come here to meet, her oldest foster brother, Sullivan.

Not that she'd ever thought of him as a brother. He was ten years older than her and had been sent to boarding school when she was all of two and then joined the Navy when she was eight. So apart from brief visits during school vacations and when he'd been on leave, they hadn't exactly been brought up together.

A gust of wind brought more stinging rain with it and she shook herself, gripping the icy rails of the steps and starting down them. The rain and the cold didn't bother her so much—winters in Wyoming weren't any worse than this— but for some reason meeting Sullivan was getting to her.

Nothing to do with that massive crush you had on him back when you were sixteen and the fact that you're pissed with him about the whole "not visiting" thing. Nope, nothing to do with that at all.

No, of course it wasn't. That crush was old news and one she'd gotten over years ago by the simple expedient of having an affair with Jason, one of the ranch hands. And as for him not visiting, well, she'd been so busy with the ranch she'd barely thought about him.

Stopping at the bottom of the steps, Chloe pushed her freezing hands into the pockets of her old and worn leather jacket, curling her cold fingers into her palms. Then she walked slowly toward the tall figure standing on the tarmac, a long black car waiting beside him. His stillness was unnerving and with that annoying light behind him, she still couldn't see his features.

Squinting against the rain and the wind tangling her hair, she eventually pulled her hand out of her pocket and pushed her hair back, wiping away the rain and shading her eyes. "Sullivan?"

At that moment one of the plane's lights flickered, illuminating his face for a second. High forehead. Carved cheekbones. A strong jaw, dark with black stubble. A wide mouth, set in a hard line. Hazel eyes, the color striking against thick, inky lashes.

Something kicked hard in Chloe's chest, which was a ridiculous reaction considering she'd seen him at her father's funeral only a couple of weeks earlier. Then again, that funeral and those subsequent weeks had been a bit of a grief-soaked blur, so maybe her reaction wasn't so surprising after all.

"Hey, pretty," Sullivan said, his voice deep and dark as the night around them.

And a sudden burst of memory hit her.

He'd been seventeen, all shaggy black hair and long lean muscle, and those hazel eyes, the color caught somewhere between a brown so light it was nearly gold, and green, like the light on a pond in the deep forest. He'd taught her to ride her first pony, lifting her up on the saddle with his big hands, so patient, making her want to do her very best to impress him.

No, he'd never felt like a brother to her, not when he was so much older. He'd been more like a teacher she idolized, or like her dad, a distant, awe-inspiring figure, coming into her life for brief moments at a time and then leaving again. He'd taught her to ride; how to take care of the tack; how to groom her horse and muck out the stable; how to feed her favorite pony an apple, holding her hand flat so the big soft lips of the animal could scoop it off her palm.

"Pretty" . . .

The day he'd left to join the Navy, he'd crouched down beside her and ruffled her hair. "Bye, pretty. I'll see you 'round." And then he was gone, taking his warmth with him, making her feel as if winter had come early.

So you idolized him once. So what? He hasn't visited in eight years and now he owns the ranch, and getting it back is all that matters.

There was a weird tension in her gut, but she ignored it, focusing on her anger instead. "Hi," she said, using the brisk tone she adopted whenever she gave instructions to the ranch hands. "I gather you needed to see me urgently."

"I did." He was silent for a long second, and she had the sense that he was studying her the way she'd been studying him. "You okay?"

Strange question. "Yes, of course." She stood a little straighter, ignoring that odd tension crawling between her shoulder blades. If she'd been at home she might have put it down to that feeling of having a cougar watching her. Except there were no cougars in New York.

But there are predators. And he's one of them.

A shiver that had nothing to do with the rain passed over her skin.

No, that was stupid. Sullivan wasn't a predator and he wasn't dangerous. She was being an idiot.

An awkward silence fell, which he made no move to break.

So, was her answer not what he'd expected? What did he mean by 'Are you okay?' anyway?

Chloe lifted her chin. "Did you expect me not to be?"

He didn't move, seemingly impervious to the wind and rain. "I wasn't sure." The light had gone, his face falling into shadow once again. "I didn't get much of a chance to talk to you at the funeral."

The grief she'd been shoving aside clenched tightly behind her breastbone, but she ignored that too. She wasn't going to have a conversation about it now, not out here in the rain on the tarmac with a man she hadn't seen in eight years, a man who was now in possession of the only thing that meant anything her.

"Well, I'm fine." She tried hard to make it sound like she was.

THE DANGEROUS BILLIONAIRE 21

Another silence, his head tilting as if studying her.

Irritated, Chloe let out a breath. "I presume you want to discuss the will. I mean, that's the whole reason I'm here, right?"

"Yeah," he said after another moment. "But let's get you out of the rain first." Abruptly he turned and reached out, pulling open the car door. "You'd better get in. I'll get your bags."

Chloe lifted the shoulder that had the bag slung over it. "This is all I bought with me."

He paused. "Seriously? One bag?"

"I don't need much." She'd never been a clothes kind of girl, had never needed to be, out on the ranch. A couple of pairs of underwear, jeans, a sweater or two, toothbrush and comb, and she was good to go. Did she need anything more than that?

Except his long silence indicated surprise, making heat climb into her cheeks. Though why she should feel embarrassed by her lack of luggage, she had no idea. Okay so, this was the first time she'd actually been out of state, but so what? She'd been busy with the ranch. She had no time for travel.

"I'm not going to be here long anyway," she said, not sure why she felt the need to justify herself and annoyed that she was doing so. "I only want to discuss the will, then go back home. Besides, you didn't say how long—"

"It's fine," he interrupted, his deep voice curt. "Come on, get in the car. You're getting wet."

The irritation inside her needled, even though it was true—she *was* getting wet. It had been a long time since anyone had told her what to do, and she didn't appreciate it. Good God, it wasn't as if she was ten anymore.

"I don't care about the rain," she said tartly. "Unless you do."

The lights of the plane behind her flickered once more,

passing over his face, making that strange feeling kick in her chest again.

She'd been sixteen, and Wolf—the last of her foster brothers to leave—had been gone three years already. The ranch had been quiet. Since she'd gotten older, her father only visited sporadically from his New York base, so when Sullivan had arrived for a week's leave, she'd been thrilled.

Then she'd seen him out by the stables, crouching down by one of the horses, its front hoof held in one of his big hands as he cleaned something out of its shoe. He hadn't been wearing a shirt, and the sun gleamed on his tanned skin, outlining the strongly muscled lines of his back and shoulders. Then he'd straightened, one hand absently stroking down the horse's neck, and in one smooth movement, he'd swung himself up into the saddle.

She hadn't been able to stop staring at him. At the shift and flex of his muscles. At the dark ink of an eagle and a trident tattooed across his chest. There was another tattoo curling around his right upper arm too, with what looked like a skeletal frog in the middle of the design.

The sight had made her feel restless and hot, and it had taken her a good week and a half to figure out exactly what that feeling was.

Desire.

She did not want to feel it again.

Sullivan's eyes gleamed as the light hit them, more gold than green, and one corner of his mouth turned up, the hard planes and angles of his face relaxing a fraction. "No," he said, a note in his voice she didn't understand. "You don't, do you? I remember."

She stared at him. Hell, was he talking about that particular memory? Oh, God, she hoped not. She'd worked very hard to hide her crush from him and even now the thought of him knowing made her feel embarrassed.

"Remember?" she asked warily. "Remember what?"

"The day I first put you on a pony. It was raining and I told you we could do it another day if you wanted."

Relief shifted inside her. "Um . . . no."

"And you said that you didn't care about the rain. You just wanted to ride the pony."

How odd. She really *didn't* remember that.

It must have been obvious to him, because he gave a soft laugh, deep and rough, that made the feeling in her chest kick once again, for absolutely no reason that she could see. "Ignore me. It was years ago. Come on, let's get you home."

Chloe said nothing as Van pulled the featureless black sedan his father had apparently preferred to drive up to the curb. She had her head tilted back, staring up at the stately historic building they'd just parked outside, her eyes widening for a brief second in what looked like surprise.

Then, as if she knew he was staring at her, her expression abruptly changed, something more guarded taking its place.

Pretty much the same expression she'd been wearing the moment she'd stepped off the plane and had continued to wear the whole drive back from the private airfield where he'd picked her up.

Van turned off the engine and leaned back in his seat, staring at her.

He'd been expecting anger to be honest, especially considering how their father had cut her out of the will. But no, she'd merely given him that slightly suspicious, guarded look.

Very different from the eight-year-old he'd taught to ride. A small, narrow-shouldered kid, with long black hair and wide dark eyes. Who'd been shy of him at first, but then that had been understandable since he hadn't spent much in the way of time with her. He'd been so much older and away at school while she was growing up.

She'd gradually lost that shyness though, her face always lighting up to see him on his rare visits to the ranch. She had a beautiful smile. It used to illuminate her like a candle inside a lantern, and the way she reached out to him to grab his hand, pulling him along to the stables to "show him the horses" before he'd even set a foot inside the house, had slowly become one of the ways he knew he was home.

Once, just before leaving on his first deployment, she'd given him a rock, a "special one" she'd found on Shadow Peak, so that he'd have something of "home" to take with him.

He still had that damn rock, but the Chloe he remembered, that passionate, fierce, excited little kid, was long gone. And maybe, given the contents of his father's letter, that was a good thing.

He tilted his head, studying her.

He recognized parts of the child she'd once been—the long black hair in loose tangles down her back and her big dark eyes, thickly fringed with soot-black lashes. Back then her face had seemed too small for all that hair and those eyes, but now it had filled out, matured. Her features were delicate, pointed, with a lush, pouty mouth and an obstinate-looking chin. She had the most incredible skin too, clear and fine-grained, the remains of a summer tan in her cheeks and neck.

Beautiful. She was beautiful.

Something inside him tightened, something familiar. Something he was *not* going to think about or even examine right now. Or ever, in fact.

Chloe's head turned and she met his gaze, the lights outside the car highlighting the purity of her features. "This is Dad's house, right?" Her voice was light with a slightly smoky quality to it that he liked very much indeed.

"Yeah," he said. "You never saw pictures of it?"

"I did, but . . ." She turned back to look out the window again. "Being here is different."

Van studied her again, noting the duffel bag on her lap and the delicate fingers splayed protectively over it. There were scars on her skin, plus a few fresh scratches and scrapes, the marks of someone who worked with her hands. Which was expected, given she worked on the ranch.

It hit him with a weird jolt all of a sudden, that the shy, wide-eyed little girl he'd once taught to ride, was now this beautiful, self-possessed young woman. Who managed the Tate ranch single-handed and had in fact been doing so for the past couple of years.

He shifted in his seat, feeling restless for some reason. "Dad never brought you to New York?"

"No." She tilted her head back, peering up at the building again. "This is my first time out of state."

Van frowned. "Seriously? You've never been out of Wyoming?"

She gave him a brief irritated-looking glance from underneath thick black lashes. "Didn't you listen? Like I said, this is my first time out of state, which means no, I haven't been out of Wyoming."

There was the faintest edge of impatience in her voice, as if he'd asked her the stupidest question ever. Which, if he was honest, he kind of had.

Maybe it was the shock of seeing her again and how different she was.

"Why not?" he asked bluntly, a little irritated at her tone.

"I've never needed to. Anyway, I can't afford to be away from the ranch for too long. Plus, there would have been the usual protection issues and I didn't want to have to deal with bodyguards and all of that." Her gaze returned once more to the view out the window. "He used to tell me about

New York though, send me postcards, stuff like that. It sounded pretty cool . . ." She stopped, her fingers tightening on her bag, and he didn't miss the faint note of pain in her voice.

Of course. She must be grieving. Noah's death had happened only three weeks ago, barely any time at all.

She's not going to like what you have to tell her either.

Yeah, that was pretty much a definite. She was not going to like it *at all*.

Anger threaded through him, aimed squarely at the man who'd caused all of the current bullshit Van was now having to deal with.

Noah and his feud with his old friend turned bitter enemy, Cesare de Santis, a billionaire weapons manufacturer and the source of the threat that had been hanging over the Tate family for most of their lives.

A threat that could loom even larger now that Noah was dead.

It was one of the reasons Van had called Chloe to New York, and he had another, even larger, secret that he had no idea how he was going to tell her.

Except not right now, not in the car when she'd only just gotten here.

Van narrowed his gaze at her, searching her face for the signs of grief he'd heard in her voice. But there were none. Still, he wondered if he should offer her some words of comfort, even though he'd never been that type of man. Moral support and encouragement sure, but comfort definitely wasn't his thing. Then again, he hadn't seen her for eight years. What did he know about what she needed? So all he said was, "Are you sure you're okay?"

She stiffened, but didn't turn. "Yes."

The flat way she said the word was indication enough that she didn't want to talk. Fine, he wasn't going to push. He didn't particularly want to talk about Noah's death either.

Van reached for the keys and pulled them out of the ignition. "Come on. Let's go inside and I'll show you around."

Getting out of the car, he came around to the passenger side and opened her door. She stepped onto the sidewalk clutching her bag, that guarded look of hers dropping for a moment as she stared up at the old, turn-of-the-century limestone building.

It wasn't raining like it had been out at the airfield but the air was pretty frigid and he could see moisture on the ratty leather jacket she wore. One long, inky strand of hair was stuck wetly to her cheek and even though it didn't appear to bother her, she must be starting to feel the chill at least.

She was very small, very slender. As if a strong wind would blow her away.

An old protectiveness shifted in his chest, which was pretty damn annoying since feeling protective over vulnerable-looking women wasn't something he needed right now. Still, it had been years since Columbia. And it *was* cold. And apart from anything else, he had some shit to tell her that she wasn't going to be pleased about, especially not on top of all that will crap.

She needed to get inside and perhaps eat something too. He had no way of knowing how she'd deal with what he had to tell her, but sometimes things were easier to handle when you had food in your belly.

Anyway, hanging around outside was a bad idea. Especially given the reason he'd asked her to come to New York as soon as she could.

"Chloe"—he pitched his voice low—"the weather's too shitty to be standing around out here on the sidewalk. We need to get inside." Glancing down the street, he did a reflexive perimeter check to be on the safe side. Luckily, it seemed clear.

She blinked, her jaw taking on a determined slant once more. "Uh, sure."

Van pushed away any lingering protectiveness, headed up the steps to the front door, and unlocked it. The security in the Tate mansion was pretty good, but he was obviously going to have to get it upgraded now that Chloe was here.

Noah's letter had been very clear: the danger to her was real and imminent, and whatever Van's personal feelings were about having someone in his care again, there was a threat and he had to take it seriously.

In this instance, he took it very seriously indeed.

"So. Dad's will." Chloe's soft footsteps came up behind him as he pushed open the door. "We need to discuss what we're going to do about it."

"Uh-huh." Van gestured for her to go inside.

But she remained on the threshold, looking up at him, an intense expression burning in her dark eyes. "The ranch is mine, Sullivan."

Great. He really did *not* want to have *that* discussion right now either. Because he hadn't brought her here to talk about the will or the ranch, though he had words to say about both topics. He'd brought her here because Wyoming was no longer safe for her. Not that New York was any less safe, but at least New York had him. Had Lucas and Wolf too.

And that was another issue. He hadn't heard from either of his brothers since Leo's a whole five days ago. Neither of them had come back to the mansion, and Van had no idea where they'd gone. Whatever had been in their respective letters had obviously been pretty fucking serious, which was a worry. He'd sent them a number of texts, plus left messages on their voicemails, but all he'd gotten was silence.

Assholes.

If they didn't call in soon, he was going to have to go find them, which would *really* piss him off. Especially since they were due for a directors meeting at Tate Oil and Gas in a couple of days where they would deliver the happy news to the rest of the company that the Tate brothers were taking over and everyone's ass was fired.

Yeah, that he was *not* looking forward to.

"Go sit in the front room," he ordered, gesturing to the doorway on the right, irritation at his brothers creeping into his voice. "I need to talk to you about something."

Chloe bristled, her finely drawn black brows drawing down in an abrupt scowl. "Hey, watch your tone. I'm not a damn dog."

Van was used to taking control of a situation—he was a SEAL after all, and he was used to commanding his own team. He was also used to being obeyed without question, and that definitely included *not* being talked back to.

He opened his mouth to tell her exactly what he thought of *her* tone, then stopped himself at the last minute. Taking his annoyance at his brothers out on her wasn't a good idea, plus she wasn't one of his men. She wasn't a soldier. She also wasn't that little girl who used to light up with smiles whenever he returned to the ranch, who used to be so excited to see him. And she certainly *wasn't* a damn dog.

No, she was a woman now, grieving the loss of their father and who'd been given a bitter pill to swallow in the shape of ownership of the ranch.

A ranch that he was going to have to explain to her that he couldn't simply hand over. Which was not going to make her any happier.

Biting back the flat command he was used to issuing, he said instead, "Go sit down. *Please.* You need to get warm and you probably need some food too."

He'd kept only one of the quite frankly ridiculous number of staff his father had employed to run his household, and that was Linda, the housekeeper. He didn't even want to keep her—he could tidy up after himself and organize his own meals thank you very much—but given that he simply didn't have the time to keep such a large house maintained, he'd decided she might as well stay. With the proviso that she knocked off at five and didn't have to come in over the weekend.

Linda herself had been more than happy with this arrangement—especially seeing as how he was paying her exactly the same—and had cheerfully gone home at five that afternoon. Which meant that if he wanted food for Chloe, he was going to have to get it himself.

She made no move toward the sitting room, still scowling at him. "I don't need food. I ate on the plane."

"You don't have to eat it."

"Then what's the point making it?"

He gritted his teeth. Great, an argument about food was exactly what he needed right now—not. "Because I'm a gracious fucking host, that's why."

"I don't care what kind of host you are. I'm only here to sort out this will bullshit, then I'm leaving."

There was a defiant gleam in her eyes, which for no apparent reason sent a small electric thrill down the length of his spine.

Shit. Where the hell had that come from?

Not wanting to examine the feeling, Van shoved it away as he turned toward the kitchen. "Sit," he growled over his shoulder, not caring how it sounded this time. "I'm going to get some food. Then we'll talk."

CHAPTER THREE

Chloe glared at Sullivan's retreating back, his black over-coat swirling out behind him. Had he always been such an autocratic bastard? She couldn't remember. Perhaps he was simply grumpy. Or maybe he didn't want her here or something. Whatever, he was the one who'd demanded her presence in the first place, so it was weird of him to get pissy about it now that she was actually here.

Maybe getting snippy with him isn't the best idea?

Possibly not. Then again, she was used to running things, and being ordered around by some guy—no matter that he was older and some kind of super soldier—had never been high on her "shit she had to put up with" list.

Clearly he thought she was still ten years old.

So? Show him you're not.

Yeah, he could probably do with a lesson. Because one thing was for sure. She wasn't going to let him strong-arm her into accepting the status quo when it came to the ranch.

Filing that thought away, Chloe took a look around at her surroundings.

So she was here. Finally. New York. Her father's house.

He'd talked about the city a lot whenever he visited the ranch, telling her tales of soaring buildings and glittering lights. Green parks and crowds of people.

The day Sullivan had gone away to the Navy, she'd

asked her father whether she'd ever get to go away too, whether he'd ever bring her to visit New York the way he'd taken her foster brothers. At the time, he'd assured her he would—when she was older. But when she'd gotten older, things had changed. He'd kept promising he'd bring her, yet somehow there had always been a reason not to. The main reason being that the feud with Cesare de Santis, his old enemy, had gotten even more bitter and there was a real risk that de Santis would target her as Noah's only surviving flesh and blood.

She hadn't been happy about that, not one bit. She'd wanted all the things her brothers had had—trips to New York, a chance to see the world, boarding school, college. But her father had nixed all of them. "Your place is on the land," he'd told her. "The boys have their responsibilities. The ranch is yours."

Perhaps it should have made her angry that she'd been denied all those things. But she'd decided long ago that it was easier to accept the role her father had given her rather than fight it, especially when it had made him happy. And making him happy, making him proud, had been important to her. It wasn't a big sacrifice anyway, not when the land and the horses gave her so much joy.

Still, now that she was actually here in New York, she was kind of curious.

Taking a couple of steps into the middle of the long gallery, she looked around at the magnificence surrounding her.

The ranch house back in Wyoming was a massive, sprawling place, but it wasn't particularly fancy. Certainly it wasn't like this, with its gleaming parquet floor and a massive staircase with elegantly curving banisters. A huge painting of what looked like Shadow Peak covered one wall, while on a long console table beneath it were arranged various lamps, plus a few vases of white camellias.

Gold gleamed off various surfaces, as lights made to look like candle wall sconces gave off a warm glow and softened the white walls.

So this was Tate House. It was, she had to admit, amazing. Beautiful even.

Grief ached at the reminder of her father, a grief that was as much to do with anger as it was with loss. At yet another empty promise he'd made to her.

But no, she wasn't going to think about that now. She had to concentrate on what was important, and that was talking to Sullivan about the ranch. The rest of her feelings she could deal with later.

Chloe swallowed back the thickness in her throat and ignored the ache in her chest, glancing off to her right, to where the door to the sitting room was.

Okay, might as well go and sit down since there wasn't much else to do.

Going over to the door, she pulled it open and stepped inside.

The sitting room was as elegant as the gallery outside it, decorated in shades of white and cream. There was a sofa set before the fireplace, upholstered in white linen, with matching armchairs arranged beside it. A huge antique mirror was displayed above the white marble mantelpiece, reflecting the light from expensive-looking lamps positioned around the room plus the massive crystal chandelier that graced the vaulted, ornate ceiling. Art covered the walls—paintings by artists Chloe didn't recognize as well as a few artsy photographs. Along one wall were huge windows that looked out over the streets but were now covered with thick, white textured curtains.

It was all grace and elegance. However, on the coffee table in front of the couch were signs of Tate House's new occupant—an open pizza box with a single cold pizza slice in it, a couple of cans of beer, and, incongruously, what

34 JACKIE ASHENDEN

looked like a gun that had been taken apart, the pieces all
laid out carefully on a length of white cloth.

Ignoring the interesting-looking bits of metal for the
moment, Chloe moved over to the fireplace, dropping her
duffel bag beside the couch as she went, her attention caught
by the framed photographs sitting on the mantelpiece.
They were all of her father with various important-looking
people, including one of him with three men in uniform.

Noah Tate was a tall man and yet even he was dwarfed
by his three adopted sons, all of them six-two at the very
least. There was Wolf, the tallest, his uniform straining
over his massive shoulders and his different-colored eyes
vivid against his olive skin. Beside him was Lucas, his
heartbreakingly handsome features saved from complete
prettiness by the strength of his jaw and the icy gleam of
his silver-blue eyes. And Sullivan, about the same height
as Lucas, but not as pretty. His dark brows were straight,
his hazel gaze staring straight at the camera with more
than a hint of defiance. Noah was standing beside Sullivan,
his hands folded in front of him, his craggy features typi-
cally stern.

The thickness returned to Chloe's throat. He always
looked good, did Noah, holding his own against his handsome foster sons with a full head of silver hair and a proud
beak of a nose from some Roman ancestor. There was a dy-
namism to him, a charisma that had helped take him from
poor rancher to oil magnate within the space of thirty years.

He'd been an absent father. Hardly around while she
was growing up, leaving her mainly in the care of the ranch
housekeeper while he spent long periods in New York at
Tate Oil and Gas. But the rare times he visited, he'd always been attentive if emotionally distant toward her, and
once she'd started managing the ranch herself, he'd even
been openly approving.

Which made it so strange that he'd given the ranch to Sullivan.

Noah had told her it was her responsibility, had told her that it would pass to her, and certainly he'd known how much that place had meant to her, how much she loved it. And the obvious backtrack of that will made no sense.

She didn't care about his oil billions. She didn't give one single fuck about his company, or his power, or whatever else he'd had. It was the ranch that she wanted. The ranch that was everything to her. And he'd promised . . .

You know how much his promises are worth.

Chloe shoved that thought away, allowing herself a moment before taking a look at the other pictures sitting there. They weren't of anyone she recognized. And then another unexpected disappointment curled in her gut as she noticed something else.

There were no pictures of her. Not one. Not anywhere.

Weird. Did he not have any photos of her he liked? Or did he just not think of her while he was here? He had a photo of the boys, so why not of her?

Behind her came the click of the door, and she turned around sharply to find Sullivan had come back in. He was holding a plate with a sandwich on it in one hand and carrying what looked to be a glass of milk in the other. Kicking the door shut unceremoniously behind him, he walked to the coffee table and bent over it, pushing aside the pizza box and putting the plate and glass down. Then he straightened and looked at her. "Food," he announced. "Which you don't have to eat."

Chloe glanced down at the plate. It looked like . . . Holy crap. "Peanut butter and jelly? Really?" She lifted her attention back to him. "I'm not eight anymore, you know that, right?"

He was standing on the other side of the coffee table with

his arms folded, dark brows drawn down, a ferocious-looking expression on his strong face. With his shorn head, massive shoulders, and black overcoat, he looked like something lethal out of the Matrix. All he needed was sunglasses.

"I know how old you are." His voice was flat.

"That would be twenty-five," she reminded him, in case he actually didn't.

For some reason this only made his expression turn even more ferocious. "It's all I had in the fridge. Just eat it."

Chloe ignored him. "I'm not here to eat sandwiches. I'm here to talk about the ranch. About the fact that Dad left everything to you."

He stared silently at her a long moment then turned, shrugging out of the overcoat before throwing it carelessly over the back of the sofa. Underneath he wore a pair of worn dark blue jeans that sat low on his hips, plus a long-sleeved black T-shirt that pulled tight over his heavily mus-cled shoulders.

Flinging himself down in one of the armchairs, he leaned forward, his elbows on his knees, long, tanned fin-gers loosely linked between them. A big, powerful man, he made the chair he sat on look small and delicate.

That feeling that had kicked her at the airfield kicked again, making it difficult to tear her gaze away from him. Disturbed, she forced it down, crossing her arms over her chest.

"Well?" she demanded when he didn't speak. "You're going to give the ranch to me, aren't you?"

"You're wet." His deep voice hit a place inside her she wasn't quite comfortable with. "I hope you've got more than one change of clothes in that tiny bag."

Irritated, Chloe shifted on her feet. "I've got another pair of jeans, if that's what you're worried about."

"Two pairs of jeans? That's it?"

"Was I supposed to bring more?" She glared at him. "Are you going to keep on ignoring me or what?"

His jaw hardened. Noticeably.

Too bad. He might be used to calling the shots with other people, but that wasn't going to work with her. She hadn't left Wyoming and flown over half the country purely to sit on the couch, eat a sandwich, and passively listen to him tell her what to do like a good girl. She was here to get her ranch back and that's all.

She met his gaze, lifting her chin slightly, letting him know she wasn't up for any kind of male bullshit, while he stared back, his black brows drawn down, somehow looking even more dangerous than he had out on the airfield tarmac.

A strange, electric kind of jolt pulsed down her spine, a cautious part of her whispering that maybe challenging him like this wasn't such a great idea.

Chloe ignored the whisper. She managed a whole damn ranch and a bunch of male ranch hands, and she wasn't about to let her own idiot foster brother get the better of her no matter how dangerous he looked.

"Okay," Sullivan said after a long moment. "Have it your way. I didn't bring you here to talk about the ranch."

Surprise rippled through her. "What? But I thought—"

"You're here because you're in danger."

Chloe's dark eyes narrowed. She stood across from him near the fireplace, her arms folded, her shoulders hunched, all prickly and annoyed.

Again, he couldn't blame her. Hearing what he had to say was going to suck, especially when he gave her the truth about the ranch too. But shit, he didn't have a choice about this and neither did she, not if she wanted to be safe.

"So what?" she said. "According to Dad, I'm *always* in danger. How is this any different from any other time? And what has that got to do with the ranch?"

Their father had always been—in Van's private view—a little overanxious about threats, both to his company and to his kids, especially Chloe because she was so much younger and . . . for other reasons. Noah had even employed private security guards to patrol the perimeter of the ranch, paying them well to stay out of sight and keep a low profile. The guards were all hardened mercs, who did their job and did it well. You wouldn't even know they were there even if you were looking for them.

When Van was younger, he hadn't questioned the need for guards, had simply accepted it as the price of having a wealthy, powerful father who had an equally wealthy and powerful enemy. But as he'd gotten older, he'd started to wonder if de Santis really was as dangerous as his father made out. Whether there was an actual reason to have armed guards everywhere, all the time, or whether his father was simply paranoid.

Even now, after reading that letter, he wondered. But even so, he couldn't afford to dismiss it. If anything happened to Chloe while he was supposed to be protecting her . . .

Nothing will happen to her. Not if you do your job properly.

Yeah, and he would. End of story.

"It's got nothing to do with the ranch," he said, holding her gaze. "It's about Cesare de Santis."

"And?" She didn't look surprised and why should she? Noah had brought them all up on tales of the de Santis family and the feud that had been going on between him and Cesare for over twenty years. How they'd once been friends until Cesare had tried to claim Noah's oil strike for himself. How their friendship had subsequently dissolved into a bitter rivalry that was still going on.

Van eyed her. "Dad's lawyer gave me a letter from Dad that was apparently only supposed to be given to me on the occasion of Dad's death. It was a set of instructions." He paused to let that sink in. "Instructions for protecting you."

She blinked, thick, silky lashes fluttering. "You got a letter?"

Still thinking about the danger part of it, Van didn't immediately notice the slight edge in her voice. "Yeah, Lucas and Wolf and I each got one."

Her mouth opened, then shut, a spark of an emotion he couldn't identify glittering briefly in her eyes. "I didn't get a letter."

He studied her. *Hurt.* That's what it was. She was hurt. And no wonder. What the fuck had Noah been thinking? Van knew why Chloe hadn't been given the ranch, but why Noah hadn't sent her a letter of her own to explain a few things, Van had no idea.

In fact, the whole situation was tricky, because Noah had been very clear that Chloe wasn't to know the specific reason why she in particular was being targeted by de Santis. Personally Van didn't agree. If someone was in danger, they deserved to have all the information at their disposal so they could act accordingly, not be kept in the dark. But Noah's letter couldn't have been plainer; Chloe wasn't to know the truth until the danger had passed.

It was a truth Van was having difficulty getting his head around himself and he preferred not to think about it, not when he had more pressing things to worry about.

He didn't know what to tell her about the fact that she hadn't gotten a letter, so he went on as if she hadn't spoken. "Dad made it very clear you were in danger and that the ranch wasn't safe for you anymore."

Her eyes widened at that. "Not safe on the ranch? What the hell?"

"He was certain that if anything happened to him, de

Santis would make a decisive move. And that you should be here in New York, where you could be better protected."

" 'Better protected,' " she echoed, frowning even harder. "By who?"

"By me."

For a second the frown vanished, then a brief look of shock passed like lightning over her face. "What?"

Before she'd arrived, Van had expected that when he told her about the danger she was in, she'd fall into line the way everyone else fell into line when he told them what was going to happen. But that had been before she'd stepped off the plane, before he'd gotten a glimpse of her anger and her stubborn determination. Before he'd fully understood that she wasn't the excited, joyful little kid he'd once known.

Yeah, she wasn't that anymore, and he had a feeling that she wasn't going to fall in line like he'd hoped she would either.

"I have to protect you, Chloe," he said. "It was in Dad's letter. He wanted me to bring you to New York and protect you until I've managed to neutralize the de Santis threat."

She stared crossly at him. "But I can't stay here. You understand that, right? We're in the middle of building a new stable complex and I need to be back there to oversee it."

Shit. He was right. There *would* be no falling into line.

"I don't give a crap what you need to do. Dad thought you were in danger and that you needed to be in New York where I could protect you."

"I don't think you get it." Her lovely mouth had thinned. "I'm the manager. Of the entire ranch. I've got O'Neil taking care of things while I'm away, but he can only do that for a couple of days. This stable complex is—"

"Let me ask you something," Van interrupted, trying to

hold onto the threads of his fraying patience. "What's more important to you? Your life or the ranch?"

She gave a short laugh. "No one's going to kill me. Anyway, I asked Dad to reduce the number of guards patrolling the ranch a few months back since we didn't need them. He wasn't happy about it, so he didn't. I have the full complement of men out there, which means I have more than enough to protect me. I certainly don't need to be here."

"Yeah, with a bunch of mercs who've got nothing to do all day but walk around checking perimeters and shooting at rabbits." He leaned back in the armchair. "While here you'd be with a Navy SEAL whose last deployment was a couple of weeks ago in Eastern Europe taking out human traffickers."

Chloe's dark gaze didn't waver. "I don't care what your last deployment was. My ranch is in Wyoming, not New York, and that's where I need to be."

Stubborn woman. How could he have forgotten that? Even as a kid, she had been. Back then, he'd been impressed by it. How every time she fell off that little pony he'd been teaching her to ride, she'd get to her feet, dust herself off, and climb back up on its back again. Her chin would jut and she'd get that look in her eye, the one that was in her eyes right now. The one that said she was going to do what she wanted to do come hell or high water.

Unfortunately for her, this was one time when her determination wasn't going to win.

"But it's not your ranch, Chloe." Van kept his tone calm. "It's mine."

Another expression blazed across her face—shock or rage or hurt, or maybe a combination of all three, he couldn't tell. Then she looked away, her jaw tight, her shoulders hunched, as if trying to keep all that emotion locked up tight inside her. "It's my ranch," she repeated, as if saying it would make it so. "It's *mine*. I've been pouring my own blood, sweat, and tears into that place for the last five years." She shot him a dark glance. "When was the last time you even set foot on it?"

Van shifted uncomfortably in his chair, because he had a feeling she knew as well as he did exactly how long it had been. But there had been reasons for that, reasons he wasn't going to share with her right now because quite frankly there were more important things at stake than how long he'd been away from the fucking ranch.

"It doesn't matter when I last set foot on it." He tried to ease the tension in his posture. "What matters is that you're in danger and the ranch is no longer safe. Which means you're staying in New York until this is over."

Something in Chloe's dark, bitter chocolate eyes flared. "And how long will that be? Weeks? Months? Years? Dad and de Santis have been enemies for twenty years. So if you're telling me I have to stay here—"

"It won't be goddamn twenty years," he snapped, not sure why he was letting her aggravate him quite so much, only sure that she was very definitely aggravating him. "And if you think I like this any better than you do, then you can think again."

A mutinous expression crossed her face. "I'm not staying here, Sullivan. I'm not. And you can't make me."

Fuck.

"So you don't give a shit about your own life?"

She snorted. "Of course I give a shit. You just haven't given me any compelling evidence that I'm better off here than I am at the ranch. And since you haven't, I'll be damned if I stay here any longer than I have to."

Double fuck.

Anger glowed like an ember just behind his breastbone. He didn't want to have to deal with this shit. What he wanted was to fix the mess Noah's death had left at Tate Oil and

Gas, find a new CEO to run the company, then head back to base and the military career he'd thrown his whole heart and soul into.

What he did *not* want was Chloe being argumentative when she was under threat. Especially when short of locking her up in one of the upstairs rooms, there wasn't any way he could keep her here if she wanted to leave. Though, quite frankly, if it did come to locking her in a room in order to save her life, then that's what he'd do.

Alternatively, you could let her go, since she's right— she does have some protection at the ranch. And since when did you pay any attention to the old man's wishes?

Good point. His relationship with Noah had deteriorated so badly after the fiasco in Columbia, Noah making no concessions for him whatsoever. So why should he slavishly obey the old bastard's wishes now that he was dead?

He stared over at Chloe standing beside the fireplace. Her chin jutted, a fierce kind of defiance glittering in her eyes. There was still moisture on her leather jacket and her damp hair was curling in the warmth, and even though she was angry and making no attempt to hide it, there was something vulnerable about her.

The protectiveness he'd felt as she'd gotten out of the car earlier shifted inside him again, even though he didn't want to feel it. Christ, he couldn't let his own issues with his father influence him here and he knew it, no matter how tempted he was simply to let her do what she wanted. The de Santis threat was real. Cesare de Santis owned the foremost weapons design and manufacturing company in the country. He was rich, incredibly powerful, and very, very dangerous, and he had good reasons for coming after Chloe.

Van could *not* let that happen.

She was his little foster sister. And even though he hadn't seen her for nearly a decade, he still carried around that little stone she'd given him all those years ago. A reminder of home.

He had to keep her safe.

Slowly, he pushed himself out of his chair, skirting the coffee table and the food—which looked like he was going to have to eat himself if he didn't want it to go to waste—coming over to where she stood. Chloe watched him approach, her gaze turning wary, her posture tensing though why he had no idea.

He came to a stop, staring down at her, into the black depths of her eyes. Fire glowed there, a small angry blaze.

The ranch was important to her, he got that. And he could understand it too, since his own career was pretty important to him. She was also furious, and it was obvious that some of that anger was directed at him. He didn't blame her for that, not at all. If he'd been her and the ranch had been given to someone else, he'd have been furious too.

Which gave him an idea.

"You know I could pick you up, take you upstairs, and lock you up in one of the bedrooms, don't you?" he asked quietly.

The blaze in her eyes leapt higher. "Try it, asshole."

"I know you're angry, pretty. I know you hate my guts right now, and Dad's too, and hell, you have reason. But this shit's real, understand?"

She glared at him. "Don't patronize me. I've lived with 'this shit' my entire life, and quite frankly since you haven't been here for eight years, how would you know how 'real' or otherwise it is?"

Okay, he'd assumed her anger was all about her not being left the ranch. Except it sounded right now as if she was angry he hadn't been there. Which was strange since he hadn't thought that their relationship had been close.

And whose fault was that?

Van ignored the thought. "Yeah, I get it. You're pissed off. So what about this for a proposition? You stay in New York, let me keep you safe, and when Cesare de Santis is no longer a threat, I'll give you the ranch and you can go back to Wyoming."

Chloe opened her mouth. Shut it. Glared at him a bit longer. Shifted on her feet, the wind very obviously taken out of her sails. "You don't want it?" she asked, after a tense moment. "The ranch, I mean?"

"Shit no. I've got Tate Oil to deal with first up, and then I'm planning on heading back to base after this. I don't want anything tying me down, understand?"

Her gaze narrowed, studying him shrewdly. "How long will it take? To deal with Cesare de Santis?"

"I've got no fucking idea. Securing you was my first priority."

"But it could be days, right? Or weeks?" Her damp hair was starting to dry in soft black waves down her back, covering her narrow shoulders. "I can't stay here that long."

But Van was used to playing hardball. He lifted a shoulder. "Then you don't get the ranch."

She scowled. "But I can't leave the place for however long it's going to take to deal with that bastard. The new stable complex is—"

"I don't give a shit about the new stable complex. You don't stay here and let me protect you, you don't get the ranch. It's that simple, pretty."

Chloe bit her lip, and for some reason he found himself watching her while she did it. Her teeth were very white, sinking into the cushiony softness of her very red lower lip.

Something tightened right down low inside him and he had to force his gaze away.

Jesus Christ. Whatever the hell that was, it was *not* welcome.

"Okay," she said, very clearly reluctant. "I'll stay. But I'm going to need internet access so I can keep in touch with O'Neil while I'm here. And I want your word that you'll sign over ownership of the ranch to me as soon as de Santis is handled."

Tenacious little thing, wasn't she? Not to mention gutsy. People didn't usually question him, still less demand his word on something. They wouldn't dare.

"You have my word," he said slowly.

"Good. Then I'll—"

"And in return, I'll need your word that you'll do exactly what I tell you when it comes to keeping you safe."

She gave him another narrow look, clearly not happy with that. "I don't like being told what to do."

"No one does. But you're not the soldier here. And if I'm in charge of protecting you, then I'm in charge. End of story."

Chloe let out a breath and glanced away, obviously irritated. But too bad. He was going to get her agreement on this because he didn't want to be fighting her every step of the way. Not when that could put at risk his ability to protect her.

"All right, fine." Her shoulders hunched even more. "But just so you know, I'm not happy with it."

"I do know. And I'm not any happier about it than you are."

A flicker of surprise crossed her face. "You're not?"

He didn't see any reason not to tell her. "You're not the only one who had a whole pile of shit handed to them in Dad's will."

"'A pile of shit,'" she echoed, an odd note in her voice. "So is protecting me included in that pile of shit?"

Ah Christ. Why had he said that?

He shoved his hands into his pockets. "I didn't mean it like that and you know it."

"Of course not." She looked down at her feet. "It doesn't matter."

But he had the very distinct impression that it did.

Have you really forgotten who she once was to you?

It had been a long time since he'd been back to the ranch. A long time since he'd seen her. But the memories he carried around with him were still there. Teaching her to ride. Her somehow seeing his nervousness before he'd left on his first deployment and pushing that stupid rock into his hand so he could take a piece of home with him. Her racing out the front doors of the ranch whenever he arrived on leave, flinging herself into his arms for a hug, then reaching for his hand, ready to drag him off to show him whatever it was that she'd been doing that day.

His father had always treated Van like a warrior, a soldier. Treated him like he expected him to act. Hard and emotionless. But Chloe never had. She'd always treated Van like a person. A person she liked to be with. He couldn't forget that. He couldn't simply pretend those memories didn't exist, that she was a stranger he didn't know. And he'd been treating her as one from the moment she'd arrived here.

Sure, she wasn't that kid anymore, but she was still his foster sister and he still cared about her.

Responding to an urge he didn't really understand, since he wasn't used to offering comfort, Van reached out and gently took hold of her shoulders. Then he pulled her into his arms.

She went rigid and there was a second when he thought she was going to pull away. But she didn't, though she didn't relax either.

He held her lightly, because she was very small, her head only just level with his heart. "I'm sorry." He tried to sound gentle. "I know this is tough for you."

Chloe said nothing.

He looked down. She had her cheek turned against his chest, her lashes lowered so he couldn't read her expression. Black hair lay across his forearms, glossy as a streak of oil in the light, and she felt fragile in his arms. Breakable even. And yet warm. Very, very warm.

Van blinked, conscious of her scent all of a sudden, dry hay and sunshine, and for some reason it hit him like a sucker punch. Reminding him of the wide-open pastures and the soaring mountains of home, of when life had been so much simpler, so much easier. A brief moment of paradise in between the gritty streets he'd grown up on as the child of two drug addicts and the hard reality of war where he'd become a man.

She tilted her head in that moment and looked up, and for some reason when her dark eyes met his, it felt not so much like a sucker-punch as being hit by a goddamn train. And his body, that traitorous asshole, instantly hardened.

Oh *shit*. No denying this feeling, no pretending it wasn't there or that it was something else. He knew. And it was wrong, wrong, *wrong*.

Chloe was his foster sister. His *much younger* foster sister. He must be insane. It was either that or he just needed to get laid. Yeah, it had to be that. Had to be.

With a suddenness that took them both by surprise, Van let her go, stepping back and turning away from her, shoving his hands into the pockets of his jeans. Time to get out of here. They could continue this discussion in the morning. It was late and clearly he needed to go find himself a little relief.

"Your bedroom's on the second floor," he said curtly over his shoulder, making for the door. "We'll talk about the rest of it tomorrow morning."

"But"—she sounded almost unsure—"what do I need to do? How long am I supposed to be here for?"

He reached the door and pulled it open. "Like I said, we'll discuss it later."

"Sullivan, you can't just—"

"My name's Van," he growled and stalked out of the room before she could say another word.

CHAPTER FOUR

Chloe opened her eyes and stared at the ceiling. Then she frowned, puzzled, because the ceiling was white and flat, not the dark, exposed beams of her own bedroom back in Wyoming.

Yeah, because you're not in Wyoming anymore, remember?

Oh God, that's right. She wasn't. She was in New York, in her father's house. And she felt like shit because she'd only had a couple of hours of sleep.

Used to the dead silence of the ranch at night, New York was a whole new experience. Even with the excellent soundproofing, she'd still been able to hear the noises of the city outside. Apparently New York really was the city that never slept and it made damn sure that she didn't sleep either, what with the sirens and car horns and trucks and a whole host of other sounds she wasn't used to.

Letting out a soft groan, she turned over, preparing to snuggle back down under the comforter, then caught a glimpse of the time on the clock on the nightstand.

Holy shit, it was eight a.m.

She *never* slept that late. Normally she woke at six, regular as clockwork.

Sighing, she pushed back the covers and sat on the edge of the bed, looking for her clothes. Automatically she began running through her head the tasks for the day, only to realize that in fact she didn't have any tasks for the day.

Because she was in New York.

Because last night she'd agreed to do what Sullivan—*Van*—said, to let him protect her from Cesare de Santis in return for him signing the ranch over to her.

God, she hoped she hadn't made a giant mistake with that decision. But she simply hadn't been able to pass it up. No, she didn't like being away from the ranch, not with so much going on, and she really didn't think this whole threat thing was as serious as Van said it was.

Then again, *he* was certainly taking it seriously.

"I could pick you up, take you upstairs, and lock you up in one of the bedrooms . . ."

The memory of his deep voice, calm and certain, rolled through her and she had to hold herself very still to stop the shiver that threatened. Though why she should feel shivery about being picked up, taken upstairs, and locked in a bedroom she had no idea. Being outraged was way more logical.

Chloe glared at the floor. Autocratic bastard. Did he really expect that she'd meekly accept the fact that she was in danger and do whatever he said? If so, he was shit out of luck. Her father had been talking about the de Santis threat for years, yet she'd never seen any evidence of it herself. Admittedly, even when she went into Blaketown, the little community closest to the ranch, she took a bodyguard with her—mainly to keep her father happy—but even so. No one had ever threatened her. Which made the thought of not being safe at the ranch seem slightly ridiculous.

Though really, the threat wasn't the important part. What was important was getting the ranch back under her control and if that meant she had to put up with Van ordering her around, then she'd put up with Van ordering her around. It would only be for a couple of days anyway.

If it turned out to be a couple of days, that was.

She really needed to talk to Van to see what his plan was for neutralizing the threat de Santis presented, perhaps get some answers as to why she in particular was being targeted. If she knew that then she could arrange for better security at the ranch, which might actually make Van happy too since he'd made it clear he wasn't all that thrilled with having to protect her.

Something caught inside her at the thought, but she ignored it, scanning around the bedroom instead.

It was just as massive as the sitting room downstairs and was similarly decorated. Creamy walls, soft cream carpet, massive white bed heaped with pillows of varying sizes, all in various shades of cream. The furniture—two nightstands and a sofa pushed underneath the windows—were also white.

Walking into it the night before had been like walking into a cloud.

Her clothes, along with her duffel bag, were lying on the carpet in the messy heap she'd left them in the night before, and when she padded over to grab them, she realized they were still a little damp.

She picked up the black thermal she'd been wearing underneath her blue plaid shirt, and gave it a cautious sniff. But it didn't smell bad, which meant the rest were good to go.

Pulling off the old T-shirt she'd brought along as a nightie, she dropped it on the floor then rummaged in her bag for a fresh pair of underwear. Five minutes later she was dressed. Mrs. Jenkins, the housekeeper back at the ranch, was always on her to take a bit more care in her appearance, especially since she was apparently a "beautiful girl." But Chloe didn't much care about how she looked. Looks weren't important when it came to managing a ranch and besides, no one apart from Mrs. Jenkins cared what she looked like.

Van might care.

The thought hit her unexpectedly, making her breath catch as she did up the last button. No, that was ridiculous. Van wouldn't care. He was her foster brother for God's sake. And anyway, she'd gotten over worrying about what he thought a long time ago.

You're seriously not going to think about that hug he gave you last night?

Chloe gritted her teeth. Great, why did her stupid brain have to remind her about that now? After she'd been doing very well *not* thinking about it so far.

Not that there was anything to think about. It had simply been a hug, unexpected and very unwelcome, yes, but only a hug. And really, did it matter that she couldn't remember the last time anyone had hugged her?

Her father wasn't a hugger and neither was Mrs. Jenkins. And since she pretty much spent all her time on the ranch in the company of her horses, the ranch hands, or O'Neil, she didn't have much in the way of friends who doled out hugs either.

As for Jason, well, he'd purely been about the sex. There had been no hugging involved.

But when Van had put his arms around her . . .

He'd been so big, his body like a massive, granite wall, and he'd been hot too. She hadn't realized how cold she'd been until he'd pulled her against him, completely surrounding her with hard muscle and male heat, and the scent of something fresh and clean, with a warm undertone to it. Like a forest after rain.

It had been the first time he'd touched her since she'd been a kid, and even though she knew she should have pushed him away, there was a moment when all the blood had rushed to her head, and she'd felt dizzy, unable to move. Then he'd let her go, so suddenly she'd nearly fallen, turned around, and walked out of the room.

She didn't even know why. Had it been the hug, or something else?

An uncomfortable feeling gathered in her gut, one she didn't like, so she looked around, trying to find something else to focus on instead.

Her gaze settled on the rounded lump of the snow globe sitting at the bottom of her bag.

After a moment she reached down and took it out, gave it a shake, and watched the snowflakes whirl around inside.

She still didn't know why she'd brought it with her. The summons from Van had come, and she'd been so full of rage that she'd barely paid attention to what she'd stuffed into her bag. After eight years of silence, that terse email was the first time he'd contacted her—if you didn't count that awkward meeting at their father's funeral, and she didn't.

God, it had pissed her off. Yes, she'd known he'd be away doing military stuff for the Navy so any contact was always going to be sparse, but nothing at all for eight years? Not even one measly email?

He hadn't even contacted her about the will, and she'd been expecting him to, because surely he would have known how much the ranch meant to her. How much it would rankle her that their father hadn't left it to her after he'd promised to. Yet Van hadn't. No, his first contact in eight years was all about a threat she'd been living with for years already and some demand she come to New York so he could protect her better.

Why does that matter? Why do you care so much? Sure you had a crush on him once, but it's been years since you've seen him, and you've moved on.

Irritated with herself, Chloe put the snow globe down on the nightstand then sat down on the side of the bed with her duffel in her lap. Grabbing her hairbrush out of it, she began pulling it through the tangles in her hair, scowling at the floor.

It was true, she *had* moved on. And all this anger was to do with the ranch, not actually with him. She didn't care about him the way she used to, not anymore. She'd been managing things fine all by herself and would continue to do so. She didn't need anyone.

Careful to not examine her reasons for brushing her hair, Chloe pushed the by-now straight and glossy strands behind her ears then slipped off the bed and went out of the room.

The house was silent, and she didn't quite know where to go first. Upstairs to see if she could find Van or downstairs to get coffee—if indeed downstairs was where the kitchen was.

Like there was even a choice after the kind of sleep she'd had—coffee it was.

Feeling gritty eyed and with a burgeoning headache from lack of sleep, Chloe went down the grand staircase, creeping down the hallway at the bottom and heading toward the back of the house, since that's where she guessed the kitchen would probably be.

Passing through a wood-paneled and very formal-looking dining room, she went through another door that, sure enough, opened into a massive, gleaming kitchen that was all stainless steel and white tile.

A kitchen that was already occupied by a very tall, very broad-shouldered man currently leaning back against the counter of the kitchen island, a coffee mug in one hand, a sleek silver phone in the other. His black head was bent, his attention on the phone.

Van.

Chloe stopped short in the doorway, staring at him because she simply couldn't seem to drag her gaze away.

He wore suit pants today, dark charcoal wool that sat low on his lean hips in much the same way as the jeans he'd been wearing the night before had. Instead of the long-sleeved black T-shirt, he wore a plain white business shirt. It was unbuttoned, leaving a large quantity of bronzed chest and abs on show.

Her mouth dried as she was catapulted back to when she'd been sixteen, staring at him as he'd checked that horse's hoof while shirtless, mesmerized by all that finely carved muscle and tanned bare skin. He looked . . . even more incredible now if that was possible. Like someone had taken to his torso with a chisel and sculpted the perfect male form.

She blinked, focusing on the chain around his neck instead of his sharply defined pecs and the corrugations of his abs that almost seemed to beg for a set of fingers to run lightly over them to confirm they were as hard as they looked. It wasn't a necklace as she'd first thought. It was his dog tags.

The tight feeling in her gut got even tighter.

"If you're going to come in, come in," he said without looking up from his phone. "I won't bite."

His deep voice came as a shock, and Chloe felt her cheeks heat. Wonderful. He'd caught her staring at him. How irritating.

"I was just trying to find out where to get coffee," she muttered grumpily, taking a few steps toward the kitchen island where he was standing, scanning about for a coffee machine.

Van shifted, putting his phone down on the counter then pulling out one of the stools. "Sit down. I'll fix you something."

It was another of his orders, issued with the same calm

authority he'd used the night before, as if he absolutely expected her to do what he said without argument.

It made her hackles rise.

"What is it with you and food?" She couldn't quite keep the snappish note from her voice. "I can make my own breakfast, thank you very much."

He gave her a look. "Didn't get much sleep, huh?"

"What?"

"You've got dark circles under your eyes and you're as grumpy as fuck."

She bristled, not liking the observation for reasons she didn't care to examine too closely. "I am not."

Van sighed. "Look, how about instead of arguing, you sit down and let me fix you some breakfast, okay? I'm making myself something anyway." He didn't wait for an answer, already moving around the kitchen island and going over to the fridge, pulling it open and scanning the shelves.

Unreasonably annoyed, Chloe debated arguing further, then decided against it. She didn't know where the food was and if he was making himself breakfast anyway, it seemed like a stupid hill to die on. Maybe they could have a little chat about orders and such after she'd finished eating.

Moving over to the stool he'd pulled out for her, she sat down on it, leaned her elbows on the counter, and watched him get out some eggs and milk from the fridge. Setting them down, he then pulled open a drawer and took out a bowl, plus several other kitchen utensils.

"So what's your plan?" she asked as he started cracking eggs. "For getting rid of the de Santis threat, I mean."

"I don't have a plan yet. I'm still at the gathering intel stage."

"But you've had a whole week."

"Yeah and I've had other shit to do." He began mixing

up the ingredients, and she found she had to concentrate her gaze on the movements of his hands, because the flex and release of his abs was way too distracting.

Already she could feel frustration eating away at her, making her antsy. She wasn't used to sitting around and letting other people do stuff for her. She wasn't used to sitting around, period. God, what the hell was she going to do all day?

"Well, can I do anything?" She folded her arms on the counter to stop herself from drumming her fingers impatiently. "I mean, I have to do something, right?"

He glanced up, his clear green-gold eyes momentarily making her catch her breath. "Other than sit there and wait for me to serve you some food? No."

"Yeah, but I can't sit here all day."

His mouth curved. "I thought you had to speak to O'Neil about the new stable complex."

There was amusement in his tone, which should have annoyed her since he was quite clearly teasing her. Yet she found herself looking down at the counter instead, somehow short of breath.

It was that smile of his. She remembered it. Warm and generous, and as a lonely kid looking for a connection to someone, she'd found it incredibly reassuring.

He'd smiled like that at her when she'd given him that dumb rock she'd found on one of her rides around Shadow Peak. It had been just before he'd left to go on his first deployment and somehow she'd sensed that he was afraid, though he was trying hard not to show it. She felt afraid too, for him, and so to make them both brave, she'd found a little piece of Wyoming to take with him.

It had made sense when she'd been ten, but as an adult, she cringed remembering it.

Her feelings about his smile as an adult too were cringeworthy. Yes, Van was hot, but that was no reason to feel all breathless and weird about it. Jesus, she wasn't sixteen anymore.

Been a while since Jason, though.

Yeah, that was true, but she was in no hurry to find another guy to fill his shoes. He'd started to get possessive and she wasn't into that. She preferred being on her own and anyway, sex wasn't that big of a deal. She could do without it just fine. This weird reaction to Van must be a holdover from her teenage years and possibly it was a grief thing. Or even an anger thing. Who knew?

Whatever, she had to ignore it before she embarrassed herself.

"I'm not quite sure why you think me getting angry about not being at the ranch is funny." She kept her gaze on the white marble countertop. "Maybe you've never poured your heart and soul into anything the way I have."

Van paused in his mixing. "I don't think it's funny, and actually I have poured my heart and soul into something. Why do you think I'm going back to base the first moment I can?"

She looked up, momentarily distracted. "What? Being a soldier?"

"Being a SEAL, yeah."

"Is that why you never called me? Never even sent an email?" As soon as the words were out, she felt herself start to go red, because she hadn't meant to say it so sharply, like an accusation almost. But now that she had, there wasn't any point trying to take it back.

Van stared at her. Then he put down the whisk he was holding with a very precise movement and leaned his hands on the edge of the counter, his dog tags swinging. "Is that why you're so pissed at me? Because I never sent you an email?"

The heat in her cheeks climbed even higher. "I'm not pissed at you."

He raised an eyebrow. "Sure you're not. You've been prickly and irritable since the moment you got off the plane."

"Are you surprised? I hear nothing from you for eight years, not even about the damn will, which you must have known would be a problem for me. And then the first thing I get is some short email telling me I have to come to New York immediately, without any explanation whatsoever." She stopped, aware that her voice had started to rise. Crap. This wasn't supposed to matter and yet here she was, making a big deal out of it.

Something glinted in Van's eyes, as if he knew exactly what she was thinking. It made her go even redder.

"Not that I care," she added quickly, before he could say anything. "I just want the ranch back. That's the only thing I care about."

There was a brief silence.

"Uh-huh," Van murmured finally, an entire universe of sarcasm contained in the two wordless syllables.

She had to look away again, the way he was staring at her making her feel oddly vulnerable, as if she'd accidentally shown him a piece of her soul. Which was annoying, because hadn't she told herself she didn't care what he thought anymore? Once, she had. But that had been back when she'd been sixteen and in the throes of a massive crush. She'd gotten over that like she'd gotten over the loneliness that had been her constant companion since childhood.

She had the ranch and that was all she needed.

Van studied her as if she were a piece of machinery he was assessing for defects, then without a word, he turned and went over to the stove, picking up the coffeepot and bringing it back to the kitchen island. He grabbed a cup from a cupboard and put that beside the pot, moving the milk carton alongside it too.

"Coffee," he said neutrally. "Get yourself a cup while I make this breakfast for you. I have to go out to do some business shit soon, but if you've got any questions about the will or Dad's letter, I'll explain what I can before I leave."

The coffee smelled good, and suddenly caffeine seemed the perfect antidote to the vulnerable feeling sitting in her chest. Reaching for the pot, she poured herself a cup, adding a bit of milk. There didn't seem to be any sugar about so she had a sip without it, the hot, bitter liquid calming her somewhat.

She gripped the cup, the heat of it burning her fingers, but she didn't let go.

Van had turned back to the stove and she heard the hiss as he poured the omelet mixture into a pan. He didn't say anything and he didn't turn around, all his attention centered on what he was cooking.

Silence descended in the kitchen and for some reason the vulnerable feeling began to ebb. But then, she'd always found Van's presence reassuring, hadn't she?

Before she'd learned to ride, she'd been afraid of horses. Of their size and their hooves. Of their big teeth. There hadn't been any reason for it, she'd just found them a bit frightening. Her father had been busy with work and had no time to deal with what he called her "irrational fears," so he'd made Van take charge of her riding lessons.

At first she'd been upset about that, wanting her father because she never saw enough of him as it was and she didn't know Van very well since he'd been away at boarding school. Yet when the time had come for her lessons, Van had been so calm, so patient, and so utterly reassuring that she'd soon lost her fear of horses, coming to love them instead. Just like she'd come to idolize her big foster brother.

That familiar reassurance threaded through her now as

she sat on her stool, sipping coffee while Van cooked. It was a seductive, insidious feeling, one she shouldn't give into. Because relying on someone else for support, to be there for her, only ended in disappointment, and she of all people should remember that.

She tried to ignore the sensation, concentrating on what questions she might have about the will and the de Santis threat instead.

"Why me?" she asked after a moment. "Why am I a target and not you, or Wolf or Lucas?"

Van didn't answer immediately, getting out a plate and slipping a perfectly folded omelet onto it before pushing it toward her, along with a knife and fork. Then he came around the counter and pulled out a stool next to her, sitting down and reaching for the coffeepot to refill his own cup.

"For a start, you're a soft target," he said, the deep rumble of his voice echoing around inside her in a way that made her feel strangely restless. "The most easily accessible and the weakest link."

She was the weakest link. Great. "I can take care of myself," she muttered irritably.

"I didn't say you couldn't. I said that's likely why de Santis wants you instead of Lucas or Wolf or me. We're SEALs. We're not exactly easy to take down."

Picking up her fork, Chloe stared at the omelet in front of her. It smelled delicious, and she had no doubt that it would taste delicious too. But she suddenly wasn't hungry. "What does he want me for?"

"De Santis? A ransom demand of some kind probably." He sounded calm, as if this shouldn't be a shock in any way.

And hell, it kind of wasn't. Her father had been worried about this very thing for years.

She poked at the omelet. "But why now? Why after Dad's gone?"

"I suspect Dad and de Santis had some kind of detente

and now that Dad's dead, that's over." Van's long fingers cradled his coffee mug in a way she found oddly distracting. "Dad's letter wasn't very specific, unfortunately."

Ah yes, the letters. Which each of her foster brothers got, but she didn't.

She poked at the omelet again, conscious of a curious tightness in her chest. It wasn't the same kind as when she looked at Van. No, this was different. Painful. Like when she'd found out about the will, about how her father had left her out of it entirely. As if nothing she'd done on the ranch had mattered.

As if you don't matter, right?

"What do you mean it wasn't very specific?" she asked, ignoring the voice in her head. "What did it say?"

Van was silent for a long moment, staring down into his mug, a certain tension in his posture, a tension that was bleeding into the air around him.

The tight thing inside her coiled into a hard knot of inexplicable dread.

She dropped her fork, letting it clatter against the plate, her heartbeat suddenly accelerating. "What was in that letter?"

He sat so still, his gaze on the liquid in his mug, not saying a word.

"Something's wrong." The dread coiled even tighter, crowding out all the air in her chest, making her feel breathless. "What was in it, Van?"

His head lifted and turned, those piercing green-gold eyes catching hers, a terribly sympathy in them. "Chloe . . ."

"Tell me." Her fingers had curled into her palms, her nails pressing down into her skin.

He was going to tell her something awful, she was certain of it. Something she wasn't going to want to hear.

"Dad didn't want you to know," Van said, his voice quiet. "He didn't want me to tell you."

"Tell me what?" She tried sucking in a breath and failed, her heartbeat thundering in her head.

Van's gaze was unwavering. "Are you sure you want to know now?"

She didn't even have to think about her response. "Of course I want to know now. Tell me, for God's sake."

He put down the mug and turned to face her, a certain fierceness in his eyes. "There's a reason de Santis is moving now and there's a reason you're his target. You're his daughter, Chloe. You are Cesare de Santis's blood daughter."

She almost laughed, a flood of relief almost making her dizzy. "Don't be stupid. Noah's my father. He had an affair with my mother, and she died having me."

Yet Van didn't laugh with her. He didn't even smile. He only looked at her with that piercing hazel gaze. "Dad was infertile. He couldn't have kids. There were test results in his letter that confirmed it. There was also a paternity test." He paused, his gaze searching her face. "It's true, pretty. You're de Santis's kid."

Her brain wanted to protest, to tell him he was wrong, that her father had lied. But somehow, deep down, she knew that wasn't the case.

Her relief ebbed away, that tight thing inside her clenching so hard all the air vanished from her lungs entirely. She couldn't breathe. As if the truth had sucked the oxygen from the room.

Oh God, she had to get out. Get some air.

Her hands shaking, Chloe shoved back her stool and slipped off it, stumbling from the room before Van could say another word.

It took everything in him not to go after her, but instinct told Van that she needed a bit of space and that it was better to let it lie. So he stared down at the mug in his hands and not at the doorway Chloe had disappeared through.

Why the fuck did you tell her?

Noah had instructed him not to say a word to her, that she would have too many other things to deal with following his death and that the knowledge that she wasn't his daughter would be too much for her to bear at an already stressful time. Better to wait until de Santis had been neutralized.

Which was bullshit and another sign of his father's emotional cowardice.

Not knowing would only delay the hurt and possibly make it even worse. Christ knew that he'd be pretty fucking pissed if a truth like that had been kept from him, especially if it was delayed further because of some spurious concern for his emotional well-being.

Noah hadn't been interested in anyone's emotional well-being—he just hadn't been that type of father. And to pretend he gave a shit about Chloe only added insult to injury.

No, the truth was better than that and she deserved to hear it. She deserved to know why Noah hadn't been able to leave anything at all to her too, that he couldn't because of her blood tie to de Santis. And perhaps even more than that, she deserved to know that her father had been a goddamned liar for over twenty years.

Just because you're pissed with him doesn't mean you need to take it out on her.

Van reached out for his coffee mug again, holding the hot ceramic between his fingers, his jaw gone tight.

He wasn't fucking taking it out on her. Yeah, he'd been pissed with Noah and he still was. But this wasn't about him and his relationship with his father. This was about her. About the flash of hurt he'd seen in her eyes the previous night when she'd realized she hadn't gotten a letter like the rest of them had. About the anger in her voice as she'd bargained with him for the ranch, and the fierce way she'd talked about it.

"I've been pouring my own blood, sweat, and tears into that place for the last five years."

Yeah, she deserved to know the truth, even if it was yet another hurt on top of a whole pile of others. And hell, he knew how that went. He was still struggling with the revelation himself and had been the whole week. And not even so much that Chloe wasn't actually Noah's daughter. No, the real shock was his own lack of surprise. It was almost as if he'd expected it. Noah had always been a secretive bastard, both in his business practices and in his personal life, so the fact that he'd been lying both to Chloe and to his sons all this time wasn't that big of a revelation.

Clearly it's a shock to her.

It certainly had been. But then she'd always had more faith in Noah than Van ever had.

A feeling he'd thought he'd long put behind him twisted, making him have to take a deep breath to get rid of it. No, he fucking wasn't going down that route again. Empathy he could allow himself, but he wasn't going to feel sympathy for her, no damn way. Hadn't he learned that in Columbia? Getting involved emotionally was *always* a mistake. It led to errors of judgment, and he couldn't afford that, not with her. *Especially* not with her.

Van put his mug down and placed his hands flat on the counter, consciously trying to relax. Christ, he really had to get on to dealing with the whole mess Noah had left him. The bereavement leave he'd managed to swing allowed him a month, but then he needed to be back on base and training for the next deployment.

He didn't have time to screw around, not with figuring out how he and his brothers were going to manage the sudden responsibility of the company, not to mention getting a handle on de Santis and the threat to Chloe.

At that moment he heard a noise coming from the front of the house, the faint and yet unmistakable sound of the front door closing.

Was that Chloe leaving? Or was that someone coming in? Either way . . .

Years of training kicked in and he was up and off the barstool, heading out of the kitchen, moving fast down the hallway, extending his awareness in the way he'd learned to do. Sensitive to every sound, to the brush of the air over his skin and the taste of it around him, alert to the slightest movement.

There was nothing but silence as he reached the front door, but by then he already knew—he was alone in the house. Which meant Chloe, the little idiot, had run out.

He didn't bother with a weapon—shit, *he* was a fucking weapon—throwing open the door and moving down the steps. Pausing at the bottom, he scanned the street, and sure enough, there she was, a small figure walking very fast down the sidewalk, heading toward Central Park.

Van didn't run—no point in drawing too much attention since the traffic was starting to build and there were people around—but he started after her, moving faster than she was since her legs were shorter. As he walked, he checked his environment, on the alert for any kind of threat. Luckily for her there didn't seem to be any, but still. . . . What the fuck was she thinking?

He'd told her that she was in danger, and yet what was the first thing she did? She ran out of the goddamn house.

Come on, she's in shock. Especially after what you just told her.

Anger began to gather inside him, thick and hot. Perhaps he shouldn't have said anything after all. Certainly he should have gone after her the minute she'd left the kitchen, and damn giving her her own space. Because quite frankly, the last thing he needed right now was her running outside during a threat situation, especially if she was having a meltdown.

You really shouldn't have told her.

Furious all of a sudden and this time with himself, Van powered down the street after Chloe, gaining on her. Some sixth sense must have alerted her because she turned, glancing behind her. The color drained from her face and her dark eyes widened as they spotted him coming, and she turned back around and began to run.

But it was too late. He had her in his sights and there would be no escaping him.

Shifting into an easy lope, Van got closer and closer until he was right behind her. Then he reached out and looped an arm around her waist, pulling her up short. She gave a gasp, her hands coming down, clawing at his forearm and trying to pry it away from her, wriggling in his grip. But she wasn't getting away from him, not again.

Van jerked her back against him, bending his head to growl in her ear, "Keep the fuck still."

She didn't, her nails digging into his forearm, her back arching in an effort to shake him off. "Let me go!"

"No." He pulled her in tighter, letting her feel his strength so she knew that struggling was pointless. "I know that was a shock, but you're supposed to stay in the fucking house. It's not safe for you to go outside."

"I don't care!" She gave another violent wriggle. "Just leave me alone!"

Oh Christ. That this wasn't going well was an understatement. Several people passing them were giving him funny looks, and he knew that if he didn't lock this down right now, he was going to get a 911 call pretty damn soon.

"Chloe." He made her name an order, hard and flat to cut through her obvious distress, then he wrapped both arms around her and held on tight to keep her immobile. "Keep still."

"Fuck you, asshole." Her voice this time sounded fragile and he became aware that the soft, warm body in his arms was trembling.

Jesus. She really was upset. His anger drained away, the sympathy he was trying so hard to ignore taking its place instead.

He bent his head and gentled his tone. "It's okay, pretty. We'll talk about this later, but right now, I need you to come back into the house."

She went still in his arms, the resistance bleeding out of her. And he became conscious, slowly, of her heat. Of the scent of her hair, like apples, and beneath that a light, musky smell that had something very primitive and very male suddenly coming alert inside him. The way it had the night before when he'd hugged her.

Which was very, *very* wrong.

"I don't want to stay inside," she whispered. "I can't breathe in there . . ."

He needed to let her go, he *really* needed to. But he couldn't, not when she sounded so lost. Not when he'd just taken apart the very fabric of her life.

With an effort, he forced his focus onto what she was saying and not the feel of her body against his. But it was difficult because it had been a long time since he'd felt that kind of softness and warmth. His last mission had been a months-long human trafficking operation in Eastern Europe, and there'd been precious little in the way of warmth or softness of any kind out there. Not that he required it, but there had been times he'd craved . . . something. And sometimes a woman would ease the craving, and sometimes a woman would only make it worse.

And sometimes it was better to pretend he didn't feel it at all.

Yeah, and he wasn't going to be thinking about that kind of shit, not now.

"I'm sorry, Chloe, but you *have* to get inside the house." He eased his grip on her so she wasn't right up against him. "We can talk once you're safe."

There was a moment when he could feel her muscles go tight and he thought she might be on the verge of running again. But then, taking him completely by surprise, she turned around and pressed her head against his chest, a great hiccupping sob tearing from her throat.

And just for a second, he was back in the jungle. The hot thick air. The rain that never stopped falling. The darkness. The terrain that seemed hell-bent on killing them with every step. The girl, whose hand in his was so small. She'd been so brave, that girl. She hadn't cried once. Except for that final night, out of fear and exhaustion, and he'd held her and told her it would be okay. Told her that he'd save her. He'd meant it with every fiber of his being.

But it hadn't been okay, and he hadn't saved her.

And he couldn't do it again, he just couldn't.

Chloe gave another sob, pressing her face hard against him, the sound so full of grief that it was all he could do not to shove her away. Shit, he had to get a hold of himself. He wasn't in fucking Columbia anymore, that had been ten years ago and that girl, Sofia, was long dead. This was Chloe, his foster sister, and she was crying not because she was afraid, but because the man she'd always believed in had lied to her for over twenty years.

He couldn't push her away. He had to fucking handle the situation, and that wasn't by letting the past get to him.

Van put his hand on the back of her head and let it rest there, then he tightened his other arm around her. She trembled as another hiccupping sob shook her, then another and another, deep and wracking, like bitter grief.

She'd cried like this once before, when she'd taken her first fall from that pony he'd taught her how to ride. Her tears hadn't been quite as wild as these, but she'd cried all the same. He'd crouched down beside her, instinctively putting his arms around her. She'd been the first person he'd hugged since he'd left his childhood behind, and the instinctive way she'd buried her head in his chest, responding to his comfort, had made him feel . . . good.

An echo of that feeling caught him now, edged as it was with the grief he kept buried so far down he normally didn't feel it at all. But he ignored that, keeping it firmly behind the walls he'd built around it and all the rest of his emotions. This wasn't about him anyway, it was about her. And besides, these days he lived by the rule of keeping himself as unemotionally involved as possible. It was easier that way.

People were looking at them, but Van kept her head pressed to his chest so her face was hidden and stared them all down. They really needed to get back inside, but giving her a moment to cry wouldn't hurt.

He stroked her hair absently as her sobs began to wind down, the black strands all soft and silky against his palm. There was damp heat against his chest and he realized, with a sudden jolt, that her cheek was pressed to his bare skin because, of course, he'd left his shirt unbuttoned.

He stilled, his heart speeding up, his cock—the stupid shit—hardening against the zipper of his suit pants. Jesus. She was his goddamn foster sister and if that wasn't bad enough, she was grieving, for fuck's sake. There was nothing about this picture that was right in any way, shape, or form.

Her hands moved, coming to his waist. Her cool fingers

on the bare skin of his hips shocked him. Made it abruptly hard to breathe. If she moved her head just a touch, her mouth would be on him . . .

Christ, she shouldn't be touching him. Why was she touching him? When he'd given her nothing but bad news after bad news?

Push her away, dick. Before you embarrass both yourself and her.

But he couldn't do that, not when she was sobbing on him. That would hurt her and he sure as hell wasn't going to do that, not after the bombshell he'd just dropped. And apart from anything else, he wasn't a teenage boy. He was a goddamn SEAL. He could control one wildly inappropriate hard-on.

Ignoring his thudding heart and the tightness in his groin, he adjusted his grip on her yet again so she'd stop giving his cock any more ideas. "Come on, pretty. Time to go in."

She raised her tearstained face from his chest. Her cheeks were shiny and there was moisture caught in her lashes. For a moment she stared up at him, grief and pain laid bare in her reddened eyes. Then abruptly her expression shuttered and she pulled herself out of his grip, looking away and swiping at her face with one hand. Without a word, she turned and began to head back to the house.

Ignoring the weird urge he had to pull her back into his arms and hold her, soothe her obvious distress, Van glanced down at his watch then cursed. He'd hoped to be able to explain further the implications of the de Santis threat when they got back to the house, but he was due at the fucking lawyer's in an hour. Which meant it was going to have to wait.

Following her back, he reflexively watched the streets as they made their way up the steps and through the front door. But there were no obvious threats and nothing out of the ordinary happening. Looked like her impromptu tour of the sidewalk hadn't had any immediate consequences, thank God.

After they'd gotten inside, he closed the door very firmly behind them, then turned to find her heading in the direction of the kitchen.

"Hey," he called after her. "Chloe, wait."

She stopped, but didn't turn. Her shoulders were hunched and she had her arms wrapped around herself as if in pain. It made him want to go over to her and pull her back into his arms, let her cry some more until it didn't hurt. But he didn't have time.

You shouldn't anyway. You need to stay uninvolved, remember?

Yeah, that too.

So all he said was, "We're going to have to talk about this later. I need to go to the lawyer's, and I'll probably be a couple of hours.

She said nothing, only nodded.

Ah, shit, he didn't like that she'd suddenly closed up on him. "Chloe," he ordered softly. "Look at me."

A few moments passed where she didn't move. Then she turned her head, giving him the unbelievably pure line of her profile.

"You'll be okay?" He had to know. He didn't want to leave her like this.

"Yes, of course." The words were defiant. As if daring him to tell her otherwise.

He narrowed his gaze at her. She wasn't okay, not if that meltdown outside was anything to go by, but he didn't have time to push it, not now. "I'll try not to be too long, but there's a TV in the living room on the third floor if you get bored." He paused. "De Santis doesn't know you're in New York and I don't want him finding out. Which means you can't go outside. I'm pretty sure he hasn't got this place under surveillance just yet, but I don't want to take any chances. Understand?"

"Yes." This time the word was flat.

"Not even to look around," he persisted. "Not even if you—"

"I get it," she interrupted. "I'm not a child, Van. Stop treating me like one."

He let out a breath. "I'm not. If I was treating you like a child, I wouldn't have told you the truth about de Santis."

Chloe turned her head away. "Can I go now? Some dick made me an omelet and if I don't eat it now, it'll get cold."

And before he could say anything more, she disappeared down the hallway.

CHAPTER FIVE

Chloe pressed the button on the remote, frustratingly clicking through yet another lot of channels that seemed to be nothing but soap operas and shopping, neither of which she was interested in. She wasn't generally interested in television, period. But she'd already called O'Neil and dealt with the various construction issues that had come up over the past couple of days, gone over some spreadsheets, handled a few questions from breeders, problem-solved a ranch hand's preference for beer over work, answered all her emails, and now she had nothing to do but sit.

The day before, while Van had been at the lawyer's, sitting and watching TV was exactly what she'd wanted, escaping into a different reality for a couple of hours and not thinking at all about what he'd told her—the truth that had left her feeling battered and bruised and not a little betrayed.

Her father had never been a physically affectionate man and he'd always been reserved, preferring to keep the world at arm's length where he could observe it without having to interact with it. When she'd been a kid, she'd sensed that distance, battering at it as if it were a pane of glass she could break if only she threw herself against it hard enough. And there had been times when it felt as if she had, some very rare occasions when he'd look at her with real warmth, with actual, honest-to-God emotion that wasn't the pleasant, business-like smile he reserved for all his dealings with people.

But those moments never lasted. And in the end, she'd stopped throwing herself against that glass and had thrown herself into the ranch instead, because at least the ranch gave something back.

So the fact that he'd lied to her so completely and for so long shouldn't have come as a surprise, since it wasn't exactly the first time she was aware that he hadn't been honest with her. It certainly shouldn't feel like her heart had been ripped out of her chest. After all, hadn't she kept that snow globe he'd given her as a reminder of what a liar he was? And that his promises were always empty ones? "Later," he used to tell her when she'd begged to be taken on one of his trips to New York. "When you're older," or "Next month, when I don't have so much work," or "Maybe in January, when things have quieted down."

He'd never taken her anywhere, never treated her as his own flesh and blood, despite telling her that she was. No, he hadn't even treated her as well as he'd treated his foster sons. She was always an afterthought. And now she knew why.

Pain she didn't want to acknowledge curled in her heart, but she concentrated instead on the woman on TV displaying a pair of tacky-looking diamond earrings. She really needed to stop sitting here, go find Van, and have the conversation she'd been avoiding. Get the facts.

Except then, you'd have to deal with what happened yesterday.

Yeah, and she didn't want to think about that either. Her making a giant fool of herself by running outside then breaking down and weeping pathetically against his chest.

The memory made her cringe. She couldn't imagine why she'd suddenly lost it and sobbed like a small child as soon as he'd put his arms around her. Sure, the news he'd given her had been a shock, but even so, she was usually way more self-contained than that. She didn't let her emotions get the better of her, not these days. She wasn't the little kid throwing a tantrum because her dad wouldn't take her to New York, not anymore.

Chloe glowered at the TV, trying to interest herself in that instead of the memory of Van coming after her, all sleek muscle and long, lean power. Gaining on her with such ease, as if she was running in quicksand while he had nothing but hard concrete underneath his feet.

She'd only wanted to get outside, get some air. She certainly hadn't meant to run like an idiot. But for some reason that glimpse of him behind her had turned her shock into a flood of adrenaline. Made her run and run hard.

And then he'd caught her, his arm like an iron bar around her waist, jerking her up against the intense heat of his body, holding her so tightly she could barely move. She'd almost forgotten about her father in that instant. All she'd been conscious of was the drumming sound of her heartbeat and his hard-muscled torso against her back. His naked torso. She'd trembled, unable to help herself, the adrenaline and shock turning into something else, that desire she thought she'd gotten over years ago.

It was all so wrong. First of all, she'd just had some pretty terrible news dumped on her, so she shouldn't be feeling all hot for a guy anyway. Second, he was her foster brother. Third, there was the fact that she'd already been down that road with him when she was sixteen, and it had been hideous.

He'd been at home on leave a whole two weeks and she'd barely been able to speak to him, too dazzled and overwhelmed by pretty much everything about him. He'd noticed her weirdness, of course, no matter how hard she'd tried to hide it, and in the end she'd started avoiding him purely so she wouldn't give herself away by blushing and stammering every time he tried to talk to her.

The only time she'd felt even semi-normal had been when she'd been out riding one afternoon and had accidentally met him doing the same thing. They hadn't said a word to each other. He'd only met her gaze, a challenge in his eyes, and all her self-consciousness had fallen away. She'd grinned, turned her horse around, and raced him back to the ranch house.

He'd won by a nose, giving her the smile she'd remembered back from when she'd been a kid as he'd gotten down off his horse. But this time there had been something wild and wolfish about it that had set her heart on fire.

She'd had to turn her horse around and ride right back out again, because she simply hadn't been able to deal with the intensity of her feelings.

Hell, she couldn't deal with them now.

The woman on TV smiled and talked about a free necklace with the earrings, but only if you order *right now,* and Chloe scowled and turned the stupid thing off.

She didn't want to be sitting there watching TV. She wanted to be at home, where she could go outside. Where she could work or go down to the stables and spend time with the horses. Where she could saddle up her favorite mare and go for a gallop, breathe in all the fresh Wyoming air.

Where she could do something with the hot coal sitting just behind her breastbone, burning her right through.

But she wasn't at home. She was in New York, stuck in a house, a virtual prisoner, and that hot coal wasn't going anywhere.

And all because Cesare de Santis had apparently targeted her.

Because you're his daughter.

Her gut churned, reminding her that sitting here distracting herself with dumb TV wasn't exactly dealing with anything.

Letting out a breath, she flung the remote down on the couch then pushed herself out of it, turning toward the doorway.

The night before, after Van had gotten back from the lawyer's, he'd clearly wanted to talk to her about the bombshell he'd dropped on her, but she definitely hadn't. So she'd locked herself in the bathroom and taken an extralong bath. By the time she'd gotten out and had done a cautious check around to see where he was, she'd heard his voice coming from the office on the second floor. She'd taken a quick glance inside and saw him standing with his back to the door, looking out the window as he talked to someone on the phone.

A small part of her—still reverberating from the shock of the news and hungry for something, though she didn't know what—had wanted to linger, to watch him, to listen to his conversation. But she'd forced herself to head upstairs and go to bed instead, avoiding him, avoiding everything.

But she knew she couldn't keep doing it. If she wanted answers, she was going to have to face asking questions. And she did want answers. The basic facts. Because how was she going to make any decisions concerning the ranch when she didn't know anything?

No, she had to know, and she didn't understand why she was avoiding it. After all, it wasn't as if it hurt *that* much. Not when she'd stopped allowing herself to be hurt by her father years ago.

Taking a breath, Chloe strode from the living room and began looking for Van.

He wasn't anywhere on the first floor or in the office on the second, and she knew he hadn't gone out that day, which left him somewhere upstairs.

The third floor had a living room and a small movie

theater, and he wasn't there, so she continued going up, past the bedrooms on the fourth, fifth, and sixth floors, to the seventh floor at the top of the house.

There was a massive bedroom, the floor-to-ceiling windows showing off magnificent views of the city, and a high-spec gym that not only had the same kind of views, but the added bonus of the view of the man working out inside it.

Chloe stopped in the doorway, leaning against the door-frame, everything in her head vanishing as she took in the sight of Van wearing nothing but a pair of workout pants, doing pull-ups on the steel bar above his head.

He had his back to her, his long hard body suspended, his biceps flexing as he pulled himself up, the play of his powerful back muscles mesmerizing her as he let himself back down. Then he did it again. And again. Up and down, every movement slow and expertly controlled.

She should say something, let him know she was there, but for some reason she couldn't seem to find her voice. Couldn't seem to stop looking.

His tanned skin was oiled with sweat, gleaming in the light pouring through the windows and bouncing off the white walls of the gym, every perfect muscle outlined. He was the ultimate female fantasy come to life, all wide shoulders, sculpted lats, and lean hips. And God, there was something hypnotic about the way he was raising himself up then lowering himself back down, something in the discipline required to keep those movements unhurried and restrained. Something in such an obvious display of strength.

You know how strong he is. You felt it yesterday when he put his arms around you.

Chloe swallowed, the memory from the day before returning yet again. His hot skin against her back, the power in his arm as it had curled around her waist, the feel of his hard torso pressed to her spine . . .

A helpless shiver went through her just as Van let go of the bar, landing lightly on his feet. He reached for the towel hanging on the bar above him, swiping it over his face, and without turning around he said, "Are you ready to talk now?"

She blinked. How did he know she was there? She hadn't made a sound, she knew it.

He's a SEAL. He has superpowers. He probably knew the moment you came into the gym.

Irritated at herself and not wanting to think about how he must know exactly how long she'd been standing there staring at him, Chloe took a couple of steps into the room and folded her arms. "I have questions."

"Of course you do." Van slung the towel around his neck and bent to pick up the water bottle sitting on the floor next to him. Then he turned around, and she was faced with that magnificent chest and the eagle-and-trident tattoo splashed across it, gleaming with sweat.

Heat began to creep up her neck and into her cheeks, and she had to look toward the windows, trying to ignore the furious beat of her heart. Jesus, he was only a shirtless guy and she'd seen plenty of shirtless guys before. There was no reason she should find him in particular so affecting.

"You okay, pretty?"

The deep gravel of his voice and the pressure of his gaze made her feel oddly exposed, so she kept her attention on the buildings out the window. She wasn't going to break this time, she just wasn't. "I'm fine, thanks."

There was a brief silence.

"Okay." His tone was neutral, for which she was grateful, because if he'd pressed her, she might have turned around and walked right back out again. "Ask me your questions then."

She took a small, silent breath. "How do you know it's true? About Dad?"

"I think I said yesterday. There were test results proving his infertility in the letter I got. Plus there was also a paternity test."

Oh yes, he'd said something about that, hadn't he? She'd still been reeling from that first hammerblow, too shocked to take it in.

The coal behind her breastbone smoldered painfully, but she ignored it. "So it's definitely true?" She made her voice sound strong, pulling her gaze from the window to look at him, to prove that she was absolutely and completely fine. Because this didn't hurt. At all. "I'm really a de Santis?"

Van's gaze was steady. "You are."

There was a heavy finality to his tone that gave the words sharp edges. Yet there was also something in the way he'd said them, without hesitation or looking away, that showed he knew she was strong enough to take it.

She appreciated that, if nothing else.

"How?" she asked. "How did it happen? I mean, he didn't tell me much about Mom, only that she was a barmaid in his hometown."

Chloe had never known her and Noah hadn't liked talking about her, but Chloe had managed to get the odd bit of information out of him. Charlie Price, the barmaid at the local pub in the town Noah had grown up in, and whom he'd been instantly smitten with. Theirs had been a brief love affair though, because Charlie had died of complications soon after Chloe's birth. Noah didn't talk about that either, and Chloe had always gotten the sense that her father still deeply grieved for her.

Van took a sip from his water bottle, and she found herself staring at the strong column of his throat, at the movement it made when he swallowed. And this time she didn't fight the urge to keep on looking. Because that was far easier than listening to what she knew was going to be hard to hear.

"Okay," he said, lowering the bottle. "So your mom wrote Dad a letter telling him she was pregnant and when he wrote back telling her that he was infertile, she admitted that she'd had a one-night stand the week before she and Dad had gotten together. The guy had only told her his first name—Cesare. Dad knew it couldn't be anyone else but his old enemy. He got that paternity test not long after you were born, and the results were conclusive."

There was a lurching sensation in her gut. She ignored it.

"So Cesare de Santis is my father." The words sounded strange out loud, and came out thick, as if her mouth was full of cotton balls. "Okay, but if Dad knew, why did he keep me? When de Santis was the enemy?"

Van took another sip from his bottle before putting it down on the floor beside the weight bench, leaning his elbows on his knees. "You're not going to like the answer to that, pretty. Are you sure you want to hear it?"

The lurching sensation got even worse, this time followed by a sudden flood of nausea. She gritted her teeth against it. "Tell me."

Something changed in his expression, a golden glint in his eyes that she recognized from years ago, from when she'd fallen off her pony at that first riding lesson. He'd asked her if she wanted to stop, and she'd said no. He'd had that same glint then. The one that told her he was impressed, that he approved.

It shouldn't matter what he thought of her, not when she'd told herself she didn't care. Yet seeing that glint made her feel a little less sick.

"You're right. De Santis was the enemy." Van's gaze was steady on hers. "But Dad thought that keeping his daughter would protect our family. A hostage so de Santis would leave us and Tate Oil alone."

So that's what she'd been? Her father's little hostage? His insurance policy? The coal burning inside her flared in response, a bright spark of pain, and she had to dig her fingers into her upper arms to stop it from leaking out.

She thought she'd inured herself to all the ways her father had hurt her, but apparently she wasn't as immune as she'd thought. Apparently she still carried a few shreds of hope around inside her. The hope that one day he'd keep at least one of his promises, that he'd show her she actually meant something to him.

Clearly *that* was a mistake, so why the hell was she still letting herself expect things from him? Why was she still letting him hurt her?

Van watched her silently, and that sympathy she recognized from the day before was back in his gaze, as if he knew exactly what she was feeling. It made her throat close up tight.

"I know it's hard to hear," he said quietly. "But you're not alone, okay? Dad's always been about looking out for the business first and foremost. Why do you think he adopted Wolf and Lucas and me? It wasn't because he wanted kids to love. It was because he needed someone to protect his legacy, because he needed heirs."

Something bitter edged his voice, distracting her for a moment.

"What? You didn't want to be his heir?"

He shook his head. "Hell no. I wanted to stay in the military. Do my part to protect the country, not protect his bottom line." The warm golden gleam in his eyes was gone, leaving behind a cold, green light. "That's why I'm not going to be here any longer than I fucking have to."

Chloe studied his strong, handsome face. Okay, so she wasn't the only one with Daddy issues. Van had them too.

Curiosity stirred inside her and she was tempted to ask him what was really so bad about protecting Noah's bottom line. But now wasn't the time to have that conversation. He probably wouldn't tell her anyway and besides, she still had other questions. "How long have you known? That Noah wasn't my father?"

"Only since I got that letter. Like I said, he told me not to tell you about it, but I thought that was bullshit. I thought you needed to know." He sat up straighter, his gaze piercing. "Was I wrong?"

She lifted her chin instinctively, as if the question was a challenge. "No. I'd much rather know the truth than be lied to. And Dad always did tell a lot of lies."

Van's gaze ran over her, doing that checking thing again, as if scanning her for injuries. She didn't like it. It made her feel like she wasn't as fine as she told herself she was.

"Don't look at me like that," she snapped. "I'm okay, I told you."

He didn't react, his cool stare meeting hers. "What other lies did he tell you?"

But she didn't want to talk about that, not right now. Ignoring him, she said, "So I guess that's why Dad couldn't leave me the ranch, right? Because de Santis might potentially use me to get it for himself?"

"Yeah. That's pretty much it. You're de Santis's target and while that's the case, Dad couldn't leave you anything."

De Santis was targeting her. De Santis, her father, was targeting her.

That sickness twisted again inside her and she had to turn away all of a sudden, taking a few steps toward the windows, keeping her arms wrapped tightly around herself. "What did Dad think de Santis was going to do?" She had to force the question out.

"Think about it." Van's voice came from behind her, much closer than she'd expected, and then she became aware of his scent, the spiciness of a rain-soaked forest and the musk of clean, male sweat. It made it difficult to concentrate on what he was saying. "If you owned the ranch, guess who your closest living relative is?"

"I get it." She stared unseeing at the buildings opposite, her awareness helplessly centering on the man standing just behind her. "Dad didn't want to risk leaving me anything in case de Santis had me killed so he could inherit it." It was a brutal truth, but she saw no point in trying to soften it.

Van said nothing, but then he didn't have to. It was obvious.

The building opposite began to waver, and it was strange how the expanse of brick seemed to shudder in the air while the ground beneath her feet remained completely stable. And then she realized that it was wavering because of the tears in her eyes.

This was stupid. Finding out she wasn't Noah's daughter didn't change anything. Didn't make any difference to a relationship that hadn't really been there in the first place.

Yeah, but that blood tie was the only connection you had with him.

"Chloe." Van's voice held a warm note and she had a sudden, intense urge to turn around and put her head against that strong chest of his the way she had yesterday.

Not that she would. She had her pride. She wouldn't let herself be vulnerable again and she certainly wasn't going to let herself be hurt again, not by anyone.

"I know you keep wanting to make sure that I'm fine." She turned around and met his gaze head-on. "Well, I am. Got it?"

She wasn't fine, though. He could see it in the way she stood—the way her shoulders hunched as if bracing for some kind of impact—the tight expression on her face, and the brittle quality to her voice.

No, if anything, she was just barely holding it together.

But that was good. He didn't want her to fall apart the way she had yesterday, because he wasn't here to comfort her. He was here to protect her, and telling her the truth, giving her all the facts, was part of that. Plus, there was his weird physical reaction to her when he'd put his arms around her the day before, and he *definitely* didn't want that coming back.

It was partly why he'd let her have her space after he'd gotten back from his meeting with the lawyers yesterday. If she hadn't wanted to talk, he hadn't been in the mood to press her, plus his brothers had finally gotten back to him, promising to be at the Tate Oil meeting he'd scheduled to finally face the board. Neither of them had told him jack shit about what was going on with them, which hadn't done his temper any good, and so it seemed prudent to keep some distance between him and Chloe. Because God knew she didn't need him being a grumpy fuck, not when the equivalent of a stick of gelignite had exploded in her life.

So what he should be doing right now, since he'd given her all the facts, was to leave her alone to deal with those facts and to keep himself uninvolved.

Yet he found himself simply unable to walk away.

She looked small and fragile, her face white, dark circles under her big dark eyes.

He'd always known that Noah had cared about his foster kids more as abstracts than as people. As heirs, as guardians of his legacy, as tools to protect his real love: Tate Oil.

But Chloe clearly hadn't known that, and for some reason Van didn't like that thought. It wasn't her fault Noah had been a lying asshole, and it made him angry that Noah had clearly done something to make her think he was a better man that he actually was.

"You're not fine," Van disagreed, scanning her pale face. "You look like hell."

Something burned in the darkness of her eyes, a hot flame. A familiar anger. "Yeah, well, I didn't sleep all that great. That bed is really uncomfortable."

"Bullshit. It's not the bed."

Her chin lifted higher. "Of course it's the bed."

"So you sobbed all over me yesterday because you had a shitty night's sleep. Right. Totally nothing to do with the fact that you just found out your father was a fucking liar not to mention not actually your father."

She flushed. "Yesterday was an aberration, so don't worry, it won't happen again. Besides, like I said, I always knew Dad was a liar. This isn't as big a surprise to me as you apparently think it is."

He stared at her, trying to read her expression. "You don't have to be embarrassed about it. You know that, right? You'd just had a hell of a shock."

Her cheeks went even redder. "You know what? I think I'm done here. Thanks for the chat." She turned, making as if to go past him toward the door.

And he didn't know why he didn't let her. Didn't understand what made him reach out and take that stubborn little chin in his hand. What made him hold her gently but firmly, turning her face toward his so he could look at her.

Her eyes had gone wide and there was no disguising the angry glow burning in their depths.

No, she wasn't fine. This hurt her. This *really* hurt her. But she was pretending very very hard that it didn't.

"Noah lying to you was a shitty thing," he said, because it was and because he wanted her to know that he knew it was. "It's okay to be angry about it."

"Yeah, well, thanks for the validation, but I don't need it. I couldn't give a crap whether he's my father or not."

Little liar. Why was she pretending this didn't matter to her?

"Oh, come on." Her skin was very warm beneath his fingers, very soft. "You think I can't see how furious you are?"

Her mouth flattened and she tried to jerk her head away. But something in him wouldn't let her go, wanting to help her, protect her. Comfort her.

Stupid. He knew he shouldn't be doing this, that he should be letting her walk away. Yet the skin beneath his fingers was so smooth. So fragile.

She'd broken apart yesterday, right out there in the street. Had put her head on his chest and wept. Apparently not caring about the fact they hadn't seen each other for eight years and were virtual strangers. No, she'd done it as if she felt safe with him. As if she trusted him.

And you know what happens to women who do that, don't you?

He felt cold all of a sudden. Fuck, of course he knew. They died.

"I'm not angry," Chloe snapped. "Let me go, asshole."

She was standing close to him, probably too close, and he didn't know where this urge to push her had come from. And what was worse, he wanted to keep doing it, to find out why she was protecting herself so fiercely, why she'd broken yesterday, and why she was now trying to pretend that that hadn't happened.

These things don't matter. Why are you letting them?

Fuck if he knew.

"Yeah, you are," he murmured. "But what I can't figure out is why you're pretending you're not."

"Like I said, I'm not having this conversation now." Her dark eyes glowed hot. "Let me go, Van."

He could feel the tension in her jaw and in her neck.

Could feel it gathering in the space between them too, a thick, heavy kind of tension that shouldn't be there.

Did she feel this? Or was it just him?

He found himself staring as she swallowed, his attention caught by the elegant column of her neck before settling on the beat of her pulse at the base of her throat.

Was it getting faster or was that his imagination?

What the fuck are you doing? Let her go, dick.

The tension pulled tighter, the hot anger in Chloe's eyes wavering as she glanced, oh so briefly, at his mouth.

He knew that look. He'd seen it many times on the faces of the women he picked up while he was on leave. Women who didn't want anything more from him than a night of hot, commitment-free sex. Women who simply needed a hard-muscled body to fuck before going off to do whatever else it was they did, which was the way he preferred it.

Yeah, those women looked at him the way Chloe was looking at him right now—wanting him.

Something dangerously like satisfaction clenched deep inside him. Which was just so fucking wrong. She was his goddamn foster sister and Jesus, apart from anything else, he was supposed to be protecting her.

And that includes protecting her from you.

Fuck.

It took far more effort than it should have to let go of her chin and take a step back, away from her. But he did it.

"Fine." He tried to ignore the fact that his voice sounded husky. "Have it your way. But now you know the truth, you'll understand why it's important that you do exactly what I say. De Santis is dangerous and we can't let him know you're here. I need more time to figure out just what the fuck we're going to do about him."

There was color in her cheeks now, and he didn't think it was purely lingering embarrassment from him mentioning the day before. But she didn't look away this time.

"Why? What the hell do you think he's going to do? I don't own anything, so I'm of no use to him at all."

"Yeah, but he doesn't know that." The warmth from her skin lingered on his fingertips and he found he'd curled them into a fist, as if he could keep hold of her heat. Surreptitiously he straightened them. "And even if he does know you were cut out of the will, that doesn't stop you from being a useful hostage."

A muscle in her jaw tightened, her shoulders hunching even more. "So, what? I continue to be trapped here? Until you deal with him?"

Once again he felt the oddest urge to take her in his arms, because beneath the anger she steadfastly refused to acknowledge, he caught a glimpse of what he thought was fear.

Christ, it really was time he got out of here. He didn't need her getting under his skin any more than she'd already done.

"Pretty much," he said shortly, stepping back and turning toward the door.

"But what am I supposed to do? I can't just . . . sit here in front of the TV."

"Then use the gym." He didn't wait for a response. He simply strode out before she could say another word.

It was only as he was standing beneath the shower, letting the water clean away all the sweat from his workout, that he realized he could still feel the smooth warmth of her skin beneath his fingertips.

CHAPTER SIX

Use the gym, Van had said the day before.

"Fuck you," Chloe muttered as she sat on the edge of the bed, watching the flakes in the snow globe whirl around the miniature ice rink.

She didn't know why she was looking at it, but O'Neil hadn't needed anything from her when she'd called the ranch that morning, and she'd gotten sick of watching television. Exploring the mansion had taken all of ten minutes, and after a cursory search through the library had turned up nothing to read but classics and books on business, the only thing left was to sit on the bed and fiddle with her stupid globe.

She shook it again, the snowflakes a blizzard against the glass. She still remembered her father giving it to her. How she'd had her bag packed the whole week, just like she always did whenever he made his "this time you can come to New York" promises. She'd been so excited, thinking that this time he really meant it. He'd organized a chopper to pick her up from the ranch and from there she'd be taken to the airfield where the corporate jet would fly her to the city. She had her bodyguards with her, and her dad would be waiting for her at the other end so there wouldn't be any danger.

She'd waited for the chopper to come sitting on the

staircase with her suitcase on her knees, almost vibrating with excitement. But the time for it to come slowly passed and still there was no sound from the sky, none at all. She sat there a whole two hours, the pit in her stomach getting wider and wider, until the front door of the ranch house had opened and one of her dad's employees came in carrying a box with a small note attached.

In the box was the snow globe, and the note attached had merely said that he was sorry but this visit wasn't going to work out. That maybe she should come later in the year, when he wasn't so busy, and here was a little piece of New York to keep her company instead.

She'd unpacked the snow globe, tears of disappointment streaming down her cheeks, hating herself for continually believing that this time would be different. Believing that one day he'd actually do what he promised.

Because it wasn't really about going to New York. It was about whether her father actually cared about her. And the fact that he kept building up her hopes only to dash them at the last minute proved that he didn't care, that he was happy with the distance he consistently held her at, and that she would never bridge it.

It had been in that moment that she'd decided. She wasn't going to believe his empty promises any longer. She wouldn't hope that things would change. She would let him keep his distance and she would find something else to channel her love into. And she'd keep the snow globe to remind herself of the danger of believing anything her goddamn father said.

Chloe sat there staring at the stupid thing.

She didn't understand why she'd even believed him at all when he'd told her that she was his own blood. In fact, why had he even said it at all? Why had he pretended that she was his when she wasn't? It didn't make any sense.

She should have asked Van the day before, but he'd

walked so abruptly out of the gym, she hadn't had the chance. She still didn't know what had happened to make him leave, but he'd shut himself in his office for the entire day afterward, making it pretty clear he didn't want to have any further discussion.

You really don't know why he left?

Chloe's breath caught, the memory of his hand holding her chin sweeping through her. His grip had been gentle yet firm, and he'd looked down at her with a hot gold flicker in his eyes.

She'd felt the tension between them, dense as the atmosphere before one of the wild storms that sometimes came in over Shadow Peak. And she'd felt her attention drift helplessly to his sensual mouth.

She couldn't kid herself that she didn't know what that tension was, or what it might mean. Sure, she was pretty inexperienced when it came to men, but she knew what sexual tension was. She knew what it felt like.

Abruptly, she put the globe back on the nightstand and stood up.

No, she wasn't going to think about the look in Van's eyes, or the way he held her, or the heat of his body, oiled and gleaming, so hard and muscled and perfect. She wasn't going to think about the part of her that knew he'd felt the tension between them as well. And had liked it.

No, shit, she *definitely* wasn't going to think about that.

God, what she needed was air, just a single hit of fresh air. She hadn't been outside for a good three days and she was going stir crazy. Maybe that was why she was feeling this way, nothing to do with that hot coal in her chest, the one that kept burning and burning and wouldn't go out.

Chloe left the bedroom and went out into the hall, glancing up the stairs. When she'd found Van in the gym the day before, she'd caught a glimpse of a rooftop terrace beyond the windows of his bedroom. Sure, he'd told her not to go outside, but surely standing on the roof would be okay? No one could see her up there and besides, she wasn't going to be out there for long. Just enough to cool that hot, burning feeling.

Van would be pissed, but hell, he wasn't here. He'd gone by the time she'd woken up that morning, leaving her a note that he would be out most of the day. So what he wouldn't know, wouldn't hurt him.

Chloe stomped up the stairs to the top floor and into Van's bedroom.

It was incredibly tidy. The bed was made and there were no clothes lying about. A large black bag was sitting on an armchair near the window. She could smell the slight hint of his fresh, forest scent and found herself inhaling for no particular reason she could see.

Stupid, she was being stupid.

Down one end of the bedroom, near the black bag, was a row of floor-to-ceiling windows with a view out onto the terrace. There was a door handle in one of the windows.

Chloe moved over to the door and tested the handle. It was locked. There was, however, a small lever that after a quick fiddle solved the problem.

She pushed it open and stepped out, and for a moment simply stood there, inhaling the scent of the city. It wasn't sunny—the sky an intense, heavy gray—there was a cold wind blowing and a bite of rain in the air, but Chloe didn't care.

She sucked in one breath and then another, enjoying the brush of wind on her face and raising goose bumps on her skin. The city smelled heavily of exhaust fumes, trash, and wet asphalt, which she didn't much like, but being out in the open air was worth it.

Closing the door behind her, she walked farther out onto the terrace, shivering in the cold wind. The area was bounded by a brick parapet with lots of potted shrubs and trees, and there was an arrangement of outdoor furniture down one end—a sectional sofa plus some armchairs and a table.

Chloe wandered over to the side of the terrace and leaned her elbows on the parapet, staring out over the city, blinking at all the buildings. She'd never been in a city. She'd never even been to Buffalo. And New York was . . . well, she had to admit it was something.

There was the Chrysler Building. And there's the Empire State. And wasn't that Rockefeller Center where they have a skating rink in the winter? Just like in her snow globe?

Her throat tightened.

She was here, finally, after all those years of broken promises. But this time it was without Noah. Because Noah was dead and gone.

The coal in her chest smoldered painfully, and suddenly she didn't want to be out here looking at a view she should have been sharing with her dad. Perhaps watching TV hadn't been such a bad idea after all.

Then something caught her attention, a flash, like light reflecting off a window. She squinted, leaning out slightly, trying to figure out what it was. It had come from the building opposite, she was sure.

"Chloe," a deep, male voice ordered harshly from behind her. "Get the fuck away from the parapet."

Chloe was bent over the edge of the damn building, her black hair blowing around in the wind, revealing herself to anyone who might be watching. Van didn't know if de Santis had the building under surveillance yet, but he did know that de Santis was a man who left nothing to chance and that Chloe was tempting fate.

At the sound of his voice, she straightened and turned sharply, her eyes going wide as he slammed the door shut behind him and headed toward her.

Jesus, what the hell was she doing out here? He'd thought he'd been clear about the whole going outside thing. Sure, he hadn't actually specified that the rooftop terrace was out of bounds, but he'd thought she'd have understood the nature of the danger.

It put him in even more of a foul temper than he already was.

The day had started badly with the meeting of the board at Tate Oil and Gas. Wolf had been late and then, when Van had explained the purpose of the meeting to the board—which was to fire the lot of them—his youngest brother had nearly gotten into a fight with a board member who'd taken exception to being let go.

Van had had to do some pretty quick negotiating in order to defuse the situation, while Lucas had sat there with his arms folded, sweeping the room with a look that promised death to anyone stupid enough to cause any more trouble.

Van hadn't wanted to handle all the company bullshit by coming in and handing out orders like a damn dictator, but he'd realized the moment he'd walked into the meeting room, his brothers at his side, that unfortunately that was exactly what he was going to have to do.

None of the board members were happy with the brothers coming in and screwing around with their cushy corporate jobs and their fat corporate paychecks, but Noah Tate's word was law. And if the brothers were now the board, then the brothers were now the board.

Even if the brothers themselves weren't happy about it.

After the meeting, they'd spent all day closeted in the board room with a couple of Noah's trusted managers, getting the lowdown on the company and where it was at. And unfortunately for all of them, the news wasn't good.

Someone very, very powerful had been in the process of buying up Tate stock, and it looked like that someone was now angling to stage a hostile takeover. But it wasn't clear exactly how much stock they actually owned.

They all knew, of course, who it was buying it.

Cesare de Santis, their father's bitter enemy and past owner of DS Corp, one of the country's biggest defense companies. Oh, and Chloe's father.

The man who'd tried to steal Noah's claim on the oil strike that had made the Tate fortune. A man the Tates needed to be careful of. One day, Noah had said, de Santis would try to bring them down as sure as the sky was blue.

Well, the sky wasn't fucking blue today and Cesare wasn't going to touch anything Tate—and that included Chloe. Who was glaring at him and very definitely *not* getting away from that fucking parapet.

"Didn't you hear what I said?" Van growled, stalking over to her. "Get away from the edge."

"Why?"

"Because if anyone's watching this house you've just announced your presence to the whole damn world."

"What?" She frowned, but took a couple of steps away from the parapet all the same, thank Christ. "I don't know that they. . . ." She stopped, her face gradually going pale. "Oh."

Van did *not* like her expression one bit. " 'Oh'? What do you mean 'oh'?"

She glanced at the view behind her. "I thought I saw a flash of something in the building opposite just now. I was trying to spot what it was but . . ."

Foreboding turned over inside him, cold and heavy. "What kind of flash?"

"Um, like a reflection, I think. Off glass or something." Her brows drew together. "It couldn't have been anything."

Of course it could've.

Cesare de Santis was finally making his move on the

Tates now that Noah was dead; both on the company and now on the family.

This was not good. The man was hugely wealthy, hugely powerful, and as one of the biggest suppliers of weapons to the military, he had friends in very, *very* high places. If he wanted the Tates taken down, then he would take the Tates down.

And, Christ, Chloe . . .

Instantly Van was in military mode.

"Get into the house," he ordered and she must have heard the don't-fuck-with-me note in his voice because this time she went without a protest.

Van reached around and took out his Glock from the back of his suit pants, moving over to the edge of the roof while keeping his gun low and out of sight. He didn't bother to look like he didn't know what was going on—no point now if Chloe had been spotted—leaning out and scanning the building opposite. He couldn't see anything, but as he was about to go back inside, someone came out of the door at street level and began walking away.

It wouldn't have looked at all suspicious if Van hadn't been alert to the fact that the timing was pretty weird and if the guy hadn't glanced up at the Tate building as he stepped out. But the man did and as soon as he spotted Van, he began to run.

Van didn't waste any time. He leapt up onto the parapet and was over the side of the building before the man on the ground had taken more than a couple of steps. Luckily Van knew the Tate building well. He knew all the entrances and exits, which windows were accessible and which were not, where all the pipes were, and even how the fucking place was wired. So he knew there was a fire escape just below the parapet and he knew he could climb down it because he'd practiced it many times, during the day and in the dark. He could fucking climb it with his eyes closed—in fact, he had.

So it took him no time at all to launch himself down the side, reach the sidewalk, and take off after the guy. The man had maybe a minute's lead, but obviously hadn't trained as frequently or as well as Van because Van found himself gaining on him pretty rapidly.

His instinct was to take out the guy's legs with a couple of well-placed shots, but he was in broad daylight, in the middle of the city. And even though it was New York, people would probably notice. So he kept his piece down and low at his side as he ran, his focus on his target. Who was unexpectedly slowing.

Van put on a burst of speed, but it was too late.

A car was parked by curb up ahead, and the man pulled open the door and flung himself inside before Van could catch up. Van made a grab for the door, but the car pulled away with a screech of tires, leaving him grabbing at empty air.

He cursed, coming to a halt, adrenaline raging inside him, suddenly aware that there were a whole lot of people standing around looking at him. Oh yeah, this was going to look good. The Tate heir running around like a madman on the streets with a fucking gun. Great. His CO was not going to enjoy him drawing attention to himself, that was for fucking sure.

Sliding his Glock into the pocket of his jacket, he settled his clothing back into place and, ignoring the stares, managed a sedate walk back to the house as if nothing had happened.

Chloe was standing in the entranceway with her arms folded, her chin at a belligerent angle. She looked angry, yet her face was pale. And if he wasn't much mistaken, concern glittered in the depths of her dark eyes.

Yeah, well, she *should* be concerned. By taking a tour

around the rooftop terrace, she'd just alerted a very dangerous man to her presence in New York.

"Are you okay?" she asked in cross voice. "What happened? I saw you go over the side of the building."

He stared at her. Why the hell was she asking about him? He was a goddamn SEAL. He was fine. It was her own personal safety she should be worried about.

She saw you go over the side of a building, holding a gun. It might actually be you she's worried about. Ever think of that?

No, quite frankly he hadn't. And it struck him weirdly, because he couldn't remember the last time someone had worried about him.

Certainly his father never had. The old bastard never showed anything beyond a curt nod when he approved of something or a slow shake of his head when he didn't. Praise wasn't something he gave out, and as for a smile, or even a pat on the back, forget it. He'd been very much of the "hard work is its own reward" school of parenting.

Van had come to hate it, of course. Nothing had made him feel more like a figurehead, the Tate heir, than Noah's lack of anything resembling fatherly warmth or affection. Many times all he'd wanted a simple heartfelt "Well done, son." But he'd never gotten even that, not matter how hard he'd worked for it. In fact, the only affection he'd ever gotten had been those few hugs from Chloe.

Back then, her open-hearted acceptance of him had been balm to his soul, but now? After the mission in Columbia where he'd lost Sofia?

Yeah, after that he'd hardened the fuck up, and he didn't need anyone worried about him or any of that "feelings" bullshit that went along with it these days.

"There is a fire escape down the side," he said brusquely, shoving away the strange sense of exposure Chloe's worry had uncovered and filling the hole it left with anger. "Some asshole in the building opposite must have seen you, because I saw him leaving. And when he spotted me, he ran. I went after him, but I didn't catch him unfortunately."

"Oh." She unfolded her arms and shoved her hands in her pockets. That's not so good."

"'That's not so good'?" he echoed, fucking pissed now, the adrenaline pumping through his system desperately needing an outlet. "What the fuck were you thinking? I told you not to go outside."

Her chin came up, her shoulders going back, squaring herself off as if defending herself against an attack. "You didn't say anything about the roof garden. And how the hell was I supposed to know there would be some asshole watching the whole damn building?"

He normally had no issues with keeping hold of his patience when things were going all to hell—as a commander he had to. But for some reason, today that patience felt slippery and difficult to grip, and he wasn't sure why.

Yes, he'd had shitty days before, plenty of them. Wasn't one of the SEAL creeds "The only easy day was yesterday"? So all this crap going down at Tate, plus the fact that Chloe's location had been revealed, shouldn't have made him so angry.

Yet he was. Suddenly, he was goddamn furious.

He took a couple of slow, stalking steps toward her, "The roof garden *is* outside, you little idiot." He took another step. "Is this a game to you? Did you think I was kidding when I told you to stay inside? That that was some kind of test?"

She held her ground, scowling. And like always, there was a part of him that admired her sheer guts. She was so much smaller than he was and he was obviously very angry, and yet she wasn't backing down, a gleam of defiance in her bitter chocolate eyes. "No," she said. "Of course it isn't a game. I just wanted some fresh air and didn't think anyone would see me on the damn roof."

A stain of color had appeared on her cheekbones, her hair a black tangle around her shoulders. She looked wild and something like free, and he was suddenly back at the ranch, almost ten years earlier, when the Navy had forced him to take some leave after what had gone down in Columbia.

It had been a mission to bust open a sex-trafficking ring and it should have been an easy one, but for various reasons the whole thing had gotten fucked up. Van ended up having to take one of the women on the run in order to protect her. For three days they'd gone deeper and deeper into the jungle in an attempt to shake their pursuers. For three days he'd promised he'd save her, get her back to her fiancé. Only to lose her. There had been ten of the pricks and Van had killed every last one, but none of that made any difference. He hadn't saved Sofia.

Back home, he'd suffered nightmares and all kinds of shit, and as much as he'd hated having to take leave, going back to the ranch, spending time riding and helping out with ranch work had helped.

One day he'd been out exercising one of the more restless stallions and he'd unexpectedly met Chloe coming down one of Shadow Peak's trails. She'd had the same expression on her face then too, color in her sharp little cheekbones, all black hair and bright gleaming eyes.

Seeing her had been a jolt, an electric shock. She'd been weird with him the whole time he'd been home and he'd gotten the impression she was avoiding him. It hadn't made him feel any better about himself, he had to admit, even though she wouldn't have known what had gone down on that mission.

And he hadn't known what it was, but suddenly she'd

given him a grin as if she hadn't been able to help herself—
the bright, open grin from when she'd been a kid—and
then spurred her horse past him, galloping off down the trail
like she was riding the Kentucky Derby. He'd watched her
for a second, the pain of his failure with Sofia still sharp
enough to draw blood, and all of a sudden racing Chloe
home had seemed like just the distraction he craved. So he
had, urging his own horse after her, racing her all the way
back to the house.

*You don't want to race her right now. You want to do
something much worse.*

Ah, fuck.

She was only a couple of steps away. All it would take
was for him to take those steps, close the distance, take
her chin in his hand the way he'd done the day before and
tip her head back . . .

Kiss her. Taste her. Pick her up and take her upstairs . . .

No, *shit,* what the fuck was he thinking? Noah had
charged him with protecting her, and Van was pretty sure
that protecting her meant not touching her. Ever. He was the
Tate heir, for God's sake. And, Christ, if the old bastard
knew what Van was thinking right now, he'd kill him.

Getting himself under control—which took far more
effort than it should have—Van reached into his back
pocket and grabbed his phone. "Yeah, well, someone *did*
see you on the damn roof. Which means that Cesare de
Santis knows you're here."

She shifted on her feet, looking both angry and defensive.
"I'm sorry, okay? I didn't know this was going to happen."

But Van was in no mood for apologies. "Whether you
did or not, we need to get out of here right now."

"We have to leave? Why?"

Ignoring her, he typed a two-word text to his brothers
that read *Leo's. Now.* Then he pushed send and pinned her
with a look. "Go get your stuff, we have to move."

CHAPTER SEVEN

Chloe's first instinct was to tell Van where he could stick his goddamn orders, but his eyes had gone from hazel to pure green with anger, so she knew that being stubborn now was probably not the best course of action. Not after she'd clearly screwed up by stepping out onto that terrace.

Guilt twisted inside her, which she hated, so she reached for anger instead, opening her mouth to demand he tell her where they were going at least.

But he forestalled her with a curt, "Now, Chloe."

She wanted to argue, but the look on his face was downright terrifying in its contained fury, and since pissing off an already angry stallion was never a good idea, she turned for the stairs and did as she was told.

Getting her stuff together didn't take long, mainly because she didn't have much stuff to get together, and she was back downstairs within ten minutes to find Van already waiting for her.

He was in that dark gray suit again, with a white shirt, except this time the shirt was buttoned up and he had a forest green silk tie around his neck that made his eyes look greener than they actually were.

God, he was hot. She really couldn't deny that he was, not anymore.

She'd gotten the shock of her life as she'd watched him

go over the side of the building, and she'd almost run to the parapet to see if he was okay, only stopping herself at the last minute. She didn't want to make her mistake any worse and besides, he was some kind of military superhero. He'd be okay.

Yet she found herself worrying all the same.

She'd dashed downstairs, reaching the door to go outside, only remembering at the last second yet again that she wasn't supposed to. So she'd paced around in the entryway instead, going over and over what she would do if he didn't come back. Not that she could come up with anything other than the fact that if he didn't, she would be alone. Really and truly alone.

The thought had made her go completely and utterly cold, which she'd hated. She hated, too, the realization that losing Van would mean losing the one person in the world she was closest to.

How is he close when you haven't seen him for eight years?

Yeah, and she didn't like *that* thought either. Not what it said about her and her life or what it said about her relationship with Van. Anyway, hadn't she dedicated those last eight years to *not* caring?

In fact, the thought had pissed her off so much that when the front door had banged opened and he'd come in, his expression taut with anger, his eyes glittering like emeralds, all she'd been able to do was scowl at him, trying to ignore the way her heart had given a kick of sheer relief.

And then he'd gone and ruined it by getting angry at her, not that he hadn't had good reason, it had to be said, but still. How was she to know what she should and shouldn't be doing? That there'd be some asshole in a nearby building watching the house?

Chloe gripped tight to the strap of her bag as she came down the rest of the stairs. "I still don't see why we actually have to leave," she said flatly. "I thought I was supposed to be safe here. And where the hell are we going anyway?"

The black bag she'd seen earlier up in Van's room was sitting beside him, and now he bent and picked it up, flinging it over his shoulder. "Later. Right now we need to get out of here. De Santis will know that we know you've been spotted, which means he'll be desperate to get some guys here before I can get you somewhere safer."

"What's he going to do? Kidnap me or something?"

"Ask me any more questions and we'll find out." He turned toward the door. "Come on. We need to go before they get here."

"But, what if—"

"Out," Van ordered, holding open the door. "The quicker we leave, the more time we'll have to lose them."

Biting her lip, Chloe did as she was told, going down the front steps and onto the sidewalk. Van followed at her heels, moving over to the plain, black sedan he'd picked her up in a couple of days earlier.

They both got in and a minute or so later Van had pulled into the traffic, heading downtown.

Chloe stared out the window, realizing with a jolt that she was finally out of the house and actually in New York City, passing by the famous landmarks, watching the crowds of people on the sidewalk. Then they were on a much wider road with lots of lanes, the river on one side, a wall of buildings on the other.

"Keep your head down." Van's deep voice held that same note of authority. "There's unlikely to be anyone watching now, but no point in making it easy for them."

Chloe's jaw tightened. "I can't even look out the window?"

"No. We'll be there in fifteen minutes anyway."

"Be where?"

But he didn't answer, pulling out from behind the slow truck he was tailing and putting his foot down. The car gathering speed as it moved sleek and fast through the traffic.

Okay, he was pissed at her—she got that loud and clear. And sure, he had something to be pissed about. If she'd really thought about it, she might not have gone out on the terrace. Then again, she truly hadn't expected the whole damn house would be watched.

A cold thread wound through her as the reality of the danger settled in her gut.

She'd never really believed all her father's dire predictions about the threat his old enemy presented, mainly because nothing had ever happened to her. Yes, she'd been protected on the ranch and since she'd never ventured far from it, there hadn't been any opportunity for anything to happen. Still, she'd always thought Noah was overstating the danger.

Apparently he hadn't been.

"I thought I was safe with you," she said, breaking the silence in the car. "I mean, that's the whole reason you brought me here, right?"

"You *are* safe with me." Van glanced into the rearview mirror as he changed lanes. "I'm being cautious. I don't want you anywhere de Santis even knows about until I've got a plan for how to deal with him."

"You don't have a plan?" The cold thread that she refused to call fear pulled a little tighter inside her. "So what the hell have you been doing the past few days then?"

Van shot her a narrow look. "Only dealing with the potential hostile takeover of a national oil company, nothing major."

She blinked at that. "What? What hostile takeover?"

"Too complicated to explain right now. We have to get you to safety first."

"We?"

"Wolf and Lucas."

The cold thread became an icy current. Okay, it had to be *really* serious if he was involving the other two.

There were more questions she wanted to ask, but she remained silent, letting Van concentrate as he eventually pulled off the avenue and onto another side street crowded with traffic.

Five minutes later, Van drew the car up to a space by the curb and turned off the engine. Chloe glanced out the window, trying to see why they were here, only spotting the dirty windowpanes of an old-fashioned bar.

"Stay in the car," he said, pushing open his door.

Oh hell no, he wasn't leaving her alone, not after that.

Chloe reached out and grabbed his arm. "Wait. I'm coming with you."

He turned sharply, his eyes glittering. "You're fucking staying in the car and that's final. I can't risk you being spotted again."

Beneath her fingers, she could feel the muscles of his biceps go tense and hard, but she didn't let go. She wasn't going to be left behind like an afterthought, not again. And most especially not if it was her the three men would be discussing.

"No." She tightened her grip on his arm. "This is my damn life, and if you're making decisions about it, I'm sure as hell not staying in the car."

He stared at her, his gaze cold and green. She met it stubbornly, refusing to be treated like a little kid, like the youngest who wasn't ever consulted when decisions were made. The one who was always left behind and often left out.

She was an adult now and she was going to be part of this whether he liked it or not.

Something in Van's expression changed, the hard green light in his eyes fading, getting warmer, more golden. And she was suddenly acutely conscious of his heat seeping through his suit jacket and into her fingertips where they rested on his arm.

Her mouth dried, tension gathering between them, thick and hot. The same tension she'd felt in the gym the day before.

"Let go, Chloe," he said very quietly, very distinctly, his voice full of gravel.

But she didn't want to let go. She wanted to keep her hand right there, grip him tighter, test all that rock-hard muscle for herself. See what would happen if she disobeyed him . . .

Let go of him, you stupid idiot.

Right. Yes. This was insane. What the hell did she think she was doing?

Chloe jerked her hand from his arm and looked away, her heartbeat thundering in her eyes, her cheeks hot.

Van said nothing. After a moment he turned, reaching over into the back seat where he'd stashed that black bag of his. There came the sound of rummaging and then something was dumped into her lap. Swallowing, she looked down.

It was a plain, dark blue hoodie.

"Put it on," he instructed. "Then pull the hood up. That should keep your face hidden at least."

Beneath the desperate beat of her heart, she felt the tight, cold thread inside her loosen, admitting a trickle of warmth. A warmth that had nothing to do with sexual tension and everything to do with being understood.

Uncomfortable with the feeling and not wanting to examine it too closely, Chloe discarded her ratty leather jacket and pulled on the hoodie. It was massive, totally swamping her, and it smelled of him. She found herself wanting to pull it around her and bury her face in it like a kid with her favorite blanket.

You're a lost cause. You know that, right?

Okay, admitting he was hot and that she liked the way

he smelled didn't make her a "lost cause," Anyway, it wasn't as if she was going to do something about it, even if she thought he might be into it. He was her foster brother, and even if she'd never thought of him in brotherly terms, that relationship would always be there.

Van gave her a critical look then reached out and tugged the hood forward so it shaded her face. "That'll do. Come on then."

They both got out of the car and she waited on the sidewalk while he locked it. Then she followed as he headed straight for the old-fashioned bar she'd noticed when they'd pulled up.

There was a sign outside that read *Leo's Alehouse,* and as she stepped through the doorway after Van, the sound of a lot of male voices all shouting at each other and the scent of beer, sweat, and old cigarette smoke rolled over her.

The place was packed with men, most of whom were in uniform. She didn't recognize the uniforms, but she thought the guys with the white hats on were probably Navy. There were a handful of women here and there, some in uniform, but it mostly seemed to be guys.

She and Van were stared at as they entered, most of the looks directed at Van, more than a few sneers happening as the guys staring took in his suit. Van seemed oblivious to the glances he was drawing as he strode toward the back of the bar, but Chloe found herself annoyed by them. She didn't know what that was about since clearly Van didn't give a shit whether people sneered at him or not, but it irritated her. Didn't they know who he was? He could probably take them *all* out by himself—with one hand tied behind his back.

She glared at a group of sailors openly smirking, and then glowered at another group who looked like army dudes. Not that they took any notice of her, but still. She didn't like it.

Eventually Van stopped by a table where a couple of familiar guys were sitting, and abruptly she forgot about the smirks. One of the men stood, his size, short black Mohawk, and different-colored eyes unmistakable. "Chloe?" Wolf's rough, gritty voice was full of surprise. "Is that you?"

Okay, so they didn't know she was here. Why hadn't Van told them?

She shot Van a look, but the expression on his face was the same: hard and unreadable as granite.

"Hey Wolf," she said when it became obvious Van wasn't going to speak, coming around the table to Wolf and impulsively giving him a warm hug. "Yeah, it's me. I know, it's been a long time."

"Yeah, fuck, it really has." Wolf stepped back, looking her up and down. "You're bigger than you used to be."

Despite herself, she could feel her cheeks heat. "Well, I was only thirteen when you left, so I would hope so."

Wolf's grin softened. "Not by much, though. You're still little."

Chloe blushed harder, which was annoying. She'd always had a soft spot for Wolf, since he was the closest to her in age and she could remember running around after him, pestering him to play with her when she'd been about four or five. He would give in on occasion, but as they'd grown older, he'd become less and less interested in his much younger foster sister and more in what his older foster brothers were doing.

"Hi Chloe." Lucas's deep, cool voice hadn't changed and neither had the sharp edge in his silver-blue eyes. He stood up and gave her a nod, but he wasn't a man who encouraged physical affection so she didn't bother offering a hug, settling for a smile instead.

"Hey Lucas," she said, trying not to feel awkward. "Nice to see you too."

It was always this way with her foster brothers. Sometimes they seemed less like the boys she'd grown up with and more like the older cousins she barely knew.

You know Van though.

She couldn't help shooting Van another glance from within her hoodie. He was standing next to her, tall and broad and intimidating even in his suit. He radiated menace, as if he was daring the entire population of the bar to take him on, including his two brothers.

It shouldn't have made a kind of dry-mouthed excitement turn over inside her, but it did. As if she really liked the idea of him being mean and dangerous as hell.

You like the idea of him protecting you as well.

Chloe felt herself start to scowl again, because where the hell had that idea come from? She'd never been a damsel in distress, didn't think of herself as one, and she didn't like being told what to do, so why the hell would she like the idea of Van protecting her?

Yet she couldn't stop thinking about him going over the side of the building the moment he thought someone had been watching her. He'd moved without hesitation, reaching for his gun, her safety the most important thing to him in that moment.

Come on, you can't say you don't like that.

Something shifted inside her, the cold thread loosening just a little bit more, and she had the strangest impulse to go stand closer to him. Which was ridiculous, naturally.

"So?" Wolf, who was also in a suit, pulled irritably at the plain black tie around his neck and ripped open a couple of buttons on his business shirt as he sat back down again. "What the fuck is this about, Van? Didn't we sort out all the company bullshit today already? And what's with Chloe? What's she doing here?"

Van pulled out a chair and gestured for Chloe to sit, before taking the seat beside her.

Lucas sat down as well, leaning back in his chair with

his arms folded. He too was in a suit, the silver blue tie
echoing the color of his eyes. Chloe found herself staring
at him, because he was almost ridiculously handsome. Yet
there was something cold about him, something intensely
reserved that kept him from being totally hot.

He wasn't like Van, that was for sure. He didn't have
Van's rough warmth or that golden gleam in his eye, the
hint of something wilder just beneath the surface.

*Why the hell are you comparing your foster brothers
with each other?*

Damn. Good point. Why *was* she? She didn't feel drawn
to either Lucas or Wolf in the same way as . . .

What? As you're drawn to Van?

Okay, sure, she *had* been. When she'd been a little girl
and he'd reached down to put her up on that pony. When
he'd let her take his hand every time he came home on
leave and followed her when she'd dragged him down to
the stables. When he'd smile at her the way no one else
ever seemed to.

But she wasn't little now.

You're still drawn to him, don't deny it.

"This isn't about the company," Van was saying, his
voice washing over her and making it very difficult for her
to ignore the thought the way she should be doing. "You
want to know why Chloe is here? Well, guess what was in
my fucking letter?"

All three brothers went suddenly very still, a silence
falling.

"Chloe's in danger," Van went on, when no one said
anything. "The old man wanted me to protect her."

Lucas's expression didn't change, though the look in his
eyes sharpened. Wolf, on the other hand, scowled fero-
ciously.

"What the fuck?" he demanded. "What do you mean 'in danger'?"

Van was very conscious of Chloe sitting beside him, wrapped up in his blue hoodie, her dark eyes gleaming in the shadow of the hood.

He shouldn't have brought her into the goddamn bar. It wasn't likely that de Santis had anyone in here who'd spot her, but he hadn't wanted to take any chances. Until she'd gripped tight to his arm, told him that this was about her life and that she wanted to be in on the discussion. She'd looked so fierce right then, reminding him of that day on the mountain when he'd raced her back to the stables, how she'd burned with challenge. How alive she'd been, how free. How wild. And how much that had appealed to something dark and uncontrolled in him. A potent combination. A fucking lethal one.

He'd become intensely conscious of her hand on his arm, the warmth of her touch, the pressure of her fingers. Of how close she was sitting to him. Maybe it had been the remains of the adrenaline pumping through him, or maybe it was her, but all he'd been able to think about was that if he leaned forward just a little bit, he could take that smart mouth of hers, taste that wildness for himself.

Luckily he had self-control down to a fine art and he'd been able to hold himself back. He still didn't think bringing her into the bar was a good idea, but he hadn't been able to deny the fact that she was right—when they were discussing her, she needed to be here. Besides, it seemed very obvious that remaining in the car and arguing with her was a recipe for disaster.

"De Santis," Van said curtly, getting straight to the point. "He's targeting her."

"Holy shit," Wolf murmured.

"How do you know?" Lucas's tone was sharp.

"Like I said"—Van met his gaze—"it was in my letter. Dad said that in the event of his death, de Santis would make a move on Chloe."

"Why?" Lucas shot back, his gaze never moving from Van's.

What the fuck was up with his middle brother? Because something was, that's for sure. Van still remembered Lucas's response to his own letter, ripping it up into tiny precise pieces, the look on his face hard, set.

Then again, now wasn't the time for that, not when the situation with Chloe had to be dealt with and fast.

" 'Why' isn't up for discussion," Van said, closing down that little topic since he wasn't having that conversation just yet. He was going to have to tell his brothers at some point, but that point wasn't now. "All that matters is that he's targeting her and that he knows she's here in New York and has been staying at Dad's mansion."

"What?" Wolf leaned forward, his elbows on the table. "How did he figure that one out? If you knew she was in danger, wouldn't you have taken better care—"

"It was my fault," Chloe interrupted unexpectedly, her quiet voice cutting over Wolf's rough one. "Van told me not to go outside, but I don't like being inside much. And there was a rooftop garden and—"

"Someone saw you," Lucas finished for her, his icy gaze switching from Van to her. "Smart move."

There was a sarcastic note in his brother's voice that made a surge of unexpected protectiveness go through Van like a tidal wave, and he found himself wanting to put his fist straight in Lucas's pretty face. Christ, where did the prick get off speaking to Chloe like that? Yes, she'd put herself at risk, but she hadn't known someone would be watching her. That he himself had been pissed with her about it made not the slightest bit of difference. It was one thing for him to be angry with her, quite another for someone else, even his own brother.

Chloe opened her mouth to no doubt tell Lucas exactly what she thought of that particular statement, but since that would probably lead to a full-blown argument, Van decided to nip it in the bud.

"Leave her alone," he ordered before Chloe could speak, meeting Lucas's icy stare with his own. "She didn't know the house was going to be watched and I should have been clearer with her about the threat she was under."

Lucas's eyes widened slightly, as if surprised by the aggressiveness in Van's tone. But that was too bad, because Van wasn't taking it back. Chloe's safety was imperative and arguing about who was at fault wasn't going to help anyone.

"What Chloe should or shouldn't have done is beside the point anyway," he went on curtly. "What matters is that de Santis knows she's here and I'm pretty sure now that he does, he's going to make a move. Which means I need to get her somewhere safe, where he can't find her."

And that was the problem; he didn't have anywhere, not in New York. His father had offered to get him a place of his own in the city "for investment purposes" but Van hadn't been interested. He'd always thought that when he retired from the Navy, he'd head back west to Wyoming to the ranch since he wasn't a city boy at heart. Unfortunately that left him with nowhere to take Chloe. On the drive to Leo's he'd gone through several scenarios in his head, such as taking her out of the city, but he needed to be here to deal with the threatened takeover of Tate Oil, not to mention appointing a new CEO to run the company while he was on active duty. He couldn't simply leave, and certainly not if he wanted to find a way to neutralize the threat to Chloe. All of which meant that he had to find somewhere in Manhattan to keep her safe and out of the way of de Santis while he tied up all his numerous loose ends.

Wolf muttered something under his breath then said, louder, "I'd love to help you, bro, but I'm heading back to base tomorrow."

A ripple of shock echoed through Van, though he couldn't have said why. Wolf had always intended to go back as soon as the legal details to do with the company had been sorted out. Whatever had been in his letter, it obviously hadn't been enough to keep him in New York. Wolf had stuck around and attended the board of directors meeting the way Van had ordered, and now there was nothing to hold him here.

Maybe you're jealous. You wouldn't mind heading back to base too.

Shit, of course he wanted to do that too. But he wasn't going to and wouldn't, not until he'd appointed a new CEO and dealt with the threat de Santis posed both to the company and to Chloe.

"Fine," he snapped. "You've done your duty. Head on back if that's what you need to do. But my mission here isn't done and I'm not leaving until it is."

There was a silence at that.

Wolf shifted in his chair, scrubbing a hand through his Mohawk and looking uncomfortable. "Shit, man. If I had a place or something—"

"I've got somewhere you can take her," Lucas interrupted coolly.

Van went still, but it was Chloe who managed to get a word in first, her voice sharp. "Where?"

Lucas glanced at her. "A penthouse in SoHo. I bought it a couple of years back when I was on leave. The building looks like it's being renovated, but it's not. I just keep it like that so people think no one lives there." His hard mouth curved in an imperceptible smile. "I'm not a fan of unexpected visitors."

She leaned forward in her chair, her elbows on the table. "What about you?"

Lucas's icy gaze flickered. "I'm staying elsewhere for a while. Here." He pulled something out of his pocket, slapping it down in front of Van. "Take it."

A featureless black key card sat on the table.

Van picked it up, staring at his brother. "You sure?"

"Yes." There was another flicker in his brother's eyes. "You need to keep her safe, and I've got lots of extra security features installed. No one is going to get in who shouldn't be there."

Knowing Lucas, Van could well imagine that the "extra security features" were going to make the place like Fort Knox. Which was exactly what he wanted.

Shooting Chloe a glance, he raised an eyebrow. "What do you think?" Not that she was going to get much of a choice about where they were going to go, since Lucas's place was their best and safest bet. But hell, she'd wanted some input into the decision, so some input she'd get.

"Why can't we go back to Wyoming?" There was a rebellious jut to her chin and a lingering fire in her dark eyes. Clearly she wasn't happy about it.

"Because I have to stay in the city. Got too much shit with Tate Oil to deal with."

She pulled a face. "You can't send me home with a few more guards or something?"

Oh no, they weren't have this discussion again. Van gave her a hard stare, which made her expression turn mutinous, but mercifully she didn't say anything.

"I can't offer to be around," Lucas went on, ignoring their interchange. "I've got my own shit to deal with right now. But if you need anything, Van, just let me know." His gaze wasn't precisely warm—with Lucas it never was—but something intent gleamed there all the same.

Van knew what it was. Lucas might keep his emotions locked down so tight he may as well not have any, but the guy always had Van's back and always would. There was a bond between them—and Wolf too—a bond forged way back in that boys home, when Van had found one of the new kids, a skinny little blond boy crying one night in his bed. Van had been eight, already in care for a couple of years after his mom and dad had both died from overdoses, and when he'd discovered that the blond kid had lost his family to a fire, he'd decided, being older, that he would protect him.

He'd been protecting his brothers ever since.

Wolf cursed under his breath, then said, "Fucking Lucas, showing me up." He glanced at Chloe briefly then back at Van. "I gotta go, man. But you know where I'll be if you need anything."

"Yeah. I do." And he did. Wolf had his back, too, no matter how much the guy ostensibly complained. Of course, both brothers should be instantly in his face about keeping Chloe safe, and he didn't know what to think about the fact that they weren't. Then again, he wasn't sure if he wanted them involved anyway. The job of protecting Chloe had been given to him and even though he wasn't happy with it, he felt strangely territorial about it all the same.

"Hey," Wolf went on, looking at Chloe. "Van's got my number. Get him to give it to you so you know who to call in an emergency, okay?"

She nodded. "Okay."

"Me too," Lucas added. "If Van's down or there's an issue and he's not around, I'll try to get there as soon as I can."

Van made a note to program both numbers into Chloe's phone ASAP. But first, they needed to get her to Lucas's place and fast.

Five minutes later, Lucas having given him the address, Van shoved back his chair and stood up. "We better get going." He gave his brothers a look. "I don't know what's going on with you two, but I'm going to need you both to stay in touch, understand? There's this takeover happening, lots of shit going down, and we need to be ready for it."

Wolf grimaced and looked away, his jaw tight. And there was a moment when Van thought he might offer to stay, but he didn't, remaining silent instead.

It wasn't like him and it made Van wonder whether he should be insisting his brother remain in New York and help. But no, that territorial need had him in its grip, insisting that protecting Chloe was his job, no one else's.

So all he did was nod once at his youngest brother, glance briefly at Lucas in a silent thank-you, and turn to Chloe.

She was sitting there with her gaze on the table, her face pale, something a little bit lost in her expression. Something a little bit vulnerable. It made him automatically reach out for her hand.

Her eyes widened, making him suddenly aware of what he was doing. A small shock went through him. What the hell was he thinking now? After that moment in the car, touching her was a mistake and he knew it. Yet he didn't take his hand away. He didn't know why she was looking so fragile all of a sudden, but he wanted her to know that he was here. Wanted to give her some reassurance, to feel those delicate, slender fingers in his and the slight pressure of her grip. Wanted to feel her holding onto him.

You can't do this. You got Sofia to trust you and look what happened to her.

Yes, he knew that. Just like he knew his brothers were watching him in surprise and probably wondering what the fuck was going on. But suddenly he didn't care. She looked like she needed something and he wanted to give it.

He met her gaze. "Come on, pretty. Time to go."

An expression lingered in her eyes, one he didn't recognize. Then she blinked, looking at his hand outstretched in front of her. And for a moment he thought she wouldn't do it, that she'd be stubborn and refuse. But then slowly she took it, her fingers sliding between his, her hold light but firm.

A surge of electricity went through him at the touch of her skin against his, an intense kind of possessiveness filling him. Yes, she *had* needed something. She'd needed him.

Let her go, you stupid fuck. This should only be about protecting her.

Yet he didn't. And as she got to her feet, Van only firmed his grip.

Then, ignoring his brother's stares, he led her out of the pub.

CHAPTER EIGHT

Chloe walked into the main living room of Lucas's penthouse and stared up through the skylights that let the gray New York afternoon flood in.

The penthouse was as different from the Tate mansion as it was possible to get, all pristine white walls and dark, hardwood flooring. There was no art to speak of and no comfortable furniture. In fact, there was barely any furniture at all—a couple of chairs in the open-plan living/dining area, a small table down one end, and a couple of stainless steel barstools pulled up to the kitchen island counter.

It was a beautiful place, but it had a bleak feel to it with nothing but that cold, gray light coming in from above.

She could hear Van's footsteps go down the hallway as he began scouting out the place—looking at the security or so he said. But that was good, she needed a couple of minutes of silence and stillness to stand there and think.

Mainly about why the hell she'd reached out and taken his hand.

She didn't understand the impulse that had made her do it. It was only that the way the three of them had sat there talking with one another had made her feel kind of . . . alone. There had been undercurrents there, references to things she didn't know about, unspoken looks that told of experiences she hadn't shared. They knew each other in a way she never had and probably never would.

It had made her throat get tight, made her wish she was part of the connection that flowed between her foster brothers, that she was included in that sense of togetherness. She'd tried not to let it matter to her, tried not to care, because shit, she *was* part of something at the ranch. No, she'd never made particular friends with anyone there, but then she hadn't felt like she'd needed to. The running of the place consumed all her time so she'd never felt lonely, and besides, when she needed someone to talk to, the best and most patient ears in the place were the horses.

Yet despite all of that, she couldn't get rid of the ache in her heart as the brothers talked to one another, sharing a connection she wasn't part of, or the horrible isolated feeling turning over and over inside her. Then Van had held out his hand, the look in his eyes understanding. As if he'd known exactly what was going on with her. And even though she knew she shouldn't, she hadn't been able to stop herself from lacing her fingers through his, craving the warmth of his skin, the feel of a connection she'd been denied all her life.

Chloe swallowed, staring at the heavy gray sky above her.

The reality, though, was that it wasn't Wolf or Lucas she wanted to feel closer to. She didn't know them. She didn't have the same childhood memories of them that she had of Van, and they hadn't been there for her the way he had.

Van would always be someone special to her, and whether she liked it or not, being in his presence constantly was turning him into something even more than that. Making her want things she'd told herself firmly that she didn't need.

Yeah, it was a problem and she didn't know what to do about it.

"It's all looking secure." Van's deep voice came from behind her. "There's a bedroom down the hallway that's a guest room, so why don't you go settle in? Looks like Lucas didn't keep much in the fridge so I'll go out and get a few essentials while you do that."

Her hand tingled, the remembered heat of his fingers closing around hers lingering.

"Why are we at Lucas's?" She kept her gaze on the sky, curling her fingers into a fist, only half conscious of doing so. "You don't have a place of your own here?"

"No. I don't much like the city. I prefer to stay on base."

She turned slowly to face him, suddenly curious. "What about Wyoming? Is that the reason you were away so often doing military stuff? You didn't like the ranch?"

His expression gave nothing away. "I liked the ranch. And I did come back. Whenever I was on leave, remember?"

Oh yes, she remembered. The image of him shirtless and bending over that horse's hoof was painfully clear in her mind, making her face get hot. God, she really did need to stop thinking about that.

"But not the last eight years," she said, unable to keep her tone from sounding snippy. "Unless of course you had an eight-year deployment that I don't know about."

An emotion she couldn't read flickered across his face. "There were reasons."

"What reasons?"

"Complicated ones"—he shoved his hands into the pockets of his suit pants, his dark brows drawing down—"that I'm not going to get into now."

"Why not?"

"Because I don't want to talk about it." His gaze narrowed. "Why do you want to know, anyway?"

"Because I—" She stopped, aware all of a sudden that maybe pushing him about this wasn't the best idea. Not given what it could reveal about her. "It's fine," she went on after a moment. "Forget I said anything."

Something glinted in his eyes. "Because you what?"

"It doesn't matter." She turned toward the windows. "Do you think this place has a better view than Dad's?"

He didn't reply, the taut silence lengthening.

Then he said quietly, "Did you miss me?"

Her chest ached all of a sudden, her throat constricting, and she didn't know why, because of course she hadn't missed him. There had been all sorts of things happening with the ranch, the purchase of new pastures, new stock, expanding the breeding programs. . . . She hadn't had time to miss him. She hadn't even thought about him.

"No." She ignored the catch in her voice.

"That's why you're angry with me, isn't it?" he went on. "It's not because Dad left me the ranch. It was because I wasn't there."

She couldn't look at him. "Don't be ridiculous. I didn't even think about you. I had too much to do."

"You're not angry at the others, though. And they didn't visit either."

It was true, none of them had. But it was only Van who'd mattered. It was only Van who'd *ever* mattered.

But she didn't want to think about that, still less feel it. She was done with making herself vulnerable to people just so they could walk all over her.

Steeling herself, she turned from the window and met his gaze. "Where did you say the bedroom was again? Like you said, I'd better get myself settled in."

He didn't move, yet the look in his eyes pierced her straight through. "Why do you keep insisting nothing's wrong? You were kind of quiet back there at Leo's, which is definitely *not* you. So what's the deal?"

"There's no deal."

"Bullshit." He was staring at her like he was trying to

see inside. "You held onto my hand back there like you couldn't bear to let me go. What was all that about?"

Her heart was starting to beat much faster, a vague sense of threat looming over her. "I could ask you the same thing," she shot back. "Why did you even hold out your hand in the first place?"

The gold was back in his eyes, flickering like a flame. "Because you looked like you needed support."

It's not support you need from him.

She wanted to look away then because she was terribly afraid that the thick mess of feelings inside her was leaking out somehow and he could see it. Could read it. And that he'd turn away like her father had done. Because who liked having to deal with all those tangled, knotty emotions? The hungry, consuming kind. Noah hadn't. And in the end, she hadn't either.

Except she didn't want to give him the satisfaction of letting him see how he affected her, how he'd gotten to her. And the only way to do that was to pretend he hadn't.

"Thanks for the concern," she snapped. "But—"

"You're fine," he finished for her. "Yeah, I get it." The intense hazel of his eyes glinted from beneath thick, sooty black lashes, somehow pinning her to the spot. "Thing is, Chloe. You're not fine, and you haven't been fine since the moment you got off the plane. And you know what? I'm getting pretty fucking sick of you pretending you are."

The sense of threat deepened, a primitive fight-or-flight response beginning to kick in, and it took all she had not to simply walk from the room. But she wasn't going to be a coward in front him, she just wasn't.

So talk to him then.

No, she couldn't do that. Couldn't give him pieces of herself, not when she had no idea what he would do with them. Not when that could end up with her wanting something from him that he couldn't and wouldn't give her.

She didn't want to end up being that silly little girl who kept hoping for something the way she had with her dad, not again.

Instead she moved, coming right up to him, staring into his eyes, letting him see that she wasn't pretending, not at all.

"I. Am. Fine." She enunciated each word clearly, so there could be no mistake. "How many times do I have to say it?"

He'd gone very still, looming over her like a mountain carved from warm, living, breathing rock. And for some reason all she was conscious of was how cold she was, and how hot he was. So very, very hot. And that she wanted to get closer, get some of that heat for herself.

Mistake. Back away.

Yet her feet felt like they were encased in concrete, and she couldn't move. His reassuring scent was all around her and she couldn't stop staring at his beautiful mouth. There was something about his bottom lip she'd never noticed before, something about the curve of it. Sensual, yet with a cruel edge. It made her shiver.

"Why are you so angry, pretty?" His voice was as soft and dark and deep as black velvet. "You can tell me. You know that, right?"

All of a sudden, she wanted to. Wanted to tell him that yes, she was angry. Because he'd never visited and she *had* missed him. That no, she actually wasn't fine, because she was starting to realize that while he might have Wolf and Lucas, she had nobody and never had. That she was lonely. That she was hungry for something, a hunger she didn't have words for and one that frightened her in its intensity. A hunger she'd tried to keep at bay for a long, long time.

But she couldn't tell him that, because doing so would make her vulnerable and she didn't want to be vulnerable. Not again.

Except now she could feel that hunger slipping from her

grip, his nearness making it twist and turn like a half-starved beast on a chain. And she knew she should move back. Walk away.

Yet she didn't. She trembled instead.

He must have seen it because his gaze shifted, flickered, the shards of gold close to his iris suddenly brilliant.

Like a tiger's.

The thought rolled through her head and she couldn't think why she'd thought it. Or why it made everything inside her gather tight into a small, hard knot. But it did.

"Van." His name came out husky, with a desperate edge, and she had no idea why she'd said that either. Only inches separated them, and suddenly all she wanted was to close the distance, because she was cold and needed his heat. Craved it.

So she took another step toward him, and he didn't move. He only watched her as she got closer. Then closer still, so there was no space between them at all.

And the rock-hard expanse of his chest was abruptly under her palms, though she had no memory of reaching out to him, the heat of him flooding through her. And then she was sliding her hands up his chest and further, around his neck, pushing her fingers into the thick, short black silk of his hair.

His gaze held hers the whole time, saying nothing. Watching her, all bright, burning gold. Like a challenge.

A challenge she couldn't resist.

Chloe rose up on her toes and pulled his mouth down on hers.

Van went utterly still as Chloe's mouth opened beneath his, her fingers twisting in his hair, holding on. And he couldn't quite work out why he'd let her do it, why he hadn't stopped her. Why he hadn't simply turned around and walked out of the room.

But he hadn't. He'd let her get closer, mesmerized by the flicker of hunger that had woken into life in the darkness of her eyes. A hunger he felt echo inside of him, too.

Don't just stand there, asshole. Stop her.

He should. Christ, he really, really should. Yet he didn't.

Her kiss wasn't at all practiced, but her mouth was open and hot, and she tasted of desperation. It was like a fucking match to an open can of rocket fuel, exploding the desire that had been simmering constantly inside him for a couple of days now.

It ripped through him and it was all he could do to keep himself still, to not grip her by the hips and push her down on the bare wood floorboards, shove her jeans down, and get inside her as quickly as he could.

Stop this. Now.

Yeah, he had to. This was wrong on just about every level there was and then some. He had no idea what she thought she was doing or what point she was trying to prove, but it couldn't go any further. He was her foster brother for fuck's sake and apart from anything else, he wasn't getting involved with a woman he was supposed to be protecting. That was a recipe for disaster, as he already knew.

He lifted his hands ready to push her away. Except then she made a low, hungry sound in the back of her throat, arching her small, slender body against him, and he became excruciatingly aware of the soft press of her breasts against his chest and the pressure of her pubic bone against the slowly growing ridge behind his zipper.

Wrong. Wrong. *Wrong.*

Van tangled his fingers in the thick, silky mass of her hair, trying to ease her away gently. "Chloe," he murmured against her mouth, his voice far thicker than he wanted it to be. "Stop."

She ignored him, angling her head to maintain the contact instead, her hands dropping to his waist. She jerked his shirt from the waistband of his pants and reached under the cotton, cool fingers trailing over the skin of his bare stomach and then up to his chest.

His breath caught, every muscle tensing. Her touch was sweetly hesitant at first and then firmer, more needy, tracing fire all over his skin.

Van had spent years honing his will and his physical control, had been on missions where both had been tested to the very limits of his endurance.

But Chloe Tate's trembling fingers on his skin? That nearly pushed him over the edge. Even his training in Coronado hadn't tested him this much.

She was desperate for him, that was obvious, and there was something irresistible about that. He hadn't let anyone get that desperate for him in a long time, hadn't let anyone get close. He gave them what they wanted straight up and then moved on, end of story.

Maybe it was the denial that was getting to her, to both of them. The fact that they'd both been resisting. Whatever it was, the way she touched him, as if he were a drug she'd been craving and couldn't get enough of, made desire grip him by the throat and hold on so tight he could barely get a breath.

Fuck, he had to let her go. Now. Before he lost the will to even try.

Tightening his grip in her hair, he tore his mouth away. "Chloe. *Stop*."

But again she ignored him. Her touch turned frantic, her breath coming hard and fast, her fingers shaking as she slid them down to the button on his pants and fumbling with it.

"That's enough." Van grabbed her wrists, pulling her hands away from him and holding them still, his patience frayed almost all the way through. "I said *stop*."

Her head jerked back, her beautiful face flushed, the fire in her dark eyes burning bright, full of anger and desire, and beneath that, a glimmer of the pain she was hiding, a pain he knew was there. The pain she kept denying.

She lifted her chin stubbornly, trying to free her hands from his grip, but he didn't let them go.

"We can't do this." He kept his tone quiet, forceful. "I'm sorry, pretty, but we can't."

Her throat moved as she swallowed, the material of her plaid shirt pulling over the swell of her breasts and outlining the stiff points of her nipples. "Why not? It's better than talking, isn't it?"

"Chloe—"

"I've wanted you since I was sixteen." The words came out in a rush. "And we're not blood related. God, we're not related *at all*. I don't even think of you as my brother. And anyway, Dad made it very clear that I'm not part of the family, so why not?" She sucked in a harsh breath. "Unless you don't want me."

He should tell her that no, of course he didn't want her. That he'd never had anything but brotherly feelings toward her. That he couldn't do this with someone he was supposed to protect.

It would be the right thing to do, the *only* thing to do.

Yet, staring down into her flushed, pointed little face and seeing the desperation in her eyes, he couldn't bring himself to lie to her like that. Not when she probably knew already how much of a lie it was.

Sixteen. She'd wanted him since she was sixteen. Christ . . .

"It doesn't matter whether I want you or not. It's *not* happening and that's final."

The fire in her eyes blazed, full of all the passion that had always been part of her, and he braced himself for anger.

Except it wasn't anger that came out.

"Please, Van." Her voice was husky, a pleading note in it that reached into his chest and wrapped warm fingers around his heart. "Please."

He couldn't look away from the hot, wild darkness in her gaze and the sudden vulnerability in it. The vulnerability he'd seen the day she'd put her head on his chest and wept.

It slid under his guard, piercing him like an assassin's knife, and for some reason he was suddenly achingly conscious of the feel of her skin against his finger tips, so warm and soft. If he adjusted his grip on her wrists, he'd be able to feel her pulse, gauge exactly what his touch did to her by the speed of her heartbeat . . .

No, shit, what was he thinking? He couldn't, not given how vulnerable she was and what his role was here. He was supposed to be protecting her, not thinking about fucking her. Hell, if his father knew what Van was thinking, the old bastard would turn in his grave.

The old bastard is why you're here in the first place. Why she's *in danger in the first place.*

That was true. Noah had lied to her, he'd lied to them both. So who the fuck cared what he thought?

Except, Noah wasn't the only reason this was a terrible idea. She was a good ten years younger than he was and while she'd been pouring her soul into that ranch, protecting it and making it grow, he'd been learning how to kill people better than anyone else.

And all that wasn't even considering what he could give her beyond sex, which wasn't anything at all. After this was over he was going back to base, and that's where he wanted to stay. He had no room in his life for anything beyond a one-night stand, and if there was one thing he was certain of, it was that Chloe Tate needed more than that.

She needed more than he'd ever be able to give.

"No." The word was far rougher around the edges than he wanted it to be. "I'm sorry, pretty, but it's not going to happen."

She stared at him, her eyes dark as strong espresso and just as hot, framed by thick, black, silky lashes. Her hips were pressing against his, nudging the fucking hard-on that wasn't going away no matter how much he wanted it to, sending a streak of fire licking up his spine in response.

"Van, I . . . need this." There was a hesitancy in her voice now, the fragility she'd kept so well protected all laid out for him to see. "Please. I just . . . need you."

She was trembling, as if the words had been hard for her to say and she was afraid of his reaction, the shake of her slight body where it pressed to his making everything inside him clench tight like a fist in response.

It had been so fucking long since anyone had needed him, since he'd *let* anyone need him. And he'd told himself that was a good thing. He didn't want to be responsible for another vulnerable woman needing him to protect her, just like he hadn't wanted to be the figurehead of a company for an old man who'd needed a cipher, not a son.

But it turned out that something deep inside him did want it after all. Some part of him that craved to be trusted, to be leaned on, to be turned to. And not because he was someone's commander or because he was some orphan kid who somehow fitted the bill, but because they wanted *him*.

So how could he deny her? She was looking at him without that prickly anger, without all the pretense, naked need burning in her eyes, and he just couldn't find it in him to say no.

Yeah, because you want this as badly as she does.

But Van didn't want to think about that, so he forced it from his head as he slowly guided her hands behind her, crossing her wrists in the small of her back and holding them there with one hand. Then he lifted the other hand to her face, cupping the petal softness of her cheek. Her eyes widened, then she shivered. "Does that mean yes?"

Sliding his fingers along her jaw and into the silky tangle of her hair, he tugged her head back. "Why, Chloe? Why me?"

"B-Because I want you. I've always wanted you." She was still trembling, and her voice sounded just as unsteady. "I need . . . something. Someone."

He didn't quite know what he wanted to hear, he only knew that he wanted more than that. "There are plenty of other men out there. You don't need me."

"I do." Her lashes fluttered, veiling the sudden flash of pain in her eyes. "You were right. I . . . missed you. And I'm scared and I'm lonely, and I want . . ." She stopped short then looked away, as if afraid she'd said too much.

Jesus Christ, she *had* missed him. Fuck, he hadn't known how badly he'd wanted to hear that from her until she'd said it. And then there was the fact that she was lonely. Which didn't make any sense to him. How? Why? She had a busy job on the ranch, surrounded by a lot of people. Did she really not have anyone?

For some reason it hurt to think that she didn't, to imagine her isolated and alone, without anyone to turn to.

She can turn to you.

Yes, she could. Hell, he couldn't refuse her, not after that. If she wanted him, she could fucking have him.

"It's okay." He stroked her cheek with his thumb. "It's okay, pretty. You want me, you got me. But only this one time. Are we clear?" It couldn't be more than that, for both their sakes.

She took a shaky breath, staring back at him, all hunger and stark need. "Yes. We're clear."

Tell yourself it's all about giving her what she wants, that it's not about what you want too.

Yeah and he was done listening to that voice. He was a

SEAL commander and once he made a decision, he stuck to it.

Van tightened his grip on her hair, kept a firm hold of her wrists, then bent his head and covered her mouth.

CHAPTER NINE

Chloe was shaking so badly she felt like she was coming apart at the seams. His body was so hot it felt like she was pressed up against a furnace. And he was hard too, a wall of unyielding muscle that had felt smooth and firm when she'd touched him. God, she could still feel the lingering warmth of his skin against her fingertips, like a burn yet without the pain. It made her desperate to touch him again.

But now he was kissing her and this time it was different than before, when she'd been the one to pull his mouth down on hers. She hadn't known what she was doing then, since although Jason had been fairly experienced, they hadn't done much in the way of kissing. She hadn't even known why she'd kissed Van in the first place, only aware that the hunger inside her needed an outlet, needed to be fed. And she was so tired of trying to keep it contained.

She'd wanted Sullivan Tate ever since she was sixteen, and it seemed abruptly clear that she'd never stopped wanting him. Even when she'd decided to use Jason to get rid of her unwanted desire, thinking she only felt that way about Van because he'd been the first man she'd seen without a shirt.

She thought she'd gotten it out of her system, and because he'd spent the last eight years away from the ranch, she hadn't had a chance to test it out. Apparently though, that desire wasn't as out of her system as she'd thought. Now it burned inside her, raging out of control. His mouth on hers only made the fire blaze higher.

She leaned into him, pressing herself up against the wall of his body, loving how small and fragile she felt in comparison to his strength and size. It was unbearably exciting, making her want to push on his chest, test that strength for herself. Except he was holding her wrists in an unbreakable grip.

Frustrated, she put her head back instead, encouraging him to take the kiss deeper, intensify it. But he didn't take any notice of the invitation, lightly brushing his lips over hers then tracing the line of her lower lip with his tongue.

"More." She rose on her toes to increase the contact, opening her mouth beneath his. "Please, more."

Van shook his head and pulled back, his lips close and yet agonizingly out of reach. She tried to follow, only to have his grip on her wrists tighten, holding her still. "No." His voice was a soft rumble of sound that she felt deep in her chest and further down too, to the ache between her thighs. "If you want me, we do this my way, understand?"

She couldn't tear her gaze from his mouth, long and sensual and wicked. "Okay." She was ready to agree to anything as long as he kissed her with that beautiful mouth again. "Just . . . hurry."

"Oh no, I'm not hurrying." His thumb stroked along her cheekbone. "Not with you."

She wanted to protest, but then he was bending his head again, his lips brushing over hers once more and a moan she couldn't stop broke from her. It sounded so helpless and needy she would have been embarrassed if she'd been thinking straight. But she wasn't thinking straight, because he was kissing her again, touching his tongue to her lower lip, beginning to explore. The heat of him was incredible. Another tremble shook her and she opened her mouth, her tongue meeting his, desperately trying to deepen the kiss yet again. He tasted so good, an intense flavor like dark, bittersweet chocolate. There was a hard, alcoholic kick to it too, like whiskey or brandy.

She could get drunk on his kisses if only he'd let her.

Chloe made an impatient sound, straining against his hold, arching insistently into him so the aching tips of her nipples came into contact with his hard chest, the unmistakable growing ridge behind his zipper nudging between her thighs and sending tiny bolts of electricity along her nerve endings.

God, she was *so* tired of resisting this. So tired of pretending she was okay, tired of feeling nothing but anger. She wanted more than that. She wanted him. Right now. Here. On the floor. Or hell, anywhere. As long as she was naked and he was too, and he was inside her, touching her everywhere, she didn't care.

But he didn't seem to notice the urgent sounds she was making, resolutely failing to take all her hints, continuing to explore her mouth with such careful, gentle insistence she wanted to scream. Bastard. He was going to drive her insane, wasn't he?

Losing patience, Chloe rose up on her toes again and bit his bottom lip, trying to wrest back control, make him do something, because she couldn't go on like this, she just couldn't.

He jerked his head back, growling, the sound a low warning that sent a burst of adrenaline rushing through her, making her heartbeat thump hard in her ears.

She looked up at him, her pulse going wild with anticipation.

The gold in his eyes had deepened, gleaming from underneath his lashes, a molten color that heated everything inside her almost to boiling point. "Naughty girl." His grip on her jaw tightened, turning her head slowly but surely away, exposing the side of her neck. "No biting. I said we're going slow."

"I don't want slow." She strained against his hold, trying to turn her head back to look at him and failing. "I need you, Van. Now."

"I know what you need." There was heat against her exposed neck, the prickle of his stubble, and then the softness of his mouth brushing her skin, making her shiver. "Trust me."

Trust him . . .

Yes, she did trust him. She'd always trusted him.

There came the hot lick of his tongue, rough as a cat's, and his teeth, lightly grazing the tendons at the side of her neck, and she couldn't breathe for the intensity of her reaction.

She shuddered. "Van . . . *please* . . ."

He said nothing, biting her gently instead, a punishment and a warning, making her groan. Making her shift her hips against the tantalizing ridge behind his zipper, rubbing up against him. Oh, he was killing her. She was literally going to die of need right here, right now.

She sobbed a little as he bit her again, not caring if he heard as she pulled against his imprisoning hand, feeling frantic and desperate and half-scared by the power of the need blazing inside her, its intensity overwhelming.

Then his voice was in her ear, his mouth brushing her skin, "It's okay. I'll make it better, pretty thing." And he let go of her wrists, his hands coming to rest on her hips before gathering her up, shaking, into his arms.

Instantly she twisted into him, seeking relief or reassurance, she wasn't sure which, sliding her palms up that magnificent chest of his and around his neck, shifting to wrap her legs around his lean hips and press herself against his muscular heat. Then she turned her face into his throat and put her mouth over the pulse that beat strong and steady there, tasting the clean, salty flavor of his skin.

He cursed softly, his muscles tensing. "Stop that. Or else I put you down right now."

But she didn't want to stop. She wanted to keep kissing him, keep tasting him, needing his flavor in her mouth. Yet he sounded dead serious and when she looked up, his jaw was set, a dangerous glitter in his eyes.

Oh yes, he was pretty fucking serious. He meant exactly what he said.

Having him put her down didn't bear thinking about, so she turned her cheek to his chest instead, listening to the beat of his heart instead as he turned and carried her out of the living room, going down the hallway to a room that was obviously one of Lucas's guest bedrooms.

There was a bed up against one wall and Van carried her over to it then laid her on the thick white comforter before following her down. Then she was surrounded by fierce, rough, masculine heat as his body covered hers, his hips settling between her thighs, his weight slowly coming to rest on her, pressing her down on the bed in the most delicious way. He had himself braced on his forearms, looking down at her, the expression in his eyes so intense she would have caught flame there and then if she hadn't been burning like a torch already.

She lifted her hands, too desperate to wait, pulling clumsily at the buttons of his shirt, frantic to open the fabric so she could see all those incredible muscles again, get her fingers on his skin. He'd felt so good before when she'd touched him in the living room, so smooth and hard, the flex and release of his abs mesmerizing. She wanted to do it again and maybe this time run her tongue over his chest and stomach, taste him.

His dog tags swung as she finally got his shirt open and

she grabbed them in one hand, holding onto them as she trailed her other hand down his chest, over the ink of the eagle and trident, feeling the warm velvet of his skin and the prickle of crisp hair against her fingertips. She went lower, loving the way his abs tightened beneath her touch.

God, he was gorgeous. So freaking hot.

He made no move as she touched him, as if he was letting her play, but she could hear the sound of his breath getting rougher as her hand roved over him. She glanced up into his face, wanting to see what effect her touch had and sure enough, there was the stain of red on his high, carved cheekbones and that deep, molten gold glittering in his eyes.

She wasn't the only one feeling this.

The realization thrilled her, made her want to push, disturb his usual steady patience, his calm certainty. She wanted him frantic like she was, shaking like she was.

She gripped the chain of his tags in one hand, then reached down with the other to the button of his pants, trying to get it undone, her fingers clumsy, desperate.

His eyes glittered even brighter, a muscle flexing in his jaw. He said nothing, merely shifted, and before she could protest, he had her wrist in a strong grip and was pulling her hand away.

"No," she began in a voice that didn't sound like hers. "I don't want—"

"We're going to do this my way." His tone was very, very firm. "I want your hands up and on the pillow."

"No." She tried to pull her wrist away. "I *have* to touch you. Please, let me."

"You do that and you won't get what you want." With gentle, implacable strength, he drew the arm he was holding up, pressing her hand down onto the pillow by her head. "Like this. And keep it there." He paused, radiating dark threat. "If you don't, I'll stop touching you."

She shivered, because right then that seemed like the worst punishment in the entire world. And she couldn't let go his tags fast enough, bringing her arm up and resting it on the pillow beside her head as ordered.

"Good girl." The threat had ebbed from his voice, making way for an approving note that made heat break out all over her skin. "Like I said, keep them like that."

She stared up into his eyes, trembling, a sudden wash of intense vulnerability flooding through her, as if she were a soft-bodied creature without a shell, naked before a predator. She wanted to turn away, hide herself somehow, but she knew it was too late for that and for some reason that knowledge was terrifying.

But it was like he'd read her mind, because the look in his eyes changed, the hot glitter becoming a little softer, a little gentler, the hard cast of his mouth curving just a bit. "It's okay," he murmured, the warmth in his voice even more pronounced. "You're safe with me. Understand?"

She couldn't speak, could only give a jerky nod to show him she understood. Because that look in his eyes and the warm note in his voice had already begun to ease her fear.

Of course she was safe with him. She always had been.

As the scared feeling receded, she began to be conscious of other things, such as the weight of him between her thighs and the press of his zipper against the seam of her jeans, not enough to ease the ache, but enough to make it throb. All she'd have to do would be to angle her hips and that seam would be pressing against her clit.

But he must have read her mind again, because he said, his voice full of soft warning, "Don't even think about it." Then the weight of him pressing down on her increased so she was pinned to the bed, unable to move. "This is my show, remember? Now, keep still."

Her breathing had become shorter and the pressure of

him between her thighs was relentless, an itch that couldn't be scratched, making her feel like she was going to crawl out of her skin.

"Please," she panted, her body shuddering. "I need you. *Now.*"

Van leaned on his elbows, his massive, hard body lying almost fully on her, and cupped her face between his palms, stroking her cheekbones with his thumbs. "Hush," he murmured as she arched and moved restlessly beneath him, unable to stop herself. "It's okay. Like I said, we're taking this slow."

"N-No. I don't want slow." The words were frayed and husky. "Touch me. I need you to touch me."

"Shhh." He stroked back and forth across her cheekbones. "Have you done this before, pretty? Have you been with a guy?"

She wanted to be outraged by the question, wanted to tell him it was none of his damn business and what did it matter anyway? But her inexperience must be wildly obvious and maybe it wasn't actually a bad thing if he knew. So all she said was, "Yes, but only one guy."

"Okay, good." His voice was low and soft, as if she was a skittish horse he was calming. "You know what's going to happen then."

Maybe that should have soothed her. But she didn't feel soothed. She only felt even more desperate. Because sure, she may have done this with Jason, yet it wasn't the same. At all. With Van it was so much stronger, so much more powerful. So relentless.

"I c-can't. I . . . Van . . ."

"Yes, you can." His thumbs swept over her skin. "This is like learning to ride, remember? Stay calm, be patient and let the horse take you where you want to go."

She remembered. His hands on her waist, lifting her up onto the broad back of the animal. She'd been scared because she'd been so far up off the ground, but he'd given her that amazing smile of his. *"It'll be okay, pretty,"* he'd said. *"You won't fall, I promise."*

Chloe looked up at him, staring into those familiar eyes, feeling those big, warm hands on her skin, and somehow the frantic need eased off, her muscles relaxing, her breathing slowing.

"You won't let me fall?" she whispered, not even knowing she was going to say it until it came out.

That beautiful mouth of his curved, as if he knew exactly which memory she was talking about. "I won't. You're safe with me, remember?"

She swallowed. "Yes. I remember."

"Good." His hands left her face and his attention dropped to her chest. "Now. I'm going to get these clothes off you." He began to undo the buttons of her shirt, slow and deliberate, one by one.

Her heartbeat thumped as she felt the fabric part, and she wanted to put her hands over her breasts to cover herself, which was weird since she'd never had any particular hang-ups about her body. She certainly hadn't worried about getting naked with Jason. But this wasn't Jason. This was Van and it was different, and she had the oddest feeling of not wanting to disappoint him.

But he'd said he'd stop touching her if she moved, so she kept her hands where they were as the last button released and he pushed the fabric of her shirt slowly apart. She wore a bra underneath, but he almost casually ripped open the lace holding the cups together, freeing her breasts, making her cheeks blaze with sudden heat. She desperately wanted to look away and yet she couldn't, her gaze drawn to his hard, beautiful face. It was set in fierce lines, the look in his eyes intent as he gazed down at her bare breasts.

"Van," she whispered, not knowing what she wanted,

maybe just a sign that he liked what he saw, that she was beautiful to him. God, she hadn't known until right in this moment that she'd wanted to be beautiful to him.

He didn't look at her. Instead he shifted his weight onto one elbow and lifted his hand, cupping one breast in his palm. The breath hissed in her throat, the shocking heat of his touch reverberating through her like a scream echoing through a deserted house. He brushed his thumb over her aching nipple and she gasped, all the desperation she'd felt earlier rushing back.

He lowered his head, putting his mouth against the pulse at the base of her throat, the feel of his lips so hot she began to shiver almost uncontrollably. His tongue pressed lightly, his thumb brushing back and forth over her nipple, teasing her. She groaned, her spine bowing, pleasure like a live thing twisting inside her.

"Beautiful," he whispered roughly against her skin, giving her the reassurance she needed without her even having to ask. "You're just so fucking beautiful."

He didn't speak after that, too busy trailing kisses down over her skin, making goose bumps rise everywhere, the brush of his thumb maddening. Then he took his hand away as his mouth closed over the hard point of her nipple, hot and wet, an intense pressure building as he began to suck.

She groaned again, the pleasure bright and electric, her hands closing into fists beside her head. It felt so good she could hardly stand it. She whispered his name yet again, the sound raw as he teased her nipple with his tongue, then bit gently on it, making a sob catch in her throat.

He shifted his attention to her other breast, sucking that into his mouth as well as he slid one hand down the quivering plane of her stomach, to the fastening of her jeans. She lifted her hips urgently, unable to keep still, wanting to pull away from the maddening torture of his mouth and yet wanting him to suck harder, deeper at the same time.

"Hush." His breath was hot against her sensitized nipple. "I told you to keep still. It'll happen, don't worry."

She tried to do as she was told as he casually flicked open the button on her jeans and grabbed the tab of her zipper, tugging it down. Then his fingers were feathering light touches across her stomach, moving lower, sliding beneath the waistband of her panties. The breath sobbed in her throat as she felt those teasing fingers tangle in the soft, damp curls between her thighs, pulling lightly, sending tiny pinpricks of sensation racing over her skin.

She said something, she didn't know what, maybe it was his name again or maybe it was a curse, and then she forgot it entirely as his fingers slid lower, stroking the soft, slick folds of her pussy.

Her hips bucked against his hand, her head going back on the pillow. He circled her clit with one finger, teasing her. Inching her closer toward the edge of the cliff but not pushing her off.

His mouth was so hot on her nipple, licking and sucking, torturing her as his fingers stroked unhurriedly around and around her clit, then sliding down to circle the entrance of her body, almost pushing inside but not quite.

He was playing with her, making her moan and move restlessly beneath him, blind now to anything but the feel of his hands on her body and the relentless pressure that was slowly building higher and higher.

Then quite suddenly he took his hands away and she nearly burst into tears at the loss, reaching for him as she felt his weight shift up and back.

"Lie still." The rough sound of his voice rolled over her, full of command. "I'm not going anywhere."

So she did as she was told, lying back against the pillows, blinking away the stupid rush of salty tears from her eyes and watching him slide off the bed. He straightened and pulled his shirt off, then got rid of his shoes. He undid his pants, pushed them down his hips along with his briefs, and stepped out of them magnificently, gloriously naked, but for his dog tags.

She couldn't stop staring at him, following the carved lines of muscle and sinew, a work of perfect, masculine art, the eagle and trident inked across his chest making it very clear—as if his body hadn't already—exactly what he was.

Dangerous, lethal. A weapon in human form.

He bent and got his wallet out of his pants, every movement fluid, purposeful as he extracted a foil packet from it. Then he ripped the open the foil, taking out the latex inside. And as she watched, completely fascinated, he reached down and gripped his cock in one hand, rolling down the condom with the other.

Big. He was really big. And beautiful too.

Her hands itched, wanting to touch him, to stroke down the long, smooth length of his rigid flesh, feel exactly how hard he was. But then he was moving, the bed dipping as he got back onto it. And her breath caught as he reached for the waistband of her jeans, pulling the denim down her legs in short, hard jerks, taking her panties along with them, and finally slipping them both off. Then he put his hands on her bare thighs and with ruthless insistence, spread them wide apart.

Another rush of vulnerability swept over her and she half sat up, breathing fast. "Van, I . . ." she began, before stopping short, not knowing what she wanted to say.

But he was moving forward, putting his hands on her shoulders and easing her back. "Let me look." His voice had gentled again. "I only want to look at you."

She tried to relax against the pillows, letting him hold her thighs apart, his gaze returning between them. The look on his face was so hungry, making her feel less exposed and more . . . powerful almost. She liked doing that to him. She liked making him look at her as if he was starving.

He moved forward quite suddenly, coming over her, surrounding her with all that bare, tanned skin and strong muscle, his dog tags brushing against her sensitized breasts. The scent of him was everywhere, fresh, with that spicy, earthy undertone, and she was abruptly trembling so hard she didn't think she'd ever stop.

He said nothing, looking at down at her, and this time his expression was fierce with something she didn't understand. She wanted to ask him what it was, but then he slid one hand beneath her hips, lifting them, and she felt the head of his cock slide through her folds, nudging against her clit. And she forgot what she was going to ask. In fact, she lost the power of speech entirely.

All she could do was lie there, shaking and desperate as he teased her, and when she didn't think she could bear it anymore, he began to push his cock inside her, the intense stretch and burn of her pussy around him tearing a gasp from her throat.

She sobbed, because he didn't rush. He went slowly. Inch by inch. Murmuring encouragement, telling her what a good girl she was, how tight and wet and hot her pussy was, and how good she felt around his cock. The dirty talk made her break out into a sweat, the climax so near she could almost taste it, making her want to shove herself up onto him or do something—*anything*—to push herself over the edge. But he didn't let her, pinning one of her hips to the mattress with one hand as he lifted her leg up and around his waist with the other, tilting her pelvis so he could slide in deeper.

She stopped pleading, her throat too dry, her voice too hoarse. Besides, it was clear he wasn't going to do anything until he was good and ready. She could only breathe through the pleasure that was wrapping itself around her throat and squeezing tight, making her gasp, making lights burst behind her eyes.

Then he was seated deep inside her, and she found herself pressed to the mattress, pinned beneath the hot, heavy weight of him. But strangely, looking up into his beautiful face, she didn't feel crushed. She felt anchored. As if for the first time since she'd left Wyoming she'd come home in some way.

She didn't speak as his arms came around her, cradling her, holding her close against him like she was a secret he wanted to keep safe. Then he drew back his hips and thrust deep inside her.

Chloe came apart then, sobbing against his shoulder, shattering as easily and as lightly as a sphere of blown glass, the pieces of her held together only by the strength of his arms.

Keeping her from falling.

Chloe's sob of release echoed around the room, her pussy clenching tight around his cock, and it was all he could do not to lose it there and then, to push her back against the mattress and drive himself into her, hard and fast until the orgasm came for him as well.

But he didn't.

He wasn't going to lose it, not with her, because this wasn't about him. She was lonely and scared, and he wanted to make her feel good. Drown her in pleasure. At least for a little while.

The aftershocks were making her shudder, but he didn't let her go. He kept her cradling against him as he began to move again, sliding out of her tight little pussy before pushing back in, long and deep and slow.

He heard her gasp his name, her nails sinking into his

back, both legs curled tight around him, tempting him to let go the firm grip he had on his control. But no. He wanted to make her come again and he wasn't going to stop until he had.

Holy Christ though, her scent was driving him crazy, musky and feminine. And he still had the taste of her skin in his mouth, salty, sweet, delicious. It had been a long time since he'd wanted to spread a woman out on his bed and taste every inch of her body. Been a long time since he'd let himself want a woman this intensely at all. After Columbia and his failure to protect Sofia, after he'd decided he was done living up to Noah's impossible standards and his insistence on treating Van less as a son and more as the cipher he'd wanted him to be, he'd been pretty selfish when it came to sex. Sure, he made sure his partners enjoyed it because there was no point if they didn't, but he was very careful to not let it become any more than that. And he chose only women who could look after themselves. Who didn't need protecting. Who didn't need him.

Which made his reaction to Chloe so very, very wrong.

Because she was none of those things.

She'd lain there beneath him, shaking and desperate, looking at him as if she was hanging off the edge of a cliff and he was her lifeline. That shouldn't have been the turn-on that it was. Yet he'd gotten so fucking hard as he'd reached down to take her face between his palms, to soothe her, calm her, watching her relax under his touch, responding to him in a way that made his chest ache and his cock ache even more.

He'd told her he was going to take it slow and he'd meant it. She was inexperienced and he hadn't wanted to do anything that might hurt or frighten her. Only what she'd wanted, which was to feel good. So he'd ignored all her little pleas and the ways she'd tried to rush him, ignored her demands and the frantic touch of her fingers on his body. Taking things nice and slow and easy.

But shit, it had been one of the hardest things he'd ever had to do.

She was so fucking beautiful. So fucking responsive. She tasted like heaven, and the way she clung to him, the way she said his name in that hoarse, desperate voice was the most erotic thing he'd ever heard in his entire life.

She was the most perfect thing he'd ever had in his bed and it took every ounce of his considerable will not to crush her down onto the mattress and pound his way into unconsciousness inside her.

Instead he moved with great care, keeping her small, naked, silky body tucked up close to his chest. She shivered and shook, panting and gasping as he eased in and out of her, whispering things like "I can't," and "It's too much," and "I don't think I can do this."

But he ignored all of that, turning to murmur encouragement in her ear then hushing her, stroking down her back to soothe her. Because of course she *could* do this. She was clinging to him like she never wanted to let him go, and her pussy was doing the same thing to his cock, clenching around him as if wanting to keep him deep inside.

It was good to have her so desperate. To have her need him. To have her trust.

Yeah and remember the last time a woman did that?

Christ, he wasn't ever likely to forget. But one night wouldn't hurt. Just for one night, he could pretend that he was good for someone instead of being their death sentence.

He shifted position to mix things up, sitting back on the bed and gathering her into his lap. He had her sit facing him, her legs spread around his waist, easing her down onto his cock again with a firm pressure on her hips. She stared at him with glazed eyes, her mouth slightly open, her cheeks a deep rose. Her hair was tumbling everywhere, strands of it sticking to her damp forehead, so he pushed it back out of her eyes. He took his time with that too, needing the small prosaic movements to distract himself from the insane heat of her pussy. From the tight, slick grip of it around his dick.

Only once she was settled and he'd gotten his own heart rate back under control did he move her again, keeping his hands on her hips and lifting her up and down, showing her how to ride him to give her the most pleasure.

When he tilted her pelvis forward, grinding the base of his cock against her clit, her eyes rolled back in her head and she gave the most helpless, most delicious moan. So he did it again and again, lifting her up and then slamming her back down, watching her face and the raw, open pleasure that played across it.

She wasn't going to last long and thank fucking Christ for that because he was pretty sure he was going to lose it himself it he wasn't careful.

He increased the pace until she rocked frantically against him, clearly on the edge of desperation. Then he slid one hand between their slick, straining bodies and found the hard bud of her clit, pressing down at the same time as he drove himself up inside her. Chloe's head went back and she let out a hoarse scream, her whole body stiffening.

Van caught her hair in his fist at the nape of her neck and held on, covering her mouth, unable to resist the temptation to taste her as she came, take her cries for himself. Then he kept on moving, holding her as she rode out the wave, feeling it gather and tighten inside him too.

There was no reason to hold back now so he didn't, slamming himself into her over and over again, until his own climax crashed down on top of him like a fucking tsunami and dragged him under.

He collapsed down onto the bed, taking her with him, rolling to the side at the last minute so she wasn't crushed. She'd turned her face into his neck, her breath hot against his throat, and he found himself lying still in silence for a long, endless minute, listening to the sound of her breathing as he waited for his raging heartbeat to slow down. She had her hands tucked against his chest as she nestled in closer, giving a small sigh. "Thank you," she murmured at last, her voice sounding thick. "That was . . . amazing."

Yeah, it had been. Too amazing. But he couldn't let himself think about that, because this was a one-time thing. Once only, he'd told her, and he'd meant it. He still did. Perhaps even more now he knew what it was like to be with her.

There was another silence, and it took him a little while to realize that it was because she'd fallen asleep.

It was probably a good thing in many ways, because now he had no reason to linger in bed with her. And he definitely didn't want to do that, because then he might be tempted to keep doing more things to her. Make her scream again, or alternatively get that beautiful red mouth of hers wrapped around his—

Yeah, best to leave now. There were too many reasons why it had been a bad idea in the first place, and none at all for letting it continue.

Carefully Van eased himself out of her, then, making sure not to wake her, he moved away, pulling the comforter around her naked body to keep her warm. She made a soft, contented sound and snuggled into it, her breathing slowing as she fell back into a deep sleep.

Leaving her there, he picked up his clothes before making a detour to the bathroom to get rid of the condom, then returning to the living room. He dressed quickly then took out his phone, texting Lucas to let his brother know they'd arrived safely at the apartment and everything was secure.

Naturally he didn't mention anything of what had occurred with Chloe. He had a feeling Lucas would personally murder him if he found out what Van had done.

His cock, the difficult bastard, was very unhappy with the decision to get out of bed, but Van had stopped thinking with his dick back when he was eighteen, and so he ignored it. Instead he checked over the apartment once again, all the entrances and exits, making sure everything was safe. Then he went over to where he'd dropped his black bag by one of the armchairs and unzipped it, getting out the plain black spare hoodie he'd put into it. He tugged the hoodie on over his shirt, pulling the hood up over his head to hide his features, then he headed to the front door.

There was a small grocery store not far from the apartment that he'd spotted earlier, and it had all the basics. So he bought some essentials, keeping the hood pulled down low, returning to the apartment via a pizza place to get a couple of slices for dinner.

She was still asleep when he got back so he put the pizza in the oven to keep warm, then got out his laptop and set it up on the small dining table near the kitchen area. He needed to figure out how he was going to neutralize the threat to Chloe, but since de Santis's takeover bid was the most pressing, he had to handle that first, as well as go through the names of various people who could be good candidates for Tate CEO.

He spent the next few hours dealing with his emails, looking at the various strategies for dealing with the takeover that his father's management team had sent him, including figuring out how much Tate stock de Santis currently controlled.

The lack of clarity about whole situation annoyed him.

If he couldn't figure out how to move against de Santis or even if the guy was actually in a position of power when it came to a potential takeover, then what was the point of appointing a new CEO? Certainly, if he was having trouble figuring out a good defense strategy, then he didn't trust anyone else to either.

That thought was even more annoying, especially when he didn't understand why he cared so much. Clearly all the bullshit about the glory of the Tate legacy his father had fed him still had a strong hold on him.

Irritated with himself, Van shoved back his chair and paced over to the windows, reflexively checking the buildings across the street for anything overtly suspicious and failing to find anything.

This was crazy. Why did he care? He hated all that corporate bullshit, hated wearing a fucking suit, and hated sitting behind a goddamn desk. He wasn't that type of guy and he never would be, no matter how hard the old man had tried to turn him into one.

"Don't be so selfish, Sullivan," his father had said, the day Van had told him he'd be going back to base and wasn't coming back. "I gave you everything and now you can't even do this one thing for me?"

Van had just looked at him, knowing his father wouldn't listen because he never damn well listened, yet saying it anyway. "No, Dad. I gave you *everything. And you didn't want it. So why the fuck would I do anything for you now?"*

The old prick hadn't responded to that. He never had when it was Van who'd wanted something from him.

Van scowled out the window as night began to creep over the city.

Fuck Cesare de Santis. If it wasn't for that bastard, Van wouldn't be in this mess to start with. The guy was powerful and successful in his own right, so what the hell did he want with Tate Oil and Gas? Was it simply a case of the one that got away? That because he'd failed to take it from Noah all those years ago, he had to try again? It wasn't about money, Van was sure of it. It had a more personal feel to it.

More personal than Chloe?

Ah, yes, Chloe. Who'd been taken from Cesare by Noah.

Maybe this wasn't about Tate Oil at all. Maybe the takeover was simply a distraction so he could make his real move, which was to get Chloe back.

Van stared out into the gathering dusk as something heavy and solid settled down inside him. Certainty. Because there was no fucking way de Santis was getting Chloe. Not while Van had anything to do about it.

You were certain last time, too. Remember?

The heavy feeling turned to ice in the pit of his stomach, memories of Sofia running through his head whether he wanted them to or not. She'd been a prisoner of the traffickers for a long time and had been terrified of him and his team during the rescue. And when things had gone to hell, and he'd had to grab her and run, he'd had his work cut out for him to gain her trust to keep her from running off into the jungle. But he'd done it. He'd told her that she had nothing to worry about, that she was safe with him. That he'd protect her whatever happened, get her home to her fiancé. And she'd believed him. She'd stayed with him, trusted him.

Hell, he'd seen no reason to doubt himself. He was the Tate heir. He was strong and powerful, a warrior just like his father had told him he was. He always did his best at whatever he was doing so he could make his father proud, and this mission would be no different.

Except it had been. He'd gained Sofia's trust and then he'd failed her. Catastrophically. He hadn't been safe for her and he hadn't protected her, and the only place he'd gotten her to was a hole in the ground.

How can you be sure you can protect Chloe then?

Given his earlier failure, he couldn't be. Shit, maybe if he'd wanted that certainty he should have given her to his brothers to look after.

Yet as soon as the thought occurred to him, that deep possessiveness rose up inside him again, somehow even worse this time. Telling him that there was no way in hell he was giving her to anyone. That protecting her was *his* job. That she was his.

It was wrong to think that. Wrong to feel it. But just because it was wrong didn't stop the feeling from sinking its claws into him and holding on tight.

No, he wasn't giving her to anyone else. He was the one who would keep her safe, the *only* one.

Are you sure that's a good idea? You failed Sofia. You failed Noah . . .

No, fuck that. Sofia had died and sure, that was on him, but he wouldn't make that mistake again. And as for his father, well, that guy had never wanted a son anyway. He'd wanted a paragon. Nothing but the best to protect and serve the Tate legacy

Van had tried to be that once, and he'd failed. And now that Noah was dead, he had nothing to prove to anyone.

"Hey," someone said, familiar and feminine.

Every muscle in his body tensed, his cock stirring like a goddamn dog at the sound of its master's voice, and he had to take a breath to get himself under control before he turned, just in case he lost his head entirely and took her back to bed.

She was standing near the dining table, dressed only in the hoodie he'd given her earlier. It came to mid-thigh, her slender legs bare. She'd rolled the sleeves up to her elbows, but she still looked like a little girl dressed up in her big brother's clothes.

Nice analogy there for you. Since you're the big brother.

Van thrust his hands into his pockets, forcing his libido to calm the fuck down and his conscience to take a damn chill pill. "Hey yourself. Had a nice nap?"

Her mouth curved and it hit him all of a sudden that this was the first time he'd actually seen her smile since she'd arrived. It was . . . beautiful. Hell, *she* was beautiful. And so fucking sexy he wanted to cross the room, pick her up, and take her back to bed for the rest of the night.

His hands curled into fists in his pockets. Christ, he liked that smile. Liked that she felt relaxed enough to give it to him. And it was he who'd done that for her, wasn't it? He'd been the one to make her feel good. He'd been the one to make her smile.

And he wanted to do it again.

Once and once only, remember?

Of course he remembered. But did that really mean he could only have her once? Because what difference would it make if he'd meant one *night*? What difference would it make if he crossed the distance between them now and took her back to bed?

It would make no difference. No difference at all.

Van took his hands out of his pockets and moved toward her before he was even conscious of making a decision, reaching for her, pulling her small, lithe body up against his. Her smile deepened and she lifted her hands and wound them around his neck, pressing herself delicately against him. The color in her cheeks made her eyes glow and he had no idea why he'd ever thought once would be enough.

"Are you hungry?" His voice had gotten rough, but he didn't care. "There's pizza in the oven if you are."

Slowly she shook her head. "I like pizza, don't get me wrong. But . . ." The blush in her cheeks became brighter. "It's kind of not pizza I'm hungry for right now."

Fuck, he couldn't tell himself he didn't like that. Couldn't tell himself he didn't love her honesty, or the way her eyes went dark as he curved his hands over her ass, slipping beneath the hem of her hoodie, feeling silky bare skin against his palms. "Are you sure?" he asked, squeezing her gently, watching desire unfurl over her lovely face. "It's pepperoni."

She gave a soft gasp as he squeezed her again. "Can we stop talking about pizza? I actually don't care about that right now."

"Sacrilege." He bent his head, caught her mouth with his, biting down on her soft lower lip. "You should always care about pizza."

Chloe shuddered. "Shut the hell up, Van."

He laughed then shut the hell up as he gathered her into his arms and carried her back to bed.

CHAPTER TEN

Chloe bent and picked up her clothes from the bedroom floor. It was late and she knew she should probably try to sleep, but that wasn't going to be happening. Not after the last couple of intense, desperate, *hungry* hours in bed with Van. No, after all of that, she was starving, and the idea of the pizza he'd been teasing her about earlier was suddenly extremely appealing.

He'd already gotten up and left the bedroom to make sure it hadn't burned to a crisp. She'd suggested eating it in bed, but he'd been *very* disapproving of that idea, which was a shame since it was going to mean getting dressed. Or at least semi-dressed.

Reaching for the hoodie that had somehow ended up underneath the bed, she pulled it over the top of her head then made her way to the kitchen/living room area.

Where she stopped, because Van was standing at the dining table, looking down at the screen of the laptop he had open in front of him, and she wanted a quiet moment simply to stare at him.

He wore only a pair of soft, battered jeans with frayed holes in the knees that sat low on his lean hips and somehow highlighted the stark perfection of the rest of his incredible body.

Her hands itched, wanting to touch him again, run her

fingers all over the oiled silk of his skin, follow the lines of carved muscle and the black tracks of those mesmerizing tattoos. This, despite the last two hours where she'd occupied herself with doing exactly that.

So. Freaking. Hot. She almost didn't know what to do with herself.

"You can keep staring. I don't mind." Van didn't look up from the laptop, but she could see his mouth curve.

Dammit. Busted yet again.

"How do you keep doing that?" She moved over to the table, hoping she wasn't blushing too badly. "Knowing I'm there, I mean. I didn't make sound."

He glanced at her, gold glinting in his eyes. "You don't have to. I can smell you."

"Oh." Her cheeks heated whether she wanted them to or not.

"Don't worry. You smell delicious." He grinned. "Plus, I can also hear your breathing."

Great. So all those times he'd caught her staring, he must have heard her getting all breathless too.

"That's not creepy at all," she muttered, feeling herself blush even harder.

He laughed, the sound so unbelievably sexy that when he reached for her to pull her to him, she didn't protest. Instead she leaned into him, loving the hard, reassuring strength of his body against hers.

"I'm a SEAL, pretty. I'm supposed to notice these things."

"Yeah, I guess so." She couldn't look up into his face for some reason, the sight of that smile of his somehow blinding. So she kept her attention on his chest right in front of her, on that tattoo inked into his skin and the chain of his dog tags. Reminders of who he was. A protector, a guardian.

Something tight inside her, something that had been

slowly uncurling over the past couple of hours, relaxed utterly and she found herself leaning her head on that broad chest of his, taking in his heat, his strength.

She couldn't remember the last time she'd allowed herself to be held and she'd forgotten how good it felt to have another person's arms around her, to have some simple, human contact.

Yeah, like it's about 'human' contact. It's him you want, idiot.

Okay, so it *was* him. And what was wrong with that? Sure, he'd only promised her a night, but that was fine. She didn't want more than that anyway, right? He was going back to the military and she was going back to the ranch, and that would be that. One night wasn't going to change anything.

"Is that pizza okay?" she asked after a long moment. "I'm starving."

"Yeah, it's still in the oven." He released her and stepped back. "You want me to get you a plate?"

"No, I can do it." She put a brief hand on his hard, flat abdomen, just because she could, then moved past him, going into the kitchen and pulling open the oven to find a couple of slices sitting there waiting for her.

"Did you want a slice?" she asked as she hunted around for a plate.

"No." He was sitting down at the table now, his attention back on his laptop again. "Try the cupboard above the sink."

She blinked then pulled open the cupboard like he'd said, and sure enough, there were the plates. Damn man was magic.

Taking one down and putting it on the counter, she dumped her pizza on it then took it over to the table and sat down opposite him. The pizza smelled really good; pepperoni was her favorite.

She lifted the slice. "Thank you for the pizza."

"No problem."

She took a bite, chewing slowly. Tasted really good too. "You remembered I liked pepperoni."

He glanced up from the screen. "You really expected me to forget? After your twelfth birthday?"

Ah yes, she did remember that. He'd been back at the ranch on leave—the other two had still been on deployment, and her father, unsurprisingly, had been in New York—and had helped organize a special birthday dinner for her. Pepperoni pizza had been what she'd wanted, but they'd run out of pepperoni, so Van had taken the chopper and flown to Blaketown to get it since that was quicker than driving the twenty miles from the ranch.

"I guess that's pretty hard to forget." Something in her chest went all warm and liquid and melty that he'd remembered, and she had to look away to hide her reaction. Taking another bite of pizza, she nodded at the laptop. "What are you doing?" It was a graceless change of subject, but she didn't care.

"Trying to stop de Santis from making that takeover bid for Tate Oil."

Ah yes. All of that was still happening, wasn't it?

Chloe shifted uncomfortably in her seat. "Is it serious?"

"Yeah. And I need to stop that shit before I can find a suitable CEO to run the company."

"Why? Aren't you the heir or whatever?"

Van gave her a glance from over the top of the laptop. "Sure. But like I told you, I'm not running his fucking company no matter how badly he wanted me to. I'm heading back to base once my leave is over."

Of course he was and yes, he'd told her that already. Yet something inside her missed a beat at the thought, though she refused to examine exactly what it was. "You sound like me and the ranch."

"It is like you and the ranch. I don't stop being a SEAL just because Dad was stupid enough to fall off his horse and break his fucking neck."

A thread of anger ran through his deep voice, she heard it clear as day. Not that it was unfamiliar. She'd heard it whenever he'd talked about being Noah's heir. Hell, whenever he'd talked about Noah, period. And if she needed further proof that he and their father hadn't gotten on, there were the eight years he hadn't set foot on the Tate ranch, eight years of silence . . .

Carefully, she picked up the other slice of pizza and took a bite, chewing slowly. "You don't want to run the company?" She tried to keep the question casual, even though curiosity was suddenly burning her up inside.

"Does it look like I want to? No, of course I fucking don't. My career is in the military, and Dad knew that." His dark brows drew down, giving him a saturnine look that made a shiver go through her. God, he was hot when he looked like that. "Dad would have preferred me to shut up and be grateful, and do exactly what I was told, just like everyone else did. Sadly for him, I wasn't one of his employees."

Now there wasn't only anger in his voice, but bitterness too. What was his deal? Had he had the same issues as she'd had? Noah wasn't an easy man to get close to as she knew to her cost, and she'd always thought her foster brothers had a better relationship with him than she did. But maybe they hadn't.

Chloe put her slice back down on the plate and looked at him. "What did he do, Van? What did he do to make you so angry?"

Something flickered in his gaze. "He was a lousy father. But then you know that already."

It was true, she did.

She glanced down at her plate. "I always thought he

liked you guys the best. You got to go places, do things, while I just had to stay on the ranch and keep quiet, like a good girl."

There was a brief silence.

Then Van sighed. "He didn't like us best, pretty. We just all had specific roles and he made sure we stuck to them. Mine was to be the heir, and everything I did had to be about that and there was no room for anything else."

She looked up again, studying him from beneath her lashes. "But why didn't you want to be the heir?"

"I did at first." He hit a button on the keypad then closed the lid of the laptop, sitting back in his chair and meeting her gaze. "But you know Dad. His standards were impossible to meet and he was pretty fucking unforgiving when you didn't meet them. I just got sick of being expected to live up to some goddamn ideal."

She hadn't known that. Noah certainly hadn't ever had any expectations of her, and when she'd been younger, she'd found that was just another example of how much he didn't care. But she didn't say that. Instead, she asked carefully, "What kind of ideal?"

Van tilted his head, his arms crossed over his broad chest. "He wanted someone who never made mistakes, basically. The perfect figurehead for his perfect legacy." Again, there was that thread of bitterness running through his voice. "But it doesn't matter. He's dead and he can't do a fucking thing about it now."

It did matter though. It was there in that note of bitterness, that note of anger. And she wanted to ask him what had happened to make him feel like that, because obviously somewhere along the line he'd failed to meet one of those impossible standards of Noah's and hadn't been forgiven.

She couldn't imagine what that was. She couldn't imagine Van failing to live up to *anyone's* standards. He was so strong and straight up. Protective. Patient. He cared, too. She'd felt it every time he touched her.

Chloe stared at him, holding his gaze. "Whatever ideal he wanted you to live up to, whatever standard you thought you failed, you didn't, Van. If he didn't forgive you, he was wrong."

Van had gone very still, his expression unreadable. Then it softened somewhat. "Thanks, pretty. But there's a whole lot of stuff that happened that you don't know about. And I don't want to go into it now, okay?"

It wasn't okay though, and somehow she knew it.

She looked back down at her plate, not quite sure why the gentle way he'd warned her off the topic should have hurt. Yet it had. She felt the ache of it nag at her like a splinter.

Trying to ignore it, she picked up her slice and took a large bite instead, letting the silence sit there for a bit. Then she asked, in another awkward change of subject, "So what are we going to do with de Santis?" No way would she call him her father, no freaking way.

Van let out a breath. "I need to head off this takeover first, figure out what the asshole wants. Whether it's you or the company, or maybe both. Dad wasn't real clear on any of this, so we're flying blind, unfortunately."

"That was unhelpful of Dad," she muttered. "How do we go about finding that out then?"

Van lifted his hands and put them behind his head, and she got briefly distracted by the play of all that sculpted muscle flexing and releasing in response to his movements. "It's difficult. Thought about hacking into his private network, finding emails, that kind of thing. But DS Corp's electronic security is stronger than the goddamn FBI's. Hell, they *sold* that security to the FBI, which means hacking in is going to be fucking impossible."

"So that's it? We can't do anything? Might as well just ask him straight out then."

Van inhaled sharply, his chest expanding, his dog tags slipping to one side and distracting her again. "No, I didn't say we can't do anything. I said it was difficult. But now you've given me an idea."

She blinked. "I did?"

"Yeah." The flash of his smile was blinding as he straightened suddenly and reached for his laptop, opening it up again. "I might just keep you on. You're a valuable asset."

"I am?"

He had his attention on the laptop screen, typing something out, his fingers moving fast on the keys. "I'd finish up that pizza if I were you, because in one more minute I'm going to be showing you just how valuable an asset you are."

A shiver went through her at the rough heat in his voice. "Okay. And do I get to know why I'm a valuable asset?"

Van hit a key, waited a moment, then pushed the laptop screen shut. Shoving back his chair, he stalked around the table and before she could move, she found herself gathered up into his arms and held tightly against the hot wall of his chest.

"Van," she said firmly. "Tell me what you're doing. Also, I didn't get to finish my pizza."

"You said why not ask him straight up, so I did." He flashed her another of the those brilliant, blinding smiles as he stalked down the hallway. "Also, you can have your pizza later."

She placed her hand on his chest, frowning up at him. "What do you mean you asked him straight up?"

"I just sent him an email organizing a meeting tomorrow." Van's smile took on a menacing edge. "He'll come. And then I'll ask him what he wants."

"Is that really such a good idea?" Something she didn't want to admit was fear fluttered inside her. Fear for him. "He's dangerous."

"Don't worry, pretty." The sharp edge in Van's smile turned lethal as he stepped into the bedroom, making her shiver. "So am I."

Van paced the length of his father's office, came to the wall opposite, then turned around.

In front of him stood the ancient desk his father had brought from Wyoming, claiming it was some kind of family heirloom. It was ridiculous to have a rolltop desk in a modern office, but his father had been adamant it had to be there. On the wall behind it was a huge painting of the Tate ranch, Shadow Peak looming behind it.

The ranch that his father had bought for some pittance back when he'd been barely in his twenties. Noah had worked like a dog on it, trying to rescue the place from an almost derelict state, building it up into a good, solid working ranch, and that's where he might have stayed if he hadn't been looking to expand. If he hadn't unexpectedly struck oil on one of the more distant pastures.

That had been the start of the business that had grown from a small oil rig into a major petroleum company, adding gas fields and oil exploration to its portfolio as it grew. The company was massive now, brought in billions, and it had been his father's baby for as long as Van could remember.

"Fuck you," Van muttered at the desk, the simmering anger that had been dogging him all day threatening to spill over.

He'd come into Tate Oil that morning for yet another round of meetings—aka the ongoing fight with the board. The de Santis takeover bid in addition to the fact that the board wasn't happy about Van and his brothers being the replacement directors, had not made things easy and Van wasn't in the mood to deal with them. He'd had to leave Lucas's apartment before dawn to get back to the Tate mansion so it looked like he was still there, and all without drawing attention to himself and giving away to de Santis where he'd been. Because he suspected de Santis would now be on his tail trying to figure out where Chloe was.

Sure enough, he'd been followed from the mansion to Tate Oil that morning and he had no doubt at all that he'd be followed home too. Which was going to make getting back to Chloe somewhat problematic.

Ah well, he'd know more once de Santis turned up for the meeting. *If* de Santis turned up for the meeting. Van had made sure to frame it as a "discussion about mutual interests" to keep it intriguing, and he was pretty sure the asshole would come. De Santis wouldn't miss an opportunity to see how the land lay after his enemy's death, to get a look at who he was up against now.

Van bared his teeth at the painting on the wall behind the desk.

Yeah and hopefully the knowledge that de Santis was up against three SEAL brothers with not inconsiderable skills, might give the bastard pause for thought.

Van began to pace back toward the desk only to stop short at the soft tap on the office door.

"Yeah, what?" he demanded gracelessly, in no mood for politeness.

The door opened and Margery, his father's secretary, put her head around it. "There's someone to see you, Mr. Tate."

"So? Do they have an appointment?" As soon as he'd said it he knew it was a stupid question. Of course they didn't have an appointment. If they had, Margery wouldn't be here asking him about it, she'd simply be telling them to wait until he was ready or she'd be showing them in.

"No," Margery said carefully. "But apparently you asked him to come."

Van stilled. There could be no doubt who it was since he'd sent out only one meeting request in the past day or so. Cesare de Santis. Though it looked like the bastard had turned up early, and probably to make a point.

Van gave Margery a feral smile that made her eyes widen. "Show him in, Margery, please."

She gave him a slightly wary look before nodding then disappearing back behind the door, shutting it after her.

Van strode quickly over to his father's desk and sat down in the big black leather chair behind it. Then he pulled open the top right drawer and grabbed his Glock, shoving it into the waistband of his pants at his back. He didn't think de Santis would be stupid enough to try anything, but it always paid to be a good Boy Scout.

A minute later the door opened again to admit Margery—this time with a pleasant, professional smile on her face—and a tall, older man in a perfectly tailored, custom navy blue suit. He looked to be in his late sixties, with iron gray hair and a kind of heavy, Mediterranean handsomeness. The famous de Santis blue eyes were piercing as he swept his gaze over Noah Tate's office, before coming to rest on Van.

"Mr. de Santis to see you, Mr. Tate," Margery said calmly.

Cesare de Santis smiled and it would have been friendly if the smile had reached his eyes. But it didn't. That blue gaze was cold, watchful, and not a little calculating. The guy definitely had presence too, the kind of forceful charisma that a great many powerful men possessed.

Men like his father.

"Mr. Tate," Cesare de Santis's voice was all pleasantness as he moved toward the desk, his hand held out. "Please forgive me being early, but your meeting request came late and this was the only gap in my schedule. Good to finally meet you at last."

Van made no move to stand and take the proffered hand, staying exactly where he was. "Thank you, Margery," he said, his voice devoid of expression. "That will be all."

As Margery nodded and left the room, closing the door behind her, Van briefly debated how he was going to play this, whether to join in the facade of politeness, play the game. Yet a part of him, brought up on Noah's tales of de Santis perfidy, wasn't interested in pretense. This man had been Noah's nemesis for a good twenty years, starting right from when he'd tried to claim the oil strike as his own. Then there was the fact that he was on the brink of gaining control of Noah's company, not to mention threatening Noah's daughter. And yes, he was going to continue to think of Chloe as Noah's because as far as Van was concerned, this asshole wasn't her father.

"What do you want?" Van demanded, deciding he may as well start as he meant to continue—aggressively. He could, of course, have acted like the bastard wasn't a problem, but there was no point pretending that particular elephant wasn't in the room.

They both knew what was going on.

De Santis's smile vanished as quickly as it had appeared, his hand dropping back to his side. "Isn't that my line? You were the one who asked me to be here."

"Yeah and that's my question. What do you want?"

The older man put his hands in his pockets and turned toward the windows that overlooked Broadway, strolling over to them. "Hope you don't mind if I don't sit down," he commented casually. "I'm not going to take up too much of your valuable time. You've got a lot on your plate at the moment, or so I hear."

Van's fingers itched to grab the gun he could feel resting reassuringly at his back. Christ, he hated this kind of bullshit. He preferred a straight-up fight to verbal sparring, always had. And he definitely wasn't a fan of empty posturing. If you wanted to prove yourself the biggest, baddest motherfucker in the room, you simply went ahead and did it. You didn't make snide remarks or drop subtle allusions to the fact that you were engineering a hostile takeover.

Van stared hard at the other man. "Like I said, what do you want?"

De Santis turned, his sharp blue eyes meeting Van's. "You get straight to the point, Mr. Tate. I like that in a businessman."

"I'm not a fucking businessman."

"No, you're not. You're a soldier, aren't you?"

Van allowed himself a slight smile. "I'm a motherfucking SEAL, asshole. Get your facts straight."

De Santis's gaze narrowed a moment, then his expression relaxed. "You're very similar to your father, did you know that?"

The comment took Van by surprise, making him feel slightly off-balance, which he did not appreciate one bit. Sure, he could be autocratic, maybe, but as for the rest? Reserved, cold, and emotionless? If any of them were like Noah, it was Lucas.

Masking his response, Van lifted a shoulder as if it wasn't a big deal. "I get that a lot. Now answer the fucking question before I get security to throw you out." Not that he needed security.

He could probably take the guy by himself.

De Santis gave Van an easy smile. "No need to get aggressive, son. I'll give you an answer then I'll get out of your hair."

Van crossed his arms, matching the other man stare for stare. Waiting.

The smile eased from de Santis's craggy, handsome face. "You want to know what I want? I want to see my daughter."

Something electric curled around Van's spine. So this *was* about Chloe.

"And which daughter would that be?" Van asked, seeing no point in making it easy for him. "Since you already have one and all."

The other man gave a soft laugh. "Are we going to play games now? And here was I thinking you preferred the direct approach. You know which daughter I'm talking about, Mr. Tate."

Yeah, he did. The small, delicate one curled up in the guest bedroom as he'd left the apartment that morning. The one with the soft, silky skin he'd spent most of the previous night stroking and tasting every inch of, making her cry his name over and over again.

The one who'd told him that whatever it was that he'd done, whatever standard it was that he hadn't lived up to, Noah was wrong.

But of course he shouldn't be thinking of her right now, or of the conversation they'd had the previous night, because it was all supposed to be over anyway. One night, that was it.

The anger that was already glowing in his gut glowed a little brighter for no goddamn reason that he could see. Not when he'd been telling himself it was a one-night-only thing right from the moment he'd decided to take her to bed.

He'd given her what she wanted, end of story.

Yet there was another part of him, the deeply territorial, primitive part, that absolutely refused this logic. That was angry at even the thought of it. That considered Chloe as his and saw no reason why he should have to give her up at all.

Which didn't make sense, since it was exactly the kind of over-the-top emotional response he'd sworn to himself he was going to avoid.

He couldn't have her again. She was under his protection and if history hadn't already taught him what a bad idea that was, then the fact that she was in a uniquely vulnerable position should. She was alone in New York, dependent on him, which made screwing her—even apart from the whole foster sister thing—a very, very bad idea.

Too late, asshole. She's already given you her trust, let you inside her. You can't take that back now.

Van shoved the thought away. "She's not your daughter," he said flatly. "She's Noah Tate's."

"Apparently the paternity test your father ordered disagrees."

"Were you the one taking care of her for twenty-five years? No, I don't think so."

"No," de Santis agreed. "Because I didn't know her mother was pregnant." He smiled at Van, but this time there was nothing pleasant about it. "Your father stole her from me. I didn't even know she existed until after she was born."

"Right. So you waited all this time to come find her?"

De Santis tilted his head, the gray light of the winter's afternoon shining on a few of the black threads lacing his gray hair. "You seem to persist in thinking I'm the bad guy, Mr. Tate. I assure you I'm not. I had no idea I had even had a daughter until your father told me." He paused. "And I didn't wait to come and find her. Noah told me in no uncertain terms that he was going to keep my child as his hostage and if I made even so much as one move in his direction, then something might happen to her. Something I might not like."

This time it was Van's turn to laugh. "Is that supposed to shock me? I know what Dad did. He told me. He initially kept Chloe to ensure that you left our family alone. But if you're implying he would have hurt her, you're flat out wrong."

"Am I?" De Santis's cold gaze never wavered. "You're very sure of your father, Mr. Tate. Surer than you should be. Noah was a deeply flawed man, make no mistake, and he was ruthless. Believe me, I know exactly how ruthless he was."

Of course Noah was deeply flawed. Like Van didn't already know that himself. He certainly wasn't going to give this prick the satisfaction of knowing he knew.

"So is that what this takeover bid's about then?" Van met the other man's stare. "Is it revenge? Or is it simply a distraction from your interest in Chloe?"

De Santis's mouth pulled up in a sneer. "You really think I'd tell you? Why don't you work it out for yourself?"

"Revenge then." Van watched the other man's face carefully. "You want revenge because Dad put a stop to you stealing his oil."

Something flickered in de Santis's cold blue eyes, but was gone so quickly Van couldn't tell what it was. "Draw whatever conclusions you like, Mr. Tate. The facts remain that your father has been holding my daughter hostage for twenty-five years and now I want to see her, understand me?"

Oh, he understood all right. And hell, maybe in different circumstances, Van might have even felt sorry for the guy. Chloe *was* his kid after all, and it had been a shitty thing Noah had done to keep her from him.

But there was no way, no way in hell, that Van was going to let this man anywhere near her.

He moved, shoving back his chair and getting to his feet. Then he strolled casually over to where de Santis stood, reaching around to grab his Glock and holding it in an easy grip. "Sure, I get it. And here's my problem with it. If seeing your kid was all you wanted, you could have done that years ago. But you didn't, did you?" He didn't do anything with the gun, merely held it at his side as a subtle warning. "And now you've got guys hanging around my house, following me everywhere, trying to get eyes on her, and you know what that says to me? That says it's not seeing her you're all that interested in. You want her for something else."

De Santis didn't even look at the gun, his gaze pinned to Van's. "You think I'd hurt her?"

"I think you want to take Tate Oil down and I think you don't much care how you do it. And if that involves Chloe, then too bad." Van arched an eyebrow. "How am I doing so far?"

Again that flicker in the other man's eyes, and it wasn't aggression or anger. It was something colder, something that seemed to see right through Van. "You don't know, do you?" De Santis said quietly.

Van felt his jaw tighten. "Know what?"

"Why your father and I hated each other."

"Sure I do, you tried to steal his oil. Which is just one more reason why Chloe isn't having anything to do with you."

De Santis didn't say anything, merely studying Van through narrowed blue eyes. "Does she know about me?" he asked after a moment. "Does she know I'm her father?"

Van remained silent, giving nothing away, keeping his face expressionless. A hard blue flame glittered briefly in the older man's eyes.

"If she doesn't know already, she'll find out," de Santis said, his voice soft and very cold. "And she won't appreciate being lied to. She won't appreciate being prevented from meeting me, either."

Van smiled, though it wasn't pleasant. "You don't know her. So how about you don't comment on what she may or may not appreciate. Now"—his fingers tightened around the Glock—"I think we're done here, don't you? Shall I get Margery to show you out or would you prefer security?"

The older man's smile changed, becoming almost warm. "Ah, perhaps I neglected to mention the fact that if

you don't give me Chloe, I shall move on Tate Oil within
the next twenty-four hours."

Van laughed. "You can't. My management team and I
went over the details of your bid this morning. You haven't
got quite the shares you need to move yet."

"Haven't I?" De Santis lifted a shoulder. "Maybe you
know business better than I do, Mr. Tate. What with being a motherfucking SEAL and all." He turned toward the
door. "Twenty-four hours. That's all you have. And don't
worry, I expect I can see myself out."

Before Van could move, de Santis turned and strolled
calmly out the door.

CHAPTER ELEVEN

Chloe spent the day sitting at the table working on Van's laptop, dealing with ranch stuff and trying very, very hard not to think about what had happened between her and Van the night before. Especially not when it was so insanely distracting. His big hands on her skin; his hot, hard body covering hers; the way he'd felt inside her . . . God, so good.

But she really needed to *not* think about it because he'd been very clear it was only supposed to be one night. And that night was over. Which meant it couldn't happen again, and she was fine with that. Absolutely fine.

Annoying that he'd gone out before she'd even woken up that morning, though. So she hadn't even had a chance to run her hands over his incredible stomach one last time, but then you couldn't have everything.

Yes, the sex had been great but it was done now. And all that other stuff, all that messy, tangled emotional stuff she'd felt when he'd held her in his arms, when he'd given her that blinding smile of his, well she needed to do what she usually did with it. Which was to *not* think about that either.

Besides, it wasn't as if they didn't already have enough on their plates, what with de Santis trying to find her and that takeover bid that Van told her about last night. And then there was the meeting Van had apparently invited him to . . .

Anxiousness twisted in her gut, but she ignored it as she typed the last couple of lines of the email to O'Neil then pressed send.

Sitting back in her chair, she stared at the laptop for a moment, wondering what the hell she was going to do next, because she had to do something. She didn't want to sit here the way she had back in the Tate mansion, not when there was so much stuff going on.

Van was handling all of it, which didn't seem fair, especially since Wolf and Lucas were off doing whatever the hell it was they were doing and apparently not inclined to help. No, Van only had her.

And you're worse than useless in this situation.

Chloe scowled, not liking that thought. Sure, the situation they were in now was kind of her fault and even though she wasn't exactly a muscle-bound SEAL who could leap over buildings while brandishing a gun, she wasn't useless either. She had a fairly analytical brain, a good head for business, and nothing but time on her hands right now, so maybe she could start helping by finding out everything she could about Cesare de Santis.

Pulling her chair a little closer to the table, Chloe started searching.

There was a lot of information on him. As the erstwhile owner of DS Corp, a massive defense company, he was one of New York's most powerful businessmen. Or at least he used to be. A year earlier he'd stepped down from helming his company in favor of his middle son, Rafael, and had been avoiding the public eye ever since. The gossip on the web was that he was living a life of gracious retirement in between attending upper class social engagements and fundraisers, spending most of his time at the family estate in the Hamptons. He had four sons—

one illegitimate—and one daughter, Olivia. Of his sons, only Rafael and Lorenzo seemed to be heavily involved with DS Corp. Chloe was intrigued to see that Cesare's youngest son, Xavier, lived out on a ranch in Wyoming.

No surprises there. The de Santis family had come from Wyoming, were descended from Italian immigrants who'd settled there many, many years earlier. In fact, Cesare de Santis had been the one to take the family gun business into the stratosphere, growing from a small family-owned company into a major conglomerate in a few decades. It was remarkable. Then again, no more remarkable than what Noah had done with Tate Oil.

It was no wonder the two of them had once been friends. Both men seemed to be rather alike.

Chloe was still searching as lunchtime came around, pulling up as many images of Cesare as she could. He was a handsome man even now, but back in his youth, he'd been quite devastating from the looks of things. The very definition of tall, dark, and handsome. No wonder her mother had indulged herself with him.

She clicked on one of the most recent pictures, staring at it. The years had carved deep lines over his face, but they hadn't dimmed the intense color of his blue eyes and there were still strands of black in his hair. She half-raised a hand to her own face. Did she have his nose? His mouth? But then she'd thought she'd gotten her dark eyes and black hair from Noah, and that clearly wasn't the case, so how would she know?

Maybe you're only seeing what you want to see?

She grimaced at the pictures. No, she wasn't. She didn't want to see anything of him in her because she didn't like the idea of being his daughter, period.

But you have a ready-made family right there. Actual half brothers and a half sister. You'd never be alone again . . .

Her heartbeat thumped in her head, gone oddly fast, a strange aching sensation in her chest. Weird to feel like this, because she wasn't alone. She had Wolf and Lucas and Van. She had the ranch. She didn't need anyone else.

But you don't know Wolf and Lucas. And the ranch isn't yours yet. And neither is Van.

Chloe shoved her chair away from the table and got up, walking quickly into the kitchen and pressing the button on Lucas's fancy coffeemaker. Caffeine, that's what she needed. She hadn't had much sleep the night before, so maybe that's why she was feeling so weird.

Yet even with a mug of coffee in her hands, the hot liquid burning her throat as she took a sip, the ache in her chest wouldn't go away. And she found herself helplessly drawn back to the laptop, clicking through yet more pictures of the man who apparently was her father.

What kind of guy was he? He was Noah's enemy, sure, but what did that mean? He'd made a play for Noah's oil, and that had destroyed their friendship, but had that *really* been enough for Noah to have taken Cesare's daughter and keep her? And why hadn't Cesare come for her earlier? Was it really true? Would Noah have hurt her if his enemy had made a move for her?

She didn't like the way that made her feel. God, she needed Van back so she could have some distraction from the way her thoughts kept turning themselves into knots over all this crap.

Pushing away the laptop, she reached for the snow globe of Rockefeller Center that Noah had given her. She'd gotten it out of her bag that morning and put it on the table, why, she had no idea. Maybe so she'd have something pretty to look at or maybe because she needed something to fiddle with.

Or maybe because you need the reminder of what happens when you let yourself want something. When you let yourself hope.

The ache in her chest deepened, but she was sick of thinking about it, sick of feeling it, so she got herself yet more coffee, going back to the laptop and continuing with her searches to distract herself.

Eventually she heard the sound of the complicated lock on the front door of the apartment clicking and the door opening, the sound of Van's footsteps echoing down the hall. Her heartbeat sped up.

He could move very silently when he wanted, which meant he wanted to make it obvious to her that it was him and that he was home.

That nagging ache throbbed. Okay, so obviously the worst hadn't happened with de Santis since Van had made it back in one piece. It was either that or maybe de Santis hadn't showed. But still, Van was back.

Suddenly she wanted to shove her chair back and go to him, put her arms around him and hold on tight. Feel his warmth and his strength, see his smile. Have him touch her in that gentle, careful, patient way.

But she couldn't. They'd had their night and she wasn't going to ask for more. She wasn't going to want again and she definitely wasn't going to hope.

Van appeared in the living room, undoing the top buttons on his shirt then pulling at his tie as he crossed over to the dining area, and just for a second she wavered. Because the fabric parted, revealing the tanned skin of his throat and giving her a glimpse of the chain of his dog tags. And she was back again on the bed, lying beneath his big, hard body, that chain in her hands, looking up into his gleaming gold eyes. His heat around her, his scent making her crazy. Desperate for him to touch her.

There was a pulse between her legs, heavy and insistent, but she forced herself to ignore it. They'd had sex and yes, it had been great, but she didn't need it again. She just didn't.

He smiled at her, making her feel like someone had taken her heart in his hands and was busy squeezing it hard. "Hey pretty, how was today?" He moved over to the table, coiling his tie in one hand then hanging it over the back of one of the chairs.

"It was fine." She picked up her coffee mug and held it tight to stop herself from reaching for him instead. The heat burned her fingertips, but she ignored it. "What about your meeting? Did he show?"

"Oh, he showed all right." That lethal edge to Van's smile was back. "He showed to deliver an ultimatum: he wants you within twenty-four hours or else he's going to move on that takeover bid."

Shock coursed through her and suddenly she wasn't clutching the coffee mug to keep from reaching for him, she was clutching it to stop her hands from shaking. "Oh," she heard herself say, her voice sounding thin. "That sounds . . . like a problem."

Van leaned on the back of the chair, his long fingers curled over the wood, his sharp hazel gaze meeting hers. "You seriously think I'd let him take you?"

"It's not that."

"Then what?"

Ah, crap. She shouldn't have said anything. She should have simply pretended she was fine the way she normally did. But it was too late for that now. She was going to have to tell him, give away the fact that she cared. And that was always bad. Always.

Chloe looked down at her mug, trying to untangle the sudden thick mass of emotion in her chest. "I don't . . . like that he gave you an ultimatum, that he's using me against you. I don't want to be the reason Tate Oil gets taken over. I . . . don't want you to have to choose."

There was a silence.

Then she felt the warmth of him next to her chair, caught the fluid movement of his body as he crouched down beside her. "Hey," he murmured, his voice full of warm reassurance, those long, capable fingers sliding beneath her chin and turning her toward him so she found herself staring into his eyes. He was so tall that even though she was sitting down and he was crouching, they were on the same level. "He can only use you if we let him, and that's not going to happen, okay? No one's taking Tate Oil and no one's taking you, and that's final."

The warmth of his fingers on her skin was a terrible, terrible temptation and she wanted very much to lean into it. But she didn't. Instead she pulled her chin carefully out of his grip and sat back in her seat.

The look in his eyes flared in response, gold and green burning bright, and it seemed for a moment as if he was going to reach for her again. And she didn't know what she'd do if he did. Probably let him, which would be a very bad idea when she was only barely holding on to what distance she had as it was.

Except he didn't reach for her. Instead his hand dropped, though he stayed where he was, crouched beside her chair. "I'll figure it out, Chloe." The warmth was fading from his tone like heat slowly ebbing from a dying fire, the bright flame in his eyes dying out. "I'm pretty sure he can't stage that takeover anyway. It's not looking like he has a majority share."

She tried not to let the sound of that warmth escaping get to her, tried very hard to ignore it and the way it made the ache in her chest worse. God, this shouldn't be difficult. She'd had no problems at all when she'd ended her relationship—such as it was—with Jason. It hadn't even been hard. She'd simply decided she didn't want to sleep with him again and she hadn't. She didn't miss him, didn't long for him. Didn't crave his touch.

So there should be no reason at all why she desperately wished Van would reach out to her again, touch her again.

"Then how can he threaten a takeover when he doesn't have a majority share?" she asked, trying to distract herself.

"He can't. Which means he either has more stock that we don't know about or he has something else up his sleeve. Unless, of course, he's bluffing."

"So do we call his bluff then?"

Van let out a breath. "You don't have to do anything. You can sit tight here while I—"

"No," she interrupted, the thick knot of suppressed emotion pressing hard against her throat, trying to escape. "I mean, I don't want to sit here and do nothing. I don't know why Wolf and Lucas aren't helping you, but I'm not going to do the same." She stared at him, struggling to keep the intensity from her voice and knowing she was failing. "You shouldn't have to do this all on your own, Van. It's not fair."

The look in his eyes intensified all of a sudden, searching her face in a way that made her want to run away and hide. Or alternatively shrug her shoulders and pretend it didn't matter. But she couldn't seem to do either of those things. She was stuck there, sitting in her chair, the threads of fear and desire, longing and hunger, anger and grief, knotting and tangling so tight she could barely breathe.

Then something changed in his face. He reached out, gently took the coffee mug out of her hands and put it on the table. Then he gripped the seat of her chair and turned it to face him, his gaze on hers, even sharper this time. "Why should it matter to you whether it's fair or not? Why should you even care about the company? I thought you only wanted the ranch and that's all?"

He was right in front of her, holding onto the seat, his arms on either side, caging her where she sat. And there was no escape. Nowhere to hide.

So she reached for her usual protective layer of angry indifference since that was easiest and most familiar. "It doesn't matter to me," she snapped. "And yes, I just want the ranch. Can you move your arms? You're kind of in the way and I really need to go to the bathroom."

But he didn't move, not one inch. Instead he stared at her for a long silent minute as the storm of emotions in her chest knotted tighter and tighter. Then he lifted his hand and cupped her cheek, the warmth of his palm shocking against her skin. "No," he said, very, very quietly. "You don't need to do that anymore. Not after last night. It's okay to care, Chloe. It's okay for this to matter."

And horribly the threads inside her began to snap, one by one, all those wild and scary emotions beginning to tug free, making her eyes fill up with helpless tears whether she wanted them to or not.

She didn't know what to do with them or the aching mass in her chest, the way he made her feel. She didn't have the words to articulate all those emotions and she'd be way too afraid to say them even if she had.

So she did the only thing she could think of.

She turned her head and pressed her mouth to the center of his palm.

As Chloe's soft mouth brushed over his skin, a bolt of intense electricity shot straight up Van's arm and he had to stay very, very still or else nothing would have stopped him from dragging her off that chair, turning her around, clawing down her jeans, and getting inside her any way he could.

But he couldn't. He wouldn't. He'd promised both himself and her that it would only be one night. And he was afraid that if he took her now, he wouldn't be able to stop himself from justifying another night, then another, and possibly even another after that.

So? What's so very bad about that?

Too many things, not the least of which was the look on Chloe's face when she'd told him that he shouldn't have to do this all on his own. That it wasn't fair. Yeah, he should never have pushed her on that, should never have followed that urge to come close to her, to crouch down in front of her, look into her dark eyes and watch the storm break in them.

It's too late now. She's involved. So what's the point in holding back?

Fuck, she *was* involved, even though he hadn't meant her to be, and he could see it, reading the emotions playing over her face as clearly as if they were words written in the pages of a book.

She cared, but he had a horrible suspicion it wasn't the company she cared about, which would be bad enough. If it was him she cared about, then she was screwed.

He was never going to give her anything more than what they had now. He was never going to want to. He wanted the military, his SEAL career, period. They shouldn't even have had that one night together, especially considering who they were to each other.

Yet for some reason he couldn't seem to bring himself to take his hand away, as if he actually wanted those soft lips to rest against his palm. As if he actually wanted more.

"You can't care about me, Chloe," he said roughly. "Because this isn't going to go anywhere. You understand that, don't you?"

Her lashes were sooty black and silky, her eyes gleaming from beneath them. She shifted in the chair, leaning forward so her mouth was inches away from his, the sweet, musky sunshine scent of her surrounding him. "I don't care," she murmured, and he didn't know what she meant, whether she didn't care about him, or whether she didn't care whether it would go anywhere.

Then her mouth was on his and his brain ceased to function.

Desire flamed like a star inside him, white hot, desperate. And somehow even more intense than it had the night before.

But it was wrong. He had too many other things to be thinking about, too many other things to deal with. He should be pushing her away. He should be getting up and turning around, and getting out of this goddamn fucking apartment, leaving all the temptation she presented far behind.

Jesus Christ, he was supposed to be protecting her, not thinking about how badly he wanted to fuck her again.

He lifted his other hand and cupped her face, holding her still and drawing back. But try as he might he couldn't bring himself to actually let her go.

Chloe's eyes glittered, her cheekbones stained with color. She made a frustrated little noise as she leaned forward to kiss him again, only to have his grip on her tighten, stopping her. "What?" She sounded breathless. "You don't want this?"

Her skin was so unbearably soft beneath his palms, so very warm. "One night." The words were full of gravel and sand. "That's what I said. Only one night."

"I know. But . . ." This time it was her hands that lifted, her fingers sliding along his jaw, cool and gentle, her touch making his heartbeat hammer in his head. "I want to help, Van. I want . . . to do something for you. You made me feel good last night, so why can't I do the same for you?"

He couldn't stand the feel of those gentle fingers,

couldn't stand it as they curled under his jaw, finding his pulse. Finding the truth. "Oh, pretty . . ." He was getting hard, his suit pants suddenly way too tight. Everything just way the fuck too tight. "This is a bad idea."

"Why?" Her fingertips trailed down his neck, stroking. "I mean apart from the whole foster-brother, foster-sister thing."

The breath escaped him in a short laugh. "That isn't enough of a reason?"

"No." She looked so serious, the glow in her eyes heating everything up inside him. "You're taking on all this shit that Dad left you with, which includes me, and all without any help whatsoever. I just think that's wrong. And I want to do something to make it better." Her gaze intensified. "Like you made everything better for me last night."

His breath caught as those exploring fingers slid down his neck, touching his throat, light and gentle. As if he was some kind of precious artifact and not a SEAL commander who'd taken everything from gunshots to knife cuts to shrapnel wounds.

She doesn't know what you really are inside. Not like Sofia knew.

Van shoved the thought away, pushed it down hard into the box it had somehow escaped from.

"If you think I'm some kind of delicate flower that needs cosseting," he said roughly, "think again."

Anger sparked in her dark eyes. "Oh, so then is that what you thought of me last night? That I was a delicate flower that needed cosseting?"

Fuck. Why the hell had he said that? "No. Of course I don't think that."

"Asshole," Chloe muttered. Before he could move, her fingers tightened suddenly around his throat, and she pulled him in close. Then she was kissing him and there was nothing delicate about it. Her tongue pushed into his mouth, hot and hungry and demanding, and he could feel himself start to go up in flames.

No, shit no. This was a mistake and he had to stop it right the hell now.

Sliding his fingers into her thick, silky hair and gripping her tightly, he jerked his head back, trying to ignore the growling, possessive thing inside him that only wanted him to get closer.

"Seriously?" She was breathing very fast, very hard, the glow in her eyes even brighter now. "I'm not some weak little—"

"I'm talking about your emotions, Chloe," he interrupted, unable to keep the harsh note from his voice, suddenly and acutely aware of how soft her hair felt against his fingers and falling over the backs of his hands. How he wanted to grip it, wind it around his wrist, draw her head right back, and expose her long, pale throat. "Because if you're looking for someone to have a relationship with, you're looking at the wrong guy. I can't get involved, not with anyone."

She scowled at him. "Did I ask for a relationship? Did I ever, at any time, say that I was desperate for a boyfriend or whatever?"

"No, but—"

"No, because I didn't." Her fingers resting on his throat spread out, slipping beneath the collar of his shirt, making his breath catch. "I'm not expecting anything, Van. Hell, I don't want to get involved any more than you do, not when I've got to get back to the ranch when all this is over. So why not have this while we can?"

It sounded good. It sounded like exactly what he wanted to hear. And he had no doubt it was exactly what she wanted to hear as well. But he knew it wasn't true, that it was too late, that she was involved already. She'd been so passionate the night before, holding onto him so desperately, and if that hadn't been enough, there was the fact that she'd admitted to him that she was lonely, that she was scared. And he had the feeling that Chloe didn't admit those kinds of feelings to anyone.

Christ, this was so wrong. He didn't know why he wasn't simply letting her go and walking away. But he wasn't. He had his hands in her hair and he couldn't look away from the hunger in her eyes.

"You took care of me last night." Her voice was a whisper. "Let me take care of you now."

The words were like bolts of electricity, shocking him. Because people didn't take care of him, they just didn't. He was a commander, he was the one who was supposed to look after others, not the other way around. Yet here was this little woman, small and slender and wildly passionate, who seemed to think he was the one who needed taking care of this time.

Like you fucking deserve it.

He couldn't move. He couldn't seem to even breathe. And he didn't stop her as she leaned forward a third time, kissing him again, her mouth warm and searching against his. Coaxing almost, as if trying to seduce him.

Shit, there was no "trying" about it. She already had seduced him. With her gentle touches and her hungry kisses, with her desperate passion. He hadn't meant to do this with her again, and yet he found himself completely unable to stop.

He couldn't say no to her, couldn't refuse her. Couldn't push her away yet again. Couldn't tell himself that this was all for her benefit either.

He wanted this. He wanted her.

Letting this continue was possibly the stupidest fucking idea he'd ever had, but she was right. They'd already crossed the line the night before, so what was the point in holding back now? Besides, he didn't even know why he was bothering. It was like he still thought he could be the paragon his father had wanted. And he wasn't. He never had been. He was as far from a paragon as it was possible to get. So why not do this? Why not take what she was offering?

Like it was even a choice. He hadn't let her go, which meant he'd made his decision already.

Van let her kiss him, let her explore his mouth, and she was far more confident than she had been the night before. Her tongue touched his, teasing, and she shifted forward to the edge of the chair, her fingers moving to undo the buttons on his shirt and pulling apart the cotton, her hands sliding over his bare chest.

His patience, already tested by the meeting he'd had with that asshole de Santis earlier that day, began to come apart at the heat of her touch, and he wound his fingers deeper into her hair, easing her head back, taking control of the kiss.

But then she slipped off the chair completely, coming down onto the floor on her knees in front of him, one small hand tracing the lines of the tattoo on his chest, the other moving down to his stomach and then down over the front of his pants, her fingers lightly tracing the rigid length of his hard-on.

Electricity shot up his spine, erupting like fire in his head.

Holy shit. He had to take control of this, and now—otherwise he was going to embarrass himself.

Easing her mouth from his again, he looked down into her flushed, vivid little face. "Bed," he ordered, this time not bothering to keep the huskiness from his voice.

"Not yet." Her hand was doing insane things, running lightly up and down the front of his fly, making that electricity crackle along every nerve ending he had. "I want to do something for you. I want to take care of you." Her hand pressed down all of a sudden, squeezing his cock through the wool of his pants, making lights explode behind his eyes. "I want to t-taste you."

Yeah, he was done. He was finished.

Seemingly of their own accord, his fingers wound tighter in her hair, increasing the pressure so her head was pulled back even further. "You want to suck my cock, pretty?" he said very deliberately. "Is that what you want to do?"

A bright flag of color unfurled across her cheeks, the glow in her eyes suddenly blinding. "Y-Yes." The stutter was small, but she didn't look away.

"Say it." He was pushing her and he knew it. But the erotic words and the rough demand in his voice was clearly only turning her on.

"I want to suck your cock." There was no stutter at all this time, no wavering in her gaze. And shit, she almost sounded triumphant.

She'd looked like this the day he'd raced her back to the stables. All fire and challenge, and an intense, passionate wildness.

His hands curled into fists and, considering he had her hair gripped in them, it had to hurt. But she gave no sign of pain other than a minute catch in her breath, the fire in her eyes only burning higher.

He couldn't say he didn't want this. His little foster sister, on her knees, sucking his dick. So wrong. Another nail in the coffin of the perfection his father had always demanded.

"Well hell." The words came out rough and lazy with heat, but he didn't care. "Since you asked so nicely . . ." He let go of her hair then rose to his feet, turning to lean back against the edge of the table, holding her gaze all the while. "Here." He gestured to the floor in front of him. "On your knees."

She didn't hesitate, moving to obey him. Then she tipped her head back to look up at him, the hunger in her eyes making his heart race even faster. "I've never done this before," she said huskily. "I don't want to do it wrong."

That shouldn't be hot, it simply shouldn't. But it was.

He reached down, ran his thumb over her full bottom lip, testing the softness of it, relishing the feel of it against his skin. "Don't worry, pretty. I'll tell you what to do."

CHAPTER TWELVE

Chloe couldn't seem to drag her gaze from his. There was no green left in it, his irises gone brilliant gold, and she knew that was all because of her.

She loved it. Loved kneeling here in front of him, having him look at her like that. As if she was the center of the universe. As if a bomb could have gone off right beside him and he wouldn't even notice.

Had anyone ever looked at her like that before? She couldn't remember. Certainly she'd never been the center of the universe for anyone, not even Jason.

Dangerous. This is dangerous.

No, it wasn't. She knew what she was getting into and she was prepared. Sex, that's all it was. There wasn't anything emotional in it, that was for sure. No matter what he said about it.

Like you're not on your knees, desperate to touch him because you don't *want to get as close to him as you can get.*

Chloe ignored the thought, lifting her hands and putting them very deliberately on his thighs, feeling his muscles bunch beneath the wool in reaction. Sure she wanted to get close to him. *Physically* close. That's all.

The expression on his face had become lean, hungry, almost predatory, making her breath come faster, a distracting ache starting up between her legs.

God, she couldn't remember wanting anything more right now. If someone had asked her to make a decision between the ranch and Van, she wasn't at all sure she wouldn't have chosen Van. Which was worrying, but she didn't want to examine that too closely, so she didn't.

His thumb was moving lazily back and forth on her lower lip, making it feel all full and sensitive, and she was very tempted to give him a nip.

Like he'd read her mind, his mouth curved. "Bad girl. No biting."

She shivered as the rough heat in his voice rolled over her. "Tell me what to do then."

"Impatient, huh? I like it." He stroked her lip a couple more times then let his hand drop. "Okay. Undo my pants, pretty. Get my dick out."

She couldn't move fast enough, reaching up to pull on the button of his pants, her fingers fumbling only a little as she undid it then tugged down his zipper, spreading aside the fabric. Underneath he wore black cotton boxers, the hard length of his cock pushing against the material.

Her mouth watered as she leaned forward, unable to stop herself, pressing her mouth to the bared skin of his stomach just above the waistband of his underwear. He inhaled sharply, the muscles of his abs flexing, tightening.

Excellent. That was promising.

She nuzzled against his hot skin, the musky scent of him going straight to her head. Oh *God,* he smelled good. She hadn't done this with Jason because she'd hadn't felt the need to, plus she hadn't thought it would be something she'd like. But, holy hell, was she wrong. She was absolutely enthralled by him, the pressure between her thighs becoming more and more insistent, the scent and the feel of him only making things worse.

Swallowing, she lifted a hand to where the outline of

his cock pressed against the cotton, stroking him through it. Long, thick and very, very hard.

His breath hissed. "Stop playing, sweetheart. Time to do as you're told."

Chloe shivered again at the low, rough sound of his voice, at the dark, heated note in it. She didn't want to stop. He'd played with her last night, taking the pleasure to record heights, and now it was her turn to return the favor. And she planned to. With interest.

She squeezed him, obsessed with the hot, heavy feel of him in her palm, rubbing her thumb up the length of his shaft, tracing him, nuzzling against the flat plane of his stomach as she did so.

"Chloe," he growled warningly. Then he untangled one hand from her hair and thrust it down into his underwear, grasping his cock and pulling it free of the cotton, while he tugged her head back gently with the other.

Her heart began to bang hard behind her ribs, her breathing coming faster.

"Open for me," he ordered, and she did.

Then she began to tremble because he was guiding all that hard, musky heat into her mouth, pressing against her tongue. Her jaw ached because he was so big, and her sex ached because he tasted so damn good. Everything she'd imagined and more.

He made a low raw sound as she closed her lips around him, her hands gripping onto the rock-hard muscles of his thighs. It thrilled her, that sound, a reminder of her own power and what she did to him. Because she had her mouth on him and it was making him as crazy as it was making her.

The knowledge gave her the confidence to reach for him, close her fingers around the base of his cock, tilting her head back further to take him deeper, watching as the look on his face became feral. She loved that.

Loved that she could make him look that hungry, that desperate.

"Jesus," he hissed. "You're supposed to wait until I tell you what to do." There was a harsh, guttural note in his voice that made another wild thrill go down her spine.

Hell, did she have to wait?

She shook her head slowly, beginning to explore him with her tongue.

He half-laughed, half-groaned, the sound unbelievably sexy. "Fuck . . . pretty . . ."

It was exciting to be able to do this to him, to make him groan and curse, and it was exciting to taste him, a wild, salty flavor that had her wanting to put her hands between her thighs and touch herself, relieve the ache that was throbbing there. But she didn't. She wanted to concentrate on him.

Firming her grip around him, she went with her instinct, sucking him deep into her mouth, hesitantly at first, then harder as she gained more confidence. Soon his fingers in her hair were locked tight, the sounds coming from him now not so much encouragement but low, guttural noises of pleasure.

Chloe began to lose herself in it, in the taste of him. In his scent and in his heat. In the flex of the muscles of his thighs and abs, and in the sounds she was drawing from him.

She forgot about the desperate, tangled mess of emotion in the center of her chest. Forgot about the ache in her soul and the hungry thing inside her that wanted and wanted no matter how hard she tried to ignore it.

Forgot about everything, consumed by the moment. Consumed by him. By the feel of him in her mouth, the ache in her jaw, and the slick glide of his smooth skin against her palm. The insane beat of her heart and the hard, insistent pulse between her thighs.

And when he began to thrust into her mouth, holding tight to her hair, she met him, sucking harder, deeper. Pumping him with her hand, feeling his thighs get hard as his muscles tightened.

Then he made another of those raw, guttural sounds, his hips flexing, his thrusts getting wilder and more out of control. But she didn't stop, she kept going, feeling like she was trying to put a bridle on a tiger, because his big, powerful body was bucking and shoving against her.

So she slid one arm around his leg and held on, leaning her body against him, and she kept sucking him, kept teasing him with her tongue and squeezing hard with her hand until his whole body stiffened and he put back his head, a hoarse cry breaking from him as the climax hit.

She didn't pull away then either, she kept hold of him, swallowing him down, taking whatever he had to give her, loving the intense thrill of being able to do this to him. Loving the way he gripped her so tight it was as if he was afraid to let her go. Loving the way he'd called her name.

She didn't let him go when he quieted either, keeping her arm around his leg, resting her forehead against the taut plane of his stomach, listening as his breathing slowed.

Then she felt his hand in her hair, stroking her gently, and she wanted to stay like that forever. Kneeling at his feet with him touching her, at peace for the first time.

Her hair was so soft and he couldn't stop touching it, even though his fingers were shaking. Christ, everything was shaking. He couldn't remember the last time that had happened after an orgasm. Couldn't remember the last time he'd physically shook, period. Not since his training days in Coronado, he was pretty certain.

Fucking hell, what had Chloe done to him?

He tried to take a deep breath and couldn't, the orgasm

echoing around inside him like a bullet fired inside a bulletproof room, bouncing off the walls and ricocheting
everywhere.

His pretty little thing had wrecked him.

Your own fault. You shouldn't have let her do that.

Yeah, well, he had. The moment she'd gone to her knees
in front of him and looked up at him, hunger stark in her
eyes, he'd known he wasn't going to stop her. She'd been
so insistent and shit . . . he'd just wanted her mouth on him.

And he'd gotten it. Hot and wet, eager, she'd sucked him
off like a goddess, her inexperience in no way detrimen-
tal. In fact, sick fuck that he was, it had only made it even
hotter.

He looked down.

She was kneeling on the hardwood floor, her head resting warmly against his abdomen. One arm was curled
around his thigh and her hand was on his cock, idly stroking him, sending more bolts of electricity sparking everywhere. Jesus. He was getting hard again. Already.

"Maybe you should stop doing that." His voice sounded
like he'd spent all day shouting on a battlefield, all fissured
and cracked.

She looked up at him. Her cheeks were deeply flushed
and there was a very smug, very self-satisfied smile curling her delicious mouth. "Are you sure?"

Desire stirred hungrily inside him again, making him
feel feral, and he reached down and slid his arms around
her, lifting her up off the floor, turning to sit her on the
table instead. She gripped his forearms to steady herself,
staring at him as if mesmerized.

Van put his hands on the table on either side of her hips,
looking into her dark eyes for a moment, then he bent,
brushing her lush mouth with his. Her lashes fell and she
let out a soft, shaken sounding breath, leaning forward as
he drew back, trying to maintain the contact.

Christ, he got off on her hunger for him. It was so honest, so real and so sweet. It reached inside him, slid through a crack in his heart he hadn't even realized was there and heated him straight through.

Women had always wanted him, it was true, but it was the SEAL they were attracted to. The muscles and the tattoos, the fact that he was a commander. They didn't see the man. To be fair, he hadn't let anyone get close enough to see the man, but still, it had been a long time since anyone had seen him the way Chloe did. Because she didn't see him as the warrior. She'd known him as the man first of all and so that's what he was to her.

Wrong to continue to let her keep seeing the man and wrong to like it, but he couldn't change it now. More, he didn't want to. It felt like forever since he'd been anything but commander, protector, SEAL. And just for a little while, he wanted to be none of those things.

"You okay?" he murmured against her lips. "I didn't hurt you?"

Her eyes fluttered open. "No. God, no. That was . . . amazing. *You're* amazing."

No, you're not. And you'd better tell her why.

Yeah, he should. But he wasn't going to. Another example of how dishonorable he was, yet he didn't care. He liked that he was amazing to her, and he was going to take that. No reason for her to know how very imperfect he really was, how royally he could fuck up with the best of them.

He reached down to the fastening of her jeans and flicked open the button. "And your mouth could make the fucking devil believe he's a good person."

She blushed, the deep rose color of her cheeks making her eyes seem even darker than they already were. "So what happens now?"

"You'll find out." He tugged down the tab of her zipper

so her jeans were completely unfastened, then he gripped the waistband, slowly beginning to ease them down and taking her panties with them. "Lift up for me, pretty."

She did as she was told, leaning back on her hands and lifting her butt, allowing him to pull her jeans and panties right down her legs and over her bare feet. He let her clothing fall into a heap on the floor then placed his hands on her knees, applying some pressure, pushing them very firmly apart.

Chloe sucked in a breath. "Van . . ."

His name sounded desperate, and fuck, he loved that. Loved the way she was looking at him right now, as if she would die if he didn't touch her.

He held her gaze, sliding his hands up the insides of her thighs, her skin all silky and hot beneath his palms. He could smell her arousal, musky and feminine and delicious, and it made his mouth water.

Oh, the things he wanted to do to her . . .

"Keep your legs spread for me," he said softly. "You gave me something pretty fucking special and now I'm going to return the favor."

"Yes." She shifted, spreading her legs even wider. "Oh . . . please . . ."

He let his attention move down between her thighs, because he liked looking at her. She was so pretty, all soft dark hair and slick pink flesh, framed by the pale skin of her thighs and stomach. His mouth watered. Jesus, she was too far away.

Cupping her butt, he pulled her to the edge of the table. "Lean back," he instructed and she did so, sliding her hands further behind her and tilting her hips toward him. Little tremors were running through her, and he could hear her breathing getting faster and faster.

Fuck, she smelled good. He couldn't wait to taste her.

He wound his arms around her thighs, gripping her and

pulling her even further toward the edge of the table. She was starting to pant now, that pretty pussy of hers exactly where he wanted it.

Carefully, he spread her open with his fingers, feeling her quiver in his hands as he touched her slick flesh. But he didn't wait—couldn't, if he was honest with himself. He was so goddamn hungry and she was right there, so he bent his head and licked straight up the middle of her pussy.

She jerked in his grip, her gasp echoing around him, and it would have made him smile in satisfaction if he'd been at all conscious of it. But he wasn't. Because the taste of her hit him, salty and sweet and absolutely fucking delicious, and all he could think about was getting more.

So he licked her again and again, making her hips tremble and tearing another gasp from her. Then he spread her open even wider and kept her like that as he pushed his tongue deep into her pussy.

Chloe groaned and arched back, her lips lifting against his mouth. "Van . . ." His name was a broken sob. "Oh, God, Van . . ."

He would have very much liked to have taken it nice and easy, eating her out slowly, leisurely. Lingering for both their pleasures. But he could feel her trembling beneath his hands, could taste the thick, musky heat of her, and knew she was pretty much on the brink already.

So he sent her over with his tongue deep inside her, with his fingers toying gently with her clit, making her put back her head and scream, her hips bucking upward, her whole body arching as the orgasm rolled over her.

By then he was hard again and he wanted to be inside her more than he wanted his next breath. Pulling away, he got back to his feet, reaching into his back pocket for his wallet, hoping to Christ he had a condom in there because

he didn't think he had the patience to go down the street
to the CVS.

Luckily, there was a lone silver packet lurking behind
a few dollar bills, so he grabbed it and ripped it open. His
pants were already undone so all he had to do was roll the
latex down on his impatient dick and he was stepping back
up to the table.

Chloe had collapsed onto her back, lying on the table-
top with her legs hanging over the edge, one arm flung over
her face. She still wore her plaid shirt, but she was naked
from the waist down and he'd never seen a sexier or more
erotic sight in his entire life.

No, wait. He knew what could be sexier.

Nudging her legs apart with his hips, he bent and slid
his arms around her, urging her to sit up. She made a soft
sound, her arm dropping from her face as she came upright, revealing her heart-stoppingly beautiful features, the
black velvet of her eyes looking into his.

Yeah, that's what he wanted. Her looking at him. *That*
was sexier.

He didn't take his gaze from hers as he found the edges
of her shirt and pulled hard, ripping them apart. She didn't
protest, staring back at him as if she'd never seen him
before in her life. Underneath her shirt, she was naked,
those small, perfect breasts and rosy nipples just as perfect
and rosy as they had been the night before.

Tugging the shirt from her so she was sitting on the
table completely naked, he slipped his hands beneath her
knees, urging her to wrap those slender legs around his
waist, bringing her hips against his. Then he took his cock
in one hand, found the slick flesh of her pussy, and pushed,
easing his way into all that tight, wet heat.

They both groaned as he slid home, going deeper and
deeper until he was all the way in, seated right inside her.

Her lashes half-fell, her pouty, red mouth open, her hands sliding up his arms to his shoulders and holding on tightly.

She looked dazed, or drunk, or something in between, and it satisfied him on some deep level that he could wreck her as thoroughly as she could wreck him.

He kept his gaze on hers as he flexed his hips, pulling back then sliding in, slowly. Carefully.

Her breath hissed, her fingers digging into the muscle of his shoulders, the glow in her eyes getting brighter and brighter as he slid out then thrust in again, taking his time. Building the pleasure for both of them.

"Rock your hips," he murmured, low and guttural, showing her what he meant with his hands on her, guiding her. "Squeeze me, pretty. Show me how much your pussy likes having my cock inside it."

She panted, tilting her hips like he'd asked, moving with him, her internal muscles clamping down on him, making him catching his breath.

"Oh fuck," he whispered. "Yeah, just like that."

Her hands wound around his neck and she leaned closer, pressing her naked body up against his, and he found himself wishing that he'd stripped his clothes off after all. Because, Christ, he wanted to feel her against his skin.

She began to rock against him, the pleasure lighting up her face, and he almost protested when she covered his mouth with hers, because he wanted to watch her. He wanted to see her come.

Yet her kiss was so sweetly desperate he couldn't bring himself to tear her away. So he kissed her back, thrusting harder, deeper, adjusting the angle of his thrusts to give her the maximum amount of pleasure.

"Van. . . ." His name was a murmur against his mouth. "Oh my God . . ."

"That good for you? You like that?"

"Yes . . ." Her hips angled further as if searching for something. "Please . . . more."

Oh, he could give her more. He definitely could.

Van reached for her hand and brought it down between them, guiding her own fingers on her slippery flesh. Her eyes went even wider as he pressed her finger down on her clit. "Touch yourself, pretty. Ride my cock and make yourself come. I want to watch."

Something lit in her face, that wildness he found impossible to resist, and he could feel her hand move beneath his, stroking her clit as he shoved into her, lifting her hips, chasing the pleasure, letting him see everything.

He saw the moment she went over the edge, a high, wild cry tearing from her throat, her body arching up in his arms like she was trying to take off and fly. Watching the pleasure explode inside her was like seeing the northern lights. Rare. Precious. Beautiful. A gift.

He tightened his grip on her, ecstasy beginning to sink its teeth into him as well, his rhythm getting wilder, out of control. Her arms came around him, her legs closed like a vice around his waist, and she turned her face into his shoulder, her mouth against his skin. And just before the orgasm tore him into shreds, he had the oddest feeling that he wasn't holding her, that she was holding him. Keeping him from breaking into tiny little pieces.

He roared when it hit, driving himself hard into her before pressing his mouth to her exposed neck and biting, tasting salt and Chloe, hardly conscious of what he was doing, the pleasure pretty much annihilating every single thought process he had.

It was her hands on his skin, slowly stroking up and down his spine, that brought him back. A gentle, soothing touch that astonished him with how much he liked it. People normally touched him for two reasons only: because they wanted to have sex with him or because they

wanted to kill him. There were no other reasons. Certainly
no one had ever touched him the way Chloe was right
now, caressing him almost absently, as if she was simply
enjoying the physical contact. She did a lot of that, or so it
seemed, and he had to say, it was a revelation.

He let himself have it for a while, then he eased himself out of her, moving away to deal with the condom in
the kitchen wastebasket before coming back and winding
one arm around her waist to hold her against him. "Holy
shit, pretty. You're killing me, you know that?"

She smiled, leaning into him, her body warm and supple
against his. "So much for being an ultra-tough SEAL. How
the hell did you survive all those years on deployment?"

"Fuck knows." He shifted, lifting his hand and pushing a strand of black hair that had gotten stuck to her forehead behind her ear. "Sometimes the only thing that gets
you through is luck."

That gorgeous smile played around her mouth, her gaze
searching his. "Not just luck, though. You don't get to be
where you are without being good at what you do."

Yeah and he was very good. At killing people.

Not so much at protecting people.

Van smoothed more of her hair back from her forehead,
concentrating instead on the feel of her damp skin against
his and not on the voice in his head. Jesus, he could get
used to touching her. Very used to it. "This is true," he said
noncommittally. "Being good at what we do is pretty much
the definition of a Navy SEAL."

"You enjoy it, don't you?" She was looking at him like
she was trying to puzzle something out. "I mean, that's
why you want to go back to the military, isn't it?"

There was no reason not to tell her. "Yeah, that's right."

"So what do you like about it? Is it the danger? Or is
protecting your country the big thing?"

Okay, this was starting to edge into territory he wasn't

all that comfortable with. "Why do you want to know?" He hoped it didn't sound as belligerent as he was afraid it did.

Her lashes fluttered and she glanced down, one of her hands shifting to trace a pattern on his chest. "I'd just like to know. You were away for a long time and . . ." She broke off all of a sudden.

But he didn't need her to finish. He knew why she was asking, and the vulnerability of the question, what it revealed, reached inside him, wrapping long fingers around his heart.

You need to tell her about Sofia.

He didn't want to, because he hated telling that story. Hated reliving that failure, especially given the fact he was now protecting Chloe. She needed to be able to trust him, but how could she do that once she knew about how he'd let a woman on his watch die?

No, not the lie you keep telling yourself. The real *truth. The one you can't even bring yourself to think about.*

Cold shot through him, the urge to pull away and put some distance between them almost overwhelming. But she was still tracing patterns on his chest and the echo of that vulnerable little statement was resounding inside him, and he couldn't bring himself to do it. Not when it would hurt her—and God knew hurting her was the last thing he wanted to do.

She had to know that the reason he'd stayed away from the ranch wasn't because of anything she'd done, though.

Shoving the cold feeling away, he caught her beneath the chin, tilting her head back so he had her attention. "It wasn't you," he said quietly. "You know that, right? I didn't stay away because of anything you did."

Her gaze flickered away from his. "I know that."

"Do you? Do you really?"

She let out a breath. Her mouth had gone soft, and it was very obvious she didn't want to look at him. "Well . . . sometimes . . ." she began hesitantly, "I used to wonder if maybe . . . I'd done something. Said something. You know . . ."

His chest constricted, like he was doing that fucking drown-proofing test again. As part of his SEAL training, he'd had his hands tied together and been thrown into a pool. The test here is wrong. The water had pressed insistently against his chest, the weight of it reminding him of how close his own death was. It felt like that now, a weight pushing down on him, except it wasn't the possibility of death that was crushing him this time but something else—and getting away from it wasn't a simple matter of escaping the ties that bound his hands and pushing up to the surface.

He didn't know how the fuck he was going to get out of this one.

Instead he gripped her a bit tighter. "Look at me."

She wanted to resist—he could feel the tension in her neck—but after a second she did as she was told, her deep brown eyes gazing back at him with a wary look.

"Why would you think it was you?" he demanded softly. "Did you seriously believe it was something you did?"

Her throat moved, the aching vulnerability that he knew was at the core of her suddenly laid bare for him to see. "I don't know. You were around every time you were on leave, and then one day you weren't. And you didn't come back for eight years. I thought . . ." She hesitated. "I thought it was because you somehow knew I had a crush on you."

He wanted to smile at that because it was so far from the truth it wasn't even funny. But he didn't. She'd gone fiery red, the confession obviously difficult for her, and he wasn't going to belittle it.

"No." He kept his tone gentle. "That wasn't why I stayed away. I had no idea you had a crush on me."

She went even redder. "Okay. Well. Good."

He could feel her trying to turn away from him yet again, so he kept a firm grip on her chin, keeping her right there where he could see her face. "It would have taken a shitload more than a teenage crush to frighten me away. Surely you must have known that?"

Her throat moved in a convulsive swallow, a vulnerable look flickering over her expressive features. "I'm . . . a lot to handle sometimes."

Van frowned, staring at her. "What do you mean you're a lot to handle?"

She gave a small shake of her head, her lashes falling again. "Don't worry about it. Forget I said anything."

Oh no, she wasn't doing that again. Not this time.

"Hey." He stroked that stubborn little chin of hers, her skin smooth and warm beneath his thumb. "Don't do that. I wouldn't have asked you if I didn't want to know. Tell me. Who told you that you were a lot to handle?"

She was silent a long moment. Then she said, "No one. Maybe it was something I just picked up on, I don't know. It was only that Dad was never around. He was always going away to New York or L.A. or down to Houston. I used to wonder why he never liked coming home and why he never seemed all that pleased to see me when he did. He certainly didn't like me hugging him or peppering him with questions about what he'd been doing." She let out a breath. "He used to go straight to his office for at least an hour or so whenever he got back, and I wondered if it was because he was avoiding me. I think I overwhelmed him."

Her lashes stayed down, veiling her gaze, and she remained quiet for a moment. "I had no one," she said after what seemed a long time. "You guys were away at boarding school, then you were all in the military, and I had no one but the housekeeper here to talk to, no friends but the tutors Dad hired for me. I got . . . kind of lonely. And when Dad came home, all I wanted to do was be with someone who cared about me." She gave an odd little laugh. "He used to promise me he'd take me to New York, show me the city, but . . . he never did. There was always a reason I couldn't go."

Van could hear how she was trying to make it sound like it was no big deal. Hiding the pain beneath a light, casual tone. But there *was* pain, he could almost feel the sharp edges of it himself.

Christ, he'd had no idea. Chloe, brought up on the ranch by a series of housekeepers and tutors. No friends, no one to talk to except the father she saw only sporadically. A father who couldn't handle the emotional needs of one small girl.

"You know it wasn't you, right?" Van lifted his other hand, cupped her beautiful face between his palms. "*None* of it was you. You only wanted what every kid wants from their parents, a little attention. He was the one who couldn't handle it, not you."

Her eyes were very dark as they stared up into his. "You really think so?"

"He was a shitty father to me too, it wasn't just you. Dad didn't know how to deal with us. Hell, I don't even think he knew how to be a proper father, period."

Chloe leaned into him, shifting her hands to his chest and spreading them out, pressing lightly as if she needed the contact. "You know, it wasn't even visiting the city that was important. It was spending time with him. I used to get so excited about it, but then he'd tell me it wasn't safe or that he was too busy—always some excuse." She half-turned, reaching for something behind her. A snow globe of all things. He hadn't even noticed it.

"The last time he promised me he'd take me to New

York, I was almost ready to go but then one of his flun-keys turned up at the ranch with a package and a message from Dad." She shook the globe, the snow inside it swirl-ing. "Apparently it was too dangerous to bring me to New York yet again, but hey, have this snow globe instead."

Ah Christ. Fucking Noah.

Van experienced a sudden and violent need to punch his father in the face.

"Dad shouldn't have done that," he said, flat and hard with certainty, so she knew. "He should have been there for you, Chloe."

He should have been there for all of them and he hadn't.

"Noah was a shitty father, and that's not your fault."

CHAPTER THIRTEEN

Chloe held the snow globe in her hands as she looked up into Van's intense, hazel stare. There was something fierce in it, something that warmed a place inside her she hadn't realized was cold.

She was still sitting on the table completely naked, while he stood in front of her with his shirt open and his pants half unzipped, his dog tags hanging against that mesmerizing chest of his. And maybe she should have felt uncomfortable about it, especially after she'd just laid bare her soul, telling him things she'd never told anyone. Things she'd only half-realized herself in many ways.

But she didn't feel uncomfortable. Instead, she felt like she'd gotten rid of something that had been weighing her down for a very long time. And instead of feeling exposed and vulnerable, she felt understood in a way she hadn't before.

There was quiet inside her, the hungry, needy thing that kept eating away at her soul suddenly sated.

She wanted to sit here with Van, right in this moment, forever. With his palms on her cheeks and the hard warmth of his body only inches from hers. With that intense look on his beautiful, powerful features. Staring at her as if he knew exactly how she felt. She'd never had that before, not with anyone.

"Yes," she said slowly. "He *was* a shitty father, wasn't he?"

"You better believe it." His thumbs moved caressingly over her skin. "At the very least he should have brought you here to visit, not sent you a crappy snow globe as a substitute. Why did you keep it?"

"To remind myself to not believe him whenever he promised me things. To not want anything too badly."

Sympathy and understanding warmed his gaze, one corner of his mouth turning up. "Well, feel free to want me badly, pretty thing. I have no problem with that at all."

God, when he looked at her that way she felt like a cat basking in a ray of sunlight, soaking up all the heat and attention.

She almost reached up and dragged his head down for another kiss, but the globe in her hands was an unpleasant reminder of her father, of his empty promises, and of the reason she was in New York in the first place.

De Santis.

Your real father.

The warm feelings began to ebb away, and she pulled back slightly. Van's warm palms slipped from her cheeks. The loss of that heat made her feel cold, but she ignored the sensation, putting the snow globe down on the table beside her.

"What's up?" His hands settled on her bare hips instead, just resting there. "You don't like the idea of wanting me?"

Slowly, she shook her head. "It's not that. I'm thinking about de Santis."

"I wouldn't do that if I were you. There are better things to be thinking about." Heat had entered his voice, whispering over her skin and making her shiver.

No prizes for guessing what kind of things he meant, and quite frankly that's exactly what she would rather have been thinking about herself. But sex wasn't going to solve the issue.

"What are we going to do, Van?" Chloe raised her hands to his chest once more, putting her palms flat on it because she loved touching him and the time for hiding it was over. "I don't want to be used as an ultimatum."

"And I'm not going to let him use you as one."

"So, what then? You're going to call his bluff on the takeover?"

Van lifted a shoulder. "Like I said, it doesn't look like he's got a controlling share."

"But you don't know that for certain. And it still doesn't solve the problem of the threat to me anyway." She spread her fingers out on his skin, his warmth soaking into her. "I can't stay away from the ranch forever, and you have to get back to base eventually."

"Hmmm." Van shifted his hands, putting them on the table on either side of her hips, leaning forward on them, his dog tags swinging. "I've got my management team investigating the last stock buy-up, but even so, we're pretty sure he can't do a damn thing. Besides, the company is a distraction. What he wants is you."

"Are you sure?"

"Yeah. He made it very clear that he wanted to see his daughter."

That hit her in a strange place, a pang of that vulnerability echoing through her. "Why? What does he want from me?"

His black brows drew down. "I don't know. But you can bet it's not simply to catch up for old time's sake."

That little pang echoed again, almost like hurt. "Maybe," she said slowly, an idea beginning to occur to her, "we need to see what he *really* wants."

"It's revenge, pretty. Revenge is what he really wants."

"But we don't know that for certain." Chloe smoothed

her thumbs over Van's hot skin. "Perhaps I could ask him? He might tell me."

"What the hell does that mean?"

"I mean, if he wants me, maybe we should let him have me."

A sharp green light glinted in Van's eyes. "Over my dead fucking body."

"I could talk to him, find out exactly what he wants. I'm his daughter, after all."

"No." The word was hard and flat with command, his expression turning to granite.

Chloe pressed a little harder against his chest. "Van, listen. What's the alternative? You call his bluff over the company, which still leaves the threat to me hanging over my head or . . . what? Unless you have another idea?"

"Of course I have an idea. Blow his goddamn brains out."

"How? When? You can't do that and you know it."

"I'm not risking you, Chloe. I'm just not."

She took a breath, her own heartbeat beginning to race at the thought of what she was suggesting. "Look, we need to know what he wants before we can do anything to stop him. Otherwise we're just reacting and not taking control. You of all people should understand that."

A muscle ticked in his jaw and that hard green light in his eyes gleamed, a glimpse of the dangerous predator he was underneath the warm, sympathetic man he'd been the moment before. "Don't you worry. Lucas is a sniper, the best in the business. And if worse came to the worst, we can take control with a well-placed bullet."

"That's your answer? A bullet?" She looked up at him, meeting him stare for stare. "Even Dad wasn't that cold-blooded. Anyway, just think about it a moment. He won't hurt me and hell, even if that's his plan, we could set up the meeting in a public place. Somewhere with lots of people around."

His expression didn't soften one bit. "And if he has someone hidden somewhere to take you out? What about that?"

"He won't."

"You don't know that."

She didn't look away. "Neither do you."

"No." He pushed himself upright and folded his arms across his chest. "Just fucking no."

Chloe let out a breath, trying to hold onto her patience. This was their best idea, couldn't he see that? She really had no idea whether de Santis would harm her or not, but she couldn't see him trying anything if they were somewhere public. And it was a way better option than Van trying to put a bullet through his brain, if that's what he was *really* intending on doing.

"He's not going to talk to you, obviously," she went on, trying logic this time. "And you said yourself that he wants to see his daughter. So why not let him? Perhaps he really does want to talk to me."

But the look on Van's face was forbidding, every inch of him the SEAL commander. "You're not going, Chloe. And that's final."

She bit on her lip, studying him. Okay, he was supposed to be protecting her, and letting her throw herself at the enemy wasn't exactly doing that. But if his alternative was seriously him and Lucas and a bullet, she wasn't going to let him do that, either.

"Van," she said quietly. "This makes sense. What's the big deal?"

His jaw hardened even more. "The big deal? You getting killed is the big deal."

"De Santis doesn't want me dead, you know that. Then I'd be no use to him at all."

That muscle jumped in the side of his jaw again, his expression like stone, not giving an inch.

Chloe reached out, her hands settling on his hips, bringing him closer, attempting to ease his tension with her warmth. "The quicker we know what de Santis is after, the quicker we can neutralize him. And then I can get back to the ranch, and you can get back to the military." She slid her palms back up to his chest again, stroking him. "Don't you want that?"

He cursed under his breath and suddenly his arms were around her, pulling her close, holding her tight. "You can't be at risk, Chloe. I won't allow it."

"Why not? What do you think's going to happen?"

The look on his face changed, an expression flickering through it she couldn't read. There was something more going on here, she could feel it.

"What is it?" she asked when he didn't speak, keeping her hands where they were, pressed to his skin. "There's something else, isn't there?"

He was quiet for a long moment, just staring down at her, the strong lines of his face drawn tight and intense. "I had to protect a woman once, a few years ago." His voice was strangely flat. "I can't tell you the details because they're classified, but it was a mission that went wrong and I ended up on the run with a terrified civilian who I not only had to get to trust me, but to believe I would protect her no matter what." There was no gold in his eyes now. They were straight-up green as glass. "I got her trust. I told her I'd protect her, that nothing would happen to her. That she was safe. . . . And she died, Chloe." Anguish flickered briefly in his gaze. "I failed to protect her and she died."

Her chest tightened, her throat constricting, that glimpse of pain making her whole body go cold. "When? How?"

"A stray bullet in a firefight she should never have even been in. And I think you can probably guess when."

And she could. All of a sudden, she could. "Eight years ago."

He nodded, his arms still tight around her. "I didn't tell anyone, most especially not Dad. Couldn't even broach the topic. He never wanted to hear about bad grades or failures. He only wanted to know about the victories. The A-pluses. The wins. And a dead girl was definitely not a win."

She didn't know what to say. She hadn't known or even sensed something had been up with him the last time he'd come back to the ranch, since she'd been so consumed with avoiding him because of that stupid crush. And no wonder he hadn't told their dad. It was definitely *not* the kind of thing Noah ever wanted to hear.

Spreading her hands wide on his chest, she leaned in, resting her head on his warm skin, fitting her body more closely against his. "You tried, Van. But how could you guard against a stray bullet in a firefight? That sounds like bad luck, not failure."

He said nothing, his arms like iron bands around her, and for a long moment there was only silence. Then he said, "I promised her she'd be safe. I couldn't keep that promise. But I'll keep it for you, pretty. I swear it."

It was terrible that he'd lost someone he was supposed to protect, and it made her hurt for him. But there was a hard, sure note in his voice that, underneath it all, made her feel like a thirsty plant finally being given rain. As if this was a promise set in stone, unlike all the other promises she'd been given.

And maybe it was only because he'd failed this other woman that he was so driven to protect her. Or maybe it was because that no matter what he said, he was still holding himself to the standards Noah had taught him. But Chloe liked to think this mattered to him because he actually cared about *her*. Hell, he'd told her about something personal he'd told no one else, and that had to count for something, didn't it?

"I know you will," she said quietly, sliding her hands

down to his waist and around him, holding him as tightly as he was holding her. "Is there anything I can do?"

"No." The word was absolutely final.

Okay then. He didn't want to talk about it, that was clear.

"Well," she murmured, "you should know that when I meet de Santis, I'll feel a whole lot safer with you near me."

He stiffened. "Chloe—"

She looked up. "There's not going to be a firefight in the middle of New York. And you'll be somewhere nearby, waiting to rescue me if it all goes bad. But I *am* going to meet him, Van. I'm the reason we're in this mess in the first place and I have to do something. No, I'm not a SEAL, but I'm also not stupid."

Again he was quiet, staring down into her face, the expression in his eyes hard and forbidding and dangerous as hell. He was a man who liked to be in control and what she was asking of him was going to be very difficult.

"I trust you to keep me safe," she said softly. "Now you have to trust me to look after myself."

She was curled around him, pressed up against him, naked and hot, her dark eyes fierce, her chin at a stubborn angle. *Trust her to keep herself safe . . .*

He didn't want to. He couldn't.

You didn't even tell her the truth.

Yeah, and he wasn't going to. He never thought about it, hadn't told anyone about it, and he wasn't about to start now.

The problem was, her plan to meet de Santis was actually a good one. That asshole wanted to see her, so who better to get information out him than her? His team was fairly certain they'd accounted for all the stock and that de Santis definitely didn't have enough to stage a takeover, but there was an element of uncertainty about the whole situation that Van didn't like. If it was possible for Chloe to get close enough to ask the guy a few questions, then logically that was a good move.

Also, she was right about one other thing too. All the shots had been called by de Santis so far, forcing them to have to scramble to catch up and that was, quite frankly, un-fucking-acceptable.

They had to take charge of this and now.

Except that would mean putting Chloe on the line.

Everything in him rebelled at the thought. No, he hadn't wanted to protect her, had been furious at being given the responsibility, but he'd been given it all the same and protect her he would. He refused to accept any other possibility.

But if he went with her plan, it was going to be her safety on the line. No, he didn't think de Santis would actually physically hurt her, but he wouldn't put it past that guy to try something else. Take her hostage so he could use her to force Van to give him controlling share of the company, for example.

Shit, it made him cold just thinking about Chloe being in the hands of that icy-eyed bastard.

She'd be safer with him than with you.

The cold crept deeper inside him, despite the warmth of her body, a small kernel of ice sitting in the pit of his stomach. She was looking at him like she wanted an answer, and he knew he had to give her one. Yeah, he wanted to say no, pick her up, and carry her into the bedroom, maybe lock the door to keep her in there. Make sure she stayed there.

But that wouldn't solve this and he knew it. He wanted to get back to base and she needed to get back to the ranch, and neither of them could do that until de Santis had been dealt with.

With a bullet.

Yeah, well, there was always that option. Except he wasn't into cold-blooded murder, no matter how attractive the option might be or how easily it would solve everything. Of course, if that bastard ended up doing something to her, then all bets were off . . .

You'd kill for her? Really?

"Van," Chloe's voice was husky and warm, distracting him. "You know it makes sense. And apart from anything else, I want to help. You can't take this all on yourself."

Of course he could, and he did, regularly. Yet, he couldn't deny that some part of him liked how she wanted to share the burden, as if it wasn't just him for a change. He was used to carrying the load—as a commander, that's what he did. But shit . . . he had to admit it was nice to know he wasn't alone.

She'll still be in the line of fire if you agree.

Van met the fierce look in her dark eyes. She was small and slender, and there was an aching vulnerability to her that made his heart clench tight. But she was also surprisingly strong, with a will and a stubborn nature just as powerful as his. Christ, she'd managed the goddamn ranch and a whole lot of staff, on her own for years, and that took guts. That took determination and resourcefulness.

She wasn't a terrified woman held captive for years by sex traffickers like Sofia had been.

"Okay," he said reluctantly. "You have a point. But we're going to do this *my* way, understand?"

She grinned, and he felt it like the sun coming up after a cold dark winter. "You really think you're still in charge here?"

He didn't smile back. He couldn't. Because something inside him had shifted like an earthquake and now the ground was all broken and uneven and unfamiliar. And he didn't recognize himself anymore.

You are so screwed. You know that right?

"Oh pretty. . . ." He slid his hands into her hair, curling his fingers around the soft, silky locks, paying no attention to the voice in his head that he thought was probably right. "I don't think, I know."

The flame in her eyes leapt high. "Want to bet?"

"Show me then," he murmured. "Show me how in charge you really are."

She tilted her head to the side, looking at him, that sunrise smile lighting her up from the inside, making her glow like a torch.

Then without another word, she reached up and brought his mouth down on hers.

CHAPTER FOURTEEN

Chloe couldn't tear her gaze from the windows as the taxi pulled up outside Rockefeller Center. Beside her, Van muttered something to the driver, but she really wasn't listening, too busy staring at the building that reared up into the night sky above her.

It was all a little weird to be here, at the building in her snow globe. A strange choice of place to meet de Santis, maybe, but she'd thought it was fitting to meet him, her real father, at the place that signified all those empty promises she'd gotten from Noah.

Van had sent de Santis an email that morning telling him exactly where Chloe would be and what time, making it sound like he was giving in to his ultimatum. De Santis had insisted that he meet with Chloe alone—which Van had balked at in a major way. But after she'd convinced him that de Santis probably wouldn't tell them anything if Van was in the vicinity, he'd grudgingly agreed to it.

She understood his reluctance, especially after what he'd told her the night before, about the woman he'd failed to save. But this wasn't the same. De Santis wasn't going to hurt her, she was sure of it. It wouldn't be in his interests to do so and besides, it would soon become pretty clear what he wanted once they'd met, and if he intended to do something sketchy, Van would be around to make sure she was okay. He would protect her, and she trusted he would. Sure, he hadn't managed to save that woman, but it sounded like a hell of a situation and one that wasn't his fault in any case. It also was not going to happen this time around.

"Are you ready?" Van's deep voice was quiet.

She turned, meeting his clear hazel gaze. "Yes." Okay, so she was a little nervous about this—maybe more than a little—but she could handle herself.

"I won't be far away. If he does anything—and I mean *anything*—you give me the signal, okay?"

Something flickered in his eyes, something that looked a hell of a lot like apprehension. And for some reason it made her feel warm inside that he was worried for her.

Don't get too excited. You know this isn't going anywhere even if you do get out of this.

Chloe shook the thought away. Of course this affair wasn't going anywhere, she knew that. But she could be pleased that he cared about her enough to be afraid for her, surely?

"Yes," she said aloud. "Got it." They'd already worked out the signal that would alert Van if she felt in danger.

"He won't be alone, you know that, right? He's likely to have men around him, though you probably won't be able to spot them. Just be aware they're there."

"I know, Van. We went through this, remember?" And they had, numerous times before coming out.

That betraying muscle ticked in his jaw again. "Just making sure." He narrowed his gaze at her, then reached out to pull up the hood of the sweatshirt she was wearing for warmth underneath her leather jacket. "It's cold out. Stay warm."

He was sitting half-turned toward her, one hand on the

back seat near her head, the other resting on one muscled thigh. He'd changed before they'd come out, into jeans and a long-sleeved tee, with a black hooded sweatshirt and his overcoat over the top. He too had the hood pulled over his head, his features shadowed, but she could still see that apprehension there, tightening the lines of his face.

Impulsively she put her hand over his where it rested on his thigh, loving the little electric spark that leapt between them as her skin touched his. "It'll be okay," she said, wanting to reassure him. "I'll be fine."

He let out a breath and turned his hand over almost absently, interlacing their fingers. "You fucking better be, understand?"

That he didn't even pretend not to be worried made her heart tighten strangely, and she wanted to say something that was more than just a paltry "I will." But she didn't know what else to say, so all she did was smile and squeeze his fingers in return.

He didn't smile back, only stared at her, and she couldn't read the expression on his face. Then his gaze flickered to the building beyond the taxi's windows. "Okay then, let's go."

Outside it was cold, the wind whipping around her, cutting through the leather of her jacket, a swirl of snowflakes gusting in the air.

Holy shit. She was honest to god standing in her snow globe.

Ignoring the crowds of people pushing past her on the sidewalk, she tilted her head back. Looking up into the sky and the building towering above her, an odd thought occurred.

Had Noah stood here? Had he tipped his head back and looked up at that building? Had he felt the same odd vertigo she did? He'd told her once that he loved tall buildings, that they were a sign of what a man could do if he really put his mind to it—create something much larger and more lasting than himself.

Like Noah created the Tate legacy.

Chloe wiped the snow out of her eyes as she stared up at the building. Yeah, it kind of made sense in a way. The Tate legacy was Noah Tate's equivalent of building Rockefeller Center. He'd wanted to create something bigger and more lasting than himself.

Pity that it had come at the expense of his relationship with his adopted kids.

"Big projects require commitment, Chloe," he'd told her once, when he'd first gotten her to help with planning a massive new breeding program for the ranch. "You can't be half-assed about it."

He hadn't been. He'd put his legacy first and everything else had come a close second, including the kids. But that wasn't their fault, was it? That was his.

"Hey," Van's deep voice was in her ear and she could feel his warmth at her back. "Are you sure you're okay?"

She turned around. He was standing with his hands in the pockets of his overcoat, his gaze flicking around at the crowds surrounding them, his big body held tense, as if expecting an attack at any second. He had his hood pulled up, hiding his strong, handsome features to prevent anyone from recognizing him, and she knew—because she'd seen him pick it up before they left—that he had a gun hidden somewhere on him.

Tough. Dangerous. *Hot.*

"You keep asking me that." She held his gaze steadily. "It's enough to give a girl doubts."

The hard look on his face didn't ease. "Just checking. Come on. The ice rink's in that direction."

She wanted to tell him her little epiphany about Noah, that they weren't to blame for the way he'd parented them, neither of them were, but there wasn't time. So instead she only nodded.

He reached for her hand, lacing his fingers through hers as if it was the most natural thing in the world, sending a small shock through her. It felt intimate, meaningful in some way, and part of her was wary of that. But she didn't want to take her hand from his, so she didn't, enjoying the warmth of his fingers around hers instead, letting him lead her toward the rink.

She'd decided on the spot to meet de Santis, another nod to her snow globe and to Noah. And it was a good place too, very public, with crowds of people clustered around watching the skaters.

As they approached the rail that ran around the rink, a couple of people turned away, leaving some space for them to stand.

Van made sure she was closest to the rail, stepping up behind her, putting his massive body between her and the crowds.

She was sure his protectiveness was instinctive and maybe it should have irritated her, yet she found herself feeling the opposite. Like she was being taken care of, which was somehow even more disturbing.

Don't get close to him. He won't give you what you want.

Yes, she knew that and it was okay, because she didn't want anything, not from him. Or at least, what she wanted, she had already. Besides, he might be gorgeous and protective, might have given her pleasure beyond her wildest dreams, but in many ways, he was a lot like Noah. There was a core of reserve in him, as if she'd only ever be allowed so far and no further, and that was something she definitely *did not* want.

If she ever fell for someone, it was going to be for someone who'd give himself to her as fully as she gave herself to him. Not someone who'd only give her a few little pieces now and then.

She didn't want to be somebody's afterthought, not again.

"I'd love to skate." She leaned on the rail, watching a woman pirouette gracefully on the ice. "Pity we can't do it now."

"We only have a couple of minutes before he shows up. Which means I have to leave."

Nervousness twisted inside her, but she refused to give into it. Instead she kept her attention on the skater. "Okay. Maybe when this is all over then."

There was a silence behind her.

Then she felt his hands settle on her hips and she was being turned around firmly.

He was looking down at her, the lights around them casting the most fascinating shadows across his face, highlighting the proud line of his nose and the sharp edges of his cheekbones. The flicker of apprehension in his eyes had gone, a furious light burning there instead. "You fucking better stay safe," he ordered, low and intense, as if he was angry with her. "Understand me?"

But she knew he wasn't angry. He was worried. And it came to her that for all his big, tough, SEAL attitude, right in this moment, he was as vulnerable as she was.

No, he wasn't like Noah. Not in the slightest.

Her heart gave a kick inside her chest, making it difficult to breathe for a second. "I will," she said thickly. "I promise."

That fierce stare of his felt too hot, too consuming, and just when she thought she was going to catch fire right there and then, he cupped her face in his hands and bent his head, covering her mouth in a hard, hungry kiss.

There was something desperate about it, and possessive too, as if he was branding her or reminding her of some-

thing, and she found herself reaching up to push her hands
in his short hair, wanting to hold onto him. Keep him there.
But even as she did so, he was raising his head and letting
her go, stepping back and away from her before she had a
chance to touch him. Then, giving her one last intent,
piercing look, he turned away, melting into the crowd.

She shouldn't watch him go and yet she couldn't help
it, her mouth burning from his touch, unable to tear her
gaze from the sight of his tall figure moving swiftly,
threading through the knots of people with ease.

You're alone again.

Chloe gave herself a shake, then dragged her attention
away from Van, turning back to the rail once more, watching the skaters glide over the ice, ignoring the churning
sensation in her gut.

No, she wasn't alone. Not this time. She had Van and
he was out there in the crowd, ready to come for her if she
needed him. And he would, she had no doubt of that, no
doubt at all.

A few minutes passed and then there was movement at
her elbow, someone leaning against the rail next to her.

"Hello Chloe," a smooth male voice said.

And even though she'd been expecting him, a bolt of
shock raced down her spine anyway, and when she turned,
she found herself staring into a pair of very blue, very familiar eyes.

Cesare de Santis smiled at her. "I got your email."

Van moved through the crowds, his attention moving out-
ward, every sense focused on the movement of the people
around him, watching their faces, alert to their movements,
reading them for any signs of threat.

Easier to do that than to think about Chloe, standing
there at the rail by herself, waiting for that asshole de
Santis to come. All alone and unprotected.

Instinct kicked at him to turn around and go back for her, pick her up and bundle her into a taxi, take her home. Make sure de Santis never found her.

But he shoved the feeling away, moving instead to a position by the rink that was far enough away that de Santis couldn't spot him, yet close enough for him to keep an eye on Chloe and be ready should she give the signal.

If anything happens to her, it'll be your fault, asshole. You should never have agreed to this.

No, maybe he shouldn't, yet what other options were there? He couldn't risk calling de Santis's bluff on the takeover bid, not when they didn't quite have all the information, and besides, they weren't actually clear on what the prick actually wanted anyway. Which was something they needed to find out in order to deal with him once and for all.

Moving around the rink, Van paused near a large group of European tourists, standing back from the rail and casting a glance back to where he'd left Chloe.

She was standing by herself, watching the skaters. Her hood had fallen back, her hair tumbling down her back in an inky fall, black as the Wyoming night sky. She looked so small, so vulnerable. De Santis could take her so easily.

His fingers curled into fists in his pockets, but he didn't move. She was right, it wasn't in de Santis's interests to harm her and certainly trying anything here, in a public space, wouldn't be in his interests either.

But he could take her hostage. He could do that very easily. What would the old man say if that happened?

His jaw was so tight he could have ground concrete with it. Yeah, he didn't need to imagine what Noah would say. He knew.

"Don't tell me about what you didn't achieve, Sullivan,"

Noah used to say. *"I don't want to hear about the failures. Only the successes matter. Only the wins."*

There would be no wins if he lost Chloe. There would be no wins ever again. But he wasn't under any illusions that the real difficulty here was dealing not only with the past and what had happened to Sofia, but also with his own control issues.

He had to trust Chloe to handle herself. To be strong. And he hadn't realized quite how hard that would be until he'd walked away from her.

She's got you by the balls.

He tried not to think about that. Tried to ignore the tension winding tighter and tighter inside him as he forced himself to look away from her small figure. Instead he studied the crowds around her, trying to see if he could spot de Santis or his men. But either the idiot who'd given himself away a couple of days ago at the Tate mansion was an isolated incident, or de Santis had hired better security, because all he could see were office workers and tourists.

Okay, so where was de Santis? The bastard would be there somewhere around, Van was sure of it. Unless, of course, this insistence on seeing Chloe was a ruse . . .

He glanced back at where she'd been standing a moment earlier.

She was gone.

An intense cold feeling settled in his gut and began to spread out, tendrils of ice snaking through his bloodstream. Ah, Christ, he could not let this get to him. He could *not*.

Switching into military mode, calm but alert, he made his way to the terrace above the rink, scanning the crowds for anyone who even looked remotely like Chloe. There were any one of a number of reasons for her not to be by that rail of course, except he couldn't think of a single one.

Deep inside him the cold shifted, twisted harder, tighter.

See? This is what happens when you trust someone to handle themselves.

Van shoved the snide voice ruthlessly aside.

She wasn't around the sides of the rink so he widened his perimeter, moving to take in the whole of the plaza area, scanning for anything, anything at all that might be suspicious or give any clue as to where she'd gone.

He couldn't see her though. He just couldn't see her.

The cold was beginning to rise up into his chest, freezing his heart, his lungs, making them feel like he couldn't take a breath, and he had to stop for a moment to get some fucking air.

This shouldn't be affecting him as badly as it was and he couldn't seem to get a grip on himself. He'd never felt this way when he'd been protecting anyone else, not even Sofia, so what the fuck was with him now?

Because it's her. Because it's Chloe.

Maybe that was it. She was family after all.

It's more than that and you know it.

But before he could acknowledge that, suddenly, out of the corner of his eye, on the street and partially hidden by the crowds, he saw a long, low black car pulled up to the curb. A limo. There were three guys in suits standing near it, all of them built, all of them surveying the crowd with the same slow, intense focus as he'd been doing not seconds earlier.

Military, he could tell. And armed. He could tell that too.

The cold seemed to swallow him whole, because there was no question at all in his mind who that car belonged to.

Cesare de Santis. The bastard had turned up after all.

Instantly, Van was moving, pulling his Glock from the waistband of his jeans and holding it low down at his side as he headed straight toward the limo. There were so many fucking people and he didn't want to cause a scene, so he had to thread his way through the crowds without drawing attention. It hampered him, especially when all he wanted to do was to fling all these fucking idiots standing between him and de Santis out of the way and just go at the guy.

He was here for Chloe, of that Van was certain.

As he dodged a crowd of Japanese tourists, he caught a glimpse of a tall man with gray hair approaching the limo. One of the military assholes guarding the car made for the rear door, pulling it open. The tall man stopped, moving aside, making way for a small, slight figure in a dark blue hoodie.

Chloe. What the hell was she doing?

Everything fell away. The crowds, the guards, even the prick standing next to her. There was only her. Only her and the distance between them. A distance he was never going to close if he didn't start running right the fuck now.

That primitive and deeply possessive thing inside him roared to life and he did start to run, not caring about drawing attention to himself. Not caring about people or obstacles standing in his way. All he cared about was getting to her before de Santis forced her into that car and took her away from him.

Someone shouted after him and someone else cursed, heads turning as he sprinted toward the car, shoving people out of the way. But he didn't take any notice of them, all his attention focused on that small, slight figure.

"Chloe!" He hurled her name through the air that separated them and she lifted her head and turned toward him. De Santis had his hand on her back and Van couldn't tell what the expression was on her face because she was too far away, but she looked white. Christ, if she'd been hurt or scared in any way, he was going to kill someone. And he meant that literally.

The assholes guarding the car had seen him and were coming toward him now, their hands already going for their weapons. Fucking idiots. Didn't they know who he was? He'd be able to take them on one-handed even if he hadn't had Chloe to defend. But with her on the line . . . well, they'd be lucky if he let them come away with their balls intact let alone alive.

"Chloe!" he shouted again, already raising his arm as asshole number one reached him. He smashed the fucker over the face with the butt of his Glock, only just remembering that pulling the trigger in a plaza full of people would be a really fucking stupid idea. The prick went down, but number two was already on him. Luckily Van already had that covered, delivering a vicious, hard punch to the man's gut that had him doubling over, choking.

Chloe was still turned toward him, staring, transfixed. And he realized belatedly that no one had a gun on her and that de Santis had dropped his hand from her back. There was nothing stopping her from running to him, nothing to stop her escape. Yet she wasn't moving.

Asshole number three was suddenly in his face, the barrel of something small and sleek sticking into his gut. Reflexively, Van reached for it, wrenching it to the side and twisting to pull it out of the other man's grip.

De Santis had bent his head, murmuring something in Chloe's ear and she turned to look up at him.

Someone hit Van from behind, a vicious kick to the kidney, making him catch his breath. Fuck, he was getting distracted. He shifted, sending his elbow back, connecting with something hard that made a cracking sound. Then, reaching forward fast with the same arm, he grabbed the guy in front of him around the neck, pulling him down at the same time as Van drove his knee up into the man's stomach. The guy groaned, dropping like a stone to lie gasping on the ground.

Chloe had turned back to look at Van but still she made no move toward him. The guy he'd elbowed tried to trip him, but he avoided it easily, delivering a kick to the asshole he'd kneed in the stomach for good measure, starting back toward the limo again.

Maybe she was too afraid to move. Maybe she was in shock and didn't know what to do.

Footsteps behind him. Clearly, one of those pricks had decided to come back for more.

Van ignored him, raising his Glock as he moved. "Don't, Chloe!" he roared at her. "Get down!"

But she didn't. She only stared at him for one long second before turning away and getting into the car.

He shouted her name again, aiming at de Santis's head, ready to pull that fucking trigger and blow the guy the fuck away if he had to. But the bastard only smirked at him and followed Chloe into the limo as if he didn't have a gun pointed at his head by a SEAL commander full of murderous rage.

You can't do this in public, you fucking idiot. You're in full fucking view. What are the media going to say about the new heir of Tate Oil opening fire in Rockefeller Plaza?

The limo was pulling away from the curb, accelerating into traffic, and his hand was shaking with the effort to keep himself from pulling that trigger because, unfortunately, it was all true. He couldn't kill a man in public, neither could he start shooting at the car.

And actually, if he didn't get out of here now, he was going to be at risk of being picked up by the police. Yeah, his superiors would be pretty unimpressed with him if that happened.

Rage burned inside him, hot and thick and choking. And beneath that, a fear he didn't want to acknowledge.

Behind him someone was getting ready to throw a punch—he could tell by the rustle of fabric and the slight sound of an indrawn breath. Turning sharply, Van smashed his fist into the guy's face. He went down without a sound.

People were shouting, a crowd starting to gather.

Van didn't wait. His hood had fallen back so he pulled it up and turned in the direction of Lucas's apartment, fury and the terrible, sick sense that somehow something had gone wrong with Chloe flooding through him.

Something had gone wrong and he didn't know what it was.

They both knew de Santis was an enemy and that her safety with him couldn't be guaranteed, yet she hadn't given Van the signal. And she'd gotten into that car *willingly*.

She'd seen him charging toward her and she'd *still* gotten in.

A dangerous kind of feeling lurched inside him, but he refused it. He couldn't afford any feelings right now, not a single one. The only thing that mattered was getting Chloe back.

Ignoring the rage and the strange emotion that felt oddly like betrayal, Van started sprinting down the street.

He would not fail another woman. Not this time.

CHAPTER FIFTEEN

Chloe leaned back against the ridiculously soft creamy leather of the limo's interior, her heart shuddering. All she could see was Van's desperate face as he tried to get to her, the hoarse sound of his voice calling to her ringing in her ears. He'd thought she was being kidnapped . . .

You know what this will do to him.

She looked down at her hands clasped tightly together in her lap. Yeah, she knew. But going with de Santis had been the only way. He'd promised her that all her questions would be answered if she came with him. And yes, she knew how empty promises were from fathers, but it was a chance she couldn't give up.

She and Van had to know whether de Santis had enough shares for a hostile takeover and what he wanted with her.

It's not just about that. You want some answers yourself.

Well, that was true. She did. Answers about a great many things, and no one could give her those answers but the man sitting beside her.

So yes, going with de Santis without giving Van a heads-up was a calculated risk, but it was a risk she had to take. She'd asked Van to trust her to handle herself and she hoped he would. Anyway, the sooner she got the answers, the sooner Van could fulfill his responsibility to her and get back to the Navy, where he belonged.

"Don't worry," Cesare de Santis—her father—said, settling into the seat beside her. "He'll be fine."

"I'm not worried." She didn't turn and look out the back window, some instinct telling her it was better not to reveal too much in front of this man and most especially not the nature of her relationship with Van. Luckily, she'd had a lot of practice with keeping her feelings locked down.

"You don't much care for your brother?" The question was casual-sounding, almost offhand.

"Foster brother," Chloe corrected absently, studying her hands. They were white. She hadn't realized how cold she'd been until she'd gotten into the limo where it was nice and warm. "And no. He's a little arrogant for my tastes."

"Well, that's true." There was an amused note in de Santis's voice. "He wasn't happy to see you leave with me, that's for sure."

Chloe let her lashes fall for a second, a quiver running through her at the look on Van's face just before she'd gotten into the limo. Because he would have seen that she wasn't being forced into it, that it wasn't a kidnapping. That she'd deliberately chosen to go with de Santis.

But what else was she supposed to do? Van would never have let her go if she'd waited to talk to him first, she knew that for a fact.

No, he was going to have to trust her to deal with this.

Still, her mind kept replaying over and over again Van striding toward her, lifting his hand and smashing first one guy over the face, then punching the second in the gut. He'd barely looked away from her as he'd felled three men as easily as a woodcutter felling trees with a razor-sharp ax. Then he'd lifted his gun and pointed it at de Santis's head, and her whole body had gone cold because she'd seen murder glittering, a pure, deep green in his eyes.

She'd hesitated in that moment, and not because she'd

been afraid for the man standing behind her, her biological father, but because she'd seen desperation in Van's eyes. So desperate that he might risk shooting another man in cold blood, in the middle of a public square, just to get to her.

That had meant something, though she wasn't sure what. Had it only been about keeping her safe? About the woman he'd lost? Or had it been about more than that?

"He wouldn't have done it," de Santis had whispered to her, as if he'd known exactly why she was hesitating. "He's too much of a good soldier."

But no, she couldn't think about that right now. She had a mission she had to complete and that's what she had to focus on. Get answers from Cesare de Santis and somehow get those answers back to Van.

Taking a breath, she lifted her lashes again then turned to glance at the man sitting next to her.

He was different in real life than he was in the pictures she'd been studying the day before. There was a powerful charisma to him, a magnetism that was more to do with the force of a strong personality than it was with his intense blue eyes and the set of his handsome features. He was looking at her very intently, which was slightly disconcerting.

"You look like her," de Santis said unexpectedly.

A little shock prickled over her skin. "Who? My mother?"

"Yes." There was an expression in de Santis's eyes she couldn't interpret. "I loved her, you know. But I was married and I already had three sons. Anything more between us would have been impossible."

Okay, so that was unexpected.

She stared at him. "I was told it was a one-night stand."

"Is that what Noah told you?" De Santis shook his head slowly. "No. It was more than a one-night stand, Chloe."

Yet another lie her father—Noah—had told her . . .

"You said you were married. Is that why you never contacted me?" she asked.

"Partly," he admitted, "but then maybe you already know the other reason."

"My father?" She stumbled slightly over the word. Saying it out loud right now, here, in the presence of her actual biological father felt strange.

"Yes. Dear Noah liked a threat and as threats go, using you against me was a good one." He tilted his head, studying her. "How much do you know? I assume you found out I was your father only after Noah died?"

She didn't want to admit how in the dark Noah had kept her, but there was little to give him other than the truth. "That's right. Van told me."

"Ah, yes, the indomitable Mr. Tate. He's really quite persistent, isn't he?"

Defensiveness curled inside her, though she tried not to let it show. "He's a SEAL. What do you expect?"

"True." Something flickered in de Santis's blue eyes. "Though, you have to know that I would never hurt you, Chloe. You're my daughter. Family is important to me."

It sounded good, but as she already knew, some men's promises were empty. There was also the fact that as she'd discovered in the course of her research, de Santis had had another son. A fourth son, also the product of an affair. A son he'd hadn't acknowledged until he was forced to. So much for family there.

"You have four sons," she pointed out. "Not three. Or is family only important in certain situations?"

Again that flicker in his eyes. "So you've been investigating. And why shouldn't you?" He gave another slight smile. "Nero was a special case. But then we're not here to talk about my sons. We're here to talk about you."

"So talk then. Why were you trying to find me? What

do you want with me?" The questions came out too sharp, but she made no attempt to soften them, too busy trying to hide the churning sensation in her gut.

If her tone bothered him, de Santis gave no sign. "By all means, let's get straight to the point. But not here. We'll wait till we get somewhere a little more comfortable I think."

A sharp jab of trepidation pricked her. "Where are we going?"

"You'll see." His smile this time was broader and he leaned forward, patting her hand. "Don't look so scared, Chloe. I don't know what lies Noah fed you, but like I already told you, you're my daughter and I would never hurt you."

Crap. What had she told herself about not letting her emotions show?

Chloe shoved her trepidation away, giving him a belligerent look instead. "I'm not scared. Don't flatter yourself."

He gave a soft laugh, but didn't say anything as the limo glided through the Manhattan night traffic. In fact, he didn't speak again until the limo slowed down on a very grand street on the Upper East Side, pulling up to the curb outside an old, stately looking building.

"This is our stop," de Santis said, glancing out the window. Then he looked back at her. "Welcome home, Chloe."

She didn't know what to make of that, so she merely lifted a shoulder as if she wasn't terribly impressed, saying nothing as the limo door opened and she was ushered out onto the sidewalk then up the stairs to the front door of the building.

De Santis showed her inside into a massive flagged entryway and from there into a very formal sitting room. The walls were white, as was the furniture, the color a lot colder and harder than the pleasant cream of the Tate mansion. And unlike the Tate home, there were no family photos on the walls or on the mantelpiece above the fireplace. Just a few intensely colored abstracts, the white walls making the paintings look like they were hanging in an art gallery rather than in someone's home.

"I'm going to get a drink," de Santis said as Chloe sat tentatively on the edge of the white linen couch. "Do you have any preferences?"

She shook her head, the churning feeling in her gut making the idea of alcohol unpleasant. She was going to need her wits relatively unclouded if she was going to win this little battle anyway. "No thanks."

He shrugged and moved over to a long, slim sideboard where a crystal whisky decanter sat along with a few crystal tumblers. Pulling the top off the carafe, he apparently ignored her request and poured a couple of measures of whiskey into two tumblers. Then, picking them up, he came over to where she sat and held one out to her. "Go on," he said gently. "You'll need this."

Chloe eyed him. It probably wasn't worth the effort to argue solely to make a point, especially not if she wanted him to be receptive to her questions.

Taking the glass reluctantly, she cradled the heavy crystal in her hands. The room was warm, but her fingers still felt icy cold. "That sounds promising," she said, hoping sarcasm masked the faint note of trepidation she could hear in her own voice.

"Well, if you're expecting for this to be all hearts and flowers, you're going to be disappointed." De Santis moved over to an armchair and sat down, leaning back into it and taking a sip of his whiskey as he surveyed her. "Noah and I were enemies, after all."

"I do realize that." The edges of the tumbler dug into her palms. "He did talk about you, you know."

"Did he now?" There was a certain sharpness in de Santis's voice. "Can't imagine what lies he filled your head with."

Many lies as it turned out. Yet she didn't want to reveal that to the man sitting opposite her. Some shreds of loyalty were still there inside her, making her oddly defensive of Noah. "He may not have been the best father in the world, but he did the best he could."

De Santis raised a dark eyebrow. "And were you happy with him, Chloe?"

For some reason the question only made her feel even more defensive, which was strange given how she and Van had spent the last couple of days agreeing that Noah had been a shitty father.

But still. He might have been distant and emotionally unavailable, yet he'd brought her up in the world's most beautiful place. Allowed her a lot of freedom. Taught her how to be self-sufficient and self-reliant, how to be a good manager, how to keep one eye on the big picture and the other on the detail.

Those things weren't inconsiderable.

"Yes," she lied without any hesitation at all. "I was." Then she added, before he could continue on the subject, "But I'm not supposed to be the one answering questions here. That's supposed to be you."

He inclined his head as if conceding a point. "Yes, I did promise you that, didn't I? First of all, do you have your phone?"

She nodded. It was in the pocket of her jeans.

"Good. Then can you please send Mr. Tate a message telling him you're safe and well, and that you'll be coming back to him within the next twenty-four hours." He paused, blue eyes glinting. "And that if he tries to come for you before then, I'll make good my threat to Tate."

Another sharp prick of trepidation.

Making no move to grab her phone, she stared at him instead. "Oh, you mean the takeover bid? You do know that it's not really a takeover if you haven't got enough shares to actually take over, right?"

The glint in his eyes deepened. "Oh, so we have a bit of spirit, do we? Good, I like that. Reminds me of your mother."

"I'm not issuing threats to Van," she said flatly. "Especially when we both know you're bluffing."

"Yes," de Santis said slowly, "I suppose it does look that way, doesn't it?" He swirled the whiskey around in his glass, studying her all the while. "How about this then, message Mr. Tate and tell him not to look for you and that you'll be back in twenty-four hours." He gave her a quick smile that didn't reach his eyes. "I merely don't want us to be disturbed. Especially when you're after answers."

Chloe narrowed her gaze at him. She didn't trust this man. Not in the slightest. Even though he was her father and even though he'd told her he didn't mean to harm her. Even though logic had told her he probably wouldn't.

It was a stupid decision to come here.

Maybe it was. Still, she was here now and there was nothing she could do but keep going and hope he'd give her the answers she was after. In the meantime, she definitely didn't want Van to worry. He needed to know she was okay, that she was handling things.

She put her whiskey on the small side table near the arm of the sofa then took her phone out of her pocket. There were no messages and it didn't look like anyone had tried to call her, which she found vaguely disappointing. But she pushed aside the feeling and texted Van before sliding the phone away again.

Then she looked at her father, sitting in the armchair opposite her. "Okay," she said flatly. "So, talk."

Van banged open the door of Lucas's apartment and strode in, grabbing his phone from his back pocket as he did so.

He punched in his brother's number, moving into the living room and over to an armchair that sat by the windows. Hooking his foot under the chair, he jerked out his little black bag of tricks. There were things in it he could use to make Cesare de Santis wish he'd never been born.

"What is it?" Lucas answered without any preamble.

"De Santis." Van saw no reason to beat about the bush. "He's taken Chloe."

There was a silence.

"What do you mean he's taken Chloe?" Lucas voice was cold but calm.

"What the fuck do you think I mean?" The rage inside him was clawing at the walls, desperate to get out, and he was only holding on by the skin of his teeth.

Not so perfect these days are you? What would Dad say?

He bared his teeth at the bag on the floor. Dad would say nothing, because he was fucking dead, and why was he thinking of the old man anyway? He knew he wasn't goddamn perfect. He *knew.* And he should never have agreed for Chloe to meet de Santis. Never have left her by the rail alone. Shit, he should never have taken her out in the first fucking place. He should have locked the fucking door and thrown away the goddamn key, that's what he should have done.

You were supposed to trust her to handle it.

Yeah, shit, he knew that. He was also a fucking SEAL, not some stupid civilian panicking at the first sign of trouble. He commanded his own team. And the one thing a commander certainly didn't ever fucking do was panic.

"What happened?" Lucas asked sharply.

Christ. He hadn't wanted to tell the others about Chloe and de Santis, not yet. He'd wanted to do it when all of this was over, but it looked like he wasn't going to be given a choice about it.

"It's a long story." Van crouched down beside the bag, pulling it open and rummaging around inside the contents as he talked. "The letter I got from Dad, the one that told me I had to protect Chloe from de Santis, also said that he wasn't her father."

"*What?*" The edge in Lucas's voice was lethal.

"Yeah, it's a shock, I get it. But there's no time for long and involved explanations. All you need to know now is that Dad has proof Chloe is de Santis's daughter and Dad adopted her to keep de Santis out of Tate business." There was silence down the other end of the phone, so Van kept on going. "De Santis is after Chloe because he wants to see his daughter, but the guy's a manipulative asshole and I don't think that's the whole story. Anyway, we decided to contact de Santis to talk. Problem was, he wanted Chloe there alone, so I had to—"

"You went ahead and *met* with de Santis?" Lucas interrupted, his voice cold. "What the actual fuck, Van?"

Van fought to keep a hold on his patience and failed. "We still don't have all the info about the takeover situation and besides, if I want to neutralize him as a threat, I need to know what the fuck it is that he wants. Anyway, I don't have time to go through that bullshit with you right now, asshole. The issue is Chloe, getting into de Santis's fucking limo."

Proving he knew what was good for him, Lucas again was silent. Then he said, "What do you mean she *got* in? No one forced her?"

Van scowled at the bag then picked up a grenade. They were nice in certain circumstances, but probably too much of a blunt instrument for a rescue operation in the middle of Manhattan. "There wasn't a gun on her if that's what you meant, but that doesn't mean she wasn't being forced."

Maybe she went willingly. Maybe she's handling this.

Christ, he didn't know which was worse. That Chloe

had deliberately put herself in harm's way and was, in actual fact, dealing with it, or that she'd lost control of the situation and this was now a kidnapping scenario.

You need to trust her.

But the last time he'd done that, a woman had died.

Or perhaps you need to stop jumping to conclusions when you don't have all the info, asshole.

Yeah, that too.

"Did you take action?"

Lucas's voice interrupted his thoughts, forcing him to concentrate on the here and now. "Of course I fucking did. Tried to grab her, but by the time I saw her she was almost in the car. De Santis had protection too. Three assholes tried to slow me down and while I was taking care of them, Chloe was taken away."

His hand tightened around the grenade at the memory, which was a pretty damn stupid thing to do so he forced himself to put it back in the bag.

"So was all this in full view of the public?" Lucas did not sound impressed. "And you were worried about fucking Wolf punching up a bunch of marines in Leo's?"

Van gritted his teeth, fighting the inexplicable urge he had to drive his fist into something. "Maybe you didn't quite get the message, asshole. Chloe's been *taken.* By that prick Cesare de Santis. Our fucking enemy. Which means I couldn't give a shit about the goddamn public."

"You should," his brother said flatly. "We don't need the police coming down on us, and neither does the Navy."

For once in his life, Van didn't give rat's ass about the Navy. "You worry about the fucking Navy then," he snapped. "I need to go rescue Chloe." Because regardless of how she'd handled this, the chances of her being able to extricate herself were slim. Especially if de Santis didn't want to let her go.

"Hey." Lucas's tone was hard but steady. "You want to

rescue her? Then we'll go rescue her. But we need a plan
that doesn't involve either the police or the military."

His brother was right. Jesus, what was wrong with him
that he was hell-bent on charging in there with grenades
and automatic weapons? This wasn't a mission to the jungle. This was fucking Manhattan. And what he needed to
do was to keep all these fucking feelings on lockdown
before they started affecting his ability to make good decisions.

Slowly, Van rose to his feet and kicked the bag back
under the chair. "We need to find out where she is first of
all and whether she's okay."

"I'm not sure de Santis would have taken her in full view
of the general public if he was going to do something to
her," Lucas pointed out dryly. "Murder is difficult to get
away with in front of a crowd."

His brother's calm tone was infuriating, making Van
want to hurl his goddamn phone through the plate glass
window in front of him. "You don't seem to realize how
fucking serious this is," he growled. "This prick is—"

"And you're not thinking straight," Lucas interrupted.
"We have no reason to believe Chloe will be physically
harmed, especially not if de Santis is her father."

Van stared out at the night beyond the windows. He
could see himself reflected in the glass, a feral snarl twisting his features.

You're out of control.

Yeah, he was. And, worse, his brother was right. He
wasn't thinking straight.

"If he doesn't want to harm her, he might want her for
other reasons." Van had to struggle to keep his voice even.
"Such as using her against us."

"How?"

Forcing his brain away from its single track around
and around the fact that Chloe had been taken, Van tried

to think about de Santis's motivations instead. The guy had wanted Chloe, that was for sure. But what could he want from her? It wasn't a simple case of a father wanting to re-connect with his daughter, because de Santis wasn't that kind of man, not from what Noah had told him about the guy.

No, Cesare de Santis was ruthless, corrupt, and even though he might stop short of physically harming Chloe, he probably wouldn't when it came to using her to get what he wanted. Especially if what he wanted was Tate Oil.

"He wants the company," Van said. "I wondered if that fucking takeover was because he wanted to take Tate Oil down, but maybe he doesn't. Maybe he wants to keep it for himself."

"I thought he didn't have enough stock to make a move on the takeover?"

"We were pretty certain, but it wasn't absolute. There were a couple of shell companies who owned stock that the team was having difficulties finding the owners for."

"Okay, so what if he doesn't have enough? And that's why he took Chloe. As leverage to get us to hand it over."

Van cursed under his breath, a cold thread of worry somehow getting through the wall he'd placed around his emotions. It made sense. It made a whole lot of extremely crappy sense. "Yeah, fuck. I think you're right."

"Shit," Lucas muttered.

"You got that right." Van turned from the window, his brain finally kicking into high gear, turning over a whole bunch of options in his head. "One thing's for fucking sure, I'm not sitting around until we get confirmation. I want to move on this now, while he still thinks he's taken us by surprise."

His phone vibrated with an incoming text and he lowered the phone from his ear to look at the screen. And everything in him went quiet and still.

It was from Chloe.

I'm okay. I'm not in danger. Please don't worry. I'll be back in less than twenty-four hours, I promise.

The rage he'd thought he'd securely battened down flung itself at the walls he'd put around it yet again. *I'm not in any danger. . . .* Fuck, did she really think she was safe? Did she really know what kind of man Cesare was? Noah had told her he was the enemy, but she wouldn't truly understand. She hadn't had all the deals and bribes and embezzlements that de Santis had committed pointed out to her the way Noah had pointed them out to Van. Instructing Van to keep an eye on their old enemy, to keep watch, because the guy was evil and one day he'd come for Tate, and if he did, no one was safe.

"No one" being Chloe.

Come on, give her some credit. She's not stupid. She's handling it.

"Van?" Lucas's voice was tinny through the phone's speaker. "What's happening?"

Van wrestled his anger back under control and lifted the phone to his ear. "Text from Chloe telling me that she's okay and that she'll be back in twenty-four hours."

"You think that'll happen?"

"Christ, I don't know. If that's even her texting and if it is . . ." He scrubbed a hand through his hair. "We got to get a plan in place. We need to go get her before shit gets serious."

Because regardless of whether she was handling this or not, her safety was his mission goal and that's all that mattered. The *only* thing that did.

CHAPTER SIXTEEN

"What do you want to know?" Cesare de Santis was sitting back in his chair, his legs outstretched before him, idly swirling his crystal tumbler full of whiskey.

"Everything," Chloe said.

He laughed. "That's a lot all at once. Are you sure?"

"I'm sure." She reached over to where she'd put her own tumbler, on a side table next to the couch she was sitting on, suddenly deciding that maybe she could do with a shot of alcohol after all. The glass was heavy in her hands and when she lifted it to her mouth and drank, the whiskey felt like fire going down.

De Santis put his head back against the armchair and watched her. "You're a brave woman."

She lifted her chin. "I do what I have to, Mr. de Santis."

"I can't ask you to call me Dad, not when we don't know each other, but please, at least call me Cesare. So, where would you like me to start?"

The alcohol glowed warmly in her stomach, settling her. "Dad apparently took me as some kind of surety for your good behavior. He thought you were going to do something to him or the company, so he wanted a way to make you keep your distance. Is that true?"

The blue of de Santis's eyes gleamed. "Yes. Not long after you were born, I got a letter from him, along with a paternity test, informing me that he had you and that if I cared about you, I was never to come near him, the boys, or Tate Oil ever again. He didn't elaborate on the threat, but I took it seriously."

There went the vague idea that somehow Van had misread the letter Noah had left for him. It really was true. Noah really had used her as a threat to hang over his enemy.

The settled feeling vanished, leaving her cold and a little sick. She didn't let it show. "I see. So is that why you didn't try to come for me?"

"I loved your mother and I didn't want anything to happen to her child. Plus, as I already told you, I was married. Your appearance would have been somewhat . . . problematic."

Problematic. She was problematic. Story of her entire life, wasn't it?

"So you let him keep me?"

Cesare turned his palm up to the sky. "What could I do? He would have harmed you if I'd come near you."

"No," she said automatically. "He wouldn't have."

"Are you sure about that?" Cesare's blue eyes gleamed. "There's a lot you don't know about Noah, Chloe."

Apparently there was. But still, would her father really have hurt her?

You never knew him, not really, and maybe there was a reason for that. Maybe he didn't want you to know what he was capable of.

But the instant the thought occurred to her, she knew it wasn't true. Yes, Noah had kept a part of himself separate from her, but it wasn't because he was a monster who would physically hurt a child. He was a deeply flawed man, yes, but he would never have raised a hand to her. Never. She knew it like she knew all the trails on Shadow Peak.

Still, Cesare clearly thought otherwise.

"Why?" she demanded. "Give me one good reason Dad would do something like that to me?"

"Because we were enemies. He didn't trust me not to make a move on Tate Oil."

"Yes, I get that. And he had reason, didn't he? You tried to take Tate Oil from him."

He'd gone very still, the color of his eyes glittering like sharp, hard sapphires. "Is that what he told you? That I tried to take it?"

Chloe gave him a narrow look. There was a tension around him, a tension that hadn't been there before. "Yes," she said slowly. "Soon after he claimed the oil strike, you tried to argue that it was on your land."

There was silence for a long moment.

Then unexpectedly, Cesare burst out laughing.

Chloe shifted in her chair, uncomfortable all of a sudden. Had she said something particularly amusing? She hadn't thought so. "What's so funny?"

Cesare took his time to answer, his laughter slowly winding down. "My God, the gall of Noah. It's really quite impressive." He raised a finger and pretended to wipe a tear from his eye. "Let me correct a misunderstanding. I didn't try to take the oil from Noah. He took it from me."

Chloe nearly laughed herself at the preposterousness of the statement. "No, he didn't. Don't be ridiculous."

All amusement vanished abruptly from Cesare's face. "Of course he told you that. He always hated to look bad."

Her heartbeat had gotten faster, sounding loud in her head. "Told me? Told me what?"

Cesare ignored the question. "We used to be friends, did you know that?" He took another sip of his whiskey, that bitter edge corroding his voice. "We did everything together. When he bought the Tate ranch, I bought myself a little piece of Wyoming too, bordering his place. We thought we could get our properties in order together, share the load, help each other. Eventually we started to plan having families, bringing our kids up side by side." He paused, looking down at the amber liquid in his tumbler. "I never wanted to go into the gun business like my father. I wanted to work the land. And that time . . . well, it was the happiest of my life."

The bitterness had faded from his voice, a wistful note entering it that made Chloe's chest tighten. Because the life he'd described sounded . . . idyllic. Yet that wasn't the life he was living now, which meant something had happened. Something terrible.

Something she could probably guess at if she let herself think about it.

Cesare swirled the whiskey in his tumbler yet again, a slow circling movement. "We were digging drainage ditches in one of the fields. It was on my property, not even near the border of Noah's, but his shovel hit something and when we looked to see what it was, there was this black stuff welling up in the hole." He lifted the tumbler to his mouth, took a sip. "It was oil. And we both knew what that meant. We got drunk that night celebrating and I promised him a share of the money I was going to make from the strike, because he was my friend. He slapped me on the back and told me he didn't need anything." Cesare's mouth twisted in a strange kind of smile. "Then the next day there were surveyors everywhere and a couple of days after that he sent me a letter. It had been drawn up by a lawyer stating that the boundaries of my ranch had been redrawn and that the field with the oil strike was actually on Noah's side, not mine."

Chloe frowned, because this was all very familiar. "Yes, that's what happened. Except you're the one who tried to get the boundaries redrawn."

Cesare's gaze didn't even flicker. "No. I didn't."

*Noah told a lot of lies, you know that. All those prom-
ises he never delivered on . . .*

A thread of cold was twisting its way through her, the
edges of her tumbler digging into her palms yet again, but
she didn't loosen her grip. "What are you saying?"

"The properties were old and the boundary lines hazy,"
Cesare went on, as if she hadn't spoken. "And I couldn't
find any legal record anywhere that stated clearly where
they were. Noah took advantage of that and had the boundary lines redrawn in his favor. He wanted the oil." This
time Cesare smiled. "So he took it."

No. She couldn't believe that. Sure, Noah may have
been deeply flawed, but surely he wasn't that venal, that
underhanded. That dishonest.

"Of course you don't believe me," Cesare said. He didn't
sound angry about it, more . . . mildly interested. "Why
would you? No one else did when I pointed it out either. I
had no proof because he'd been quite thorough, had Noah.
He'd gotten it all locked up tight legally so I couldn't do
a thing to stop him as he claimed my fucking oil for
himself."

Except that hadn't been the way Noah told it.

"That's . . . wrong," she couldn't help pointing out. "You
were the one who took advantage of him and had those
boundaries redrawn. And at the last minute Dad found
some old plans that proved you were wrong. He said you
never forgave him and tried to sabotage the company." She
stopped.

Cesare said nothing, his expression hard, fury glittering in his blue eyes.

*Noah lied to you for years about your parentage. Why
wouldn't he lie about this?*

A kernel of doubt solidified in her chest, sitting there
in a cold, hard lump.

She didn't want to believe what Cesare was telling her.

Noah hadn't been the father she'd wanted, but he'd still been the only father she'd known. And the thought that he'd lied to her about everything . . .

How is that any different from anything else he's ever told you?

No, it couldn't be true. Could it?

Chloe studied the older man's face, trying to figure out if he too was lying. Except why he'd lie she couldn't imagine. What would he even get out of it?

The kernel of doubt got larger, the thread of cold, colder.

Was it true? Had the multibillion dollar company her father built all been on the back of stolen oil? This man's stolen oil? Her *real* father's stolen oil?

"I'd give you proof if I had any," Cesare said. "But unfortunately I can't prove it. Noah made very sure of that."

Her fingers had gone numb and she had to hold onto her tumbler very tightly to stop it from slipping out of her hands. "He wouldn't do something like that." She tried to sound as if she believed it. "Not to a friend."

"Forgive me, child. But you have no fucking idea what he would or wouldn't do. You didn't know him. I was his friend since we were both five years old. We grew up together. I knew him better than he knew himself. I was a brother to him." He lifted his tumbler, drained it. "And then the bastard betrayed me, and all because money meant more to him than friendship did."

Cesare suddenly turned and without warning flung the empty tumbler into the fireplace. It exploded in a shower of glass, the unexpected sound making Chloe jump and sending her own tumbler to the floor as her fingers lost their grip. Her tumbler cracked but didn't shatter, rolling under the sofa, but she made no move to retrieve it.

Cesare sat back in his chair, interlacing his fingers in his lap. Nothing remained of the bitterness or his sudden vicious anger, the expression on his face pleasant. "Now," he said, "is there anything else you wanted to know?"

She stared at him, her heartbeat thumping painfully hard behind her breastbone, the doubt inside her becoming certainty.

There was no denying the fury in Cesare's eyes—that wasn't an act. Noah had betrayed him. Noah had wanted a legacy more than he'd wanted friendship, more than he'd wanted family, more than he'd wanted anything. And she knew firsthand how that went.

"You wanted the company, didn't you?" she said, because it was becoming clear now. "You wanted to take it for yourself."

"Of course I wanted the company," he agreed smoothly. "Like I told you, it's rightfully mine anyway. In the early days I kept hoping your father would actually talk to me so we could sort this out like adults, come to some agreement over the boundary issue. But he refused every meeting. He didn't want to talk and when I tried to insist, he threatened legal action. He was guilty and he knew it."

The smell of her spilled whiskey was making her feel ill, but she didn't move, unable to tear her gaze from Cesare.

No wonder Noah had lied to you and to Van and Wolf and Lucas, too.

Of course. He must have been ashamed . . .

"Why did he need to use me then?" she asked. "If everything had been totally aboveboard, there's nothing you could have done to touch him."

"Well, not entirely nothing," Cesare said slowly. "I might have tried a few things that weren't exactly on the right side of the law. But he'd left me with no choice. He'd stolen from me and if there's one thing I don't like, Chloe, it's a thief."

"So he was afraid of you. That's why he took me."

"Yes, I suppose he was. A pretty cowardly move, don't you think? To use an innocent child like that."

A flawed man. A liar. A thief. A coward. And a shitty father.

Yet along the way, somehow, she'd learned enough to manage a massive spread like the Tate ranch. A role Noah had given her with no hesitation whatsoever, trusting in her abilities totally. He may not have been able to give her the emotional support she'd needed, but nevertheless he'd given her something.

"You didn't come for me," she said, not even realizing she was going to say it until it came out. "You left me there with him on purpose, didn't you?"

Cesare tilted his head, a gleam in his eye that hadn't been there before. A cold gleam. "I couldn't come to get you, Chloe. He would have harmed you."

"No," she said, with absolute certainty now. "That's a lie. If you'd wanted me, you would have come and gotten me no matter what he would have said."

Another silence fell, deep and cold as the feeling inside her. As the gleam in Cesare de Santis's blue eyes.

"I could have, it's true." His voice was steady, calm. "And I did think about it, believe me. But given the level of security at the ranch, it was going to be difficult to get you out. So I decided in the end that it would be more useful to me to have you stay where you were." His mouth twisted in another of those terrible smiles. "My own little sleeper agent."

It wasn't a shock. More like a confirmation. He didn't want her. He'd *never* wanted her. And maybe a few days ago that would have secretly devastated her. But it didn't now. Not now that she had Van.

Chloe didn't even blink. "What do you expect to get from holding me here?"

"You're a smart girl." The terrible smile on Cesare's face softened. "Work it out."

It wasn't difficult. "Let me guess. Tate Oil."

"Of course." He put his hands on the arms of the chair and pushed himself up and out of it. "I'm sorry, Chloe. I'm usually a patient man, but it's been over twenty-five years since Noah Tate stole was what rightfully mine and I'm afraid I got tired of waiting. Perhaps if my sons hadn't put me in such a difficult position with DS Corp last year, I might have been okay with waiting a little longer, but well"—he spread his hands—"a man needs a hobby in his retirement. And since DS Corp is no longer mine, I thought it was time to take back what always was."

It took some effort to keep her anger in check, but she was proud of herself that she managed it. "So I get to be *your* pawn now? Is that what you're saying?"

"I knew you were smart." He moved toward the door without any hurry. "Maybe if you'd been brought up with your own flesh and blood, it might have been different, but"—he sighed—"you weren't. You're Noah's child, which, in a way, makes this easier."

The churning in her gut intensified, but she fought it back. "I know what you're going to do," she said flatly. "You *don't* have enough stock for a takeover bid and you're going to use me to get Van to hand the company over, aren't you?"

Cesare put his hand on the doorknob and turned to her, giving her a slow, critical look. "Hmmm. *Very* smart girl. Maybe you're one of mine after all."

"So I'm your prisoner? Is that what this is?"

"Of course you are. I need some leverage after all."

"You think what you're doing makes it better?" She stared at him, refusing to give him any sign of the fear that had started to worm its way through her. "That using me makes it right?"

"No," he said coldly. "But then I don't care if it's right. The only thing I care about is taking back what's mine. And make no mistake, Tate Oil is mine."

What could she say to that? Noah had stolen from him, which made Tate Oil very definitely his.

Her jaw felt tight with the effort it took to keep her rage in check. "And me? You don't care what happens to me? Not at all?"

"Good question." His forehead creased. "I did love your mother. Very much. But you . . ." The crease disappeared, his forehead smoothing out. "Well, I don't know you. And Noah felt no compunction about using you as a pawn to get what he wanted, so why should I?"

She refused to let it hurt, concentrating instead on the last thing that had made her feel good, made her feel wanted. Van's kiss beside the rink, hard and possessive and hot. And that look in his eyes, furious and intent, and the sound of it in his voice, telling her to stay safe.

"You're a fool, Mr. de Santis." She enunciated each syllable of his name mockingly. "Van won't let you use me. He won't give you the company."

"Yes, he will," Cesare said, almost gently. "Because he'll do anything to save his foster sister." Something cruel crept into his face. "His lover."

Shock uncurled down her spine in a slow, icy lick. How *the hell* could he know? No one knew that she and Van had slept together. Absolutely no one.

That kiss beside the rink . . . in public . . .

Oh God.

And like he'd read her mind, Cesare said, "You think no one saw that kiss he gave you? My dear, *everyone* saw it."

The urge to put her fist through de Santis's smug, handsome face was suddenly overwhelming and she had to drive her nails hard into her palms to stop herself from doing so. "That's got nothing to do with anything."

"Maybe. Or maybe it's another nice little weapon to add to my arsenal. And I do like weapons, Chloe. Especially explosive ones. Which is what makes this so perfect." He leaned against the door. "Hell, I don't even need to threaten you physically. One of my men had a camera on you the whole time, which means I can just threaten to post that footage online. The idea that the head of Tate Oil has been fucking his foster sister. . . . Well, think of the scandal."

She could feel herself flushing red, but not with shame. Because she'd never thought that what she'd done with Van was wrong, not once. She'd never thought of him as a brother and it was clear he'd never thought of her as a sister. But the rest of the world didn't know that.

And neither did everyone who worked for her at the ranch. Or for Van at Tate Oil. Or with him in the military. If word of this got out, both of them would be screwed.

She ignored the fear that gathered suddenly inside her, freezing her solid. Lifted her chin instead, stubborn to the last. "Even if you do post that footage, Van will figure out some way to spin it. He's not going to let some piece of shit blackmail him. You've got nothing."

"Well, I guess we'll soon find out, won't we?" Cesare gave her a pleasant smile. "Until then, I'm sure you won't mind sitting in here for a while."

Turning the knob, he let himself out, shutting it very firmly behind him.

Leaving her alone.

"Jesus Christ," Lucas muttered, his head bent over Van's laptop, studying the paternity test results he'd demanded Van show him. "She's really his daughter."

Van stared down at the various pieces of the assault rifle he'd just stripped down and cleaned sitting on the table. They all looked good. Time to reassemble it. "Yeah," he said, picking up a couple of pieces and fitting them together with practiced ease. "She really is."

Lucas shook his blond head. "Why did Dad tell her she was his then?"

"Fuck knows." Van fitted the stock into place. "He didn't see fit to reveal that little piece of information."

"Obviously de Santis knows." Lucas looked up from the screen, his silver-blue eyes sharp. "Whose great idea was it to meet him?"

"It was a mutual decision."

"Hers then." Lucas's tone dripped with scorn. "What a fucking stupid thing to do. You should have talked her out of it."

Van's anger simmered away like a stream of hot lava under a crust of rock, making him entertain pleasant thoughts about what it might feel like to punch his brother in the face.

Because, Christ, hadn't he spent the last few hours pacing around the apartment thinking exactly that? Still, getting openly furious on Chloe's behalf would *not* be a good move right now, not when it would no doubt reveal way more than he was comfortable with. Lucas would have an aneurysm if he knew what Van and Chloe had been doing in his apartment and he was *not* going to be revealing that to his brothers anytime soon.

"Short of putting a bullet in his brain, we didn't have many options," Van said shortly. "We needed more information, and he sure as hell wasn't going to talk to me."

"Why did you assume he'd talk to her?"

"Because he's her father." Van picked up another piece of the rifle and fitted it with a snap. "And he made it very clear he wanted to see her."

Lucas stared at him, his gaze narrowing. "Since when have you been talking to him?"

Shit. His brother wouldn't know about the ultimatum because Van hadn't told him.

You want to handle this. You want to keep her all to yourself.

He did. He couldn't deny it. But it was too late to do it on his own now. Lucas was involved whether Van liked it or not, and just to be clear, he did *not* like it. And when Lucas heard what Van hadn't told him, he wouldn't like it either.

Van put the half-built rifle back down on the table and met his brother's gaze. "I met with de Santis a couple of days ago. I wanted to know what he wanted. Long story short, he wanted Chloe and threatened to go ahead with the takeover if I didn't give her to him."

Lucas's blond brows arrowed down. "A bluff, clearly."

"Yeah," Van said heavily, "well we didn't know that for sure. Plus we also needed to know exactly what he was planning and it wasn't like he was going to spill his guts to me. Chloe thought he might talk to her."

"So you just said 'Sure, go ahead'?"

Van put his hands on the table and leaned on them, mainly to stop himself from throwing that punch he'd just been thinking about straight into Lucas's pretty face. "We can't neutralize de Santis if we don't know what he wants."

"I thought it was pretty damn obvious what he wants. To take down Tate."

"If it was as simple as that, then he wouldn't have bothered with Chloe. No, he wants more. And we need to find out exactly what that is."

"You keep saying 'we.'" Lucas's tone was utterly neutral. "I presume you're not talking about Wolf and me."

Now they were getting on dangerous ground.

Van straightened, then reached for the last few piece of

the rifle, fitting them back together before checking over the weapon. "We went over that. You both told me you had shit to take care of. So no, I don't mean you and Wolf."

Placing the rifle back down on the table, he glanced across the table at his brother.

Lucas had come over immediately after Van had called him so they could discuss what they were going to do about the Chloe situation. They had, indeed, briefly considered bringing Wolf in, but then decided against it. Their youngest brother was back on base and since he'd cut short his bereavement leave, he probably wouldn't be able to get leave to come back to New York anyway. Telling him Chloe was in danger when he couldn't do anything to help would only needlessly frustrate him.

No, they were going to have to do this on their own.

Correction. Van was going to have to do this on *his* own since apparently Lucas had a "situation" that required his constant presence.

"Unless you've changed your mind about coming," Van added, studying his brother's face, trying to get a clue as to what the fuck was going on with him.

Lucas's pretty-boy features hardened. "I can't. I told you. I'm dealing with some pretty serious shit right now."

"More serious than Chloe's life?"

Unexpectedly, Lucas turned away. "I'm not answering that question. If you don't trust me—"

"Of course I fucking trust you," Van growled, irritated by his brother's recalcitrance. Christ, he'd been hoping the asshole might actually tell him what the deal was, but it looked like he wasn't going to get lucky today. "Don't get all up on your high horse. If you say you've got some serious shit, then you've got some serious shit. Like I need your pussy ass along for the ride anyway."

Lucas glanced at him and there was something intense in his gaze. Something that wasn't—for a change—all ice.

"Believe me, if it wasn't life or death, I'd be coming. But I can't leave the situation I'm dealing with right now. In fact"—he glanced down at his watch and cursed under his breath—"I'd better be getting back right now."

"Getting back where?"

"You got someone to protect? Well, so do I."

Ah, so it was *that* kind of situation. Interesting.

"Anyone I know?" Van asked casually.

Luca's piercing silver-blue gaze was completely opaque. "No."

"Don't get pissy with me. I might be able to help."

"You can't. It's also none of your fucking business." There was a note in his brother's tone that Van hadn't heard before. Almost as if the guy was worried or something. Which couldn't be right, surely? Lucas didn't care enough about anything to be worried about it.

Unless the someone he had to protect was a woman?

Yeah, you don't want to get into that kind of shit with him right now. Not when you've got your own situation with Chloe to deal with.

Good fucking point.

"Fine." Van put the rifle back down on the table and looked pointedly at the computer. "Any luck with finding her?"

Instantly Lucas was back at the laptop, pushing a button and staring down at the screen. They'd been trying to track Chloe down using her cell-phone signal, but it had been taking a while to lock onto her location for some reason.

"Okay," Lucas murmured, narrowing his gaze. "Looks like she's on the Upper East Side."

Van moved around the side of the table to look at the screen himself. "Yeah and that's de Santis's address."

He knew the place. His father had pointed it out to him on a number of occasions.

"Doesn't mean she's there," Lucas pointed out. "Only that her phone is."

"Yeah, I know that. But it's the only lead we've got, so I guess I'm taking it."

His brother gave one sharp nod then turned to the doorway. "Call me if you need anything. I can't promise I'll come, but if I can make it, I'll try."

"Got it."

"Oh, and Van?"

"Yeah?"

Lucas's eyes were suddenly intensely blue. "Try not to fuck it up, okay?"

Van let out a short laugh, ignoring the icy dread that was collecting in his gut. "That sounds like you don't trust me to do my job, baby bro. But no, fucking up is not in the mission briefing. Neither is getting caught or having this blow up in the media."

Lucas didn't smile. But then, he never did. "De Santis will know it's you if you come after her. And if he does, he'll make sure everyone else knows it too."

"Yeah, but first he'll have to catch me and then he'll have to get proof. And like I said, see the above mission briefing."

Lucas stayed silent, staring at him.

Yeah, well, he could understand his brother's qualms. They'd briefly discussed taking it to the police, since it was a civilian matter—or at least, Lucas had, since Van had told him to fuck off with that kind of thinking.

As far as the police were concerned, this wouldn't be kidnapping, Van was pretty sure. Especially since Chloe had gone with de Santis willingly. Plus, there had been no ransom demand or anything similar, which meant the police couldn't make a move since there was no evidence Chloe was in actual danger.

That left Van with only one choice. If he wanted to retain the element of surprise over de Santis, he had to move and move now. Before the guy could get Chloe somewhere more secure.

It was a risk, no mistake. If he was caught, he could face prosecution and certainly his superiors would have something to say about taking the law into his own hands. There would also be a media storm, which wouldn't do Tate Oil any favors, that was for sure.

But he had no other choice. He had to get Chloe out of there somehow, and he was pretty much the only person who could do it.

A SEAL going up against a weapons billionaire seemed like a fair fight.

As the door to the apartment closed behind Lucas, Van lifted his black bag of tricks from the seat he'd put it on earlier and dumped it on the table.

He began to sort through the stuff inside, stopping when his fingers closed around something hard, and way too small to be any type of grenade.

Frowning, he drew it out and opened his hand. Sitting on his palm was a smooth, black stone. It was familiar, the stone Chloe had given him years ago to remind him of home.

Van stared at it. Jesus, he'd almost forgotten he had it.

At that moment, his phone began to buzz. Without knowing quite why, he curled his fingers around the stone and shoved it into the pocket of his jeans before grabbing his phone. And the instant he looked down at the screen, he promptly forgot about the stone.

"Chloe," he said roughly, before she had a chance to speak. "Where the fuck are you?"

"It's not Chloe, Mr. Tate," Cesare de Santis said smoothly. "But obviously I have her, don't worry about that. In fact, she kindly lent me her cell phone so we could have this little chat."

A wash of red descended over Van's vision, the lava bubbling up from underneath. "If you fucking hurt her, I swear to God—"

"I wouldn't swear on anything if I were you, Mr. Tate. Or make any rash promises, not when I have a very serious business proposition to put to you."

Van contemplated telling the asshole exactly what he could do with his serious business proposition, especially when he had a feeling he already knew anyway. "Don't tell me," he growled. "You'll give me Chloe if I give you my Tate Oil stock."

"Actually," de Santis said, "it's even worse than that. Not only do I have your foster sister, I also have proof that you two are lovers."

Shock bolted down Van's spine like electricity grounding itself, the plastic casing of the phone creaking as his grip tightened, threatening to crush it.

"What proof?" he demanded, not bothering to deny it since no one would use that threat if they didn't already have some basis for suspecting it.

"Need-to-know basis only, son. And you don't need to know. Suffice to say that should you take it into your head to conduct a rescue mission and Chloe somehow disappears mysteriously from my custody, I will have no choice but to release my proof to the media. I'm sure they'll be delighted to have their minds taken off the current political climate by a nice little sex scandal."

"Show me," Van hissed through gritted teeth. "Show me your fucking proof."

There was no response to that, and then Van's phone beeped with a text. He looked down. On the screen was a video clip. It was focused on two people, one tall, one small. They were standing in a crowd, the rail of the ice rink next to them, and Van couldn't look away as he watched himself take Chloe's face between his hands and tilt her head back, and cover her mouth in that desperate, hungry kiss. A kiss that no one with any brains would ever mistake for platonic.

The video was very clear and it was very obvious who they were.

The clip ended.

Van raised the phone to his ear. "I'll kill you," he said pleasantly.

De Santis merely laughed. "Checkmate, Mr. Tate."

The call abruptly disconnected.

With exaggerated care, Van put his phone back in his pocket before he could hurl it through the window.

He'd never seriously wanted to kill someone before, but if Cesare de Santis suddenly appeared before him, he'd have had no problem picking up that assault rifle and pulling the trigger with a glad heart.

"Fuck," he muttered.

There was a seething mass of fury in the center of his chest and he knew that if he wasn't careful, it was going to eat him alive.

So, not only did the bastard have Chloe, that footage was irrefutable. If that went out to the media, he was screwed six ways to Sunday. The situation with Tate Oil's management was already volatile and that piece of film would light it on fire and burn the whole fucking thing to the ground.

The Tate heir sleeping with his younger foster sister? Oh yeah, that would set the whole internet blazing. He would be vilified and even apart from how it would cause huge problems with the company, the ensuing shitstorm would screw his Navy career too. The COs didn't like it when their men drew attention to themselves. Christ, he was a liability by dint of being the Tate heir already and this would make it a thousand times worse.

Then there was the way it would affect her. What would

they all think at the ranch? They'd be horrified in all likelihood.

"*Fuck*," he muttered again.

So much for being the perfect Tate heir. How many more mistakes can you possibly make?

Yeah, well, he *wasn't* perfect and he never had been, and this was proof positive of why. He'd let Chloe meet de Santis and then he'd let her get taken.

This is what happens when you fail to handle a situation.

Van's jaw was so tight it ached. Ah, Christ, he had to fix this. He *had* to.

Okay, so de Santis had apparently left him without options. If he gave de Santis Tate stock, the asshole would *still* have that footage, and Van didn't trust the man not to keep it so he could have something on Van for a future rainy day.

If he rescued Chloe, the footage would go out on the internet and the shit would hit the fan for both him and Chloe. He could possibly protect himself from that, but Chloe had to return to the ranch. How would that affect her when it came to managing the place? Christ, the ranch aside, the media were misogynistic assholes and she would be hounded anyway. Even if she left New York, she'd still find herself the center of a media storm that would be there forever. Oh yeah, and the Navy would probably ditch him and he'd never be able to go back.

There was the option of finding the footage and destroying it, but he wasn't a hacker and he suspected that de Santis would have gotten the file locked up tight behind layers and layers of firewalls that Van wouldn't have a hope in hell of getting through. Not when the man used to own a company that provided digital security to the military, which meant his own computer security would probably be at least military grade.

You really are fucked.

Unconsciously, Van's fingers curled around something hard, and he realized he was still holding the stone Chloe had given him. The little stone to remind him of home.

But it wasn't the Tate ranch he was thinking about now. He was thinking of her. She'd reluctantly put her physical safety in his hands, and then, when she'd given herself to him that night, she'd trusted him with even more.

She wasn't merely a mission he'd been given by his father, or a responsibility he hadn't asked for. She was more than that, no matter how much he hadn't wanted her to be, and she certainly deserved more than that from him.

He'd promised he'd keep her safe, and he meant it.

Which meant it was time for him to stop thinking about how quickly he could get this over with before he could go back to the Navy. Time to stop acting like the responsibilities he'd been given were simply a fucking burden he didn't want to deal with.

He had to step up. He had to take control.

He was the Tate heir and it was time to claim what was his.

CHAPTER SEVENTEEN

Chloe woke up with a start, staring at the ceiling above and wondering where the hell she was. Because she wasn't in her room at the ranch, or at the Tate mansion. And it certainly didn't look like the ceiling in Lucas's apartment either. So . . . where was she?

The memory of the night before came crashing in all of a sudden.

Leaving with de Santis, watching Van running after her, shouting her name. Then listening to de Santis talk, telling her things she didn't want to hear. All about a friendship. A betrayal. Stolen oil. Revenge. . . .

And, oh yes, de Santis was planning to blackmail Van by using her and the footage of them kissing at Rockefeller Plaza.

Yeah, she'd sure had a great evening.

She closed her eyes, for a second hoping reality would change itself to suit her better. But sadly it didn't.

Forcing herself to sit up, Chloe took a look around. She was still on the couch where she'd curled up the evening before, after it had become clear that de Santis meant to keep her there at least for the night. She felt cold, her neck sore and her back stiff, so she slid off the couch and paced around to get warm.

Glaring at the windows that faced the street, she stuck

her fists beneath her armpits to get some feeling back into her fingers. She didn't bother trying the windows again. They'd been locked the previous night and trying to break the glass with a nearby vase had shattered only the vase. Clearly they were bulletproof and nothing she had on her was going to break them.

She turned toward the door, sparing it an especially evil glare. She'd tried pulling on that too, but it had remained securely locked and she couldn't imagine that had changed overnight either.

Pacing over to the fireplace then back to the couch, she tried to ignore the rumblings in her stomach and the growing urgency in her bladder.

Okay, so she was locked in a room. What was her next step? Basically her options were either sit and wait for de Santis to blackmail Van, or sit and wait for Van to rescue her.

Dammit. She'd told Van she'd be able to handle this. Especially when rescue might be a little tricky if de Santis really did have footage of that kiss. If Van rescued her, she had no doubt de Santis would release it and that . . . wouldn't be good. A sex scandal wasn't exactly what either of them needed right now.

Even if you manage to escape, he'll release it anyway.

Well, what else was she supposed to do? Sit around and wait to be either rescued or hurt in some way? Continue to let herself be used as a pawn the way her father had used her most of her life?

No. Just no. She'd have to risk it. She had to do *something*.

Chloe turned and paced back to the fireplace.

They would come for her, that was for sure. And when they did, she needed to be ready. No, she had no fighting skills to speak of, but she wasn't completely defenseless. She'd broken in horses, fixed up fencing, helped shift hay bales, done all sorts of hard, physical labor on the ranch. She wasn't exactly some weak little kid.

However, de Santis no doubt thought of her as such, which meant they probably wouldn't be expecting her to attempt an escape and *definitely* wouldn't be expecting an offensive attack.

Chloe took a quick look around the room to see if there was anything, anything at all, she could use as a weapon. There wasn't much—a couple of glass vases, which looked too delicate to be of any use. She imagined she could smash them and use the glass shards as weapons, but she'd never used a knife or anything similar. If she got into a fight, she was more likely to get hurt than to hurt someone else.

No, what she needed was something heavy. Something that she could use to hit someone over the head to render them instantly unconscious.

There was a lamp on the sideboard opposite her, yet it looked far too big and unwieldy to handle easily. But . . . her gaze dropped to the fireplace and the set of elegant tongs hanging on a small stand. Ah, that might do.

She went over and picked them up, weighing them experimentally in her hand. They were iron and heavy, yet not too heavy to lift or to potentially whack someone over the head hard with. Yes, that could work. That could work very well.

Gripping the tongs in her hand, Chloe moved to the door and put her ear against the wood. There was no sound from the other side. She stepped back again, staring at the closed door. How long would she have to wait until they opened it? Ah, but what did that matter anyway? It wasn't like she could get out of there any sooner.

She went to stand behind the door, leaning back against the wall, keeping her fingers wrapped tightly around the tongs. Hitting whoever came in over the head and making a run for it wasn't the greatest plan in the world, especially if more than one guard came into the room or if there were more out in the hallway. She didn't think they'd actually physically harm her—at least not if de Santis wanted to use her against Van—but then, who knew? They might decide she was more trouble than she was worth and shoot her as she tried to escape.

Too bad, though. It was the only plan she had.

Her palms began to get sweaty, her mouth began to get dry, and her rumbling stomach was now replaced by an uncomfortable, churning fear.

No, she couldn't let herself think about what they might do to her. She had to believe de Santis wouldn't want her harmed. And if he did . . .

Well, if he did, she had nothing left to lose anyway.

For some reason the decision calmed her, the fear settling, making way for a kind of grim determination.

She didn't know how long she'd have to stand there, but she eventually heard footsteps, then the sound of the door being unlocked. Pushing herself away from the wall, Chloe gripped the tongs tight and raised them above her head. She wouldn't have much time before they'd discover where she was, a couple of seconds max. She had to make those seconds count.

The door opened and one black-suited man came in.

He hesitated, obviously taken aback by the fact that he couldn't see her.

Chloe didn't hesitate. Using the element of a few seconds' surprise to her advantage, she came up silently behind him and smashed the tongs down on the back of his head with all her strength.

He let out a sharp grunt then fell heavily to the floor, lying there unmoving.

She blinked, her hands shaking, slightly shocked at herself. Oh God, had she killed him?

Now is not the time to be second-guessing. Run, you fucking idiot!

Chloe sucked in a breath, spared a precious second to pick up the gun the guy had been holding, then turned and ran out of the room.

There didn't seem to be anyone immediately in the grand hallway outside, but she didn't pause to look around, heading straight toward the mansion's big front doors instead.

Please God, don't let her be seen. Please let her get out.

She had her hand on the front door when a casual voice behind her said, "I'm afraid you can't get out that way, Chloe. The door's locked."

A bolt of real fear caught her and she whirled around, lifting the gun toward the voice.

Cesare de Santis was standing behind her, dressed in an exquisitely tailored dark blue suit with a tie the same sapphire of his eyes, the very picture of a wealthy, powerful businessman. He didn't even look at the gun she had pointed at him, and no wonder since he had two goons standing behind him, each with a weapon trained on her.

Crap.

His mouth curled. "Going somewhere?"

"Yeah." She lifted her chin, not lowering her own gun one inch. "Is there a Starbucks around here because I really need a goddamn latte."

He laughed, but it wasn't a pleasant sound. "The lattes will have to wait. Clearly we'll need more of a guard, though where you're going, that won't be too much of a problem."

Trepidation twisted inside her, but she didn't let it show. "And where am I going?"

"Somewhere more secure. Not that this place isn't, but it's not really set up for . . . guests. At least not unwilling ones."

Chloe kept the muzzle of her weapon trained on his smug face, ignoring the men standing behind him and the guns they held. "Why?"

"Why take you anywhere? I don't like leaving loose ends lying around, Chloe, and you're one hell of a loose end."

"If you don't like loose ends, why not simply kill me, *Dad*?"

De Santis's eyes widened as if genuinely surprised by the question. "Kill you? No, of course I'm not going to kill you. You're my daughter and I'm not a monster. Besides, you're far too useful. I'm going to keep you for a rainy day, so to speak." He gestured to the pair of massive, black-suited men behind him. "Get her gun then put her in the car. If she gets away I'll have both your heads."

Chloe swallowed, part of her wanting to pull that trigger anyway, shoot de Santis right in the face. But that wouldn't help anything, not when his goons would then just shoot her. No, there was no point trying to get away now. De Santis had her and he knew it.

Belatedly, she tried to make a dash out the door, but the men came for her, ripping the gun from her hand and gripping her arms so she couldn't pull away. The front door was opened and she was hustled out and down the steps to where a car waited at the curb. Five seconds later she found herself sitting in the back seat flanked by the two huge guards, while a third, the driver, pulled the car out into the traffic.

She couldn't escape now, she was trapped. Even if she was able to unlock the doors, she'd have to somehow climb over one of the guards before hurling herself into traffic.

Oh God. How the hell was she going to get out of this one? She'd promised Van she would handle this, that she would be safe, and she very clearly wasn't.

You kind of fucked up.

Chloe sat back in the seat, feeling the unwelcome prick

of frustrated tears, but she swallowed them down, clenching her jaw tight. No, she refused to accept she was helpless. She was just going to have to come up with another plan.

It was morning rush hour, so the car moved slowly through heavy traffic, but the driver didn't seem worried. Clearly they weren't under any time pressure and were confident they were going to get her to wherever stupid de Santis had ordered them to take her.

They pulled up to a set of lights, the loud purr of a motorcycle engine rumbling beside them. Chloe glanced over at it, the sound distracting her. It was a massive bike, black and lethal-looking, its black leather–clad rider sitting casually astride it as if it weighed nothing at all. He had one booted foot on the asphalt for balance, one gloved hand on the handlebars, while the other hand . . .

Chloe blinked as the man drew out what looked like a long-barreled pistol. And before she'd even had time to think about what was happening, he pointed the muzzle at the driver's window and pulled the trigger. The glass cracked, the driver shouted a sudden curse. The biker pulled the trigger again and the driver slumped over as the glass began to fall away from its frame.

The two guards beside her began to react, reaching into their jackets for their weapons, and Chloe knew that this was her chance. She had no idea who the man on the bike was—*Van?*—but whatever, she had only a few seconds to get out of the car while the guards were distracted, and hell, she'd take it.

She launched herself out of the back seat and into the front. Someone swiped at her hoodie, grabbing a handful of the fabric, but she slid out of their grip and jerked open the front passenger-side door. There was a shout behind her and a curse, then the sharp, percussive sound of a silenced gun. But she'd already flung herself out of the car and onto the street. Horns blared as she stumbled into the traffic and she had to dodge a couple of cars to stop from getting run over. But she kept going, gaining the sidewalk, then sprinting down it, putting as much distance between her and the car as she could.

She didn't know how long she kept running, but eventually her lungs began to burn and her muscles started screaming, so she ducked into an alleyway and came to a halt, her breaths sawing in and out.

The low throb of a bike engine neared.

She jerked her head up and there he was, at the curb, waiting for her. The man on the huge black bike.

Van.

Her heart swelled up suddenly, huge and aching in her chest. She didn't even care that she hadn't managed to get herself out of the situation. All that mattered was that he'd come for her.

Then the man pulled up his visor and she met a pair of cold, silver-blue eyes.

Lucas.

The disappointment was so bitter she could almost taste it, which was kind of ungrateful of her, seeing as how he'd just rescued her. Nevertheless, she felt it.

She fought it back as he scanned her from head to foot, obviously checking to make sure she was whole and uninjured.

"Are you okay?" he asked shortly. "Did that bastard hurt you?"

"No." Her voice sounded breathless and husky and the question came out before she could stop it. "Where's Van?"

Lucas's eyes narrowed. "He's dealing with de Santis."

"Oh? How?"

"You can ask questions later. We need to go."

She didn't move. "What about those men in the car? Did you kill them?"

"You really think I'm stupid enough to kill a couple of assholes in the middle of the street in broad daylight? No, of course not." He jerked his head toward the back of the bike. "Stop asking questions and get on. Now."

Chloe let out a breath, swallowed down the rest of her questions, and climbed on the back of the bike.

Van stepped out of the limo, letting Walker, Noah's old driver, shut it behind him. For a moment he stood on the sidewalk, doing up a single button on his suit jacket. Adjusting the cuffs of his shirt. Smoothing his tie. Taking his time and being as ostentatious as fuck about it.

His phone went off and he grabbed it from his pocket, glancing down to check the screen, hoping it was who he expected it to be. And sure enough, it was. The message was short and sweet: *Got her.*

Lucas. Right on schedule.

Pushing aside the intense rush of relief that flooded him, Van shoved his phone back into his pocket.

Right. Phase one had been accomplished. Time for phase two.

He headed straight for the front door of de Santis's mansion.

Once he'd made the decision to act, the plan had come together easily enough. Lucas, predictably, hadn't been impressed with either Van's decision or the orders Van had issued when he'd called to give him the news. But Van hadn't given a shit. He'd reminded his brother that if he found rescuing one woman from a bunch of little boys too tough for him, then maybe Wolf might be up for the challenge. Lucas had growled at that, then said, "Fine. What do you need?"

Van had decided to keep phase three of his plan on the

down low, because he didn't need the extra aggravation that would come from his brothers once he announced it. He also needed to talk to Chloe first, since it was all a moot point if she didn't agree.

And if she doesn't agree?

Well, he'd cross that bridge when he came to it. Right now, he had to deal with de Santis.

The door to the mansion opened immediately since they were expecting him—he'd already gotten Margery to call de Santis and tell him to expect a visit. He'd decided he was going to handle this particular situation in full corporate mode, rather than as a SEAL. It was a risk since the corporate world was de Santis's battlefield, not his, but then Van had never been one to shy away from a challenge.

Plus, he liked the idea of besting the asshole on his own hill, using his own tactics against him. Start as you meant to continue and all that shit.

The black-suited man who opened the door was familiar—one of the pricks Van had smashed over the face a couple of nights previously, he could see by the bruise around his eye socket. He gave the guy a feral smile and said, all politeness, "I believe Mr. de Santis is expecting me."

A flicker of anger gleamed in the man's eyes, but all he said was, "Follow me."

Van followed him up some stairs and into an office on the second floor. The decor was very old school, lots of wood paneling and library shelving, plus a couple of landscape paintings that reminded him of Wyoming.

Over by the windows there was a massive oak desk with nothing much on it except a computer screen and a blotter. In front of it were a couple of leather armchairs.

"I'll give Mr. de Santis exactly five minutes to show his superiority by making me wait," Van said, not bothering to look at the lackey. "Then I'm leaving. Do you understand?"

"Yes," the lackey muttered.

"Yes, what?"

There was only a very brief hesitation. "Yes, sir."

Excellent. It was always worth showing pricks like this who was boss. Especially in a game of "who has the biggest balls." "Good boy. Now, run along and pass that message on for me."

The guy left the room obediently, leaving Van on his own. Which gave him a couple of minutes to case the office, not that he expected to find anything. There was no way a man like Cesare de Santis, seasoned in the art of corporate warfare, would show Van into his office only to leave something of vital importance lying around.

Still, it was a little annoying to not spot a memory stick sitting in a drawer with the incriminating footage on it, so that he could simply pick it up and put in his pocket.

After having another quick look around and not finding anything of any use, Van checked his watch. The five minutes were nearly up. If de Santis was going to push, he'd soon find out what was going on. Van's presence here was merely a courtesy call and one he didn't need to make. If the guy was going to screw around, then Van was out of here.

He turned to the door, preparing to leave, just as de Santis, looking cool, calm, and collected, came through it.

"Ah, Mr. Tate." De Santis smiled as he closed the door behind him. "Leaving already? But we have so much to discuss."

Van adjusted his cuffs unhurriedly, making the movement as arrogant as possible. "Actually this is only going to take five minutes."

De Santis's smile didn't waver, but his blue eyes narrowed. "Five minutes isn't very long, Mr. Tate. I feel sure this interview is going to take longer than that, so why don't you make yourself comfortable?" He gestured to one of the armchairs near the desk. "We have dear Chloe to discuss after all."

Van allowed himself to return the smile, making it a touch feral. "Oh, I don't think we'll be discussing *dear* Chloe at all. Not here and certainly not now."

The other man raised one black eyebrow. "I'm not sure you quite understand your position, Mr. Tate. Chloe is—"

"Chloe is now safely with me," Van cut him off, resisting the temptation to string him along a little longer since there was nothing to be gained by it. "Also, I suggest hiring a new security detail since the ones you have suck."

De Santis's expression had blanked. "What are you talking about?"

"I'm talking about Chloe, *Cesare*." Van gave an insulting inflection to the name purely because he could. "A friend of mine found her en route to fuck knows where and was able to secure her. It wasn't very difficult, hence my suggestion of a new detail. Men who actually know what they're doing."

The older man's mouth flattened into a thin line. "You're bluffing."

Van lifted a shoulder. "I couldn't give a shit what you think. I'm only here to tell you that there's no way you'll ever get your hands on Tate Oil. Not today, not next week, not next year. Not fucking ever."

A muscle ticked in de Santis's jaw, fury gleaming sudden and blue in his eyes. Without taking his gaze off Van, he took out his phone and punched in a number. "The girl," he said curtly. "Do you have her?" There was a pause, then he snapped, "No. She left here a half hour ago. . . . Christ, don't give me excuses, just find her."

"I don't like to say I told you so," Van murmured as de Santis hit the disconnect button. "But . . ."

"I'm putting that footage up online, where every media outlet in the world will be able to get hold of it." De Santis's tone dripped with ice. "Tate Oil won't survive that and neither will your military career."

"By all means try it." Van took a step toward him, the anger he'd kept carefully in check beginning to strain against the bonds he'd placed on it. This was the fucker who'd taken Chloe. Who'd threatened her. Who was using her as a pawn for blackmail, just the way his father had. The guy was lucky Van had left his Glock behind. "In fact," he added, "I'm dying to see what happens."

De Santis, in no way intimidated, didn't back away. "You know what'll happen."

Tate shareholders would riot. His military career would go down in flames. Chloe would find herself at the center of a media firestorm and even the ranch she loved would be no haven for her . . .

Dad would turn in his grave.

Yeah, he would. Because he'd wanted the perfect heir to take over his perfect company. But that was the thing. Van had never been the perfect Tate heir, yet he *was* the heir. And he had a plan for how to deal with all of the above. It wasn't perfect, but it was the best plan he had and he was going with it.

Van took another step. De Santis was tall but not as tall as Van. "The scandal will hardly be a problem, at least not for the military. And especially not since I've decided to retire from the Navy and run Tate Oil full-time."

De Santis gave a short bark of mirthless laughter. His posture was easy, loose, not at all threatened. "What? You'd really give up the Navy for a career in business?"

It wasn't something he'd wanted, no. But as he'd stood there in Lucas's apartment, clutching onto that little stone Chloe had given him, he'd realized that there were a lot of things he hadn't wanted, and most of those things related back to his father. To Noah's impossible standards and the fear he'd never live up to them. To the knowledge that after Sofia, he *couldn't* ever live up to them.

Far easier to pretend to himself he didn't want those things, he didn't care about them, and his father could go fuck himself.

But he did care. He always had. And it hadn't been until Chloe had pushed into his life, all fierce passion and determination, that he'd realized it.

She'd had her issues with Noah, but she hadn't walked away from the ranch when she could have. She'd stayed and poured her heart and soul into it, so how could he do any less with Tate Oil? How could he let his own failure with Sofia determine the course of his life?

He was a commander and he could command an oil company as well as he could command a SEAL team. Sure, the weapons in the boardroom were different and the stakes weren't as high as possibly being killed, but there were challenges to be had all the same. Challenges that before Columbia, he'd been keen to take on.

No, he could not let Sofia's death mean failure. Because she, too, deserved more than that.

And hell, apart from anything else, he'd been in the forces a good many years and eventually he'd need to consider retirement anyway. And getting out while he was still whole was a bonus.

"Sure." He grinned at the other man like it wasn't a big deal. "Why not?

"You think your shareholders will be happy?" De Santis's expression was cold. "When they discover you've been screwing your foster sister on the side? If you believe that, you don't know the first thing about business, son."

Van took one last step, getting right in de Santis's face, using his superior height to loom over him. Because it turned out he wasn't above that kind of thing after all, especially not since this bastard had threatened someone he considered his. "No," he agreed slowly, "you're right, they won't be happy. But don't worry, I have a plan."

It would have been satisfying to tell de Santis what that plan was so he could see the expression on the guy's face. But he didn't want to give de Santis a heads-up.

De Santis's expression was one of contempt. "I hope it's a good one, Mr. Tate. You're going to need it."

It was an imperfect one, but then he was an imperfect man. It also happened to be the only way he could think of to neutralize the revelation of that footage.

Screwing Chloe was one thing. Marrying Chloe was quite another.

Not only would it make the whole situation more palatable for the shareholders, it would hopefully render the media shitstorm that would follow a whole lot less salacious. It had the added bonus of keeping Chloe safe from the worst of the gossip too, not to mention making the ranch truly hers.

There were other reasons too. As his wife, she would be given other protections, not to mention having the Tate billions at her disposal—if she wanted them. And having him as her husband would hopefully protect her should de Santis try to pull another kidnapping stunt.

You also want her.

Yes, he did. No point in denying it. She was his and had been from the moment she'd risen up on her toes and kissed him.

Tate Oil wasn't the only thing he had to claim.

He would claim Chloe too.

De Santis had turned away from him, moving over to his desk. "Don't let me keep you, Mr. Tate. I've got a few things to arrange, such as a video to upload."

Van bared his teeth at the other man's back "Have fun. Let me know how that works out for you."

De Santis rounded his desk and bent over his computer screen, tapping a few keys on the keyboard. "Don't worry. You'll find out for yourself soon enough." He tapped another key. "Oh, one last thing. When you see Chloe, be sure to get her to tell you how Noah actually founded his fortune."

The statement was a strange one since everyone knew how Noah Tate had gotten his wealth. "Why the fuck would I want to do that? There was oil on his ranch."

De Santis glanced up from his screen, a strange smile on his mouth. "Yes, that's what he told you. But we all know what a liar Noah was. Just ask Chloe."

There was something in the other man's words, a veiled threat that sat uncomfortably in Van's chest. Making him want to press the bastard for answers. But now wasn't the time. There were things he needed to do before de Santis uploaded that fucking footage. Matters that needed arranging.

Like getting Chloe to agree to marry him.

"If I remember." He moved toward the door. "Oh, by the way, if you ever come near Chloe again, I don't care who you are, I'll shoot you in the head."

"Don't get too comfortable, Mr. Tate," de Santis murmured after him. "I'm not giving up that easily. I may not be a motherfucking SEAL, but I know the business world far better than you ever will."

"Maybe." Van put his hand on the doorknob and pulled it open, turning back briefly to meet the other man's blue gaze. "And maybe not. Whatever, I could use some fucking target practice."

Then without waiting for another word, he strode out.

CHAPTER EIGHTEEN

Lucas took Chloe back to the Tate mansion, much to her surprise. As she slid off the back of the bike, she glanced at him. "Here? Are you sure?"

"That's where Van wanted you. Don't ask me why." Lucas got off the bike after her, locked it, then headed straight toward the front doors, tugging his helmet off as he went. He didn't say another word, leaving her to follow in his wake.

The lack of information was making her feel . . . uncertain. Which she hated. Lucas might have gotten her away from de Santis, but there was still the issue of that footage. Of that blackmail. Would the bastard release it since she'd been rescued? Was Tate Oil and Van's military career screwed even now? And what about the ranch? What would happen with that?

The hunger that had gripped her earlier vanished, leaving nothing but an awful sick feeling washing around her stomach.

Luckily, once she headed to the nearest bathroom to relieve her aching bladder, she wasn't actually sick, and a hot shower afterward soon had her feeling slightly better. Then she wrapped herself in a towel and crept down the hallway to the bedroom she'd had when she'd initially arrived in New York. Her bag was sitting on the bed and when she opened it, all her gear was neatly packed inside, the snow globe sitting on top. Either Van or Lucas must have gotten it from Lucas's apartment for her.

She took the snow globe out and stared at it for a moment, her little reminder of Noah's empty promises. Yet for some reason, right now, the anger she usually associated with it was gone.

She only felt . . . sad.

Her father hadn't been a bad man, she knew that as surely as she knew every inch of the ranch he'd taught her how to manage. But he'd let greed blind him, and the decision to take de Santis's oil had cost him the relationship he'd had with his best friend and his foster kids.

Had he once cared about that? Had he *ever* cared?

It was a question that would remain forever without an answer.

Do you need one?

Chloe shook the globe, watching the snow whirl against the glass, and it came to her all of a sudden that no, she didn't need one. Because she was holding all the answers she needed in her hand.

In some corner of his cold heart, Noah Tate had cared enough to buy the little girl he'd disappointed a snow globe. He didn't have to, yet he had all the same.

Something tight in Chloe's chest relaxed and she looked at the globe a moment longer, simply staring at all those glittering flakes. Then she put it carefully on the nightstand beside her bed, before turning back to the bag to find some clean clothes.

Sadly there were none.

Irritated, she went over to the closet and slid the door open on the chance she'd find clothes inside. Unfortunately there were none in there either.

There were other bedrooms in the Tate mansion and she had a poke around though them, trying to find something to wear that wasn't a blanket and didn't smell, but it wasn't until she reached the top floor and Van's bedroom that she found something she could pull on—a dark gray robe made out of some thick, soft, fluffy fabric that made her instantly warm as she drew it around her.

The robe was far too big for her, and she wrapped the belt twice around her waist then rolled up the sleeves as much as she could. Then she took a breath and headed downstairs.

Lucas was pacing around in the hallway when she came down and when he spotted her, he stopped, the look in his silvery blue eyes cool. "All good?" he asked tersely.

Chloe pushed her hands into the pockets of her robe. "Yes. He didn't do anything to me, if that's what you're worried about."

Lucas folded his arms, giving her another of those ice-cold, impersonal scans. He was such a handsome man and all that black leather should have made him even hotter, but all she was conscious of was how his build was more lean than Van's and how he wasn't quite as tall. And that gaze of his wasn't at all warm, the way Van's could be, and there was nothing reassuring about him in the slightest. He didn't make her heart beat fast and he didn't make her want to put her arms around him and hold him. In fact, the way he was looking at her now only made her feel like she was an insect being studied with a magnifying glass.

It was good to know that it wasn't just any man who could make her feel the way Van did. Because if it had been, then Lucas would have won hands down simply due to his looks.

But it wasn't that at all.

She wasn't attracted to him, because he wasn't Van, period.

Why are you comparing them? What do you think is going to happen with Van anyway?

Chloe shook the thought away. "Where's Van?" she asked instead. "When you said he was dealing with—"

"He's coming." Lucas's gaze glittered. "A thank you would be nice."

"Thank you." Chloe let his tone slide right off of her. "How did you find me?"

"Van tracked your phone. We pinpointed you at the de Santis house, so I offered to stake the place out. Saw you come out this morning, so I let Van know I was going to get you while he handled de Santis."

A sudden, sharp fear clutched at her, though she fought it down. "What's he going to do?"

"It's already done," a deep, familiar male voice said.

A shiver coursed all the way down Chloe's spine, making her attention shift sharply to the front door.

Van had come in, shutting the front door behind him, tall and broad in that impeccably tailored dark charcoal suit. A massive, powerful presence.

Relief flooded through her, along with a different, bigger, more powerful emotion. One she didn't recognize yet made her feel like she might burst into tears.

"Finally," Lucas murmured. "I was wondering when the fuck you were going to get here. I've got better things to do than babysitting." He didn't look at Chloe as he moved toward the front door, his helmet dangling carelessly from one hand. "How did the meeting go?"

An urge gripped her, one both familiar and unfamiliar at the same time, the need to fling herself into Van's arms, reassure herself that he was here, that he was okay. Except she didn't dare, not with Lucas there.

"It went fine," Van said casually, but he didn't look at Lucas. He looked at her, a strange, intent expression in his green-gold eyes. "I need to speak with Chloe alone, Luc."

All her muscles went tight, anticipation making her heart race.

A dense, heavy silence fell.

Lucas stared at his brother, giving him one of those cold, penetrating looks, as if trying to figure out what was going on. Van said nothing, all his attention focused on Chloe.

She felt like she couldn't breathe all of a sudden.

"Okay," Lucas said eventually, when the tension had drawn to screaming point. "Suit yourself."

As soon as the door had shut behind him, Van said, "Come here."

Her heartbeat shuddered in her chest.

He could have been carved out of rock for all the expression he gave. Tall, dark, powerful. Like a mountain and just as contained. Except for the look in his eyes. It burned, a clear, deep gold.

She didn't hesitate, moving toward him then stopping right in front of him. She wanted to reach out and touch him, but something about the way he was looking at her made her hold back.

His gaze roved over her instead, intent and fierce, as if making sure she was all there. "Are you okay?" It sounded harsh, like a demand. "Did he hurt you?"

"No." It was hard to meet the intensity of that stare for some reason. "I'm fine."

"Good." He jerked his chin in the direction of the sitting room. "Let's go sit down. We need to talk."

A weird, uncertain feeling gathered in the pit of her stomach. He was acting strange. After that kiss he'd given her beside the ice rink, she'd expected . . . well, she didn't know what she'd expected, only that it wasn't this ferocious stare.

Perhaps he was pissed about her getting into de Santis's car?

"Look," she began. "About last night—"

"Go and sit down," he interrupted, not ungently.

The uncertain feeling twisted inside her. Okay then, fine. If he wanted her to go sit down where they could talk, then she'd go sit down.

She turned and went into the sitting room, seating herself on the comfortable cream sofa and folding her hands neatly in her lap.

She'd compared this room with the one in de Santis mansion when she was held there the night before, and she'd wished she was back here where it was more comfortable and homey. But right now it felt neither comfortable nor homey. Especially not when Van came in, bringing all that tension with him as he closed the door and moved over to where she sat.

He halted in front of her, folding his arms across his broad chest. "Are you sure you're not hurt?"

"I'm sure." She picked up the end of the belt on her robe and toyed with it to give her hands something to do. "He didn't physically hurt me, if that's what you're asking."

"Good." His gaze ran over her, as if he didn't quite believe her and had to check for himself. "Because if he had, I'd kill him."

The uncertainty inside her loosened just a bit. It was probably sick to like that fierce note in his voice, but she did all the same. He *had* been worried about her, hadn't he?

She let out a breath she hadn't realized she'd been holding. "I'm sorry I got into that damn limo. He just wasn't going to tell me anything unless I . . ."

Van abruptly crouched down in front of her, making her break off as he reached for her hands, lacing her chilly fingers with his warm ones. "That's not important right now." His gaze pinned her to the spot, made her forget what she'd been going to say. "De Santis has footage of us at Rockefeller Plaza. When I kissed you. I presume you know that?"

"Yes. He said he was going to use it to blackmail you if you attempted to rescue me." Her heartbeat got faster, louder. "Van, I don't know what—"

"Oh, he certainly tried to blackmail me." There was a hard cast to Van's beautiful mouth. "He failed."

Relief coursed through her. "What happened? Lucas said you had a meeting with him, but he didn't give me any details."

"I went to negotiate." He lightly rubbed his thumb over the back of her hand, the smile on his face the one she remembered from so long ago—warm and reassuring. "Or rather, to inform him that I don't give away what's mine. Especially not to people who threaten me or anyone else I care about."

"Oh." The word came out breathless, the brush of his thumb over her skin stealing all the air from her lungs. Making her feel needy and so aware that it had been a whole twelve hours since she'd touched him, and that that was twelve hours too long.

"You know what else is mine?" he went on in that steady voice, his thumbs stroking the backs of her hands over and over. "You are, Chloe. You and the company are both mine and I'm not handing either of you over to anyone ever again."

The words took a second to sink in. Wait, what? She was his? What did that mean?

Yet even as her brain rushed to catch up, her heart had already made the leap, throwing itself off the edge of the cliff, tumbling end over end, falling like a stone.

This wasn't supposed to happen. You weren't going to fall for him.

She swallowed, trying to get some air, the thought resounding in her head like an echo. What? Fall for him? No, she hadn't fallen for him. She hadn't.

"Here's what's going to happen," Van continued, as if

he hadn't just thrown her into absolute chaos. "I'm leaving the military, effective immediately, and I'm taking control of Tate Oil. Once the footage of you and me hits the internet, it'll be the final straw for my superiors, which pretty much means my career in the Navy is screwed. They didn't like me being the Tate heir anyway, and that footage will put the final nail in the coffin." His thumbs began to move in small, light circles. "Now, Tate Oil management won't be happy once they see that footage either, but"— he paused, the intent look in his eyes becoming even more certain—"I have a plan for how to handle that."

Her mouth felt dry, full of cotton, and she wasn't sure why. "What plan?"

"People are going to be shocked when they find out you and I have been having an affair. People are going to be appalled. Dad's adopted kids screwing around and playing with his money, yeah, it's going to look really bad. The press will be a nightmare and I can't have that."

She wanted to pull her hands away, put some space between them, because that feeling in her chest, the sound of her heart falling into the chasm, was overwhelming and she couldn't think. But the way he was stroking her, gentle and warm, sucked all the strength right out of her.

"Van," she began thickly.

"It's okay, pretty." His thumbs pressed lightly on the backs of her hands. "I'll protect you. I keep my promises, remember?"

"How? I mean . . . what are you going to do?"

There was gold in his eyes, gleaming bright. "I'm going to marry you, Chloe. That's what I'm going to do."

Van watched as Chloe's dark chocolatey eyes went wide, shock moving over her small, delicate features.

"*Marry* me?" Her voice sounded hoarse. "You can't be serious?"

He tightened his fingers around hers, feeling her skin chill and instinctively chafing it to warm it up. "Of course I'm serious. You really think I'd joke about something like that?"

Color had risen to her cheeks. "Van, that's . . . crazy."

Okay, so she was shocked. He'd expected that. It *did* sound crazy. But once he explained, she'd see that it made sense. That it was the logical step to keep both her and the company safe.

Hell, even if she didn't see that, surely she'd accept that this was also a good answer for her emotionally. She would be his, which meant she could move to New York if she wanted to, live with him here at the Tate mansion. Or hell, he could come out and visit her in Wyoming whenever he got a moment. But one thing he was certain of was that she'd never be lonely again, not if he could help it.

He stared at her, running his gaze over her once again to make sure she was okay, that de Santis, the prick, hadn't hurt her. She'd obviously just had a shower and he could smell damp skin and soap, and he wanted to put his mouth right at her pale throat where her pulse was beating fast and hard.

Christ, already the need for her was running through him like electricity through high tension wires, humming, vibrating. The need to pull her into his arms, touch her, hold her. Crush that lovely mouth beneath his and taste her.

He nearly had the moment he'd walked into the Tate mansion and seen her standing on the stairs, an intense powerful emotion crashing through the military calm that he'd maintained since leaving de Santis's place swamping him.

She'd been swathed in the gray robe he'd used a couple of times, looking so small and vulnerable, her hair in a damp black tangle down her back, and her face pale. And he'd had to hold himself absolutely still so he didn't cross the space between them and catch her in his arms, hold her close, and breathe her in. Reassure himself that she was actually here and whole and unhurt.

He couldn't, not with Lucas standing there staring a hole right through him. Jesus, the guy was going to have an aneurysm when Van got around to telling him what he intended to do with Chloe, no question.

Right now though, there was nothing between him and the woman sitting on the couch. And no one standing there watching them. They were alone.

He suddenly wanted to pull open the tie of the robe, push apart the edges of it, see if she was naked underneath. Touch her, show her all the ways she was his . . .

Settle the fuck down. There'll be time for that.

Yeah, there would. First, he needed to talk.

"It's not crazy," he said, forcing himself to limit his touch to that steady, reassuring stroke over the backs of her hands. "I told you, once it gets out that you and I are having an affair, it's going to be a goddamn media circus."

The color in her cheeks vanished. "I'm sorry. Perhaps if I hadn't suggested we meet—"

"No," he interrupted softly, not wanting to waste time with recriminations when the situation they had to deal with was the only thing that mattered. "Don't go getting into that. What's done is done. We can't change it. The only thing we can do is deal with the consequences. Hell, that was my fault anyway. I shouldn't have kissed you and I did."

She looked down at their intertwined hands, her cheeks still pale. "He told me he'd give me the answers if I came with him, so I had to go. There wasn't any time to tell you what was happening and . . . underneath all that I just wanted to meet my father. Talk to him face to face."

Van stilled his thumbs on her skin, tightening his fingers around hers. "He's your family, of course."

Her gaze lifted to his abruptly. "No," she said, a familiar glow in her dark eyes. "He's no family of mine."

Perhaps that shouldn't have made him feel as good as it did, because clearly being kidnapped by de Santis hadn't exactly been pleasant for her. Yet he felt pleased all the same. He didn't want her finding a family with that asshole, not when she had one right here with him.

"He told me stuff," Chloe went on, the glow in her eyes getting brighter. "He wants the company, Van. That's always been what he's after."

"Yes, I know," he said gently. "Which is why we need to talk about you becoming my wife."

She stared at him. "Why?"

For some reason he found the blunt question irritating. "What do you mean why? You don't agree?"

Her hands had gone still in his. "I guess I don't understand what the point of it is."

He frowned. Hadn't he explained clearly enough? "The point is to keep you safe. To protect you from the media. It'll be better when it comes to the company too, since people are already pissed about how Dad fired the board and put me and Wolf and Lucas in their place. If they find out you and I have been screwing around, it's going to make the situation even worse." He found his gaze lingering on the curve of her bottom lip, so soft and full. He couldn't look away.

"So, this is all about keeping me safe and protecting the company then?"

"Not entirely." All it would take to kiss her would be to pull her hands toward him and for him to lean forward. That beautiful mouth would be right there. "I can't imagine people at the ranch will be all that impressed, so this will protect your position there, should you want to go back. Plus, we've got some great chemistry too, don't you think?"

"What do you mean 'should I want to go back'? Of course I want to go back. That was the whole point."

The small thread of irritation wound tighter. "Chloe." He tried to keep his impatience out of his tone, because time was ticking and he didn't need her getting cold feet. "The ranch doesn't matter right now. We have to make a decision on this and quickly, because de Santis is going to release that footage and we have to have an answer ready. So, what's the issue?"

Her chin came up at that, her gaze darker than midnight. "I thought you wanted to go back to the military. That's what you kept saying. That I was a responsibility you didn't want anyway, and once you'd neutralized de Santis you were going back to base."

There was something in her tone he couldn't quite figure out, which didn't help his temper. "Yeah, I know what I said, but I changed my mind, okay? It's not like we have a lot of other options."

"Great, so you're marrying me because you don't have any other options."

This time he heard the hurt in her voice loud and clear. "No," he said flatly, inwardly cursing because it was obvious he wasn't explaining himself very well. "It's not only that. You don't have to go back to the ranch, not if you don't want to. You can stay here with me. Or I'll come and see you in Wyoming, whatever you like. Point is, you won't have to be alone anymore, okay? I'll be there for you, Chloe."

There was a flush in her cheeks now, a glow in her eyes. But it wasn't because she was happy, he knew that. "So you're giving up your military career, giving up basically everything, so that poor little Chloe doesn't have to be alone anymore. Do you know how pathetic that makes me sound?"

"That's not—"

"And then there's the fact that you're assuming I want to move to New York, when for the past week you've known how important the ranch is to me and how much I want to be back there. And we won't even go into how you, dropping in to visit whenever you damn well feel like it, isn't at all like Dad only bothering to come when he had the time. Which he never did." Her voice had become sharper, that note of pain like the edge of a knife beneath the anger.

Christ, he really *had* handled this badly.

Van firmed his grip on her hands, engulfing those cold, slender fingers in his. "You're not pathetic. And it wouldn't be like that. I have to be here for the company, but there's no reason that at some point down the track I couldn't come out to Wyoming on a semi-permanent basis. You could visit me in New York whenever you wanted anyway. I'm not going to keep you like some goddamn princess in a tower like Dad did."

But the look in her eyes didn't even flicker. "That's not what I meant."

"What did you mean then?"

"I don't want to be another mission you didn't ask for." The expression on her face was suddenly fierce. "I don't want to be a responsibility you didn't want. And I'm certainly not going to marry you because of some damn media storm or the fact that you don't want me to be lonely."

Instantly, tension gathered between his shoulder blades, a familiar possessive feeling rising inside him. Of all the times for her to get stubborn . . . He had to concentrate not to crush her fingers in his, pull her violently forward to take her mouth, kiss the denial away.

Okay, so he understood why this might be a problem for her, but couldn't she see that this was the best way to handle their situation? Not wanting to marry him didn't change the fact that the footage was still out there and they couldn't stop de Santis from releasing it.

Besides, he wasn't simply marrying her to protect her from the media or to stop her from being lonely. He wanted her too. Didn't that count for something?

"You're not a mission and you're not a responsibility." He struggled to keep the possessiveness out of his voice. "I want you, Chloe."

"I know you do." Her gaze burned into his. "But wanting isn't enough."

"What the fuck does that mean? What more is there?"

Her throat moved, her pulse beating fast beneath her delicate pale skin. "Tell me something. If none of this had happened, if there was no footage, if there was no de Santis. If there was just you and me, would you still be here in front of me, holding my hands and asking me to marry you?"

His impatience gathered tighter. "There's no point in what-ifs. That's not the reality. We have to deal with the situation as it is, not how we want it to be."

As soon as the words came out of his mouth he knew he'd said the wrong thing, because Chloe's expression abruptly closed up like a fan. "Yeah, and that's why my answer is no."

A hot, raw emotion twisted inexplicably inside him. "Jesus Christ, why not? Can't you see that this is the best decision for both of us?"

"No, Van. It's the best decision for you."

He stared at her. "What the fuck do you mean by that?"

"This scandal isn't going to affect me as much as you think it will. Yes, the ranch might be a problem, but everyone there knows me. They'll understand once I explain it to them. And as for the media, I don't care about them."

"Yes, but—"

"Don't kid yourself that this is about my protection,"

she cut him off. "This is about that girl you failed to save, isn't it? This is about being the perfect Tate heir. About Dad and living up to his standards."

He was holding her hands tightly—probably too tightly—but he couldn't bring himself to let her go. There was a hot ember of anger glowing inside him at the way she'd managed to home in on the most painful topics possible. Fuck, he should *never* have told her about Sofia or about Noah. Not if she was going to bring them up to use against him.

"That's got *nothing* to do with it," he growled. "Fucking nothing."

But the look on her face didn't change, stubborn and fierce. "Yes it has. And if you think it hasn't, you're fooling yourself."

He stared at her, furious at her point-blank refusal, the one possibility he hadn't expected in this whole scenario. "What the fuck do you want from me then?" he demanded. "What the fuck do you expect me to do?"

And in that moment he saw it, the way her mouth became soft and vulnerable, making his chest hurt for reasons he couldn't name.

"What do I want from you?" she echoed. "What any girl expects when a man asks her to marry him." There was a slight tremble in her voice. "I want you to tell me you love me."

Relief pulsed through him. Fuck, was that all?

"I do love you." He kept her fingers tight in his. "I always have. Surely you know that?"

Yet that vulnerable cast to her mouth didn't change. "No you don't. Not the way I'm talking about. Because if you did, you would have married me, de Santis footage or not."

The simple way she said it infuriated him. Hit him somewhere painful, a part of himself he'd thought he'd kept very well defended.

He had no idea what kind of love she meant, because if it was the kind of acid-drip love that Noah had given him, the kind that ate away at you, left you hollow and empty, left you doubting yourself, that made you wonder if you'd done enough, tried hard enough, then she was shit out of luck. He didn't do that kind of love. Not anymore.

"You don't need love," he growled. "All you need is this."

And he pulled her hands to him, leaned forward, and covered her mouth with his.

CHAPTER NINETEEN

Chloe's heartbeat went through the roof the moment Van's lips touched hers, the seductive heat and wicked taste of him blanking her brain completely. Making her forget the great, yawning gulf that had opened up inside her the moment he'd asked her to marry him. And the anger that had knotted tight when he'd refused to understand.

It had only been in that moment that she knew what she wanted. What she'd always wanted, even back when she'd been sixteen.

Him. She wanted him.

But not like this. Not forced into it because of some stupid video he had to protect himself from or because she was a responsibility that had been given to him, a mission he had to complete.

She wanted him to marry her because he loved her. Because she was important to him, more important than anything else. And most of all, because she loved him in return. She knew it. Felt it curling deep in her bones.

She'd told herself that she'd gotten rid of those old, obsessive sixteen-year-old feelings. But the truth was that they'd always been there, left over from the summer he'd taught her how to ride, standing strong like the foundations of an old, abandoned house almost lost beneath a tangled wild garden. His encouraging smile. His hands on her waist, his grip firm, reassuring. And being in New York with him, having him right here, touching her, gradually dropping his guard with her and giving her little pieces of himself . . .

Yeah, that house wasn't abandoned anymore and it wasn't only foundations now either. She'd put in some walls, some windows; put in doors. A roof even. She'd rebuilt it completely. And now all it needed was someone to live in it with her.

Van.

Except it looked like he only wanted to patrol the perimeter of her house, not come inside, let alone make it his. Which was pretty much exactly what Noah had done.

She couldn't live like that again, not now that she knew what it was like to be with someone without fear of holding back. Someone who took her passion and celebrated it, stoked it higher, met it with his own. Someone who held her while she wept and someone who let her hold him in return.

She didn't want to go back to that place she'd been in when she'd gotten here, forcing everything she felt way down deep inside her because she was too afraid to let it out in case she pushed people away.

No, she couldn't do it.

This time she wanted his love and she wasn't settling for anything less.

She tried to tear her mouth away, but he moved, coming up out of his crouch in a fluid movement, dropping her hands to tangle his fingers in her hair. Then he reached for her chin with his other hand, gripping it, his thumb pushing her bottom lip down, opening up her mouth so he could deepen the kiss.

Chloe shuddered as the flavor of him flooded her senses, his tongue sliding in, exploring. It was so good to taste him, so good to have his lips on hers. She wanted to reach for him, touch him, let her passion free and give him whatever he wanted . . .

But no. She couldn't give in.

He'd said he loved her, but he didn't. Not the way she wanted him to. Because if he had, that security footage wouldn't have mattered to him. He wouldn't have come back with bullshit about "the reality" and how "we have to deal with the situation how it is, not how we want it to be."

No, if he'd loved her, he would have said yes, of course he would have married her anyway. And he hadn't.

Which meant she couldn't agree to this marriage, and if he was using sex to try and convince her, he was shit out of luck.

Chloe didn't move, didn't try to pull away or shove him. He was leaning over her, holding her still as he explored her mouth, deep and hot and so blindingly erotic it was all she could do to not respond.

She clenched her hands in her lap, driving her nails into her palms, forcing herself to remain there passively until he'd finished. Until he'd gotten the message.

Sure enough, he pulled away, staring at her. His breathing had accelerated, the molten gold of his eyes brilliant. "Chloe . . ." Her name in that soft sensual rumble made her shiver, his fingers on her chin a firm pressure. "Don't say no. It would be so good, pretty thing. You could live here with me, share my room. Share my bed." He leaned forward, letting go of her hair, bracing himself with a hand on the back of the couch, his big, hard body looming over her. Releasing her chin, he trailed his fingers down her throat in a light caress that sent ripples of electricity cascading all over her skin. "And anytime you needed to feel good, all you'd have to do is ask. Any time you want me, I'd be there for you. I'd never leave you lonely." He went lower, brushing over the front of her robe to the tie at her waist. "I'd never leave you wanting."

Oh God. She had to get him to stop. She couldn't give in, she couldn't.

"No." She put her hand over where his fingers were toying with the knot at her waist. "I can't. I won't."

He went very still, staring down at her, his hand beneath hers motionless. But there was something in his eyes, in the strong lines of his beautiful face. Something hot, possessive . . . desperate.

He leaned down, brushing his lips against hers. "I want you," he whispered, then turned his head, his mouth grazing the sensitive skin beneath her ear, sending another electric shiver through her. "I want you so much." His breath ghosted over her, the heat of his body leaning over her sending cracks all through the walls of her defenses. "And I think you want me too."

She tried to be like granite, like steel. Ignoring the soft touch of his mouth as it trailed down the side of her neck. "You're right. I do." The words were hoarse and thick. "But I don't need you."

"Bullshit." He shifted, pulling aside the neckline of her robe. "You need me as badly as I need you." His lips found the hollows of her collarbones, beginning to explore, tasting her skin.

Chloe swallowed, her heartbeat almost deafening. The light touch of his mouth made goose bumps rise everywhere, and it was next to impossible to think. There was a pulse inside her, an ache, her nipples hardening, pressing against the soft fabric of her robe.

Yes, you do. You do need him.

"No." The words were a breath. "I don't."

But he must have heard the uncertainty in her voice, undermining everything she'd said like rust eating into metal. Because he didn't stop, pushing the neckline of her robe further so it was nearly off her shoulder, baring more of her skin to his mouth.

His hand moved at her waist, pulling at the ties of her robe. "Tell me your nipples aren't hard," he whispered as the fabric loosened around her. "Tell me you're not wet for me, aching for me."

She needed to get away from him, yet somehow she wasn't moving. Somehow she was letting him tug aside the edges of her robe, letting him spread it open entirely, baring her naked body to his gaze.

Her breath was coming faster now, her mouth dry. He was looking at her, but she couldn't look back because if she did, if she met his gaze, everything would be lost.

"Yes." Approval warmed his deep voice. "I was right." His fingers trailed down over the swell of one breast and she shuddered helplessly as they brushed over her sensitized nipple, making it harden even further. "You're such a passionate little thing. You do need me badly, don't you?"

She turned her face away, as if by doing that she could shut him out, shut out the things he was saying to her, the truth she didn't want to acknowledge. But his hand curved, cupping her breast in his palm, his thumb lazily circling her nipple, sending yet another helpless shudder of reaction through her.

God, the bastard was using sex to get her to change her mind, and the hell of it was that it just might work. Because who else could do this to her? Who else could make her feel this way? No one and she knew it.

"It's not just about sex." She had to force herself to speak. "Hell, I could get this from anyone. I don't actually need it from you."

It was such a lie and yet the hand on her breast stilled, a different kind of tension gathering between them. A dangerous tension.

Oh God. Why had she said that?

She kept her face averted, her breathing getting even faster, her heartbeat thumping so loud he must have felt it as he cupped her soft flesh. There was a kind of electricity in her blood, a fierce anticipation. As if she was sixteen again, staring at him as she rode past, issuing that unspoken challenge, that race back to the ranch. And the thrill she'd felt as he'd spurred his horse after her . . .

You know why you said it.

Of course she did. It was a challenge, pure and simple. She wanted him to prove it to her. Wanted him to make it clear to her that she *couldn't* get this from any other man. That only he would make her feel this way, as if she were a lit torch and only he could douse the flames.

Wanted him to prove that maybe this was enough. That his touch and his promises to protect her were all she needed after all . . .

You know it won't be.

She shut her eyes and ignored the thought, the sound of her harsh breaths loud in the space between them.

He said nothing, but his hand flexed, his fingers spreading out on her breast, his thumb beginning to rub lightly back and forth over her nipple.

The sensation was exquisite, making the breath catch audibly in her throat, making her desperate to pull away and yet desperate to stay exactly where she was.

His fingers moved again, lightly pinching her hardened nipple, tearing a gasp from her, the electricity firing in a direct hot line straight down between her thighs.

"You really think so?" The words sounded casual and yet there was a deep rasp to them that had her nearly trembling. "You really think you could get this with another man?" Another pinch, gentle and somehow all the more painful for it. "Perhaps I should call one? Call up one of my buddies and get him to join us?" Warm breath against her bare skin, the rough prickle of his stubble on her sensitized flesh. "Would you like that, pretty? Would you like someone else's hands on you?" A hot mouth covered her nipple all of a sudden, sucking hard, and she groaned, arching against the back of the couch, helpless to stop the burst of wild pleasure that went through her. Then just as suddenly it was gone.

"Would you like someone else's mouth doing that to you?" His breath again, ghosting over her damp skin. "Sucking on your nipples? Making you moan?"

She was panting now, and his lips were again near the base of her throat, brushing over her, the most delicious chills chasing everywhere. His hand slid from her breast, moving lower, over her stomach, making all her muscles clench tightly in response.

"Would you like someone else to touch you"—his fingers pushed even lower, tangling in the damp curls between her thighs—"right here?" His thumb pressed down lightly, right on her clit.

Another spike of hot pleasure hit her and she sagged back against the couch, her resistance ebbing, the need to spread her legs, let him do whatever he wanted to her so acute she almost couldn't bear it.

His thumb moved in a slow circle around the achingly sensitive nub of flesh, his mouth moving unhurriedly to her breast again, the rough lick of his tongue on her nipple drawing a needy sound from her.

"I can do it," he murmured softly. "I can call them right now. I'm sure you won't mind. Not when you can get this from anyone, right?"

She was shaking now, and behind her closed lids there were stars. The pleasure was gathering tighter and tighter, his fingers moving lazily on her slick flesh as if he had all the time in the world.

"Yes or no, pretty." One finger lightly stroked the length of her sex then circled around her entrance, almost but not quite sliding inside. "Do you want another man right now?"

Of course she didn't. All she wanted was him. And now she couldn't stop her hips from lifting, searching for a firmer touch, more friction. But he refused to give it to her.

"Uh-uh," he chided, the rasp in his voice getting deeper. "Keep still. You're not getting anything until you give me an answer." His finger glided up the wet folds of her sex, finding her clit, brushing over it, making her moan yet again. "You're not going to come until you admit that it has to be me touching you, me inside you. Me and no one else."

His touch couldn't be denied. It was breaking her down into small, quivering pieces, cementing the knowledge deep in her soul that there was only one person who could put her back together again. Only one person who could *ever* make her whole.

"Van," she whispered, unable to stop herself. "Please."

"No." He nuzzled against her breast, that maddening hand between her legs stroking her gently. "Those aren't the words I want to hear."

She kept her eyes tightly shut, struggling against the pull of inexorable pleasure, trying not to give in to the seduction of his touch, to the heat that pervaded her, stretching all her nerve endings as tight as high tension wires.

He must've been leaning over her, because she could feel him, his body, hot and hard and mere inches away. Too far, too far. . . . She wanted his skin against hers, his hands on her. His cock pushing deep inside her.

It's not enough and you know it.

But she ignored the little voice, concentrating instead on the unbelievable pleasure as he eased a finger slowly inside her, making her hips jerk and her spine bow.

"Tell me you need me, Chloe." His hot breath against

her nipple again, his thumb pressing down on her clit. "Give me the words and I'll let you come."

She shivered and shook, the words spilling out of her, helplessly, hopelessly. "I need . . . you." Small, harsh scrapes of sound. "I need you, V-Van."

He growled deep in his throat, the vibration of it echoing against her skin. "Yes," he murmured, the satisfaction in the word, the sheer triumph of it making her ache. "Of course you do." He slid another finger inside her and this time she didn't hold back, spreading her legs to give him greater access, tilting her hips to allow him to slide deeper. "Me and only me, pretty." His fingers pulled back then slid back in again, twisting to hit a place inside her that made the stars behind her eyes burst into showers of light. "Because you're mine."

She'd stopped trying to be quiet, stopped trying to resist. Yes, of course she was his. She always had been.

"What are you, Chloe?" His fingers hit that place again, his thumb on her clit adding another bright shard of pleasure to the mix. "*Whose* are you?"

"Yours." It was the only answer she had left. "I'm yours."

"Yes," he growled, the possessive rasp she'd only heard hints of before, now loud and clear. "Yes, you fucking are."

Then he closed his mouth around her nipple, sucking it in deep, and pressed down hard on her clit. Making the stars behind her eyes go nova.

Making her scream.

Van could feel her pussy clamp down hard around his fingers, her body convulsing as the orgasm swept over her. She sobbed, arching up into him as if searching for more.

Savage satisfaction clenched like a fist in his chest and he gave her nipple a last lick, raising his head and looking down at her. She'd slumped against the back of the couch, her eyes closed, her mouth slightly open. The robe had slipped entirely off one of her shoulders, the edges of it wide open, exposing her delicate curves and pale skin. Though she didn't look so pale anymore, pleasure giving her a rosy flush all over her body.

She was the most beautiful thing he'd ever seen and she was his.

And now they both knew it.

He eased his fingers out of her and she shivered, her eyes suddenly opening. They were the color of the sky at midnight out on the ranch, where no city light could wash the stars away. Thick, black velvet, dark and deep.

Holding that midnight gaze, he lifted his fingers to his mouth and licked them, tasting the delicious salt and musk flavor of her, watching as her pupils dilated even more.

He should have stopped when she'd told him she wouldn't marry him, he knew that. When she'd told him she wanted love, he should have gotten up and let her go. But he hadn't.

Instead everything in him had tightened in instant denial. She didn't need the painful sack of lies that was love. She could have this instead, all the pleasure she could handle. Pleasure didn't hurt—at least not unless you wanted it to—and it didn't demand anything from you but participation.

But then she'd said that it wasn't about sex, that she could get that from anyone, and well . . . If that hadn't been a challenge he didn't know what was, and he couldn't let it stand.

She *couldn't* get this from anyone else and she had to understand that. He had to prove it to her. And he had. Pretty conclusively he'd thought.

She needed him and only him.

Van didn't question the territorial urge that rose inside

him, the primitive desire to hammer his point home and underline it in blazing red. The primal need to make her see that there was no point denying him, no point holding out against him.

That she was his, pure and simple.

Why did she need all this love bullshit when she had him and the pleasure he could give her? She was such a little sensualist, she didn't need anything else, surely?

He straightened, lifting his hands to the buttons of his shirt and ripping them open, shrugging out of the cotton and letting it fall. 'You will marry me, Chloe," he said. "And I'll make you come like that every night." He got rid of his shoes then unfastened his pants, pulling down the zipper, his cock so fucking hard it almost hurt. "You won't ever need anything else, I promise you."

She simply stared at him, currents and tides shifting in the darkness of her eyes, watching as he shoved his pants and underwear down, and stepped out of them, open hunger tightening her features.

Yeah, she needed him all right, so why she'd been so hell-bent on denying him, he didn't know.

Getting out his wallet, he pulled a condom packet from it, tore it open, and rolled the latex over his dick.

Then he reached for her, turning her onto her front then bringing her down so she was kneeling on the floor between him and the couch, pressing her forward over the cushions.

Need for her was like the beat of his pulse, steady and relentless, an inexorable pull, but he didn't want her silence or her stillness. He wanted her soft, husky voice telling him she needed him. Telling him that only he could make her feel this way, that it was only him she craved.

He would give her all of it. All of it and more. Make her forget about the hard, painful thing called love that he had no intention of giving her—of giving anyone. Make her desperate for the pleasure that he could instead.

She lay still, bent over the couch cushions, her arms lying on the cream linen, black hair all thick and glossy over her shoulders. So beautiful she made everything inside him tighten.

He knelt behind her, reaching forward to slide his arms around her, gathering her to him so her spine was pressed against the length of his torso. She felt so soft, so hot, and yet so fragile. Christ, he wanted to eat her alive.

Flexing his hips, he eased his aching dick against the softness of her ass, loving the give of her flesh as he did so.

"Talk to me, pretty." He nuzzled against her neck, giving her a feel of his teeth against her skin, nipping at her, tasting her skin, hungry for something he didn't have words for. "Tell me how much you want me."

"I want you." She gave in to him with no hesitation this time. "I want you, Van. So much."

The words should have soothed the hot, possessive thing inside him, should have made him feel better, and yet for some reason they didn't. They only made it feel even hotter, even more possessive.

He slid his hands up to cup her beautiful tits, teasing her nipples with his thumbs, and she stiffened. "Tell me you need me." He pressed his mouth to the side of her neck then bit down a little. "Tell me there's no one else for you but me."

She arched back against him, lifting her breasts into his palms. "I need you," she said huskily. "Oh God . . . Van. There's no one else but you.'

Again, it should have been enough. Yet it wasn't.

The possessiveness deepened, threaded through with a kind of desperation, a searching hunger that had him easing her forward and putting his hand on the back of her neck, pushing her head down onto the couch cushions, holding her still so she couldn't protest and couldn't escape. So she would know how completely she was at his mercy, in his power.

But she didn't resist. She merely turned her head to the side so her cheek rested against the cream linen, accepting him. Her black hair was tumbling down her back, her skin even paler than the upholstery of the couch, her spine an elegant curve.

He had the sudden, intense feeling that she should be fighting him the way she normally did, that she should be pushing back against him, doing *something*, not simply giving in like this. Not doing everything she was told.

His heartbeat began to ramp up, the scent of her skin and her hair clouding his senses, the feel of her against his fingertips stinging like a burn.

He lifted a hand, stroking it down her spine, feeling her small, fragile bones and the satin of her skin, watching as she shuddered beneath his touch.

This was what he wanted, her on her knees and naked in front of him, telling him exactly what he wanted to hear. So why wasn't it enough?

The possessiveness growled deep inside.

"You'll marry me, won't you?" He couldn't make it sound like anything less like a demand, though he kept his touch on her back light.

Her lashes had fallen closed, lying thick and soft on her cheekbones. "Yes." It was little more than a whisper. "I will."

Again, it should have made him feel triumphant and satisfied. In control. In charge. Yet it felt more like something was slipping through his fingers. Something very, very precious.

"Chloe," he said hoarsely, though he didn't know quite

why. "Chloe . . ." He slid his arms around her, the soft curve of her ass pressing against the hard ridge of his cock, as if pulling her closer would bridge the weird sense of distance he felt opening up between them.

She was so warm, the thick fan of lashes on her cheeks fluttering, and she gasped as he slid his fingers down her stomach, cupping her pussy in his palm.

Christ, she was so wet, so hot. And all for him.

His fingers almost shook as he stroked them through her slick folds, feeling her legs quiver as he did so. She was slippery, her clit hard as a button as he brushed his fingers over it, her hips jerking in response.

Yeah, this was all exactly as he'd wanted. So why the fuck did he keep feeling as if there was distance between them? As if the more he told her she was his, the less she actually was?

Why does that matter?

Maybe it didn't. Maybe all that mattered was that he close that distance any way he could.

He took his hand away from between her legs and gripped his cock, shifting so he could rub the head of his dick all through the slick folds of her pussy and over that hard little clit, making her squirm and gasp and pant beneath him.

Making her burn like he was burning, making her as desperate as he was.

Only when she was trembling so hard it was as if she was going to come apart, did he grip her hips and position himself. Then he eased the head of his cock inside her, the feel of her pussy stretching to admit him then squeezing down hard on him making them both groan.

Ah, *fuck*, this was good. She was damn hot. She was going to kill him.

Chloe's hands were spread out on the couch cushions,

her fingers clutching onto the fabric, her eyes closed tight. Her hips flexed, urging him deeper, but he didn't move, holding himself back.

He was going to take this slow, he was going to blow her fucking mind.

She gave a groan. "Van . . . please . . ."

Ignoring her, he leaned forward, spreading one arm out so it rested on the couch cushions alongside hers while sliding the other around her waist to anchor her against him. He covered her entirely so that there was nothing between them, not even air.

Then he began to move, drawing out then sliding back in, taking it slow and deep, relishing the tight clasp of her pussy around him, the scent of her shampoo, soap and feminine musk soaking the air around him.

She quivered, her hips trying to keep pace with his. "Oh . . . God . . ."

It sounded desperate. Fuck, *he* was desperate too.

He lifted one hand to the back of her neck and swept aside her hair, pressing his mouth to her vulnerable nape, tasting her skin.

There was no distance now and nothing between them, yet he kept his arm like an iron bar around her waist, holding her hot little body close as he moved faster, deeper. Because it still felt like it wasn't enough, that there could be more, he just had to get closer.

She was making soft, desperate sounds, shoving herself back onto him, arching her back as if that would increase the contact somehow. She'd dropped one hand onto his thigh, using it to brace herself, her fingers digging into muscle. He fucking loved that. Loved how she clung to him, loved how she twisted and strained beneath him, desperate for whatever he gave her.

How could he give this up? How could he let her go?

He couldn't. He couldn't ever.

"Van . . ." she pleaded hoarsely. "Van . . . please . . ."

"It's okay, pretty," he murmured. "I know. I'm here." Keeping her pinned tightly against him, he slid his free hand around and down between her thighs, finding her clit. Making her buck and jerk and shake as he stroked her, as he continued to thrust deep inside her.

He'd make her come so hard she'd forget everything but this pleasure. Everything but the need to have it over and over again. Everything but him.

"Oh, God." she whispered. "Oh God, *Van* . . ."

He pinched her clit, driving into her as deep as he could go, leaning over her and watching her deeply flushed face against the cushions, the pleasure beginning to do its work on him too.

Holy fucking Christ, he wanted this to last forever.

Chloe gave a little sob. "I love you," she said.

And came.

CHAPTER TWENTY

She hadn't meant to say it, the words just slipped out. She simply hadn't been able to keep them inside any longer. All he had to do was touch her and she'd cave, crumble like a sandcastle before a wave, swamped by pleasure, by the feel of his body over hers and his hands touching her. By his heat, the rain and forest scent of him, the way he moved inside her, the way he covered her.

It was impossible to try to keep out a man like Sullivan Tate. He took what he wanted, and what he wanted was her. And she couldn't resist him. It was futile.

She needed too much, just like she always had. Needed what he was giving her, all that warmth and sensuality, all the passion that had been missing from her life. The passion she didn't know if she had the strength to give up.

Even though she'd sworn to herself she wouldn't let herself be so desperate for someone again, she couldn't help it. She loved him, and if he wanted her to marry him, then she'd do it.

Maybe it didn't matter if he didn't love her. Maybe he was right, that they didn't need love. They had this and maybe this was enough. She'd managed well enough without the connection to Noah she'd longed for, so why shouldn't she be able to do the same with Van?

The aftershocks of her orgasm were pulsing through

her, so it took her a little while to realize that he wasn't moving. She panted, feeling the pressure of his cock buried deep inside her, the intense heat of his muscled body at her back.

Oh God, had he heard her?

He didn't say anything and after a while, he began to move again, his hips pulling back, his cock slowly drawing out of her before slamming back in again, making her clutch the couch cushions as a hot stab of pleasure echoed through her.

She shivered. He was going to make her come again, wasn't he?

His massive body was a hard, hot wall at her back, his arm around her waist like steel, keeping her pinned against him. She shut her eyes, her breathing accelerating, her body shaking as his rhythm picked up.

He moved harder, the sound of his flesh meeting hers loud in the room, and sure enough the helpless, aching pleasure began to wind tighter and tighter again, making her moan against the fabric of the cushions.

It was as if he was on a mission to give her as much pleasure as he could, and God help her, she knew how single-minded he was when it came to completing his missions. He let nothing stand in his way.

It felt so good. *He* felt so good. And when he moved, putting one hand over hers where it clutched at the couch and sliding the other between her thighs again, it felt even better. He began to stroke her clit, timing it with his thrusts, and she was flying over the edge a second time, even before she'd had a chance to think about it, sobbing as the pleasure exploded through her.

And he didn't stop, he kept driving himself into her, over and over again, his fingers sliding all over and around her sex, building her up yet again.

"I can't give you anything," he murmured, hot and

rough in her ear. "I can't give you anything but this, understand?" He drew out, thrust in. "But that's all you'll need, pretty." Another withdrawal, another hard thrust. "I'll make sure you'll never know the difference."

Oh, Jesus, he *had* heard her.

Her throat constricted and a small, fierce part of her wanted to tell him that was wrong, that *she'd* know the difference, that he was an arrogant son of a bitch to think he could tell her what she did and didn't need. But she had no breath left, her voice too cracked and hoarse to explain.

All she could do was whisper "Yes" against the cushions as his hands and his cock began to work their magic on her again, another orgasm on the cusp of exploding inside her. And she screamed "Yes" when it hit, shaking as it began to tear her apart, sobbing the word over and over as she lost herself in the storm.

Dimly she felt him behind her, moving faster and faster, getting wild, losing control, his hands over both of hers now, their fingers interlaced. Then a hoarse roar in her ear, his body stiffening, his fingers clenching as the orgasm came for him too.

She didn't move as he slumped against her, his body covering hers completely like a big, hot blanket. Making her feel safe, as if she could lie here beneath him forever and everything would be okay.

As if he was right, and she didn't need love. All she needed was him.

Soon enough, though, he moved away, his withdrawal from her feeling like a loss, the air across her bare back making her shiver. Behind her she could hear the rustle of clothing and the sound of him moving out of the room.

She swallowed, her mouth dry. Her knees hurt too, and she was cold, and when she finally forced herself to her feet, her muscles ached. Her sex throbbed, feeling raw, and somehow her heart was raw too, tender and painful in her chest.

Bending to pick up her robe, she found her hands were shaking.

"Let me do that." Van's deep voice came from behind her, the sound of it like a shock of cold water over blistered skin, and then he was helping her back into the robe, turning her around to face him as he wrapped it around her and tied it close.

"I thought you'd gone," she said thickly, her legs feeling wobbly.

"Just getting rid of the condom." He scooped her up in his arms, took a couple of steps to the couch, and sat her down on it. Then he turned away, bending to pick up his own clothes, dressing himself in a series of short, efficient movements.

She watched him, an uncomfortable, unsettled silence filling the room.

Was there something wrong? He wasn't looking at her, his face averted as he began to do up his shirt, his gaze directed at his hands.

"Shall . . . we go upstairs?" she asked haltingly. "I mean . . . I don't mind. Though maybe I could have something to eat before we do anything else. I kind of missed breakfast."

His hands dropped from the buttons and suddenly he looked at her, the intensity in his green-gold eyes taking her breath away. "Why did you say that?"

"Why did I say what?"

"That you loved me."

She could feel her cheeks heat. She hadn't meant to say it, in fact those old, forgotten instincts had her fighting hard not to, to not reveal herself so completely. But now he was here, standing in front of her, an intense look on his beautiful face, demanding to know why, and . . . she couldn't lie. Not about this.

She meant it. She'd meant it with every breath in her. And even though he'd already made it clear he wasn't going to give it back to her, she couldn't deny it, not to him and not to herself. Her days of pretending were over.

Chloe held his gaze. "Because I do."

"Why?" It was barked like an order, a muscle ticking in the side of his jaw.

"Why shouldn't I love you?" She lifted her chin. "You're the reason I didn't die of loneliness out at the ranch, Van. You're the reason I realized it wasn't my fault Dad treated me the way he did." Her voice firmed. "You listened to me in a way no one else ever has. You made me feel important. Like I mattered to someone."

He stood there, saying nothing, staring at her, and she couldn't read the expression on his face. "I never told anyone the truth," he said harshly, abruptly. "Not my men, not my brothers, not Dad. No one."

She blinked. What on earth was he talking about? "The truth? The truth about what?"

"The truth about Sofia."

"Sofia?"

"The woman I was supposed to protect in Columbia. The woman who died."

There was something in his voice that made her heart skip a beat and sent a chill whispering over her skin. "What truth?"

"It was my fault she died." His tone was curiously blank. "I killed her."

"But you said it was a stray bullet—"

"The bullet was mine."

The chill gripping her deepened. "What?"

"We were on the run for three days, in the jungle, with

mercenaries after us. It was in the middle of the night and she was on watch because I hadn't slept for two days. She woke me up, told me that there were people nearby, that she'd heard them, so I told her to go find a place to hide. That I'd deal with the people then come find her, and she wasn't to move until I did." His hands slowly closed into fists at his sides, the look in his eyes burning with a cold, green light. "It was dark, but I managed to take the guys on our tail out. Then I went to find her, except she didn't answer when I called her name. I ended up searching for about an hour or so before I realized that what I thought was one of the mercenaries was her. She was supposed to stay put but I guess she must have gotten scared or something and tried to run." He paused. "Like I said. It was dark and I'd had no sleep, and all I saw were shadows in the jungle. But I shot her, Chloe. I shot her thinking she was one of them."

There were tears in her eyes, a terrible grief in her heart. Her chest ached at the look on his face, at the sudden anguish that burned in his eyes. He was a man who protected people, who took care of them. It was what he'd been raised for since Noah had adopted him and it was the standard he'd had to measure himself against ever since. And to have lost someone like this, to have been the agent of their death . . .

God, she couldn't even imagine.

She slipped off the couch, made as if to move toward him, her first instinct to offer comfort in some way, but he shook his head. "No." The word was flat, hard. "Stay there."

"Van—"

"I have to make it up to her. I have to make her death mean something." His eyes glittered, hard as emeralds. "That's why I stayed in the military, why I told Dad he could find another heir. It was my failure that killed her and so it was my duty to make up for it."

She swallowed, her throat aching. "Why are you telling me this?"

"So you know what I am. So you know that there will always be a mission for me, always responsibilities I have to take up. I can't refuse them, Chloe. I have to put them first, before everything. Otherwise Sofia's death will be for fucking nothing."

"I'm sorry, Van." It was pathetic and paltry, but she didn't know what else to say. "I'm so sorry that happened to you."

His strong features looked starker somehow, sharper, as if his skin had pulled suddenly tight over the bones of his face. "I'm sorry too. Because I can't give you what you want. I can't give you love, Chloe. I can't ever give you that."

"It's okay," she began thickly.

But he shook his head. "It's *not* okay. I'm going to call my secretary. Get her to ready the jet."

She didn't understand what was happening. "What? Why?"

"Because you're leaving." The look in his face was shuttered. "It's time for you to go home."

A week ago the mention of home would have made her happy, would have been a relief. But now it made something crack inside her.

"What do you mean I'm leaving?" She struggled to make sense of what was happening. "But I thought you wanted me to stay here, to marry you."

"I was wrong." His tone was clipped. "I can't marry you. And I won't force you to be with me when I can't give you what you want. I don't want to do what Dad did to you." He had that look in his eyes now, the one he got when he was giving orders, no argument possible. "You'll probably want to head back to Wyoming, but maybe it would be a good idea to head overseas for a while, put yourself out of de Santis's reach for a couple of months."

It felt like the floor had suddenly turned into ice beneath her feet and she was slipping and skidding around, her balance totally gone. "But . . . you said I was yours." Anger crept into her tone and she let it, because that was better than hurt, than desperation. "You said you were going to keep me. Or were those just more empty promises?"

His features tightened, that muscle leaping in his jaw again. "I know what I said. But I can't keep you after all. You deserve to have everything, Chloe. Everything you want and if I can't give it to you, you need to find someone who can."

Now the ice wasn't only affecting her balance, it was freezing her feet, her legs, rising up to her torso, wrapping frigid tendrils around her heart. So she reached for that anger, held onto it with everything she had.

"And the footage?" she snapped. "What about that? What about the company?"

"You don't need to worry about that. I'll deal with it."

"Van—"

"You wanted to know if I would have married you if there was no footage? No de Santis? No company?" There was something horribly final about the look on his face. "The answer is no. I wouldn't have."

Somehow, even when she'd asked that question, she'd known what his answer would be, and for some strange reason, it made something inside her settle as if a heavy weight had fallen on her.

He wouldn't have married her, she understood that. But not because he didn't want her, she was sure of that too, especially given the desperate way he'd taken her on her knees just before.

He wanted her but he wasn't going to let himself have her because of the woman who'd died. Because he was doing his best to keep saving her even though she was long dead. Because he was still trying to live up to the standards his father had set for him, even though Noah was dead too. Still trying to do the right thing, be the perfect Tate heir.

She couldn't fight that. She couldn't tell him to ignore the death he'd caused. She couldn't tell him to put *her* first.

She'd told him how she felt and he'd made a choice, and the choice wasn't her. It was duty over love for him, and now all she could do was respect the decision he'd made and do her best to deal with it. Wasn't that what you did when you loved someone? You respected their choices even when you didn't like those choices.

Her heart felt tender and bruised in her chest, and she felt a tear slip down her cheek. But she didn't wipe it away or try to hide it. These were her feelings and they were important, even if they were painful.

Crossing the space between them, she came to stand right in front of him, looking up into his hazel eyes. They'd gone dark, shadowed, but he didn't look away. "Okay," she said quietly, the heavy weight settling down inside her. "If that's the way you want it, then I'll go."

Surprise rippled through his gaze. "What? Just like that?"

"If you're expecting me to argue with you, Van, I'm not going to." She swallowed, her throat dry and sore. "I can't ask you to give up your mission and I can't demand to be put first, not after that. I understand you feel you have to do this and no, I don't like it, but I respect it."

He half-lifted his hand toward her, only to check himself at the last minute, pushing it into his pocket instead, his jaw hardening even more. "I didn't want to hurt you, Chloe. That was never my intention. You have to understand that."

Her bruised and battered heart felt like it was rubbing

itself raw against the cage of her ribs, but she tried to give him a smile all the same. "I know. I can't deny this doesn't hurt, because it does. It hurts a lot. But I'm strong. I'll be okay."

This time it was Van who looked away, his shoulders hunched, his posture tense. "I'm going to call Lucas to put you on the plane."

Chloe lifted a hand, wiping away her tears. "Fine."

He said nothing so she moved past him, heading toward the door.

"So, just like that?" The words hoarse-sounding, like they'd been forced out of him. "Not even a good-bye?"

Chloe stared at the door in front of her and suddenly her calm felt tenuous, as if it would crack straight through at the slightest touch. "No," she said thickly "I'm sorry. I can't."

And before he could say anything, she pulled the door open and walked through it, deafened by the sound of her heart shattering into a million tiny pieces.

Van completed the last pull-up then let go of the bar, landing on the floor. His muscles were screaming and he was covered with sweat, and yet it felt like he really hadn't done enough. Not nearly enough to block out the pain that was centered in the middle of his chest and the awful sense that somehow he'd made a colossal mistake.

He panted, eyeing the rowing machine for his next set.

He'd called Lucas a couple of hours ago, asking him to take Chloe to the airport and there must have been something hard in his voice because his brother didn't even argue. Which was a good thing. If he had, Van would probably have broken something. Preferably Lucas's face.

Coward. You couldn't even take her yourself.

He gritted his teeth, his jaw aching. No, of course he couldn't take her. He had to stay here and monitor the situation with de Santis. That footage would be going up on news sites everywhere and he had to be here to cope with the media storm that was going to be breaking any fucking minute.

He couldn't be heading off to the airport to say good-bye to one small woman who in one minute had revealed her strength in a way that put him to shame. She'd accepted his decision without even a protest, lifting that proud little chin of hers as she'd walked past him.

He'd been the one with desperation clawing inside him, unable to stop that last demand for a good-bye as she'd gone to the door. A good-bye she hadn't given him.

A good-bye you did not deserve.

He went over to the rowing machine and sat down, leaning forward to key in one of the most punishing programs. Then he began.

The hissing sound of the machine filled the room, the already stretched muscles of his chest and arms screaming even more.

He ignored them.

It had been the right decision to make. The only decision. She'd told him she loved him and he'd known in that moment he'd taken things too far. That forcing her to stay with him simply because he couldn't bear the thought of not having her was wrong.

She loved him. And marrying her, keeping her, without giving back what she'd so freely given him, would make him no better than his father. He refused to do that. He just fucking refused.

He'd meant it when he told her she deserved everything. She did. And if he couldn't give it to her, she needed to find someone who could. Someone who wouldn't give her all those empty promises, who would protect her and cherish her and give her the love she deserved.

But that someone wasn't him.

He hauled on the bars of the machine, the breath exploding from him as he powered through. Sweat streamed down his back, but he could still feel the pain in his heart. It throbbed like a bastard.

He'd had to send her away. He *had* to. He couldn't put someone else first, put them before the mission. Couldn't put Chloe ahead of the woman who'd died because of him. How could he? It wasn't fair to Chloe and it wasn't fair to Sofia's memory. It belittled both of them and he wasn't doing that.

Yeah, that's right. Use Sofia to excuse your own damn cowardice.

Van hauled hard on the rowing machine, his teeth bared in a feral snarl, both to that fucking pain that wouldn't go away and to the thought in his head.

He wasn't a coward. He'd fucked up eight years ago and shot a civilian by mistake, a woman who trusted him to bring her home. How the hell could he justify putting Chloe ahead of what he owed Sofia?

Christ, if he only ever did one right thing in his crappy life, then letting Chloe go was it. It was the only way to protect her from even more hurt, even more pain. Leaving her free to find someone who was truly worthy of her.

It might hurt her to start with, but she'd get over it and if he handled the situation right, the media attention that would hit after that footage went live wouldn't even touch her. He'd have a metric ton of crap to deal with himself, but he could deal with it.

He was going to have to.

Why is handling a media storm easier than telling Chloe you love her?

Van let go of the bars of the machine all of a sudden, the thing recoiling with a snap. His shoulders, chest, and thighs were screaming in agony, yet the pain he couldn't bear was the one inside him, where his heart should be.

What the hell was all this about loving her? He *didn't*
love her, at least not in the way she wanted him to. He'd
told himself not to get involved and he hadn't. End of story.

Yet even to himself that sounded hollow, an empty justification with no meaning.

"Fuck." Van got off the rowing machine, paced restlessly over to the windows then back again. There was a
water bottle lying on the floor next to the machine and he
abruptly picked it up and threw at the wall. It exploded
in a shower of plastic, water streaming down the wall.
"Fuck!"

No, he didn't feel better. Not one bit.

Trying to get a handle on himself, he stalked out of the
gym and into the bathroom, shoving the mixer shower to
cold. Then he stripped off his sweaty clothes and stood
under the stream, forcing himself to stay there as the water
turned his heated skin to ice.

That didn't help either.

He was almost blue by the time he got out, but ignoring the fact that he was basically freezing, he pulled on a
clean tee and a pair of jeans, then went downstairs to his
father's office to check the news media sites.

The house was silent. Lucas must have come and taken
Chloe away.

Good. Saying good-bye was hard and it was easier on
her if they didn't.

Another justification that sounded good, yet the pain in
his chest squeezing so hard he almost couldn't breathe told
him what a goddamn lie it was.

Fucking coward.

Van stepped into the office, slamming the door behind
him so hard the thing rattled on its hinges. He went over
to the desk and sat down, pressing a button on the computer keyboard.

No doubt that footage would be up by now, which meant

it was time to deal with the mess de Santis had created
for him.

Then he noticed there was an envelope sitting next to
the keyboard with his name written on the front of it.

Frowning, he picked it up, examining it. Who the hell
had left him this? He didn't recognize the handwriting, but
of course there was only one person it could have been
since no one else had been in the house.

Chloe.

He ripped the envelope, his hands shaking for some stupid reason, and a piece of paper slipped out. Unfolding it
carefully, she spread the paper out on the desktop.

> *Van, there's one last thing I need to tell you. It's
> about Dad and the oil. De Santis told me that it wasn't
> him who tried to steal the oil from Dad. It was Dad
> who stole it from him. The strike was on his land and
> Dad had the boundaries altered so it looked like it was
> on Tate land instead. He didn't give me proof, but I
> believe him. He had no reason to lie.*
>
> *I'm sorry.*
> *Chloe.*

Van stared at the words on the page and waited for the
shock to hit at the revelation of yet another lie Noah had
told, and waited for the anger to rise along with it.

But neither came. It was as if he already knew and,
more, it was like he just didn't care. Not about his father
or the oil or even goddamn de Santis. He didn't care
whether Noah had stolen it and he didn't care whether it
was true or not.

*He wasn't perfect, what a fucking surprise. So why the
hell are you still trying to be?*

Abruptly, he couldn't breathe. As if all the air in the
room was slowly being sucked away, and this was worse

than that fucking drown-proofing test when he'd been doing his BUD/S training. Way, way worse. There, you were in a pool and your hands and legs were tied, and all you had to do was complete a series of exercises, no biggie. But he wasn't underwater here and there were no exercises to do, he just . . . couldn't fucking breathe.

Jesus, he *wasn't* trying to perfect. He was about as imperfect as a man could get and he knew it.

Yet you're still trying to do the right thing. Still trying to save the company. Still trying to save Sofia. Still putting those standards of Noah's ahead of everything else. Ahead of Chloe.

Yeah, but he couldn't forget Sofia. It was part of his past. And he couldn't tell himself her life hadn't mattered, because it did. Yet . . . he'd thought he'd accepted that he wouldn't ever live up to Noah's vision of what he wanted Van to be. He'd thought he'd refuted it.

So why are you working yourself into screaming agony then freezing yourself in an icy cold shower? How does that honor Sofia's death? How does it help anything? How does it fix the mistake you made?

It didn't. It was only more of what he'd been doing for the past eight years. Punishing himself, martyring himself. Telling himself it was all about missions and protecting people, and all kinds of bullshit, when it wasn't any of those things.

No, all it was, was him trying to ease the guilt of a mistake he shouldn't have made, trying to be the man his father wanted him to be. And that wasn't honoring Sofia's death or being any kind of man at all. That was just fucking wallowing in it.

That was using both as an excuse not to have to admit the truth—that he was in love with Chloe Tate and it scared the shit out of him.

The realization was like someone had stuck an oxygen

mask on his face, inflating his lungs, filling them with air. Making him breathe, making him gasp. And he had to resist the urge to shove back his chair and just run the fuck after her, sprint the whole goddamn way to the airport then fall on his knees, tell her he didn't give a shit about how wrong or otherwise it was to be with her, he just couldn't bear to be without her another minute more.

But no. This required more. This required true commitment. If he was going to lay his imperfect heart at her feet, this required him to be a motherfucking SEAL and step the fuck up.

No retreat, no surrender.

Van slipped one hand into his pocket and found the small, round stone that had somehow found its way in there, and he curled his fingers around it. Then he reached for his phone.

He had something big to arrange.

CHAPTER TWENTY-ONE

Chloe stared blankly at the neon painted city as it passed by out the windows. How ironic that after years of being desperate to come with her father to New York, she couldn't wait to get out of the goddamn place.

Lucas kept shooting her narrow looks as he drove, but she ignored him.

Her heart didn't hurt anymore, nothing did. She felt empty, light as a soap bubble. As if her seat belt was the only thing keeping her anchored.

Which was fine. Numbness was preferable to pain, to the aching sadness that had filled every part of her as she'd gathered her meager belongings together and put them in her duffel.

Still, it wouldn't hurt forever and once she got back to the ranch, there would be so much to do she wouldn't have time to think about it. To think about him and what he'd meant to her, what they'd found together here.

She would get over this. She was strong.

"What's going on between you and Van?"

The sound of Lucas's voice was abrupt after the sudden silence, almost making her jump. "There's nothing going on." She didn't want to talk about it and definitely not to him.

"There's something," he disagreed. "You're looking like

somebody died and Van was grumpy as fuck. What happened?" He paused, and suddenly the note in his voice was all threat. "He didn't hurt you or anything?"

She turned from the view of the city to stare at Lucas's perfect profile. "Who? Van?"

"Of course Van."

"No," she snapped, anger stirring in the emptiness inside her. "He didn't." At least he hadn't physically. Emotionally? That was a different story. "What the hell do you care anyway?"

"Because if he did," Lucas went on, as if she hadn't spoken, "I'll kill him."

"Yeah, thanks for the support." Her tone was acid. "But I'm only sad to be going home, nothing else." She turned to look out the window again, hoping he wouldn't see the truth. "And as for Van . . . I've got no idea what he's so annoyed about."

"What about de Santis? Has all that been handled then?"

Chloe kept her gaze on the city passing by. "Yes," she said, because it was the easiest answer to give. "That's all over now."

Lucas said nothing to that, and for another couple of minutes silence reigned.

Then his phone buzzed, and he cursed.

She glanced at him.

He had one hand on the wheel, the other holding his phone, and he was glancing down at the screen, a frown on his face. "Make up your fucking mind," he muttered.

Something inside her tensed. "What's wrong?"

He didn't answer. Instead, he put the phone down and hauled on the wheel, turning the car around in a screech of tires.

Chloe blinked. "Where are we going?"

"Back," he said cryptically.

"Back where?"

"You'll see."

Her heart began to speed up. Was there another problem? Was it the footage going out? What?

She stared sharply at Lucas, but that hard, intent look that he'd had when he'd rescued her earlier that day wasn't there. No, now he merely looked pissed off, which had to mean nothing too serious was going down, right? Or maybe that was just wishful thinking on her part.

"Is there a problem?" she asked sharply

"No."

"Lucas—" Chloe began.

"Chill," he murmured, before she could finish. "It's not dangerous, okay? We're going to Rockefeller Center."

Surprise made her blink. "What?"

He lifted a shoulder. "I don't know. That's just where I was told to go.

"So . . . we're not going to the airport?"

"No."

Chloe struggled to process what was going on. "Who told you that?"

He gave her another of those piercing glances. "It's a surprise."

A surprise? What the hell did that mean? "Are you not allowed to tell me or something?"

Lucas only shrugged again, refusing to answer any more questions and falling silent.

Great. He'd told her to chill, but how was she supposed to chill when he wouldn't tell her what on earth was going on?

They headed back into Manhattan, the traffic beginning to build up, and she had a weird sense of deja vu as the streets began to get familiar. Well, of course they did. She'd come here a couple of nights ago, in the taxi with Van.

Her gut clenched at the reminder, her throat constricting.

She didn't want to be here, not where she'd been with him. Where she'd kissed him. Where everything had gone wrong.

Yet Lucas pulled the car up to the curb all the same, keeping the engine running as he turned to her. "Out, Chloe. Someone's going to be meeting you."

"Who?"

"Get out and you'll see."

"Lucas—"

"Come on." He glanced down at his watch. "I've got other shit to do."

"But what about the airport?"

"Fucked if I know. Are you going to get out or what?"

Well and why the hell not? Wasn't like there was anyone champing at the bit to see her in Wyoming. And besides, if there had been any real danger, Lucas wouldn't be telling her to get out, she was pretty sure of that.

Chloe lifted her bag, preparing to open the door, and suddenly became conscious of the weight of it dragging her down. Ah, the snow globe. She'd been going to leave it behind then had decided against it.

An impulse took her and she didn't question it, unzipping the bag and pulling out the little globe, a tiny replica of the building towering above her with an even tinier rink in front. She shook it, a flurry of white flakes obscuring the tiny skaters on the rink.

Why was she taking this with her? Did she really need another reminder of a man's empty promises? Wasn't the ache in her heart reminder enough?

Lucas frowned. "What the fuck is that?"

"It's a snow globe." She let out a breath. "But I don't need it anymore. Here." She reached over, placing it in Lucas's lap. "You can have it."

"What?" Surprise crossed his ridiculously handsome face. "But I don't—"

"Thanks Lucas," she said, opening the car door. "I'll see you 'round sometime." Then she got out, slamming the door behind her, cutting off his protests.

People streamed by her. It was cold but not sleeting the way it had been the night before, though there was the bite of snow in the air.

She looked up at the building towering above her, the bag on her shoulder feeling light as a feather, and somehow her heart feeling lighter too. As if giving away the snow globe had gotten rid of a few things that had been weighing her down.

"Miss Tate?" someone behind her said.

She turned around to find a man wearing a jacket with the ice rink logo on it standing behind her. "Yes?"

He smiled, professional and pleasant. "I was asked to come and meet you, and take you to the rink."

The rink? What the hell was going on?

Chloe eyed him. "Why?"

The man's smile didn't budge. "If you'll come this way?"

Okay, so whoever was behind this was doing their damnedest to make it a surprise. And she guessed she had nothing to lose by going along with it.

She lifted a shoulder. "Okay."

The man beamed. "Follow me, please." Then he turned and began to move through the crowds of people in the direction of the ice rink.

Chloe followed along after him, her heartbeat suddenly sounding loud in her head. Whatever was going on, it couldn't be all that sinister if it involved one of the ice rink employees, right?

The man led her down the steps but not to the ticket office. Instead, he took her to a glassed-in area, where there was a sign that said VIP igloo and lots of velvet ropes cordoning things off. Inside the igloo someone took her bag, while someone else handed her a pair of skates, ushering her to sit down while they assisted her with putting them on.

As she pulled on the laces, she looked around, trying to see what this was all about, but there was no one else in the VIP area and, weirdly, the rink seemed empty too. There weren't any people even clustered around it.

How odd.

When she'd finished with her skates, the man who'd first greeted her came back, showing her to a special door that led outside to the rink.

"What's happening?" she asked as he opened the door for her. "Where's everyone else?"

The man smiled. "It's just you, Miss Tate. You and the gentleman."

The gentleman? What gentleman?

But then the man was urging her out and so she went, shivering as she came out into the cold, frosty air.

It was empty, the ice white and smooth and perfect.

Well, nearly empty.

Down one end, standing on the ice, was a very tall man in a long black overcoat. Watching her.

Her breath caught in her throat, her vision blurring as stupid instant tears welled up, and she found herself unable to move. But it was okay because he was moving toward her, gliding over the ice with the easy, fluid grace with which he did everything.

Van slid to a stop in front of her, his expression fierce, his eyes molten gold. "You came." The familiar deep rumble of his voice made her catch her breath.

She swallowed past the lump in her throat. "Y-Yes."

"I wasn't sure if you would." His gaze roved her face as if memorizing it. "So I told Lucas not to tell you it was me. I wanted it to be a surprise."

Chloe blinked her tears away hard. "I'm not really up

to surprises right now, so you'd better tell me what this is all about. And fast."

That intent, burning look in his eyes didn't even flicker. "There are some things I need to say and you don't have to listen. But"—slowly, he held out his hands—"I'd like it if you would. Will you skate with me?"

She didn't know why this was happening, why he'd had her brought here when he'd told her he was sending her away, but one thing she did know. There was something in his face that was desperate, and she couldn't find it in herself to refuse.

So she said nothing, merely put her hands into his.

His gaze flared, suddenly brilliant, and then his long, warm fingers were interlaced with hers and she was being drawn out onto the ice.

He began to skate backward, holding onto her hands, his gaze pinned to hers.

She let herself be pulled along. "Where's everyone else?"

"There is no one else. It's just you and me."

Her heartbeat was going wild, his touch sending it galloping around inside her chest like a runaway horse, and there was no sound but for the scrape of their skates on the ice.

"I need to tell you that I made a mistake, Chloe," Van said at last. "I shouldn't have sent you away."

Oh. One of those ridiculous tears escaped and she almost stumbled on the ice, his strong grip the only thing stopping her skates from going out from under her. "I don't understand," she said, her voice almost as unsteady as her feet. "I thought you couldn't give me what I wanted. That the mission would always come first."

He was silent a moment, gliding backward, but he didn't look away from her. "I know. I was wrong."

All the breath went out of her and she found she'd

stopped skating, his momentum the only thing keeping them moving across the ice. "Why?" she asked at last, staring at him, conscious of nothing but the deep amber glow in his eyes and the feel of his fingers wrapped around hers. "What changed your mind?"

"You left me that letter, about de Santis and Dad. And I read it. And I sat there waiting for the shock to hit, but it didn't. It was like I already knew. Dad was so . . . flawed. And it made me realize that I was still holding myself to his standards, still trying to be the man he wanted me to be. But then he wasn't perfect, so why was I still trying?"

"Oh." Her voice sounded scraped raw and thready, and she couldn't think of a single thing to say.

"And then I realized something else," he went on, his fingers tightening around hers, the cold air moving softly over her face as they glided across the ice. "All this time I've been trying to make Sofia's life mean something, because I fired the bullet that killed her. Because Dad brought me up to be the perfect heir, the protector of the legacy. But sitting there, denying what I felt for you wasn't honoring her memory. It was only protecting a legacy created by a deeply flawed man. It was also protecting me."

Van pulled her closer gently, still gliding backward, effortlessly controlling their momentum. "You're not a mission, pretty thing, and you're not a responsibility. And telling you that you were, that I couldn't put you first, was just another excuse to keep myself safe. Because I'm shit scared. I'm in love with you, Chloe Tate, and I've been trying to use every excuse under the sun to not admit it." He was so warm, so strong, holding her as if he never wanted to let her go. "I can't be perfect and I can't ever atone for what I did. Christ, I was never good enough for Dad, and I'm sure as hell not good enough for you. But the only way I can think of to make Sofia's life mean anything at all, to leave Dad's legacy well and truly behind, is to tell you that I love you."

Her throat ached and either her heart had expanded or her ribs had closed up tight, because suddenly her chest was aching too. Letting go of his fingers, she slid her hands up his forearms to bring herself closer, keeping her gaze on the strong, intense lines of his face.

The air had gotten colder and it was full of snowflakes, white and fluffy, settling on his black hair and on the shoulders of his overcoat. She could feel them settle on her too, the cold breath of them against her cheek.

"You don't need to be perfect, Sullivan Tate," she forced out, her voice cracked and more than a little hoarse. "You only need to be exactly who you are. Who you always were. A protector. A defender. Honest and caring and trustworthy." She looked up into his eyes, a deep, smoldering gold. "A good man. A better man than Noah ever was."

He could feel the heat of her hands soaking through his overcoat and she was staring at him with all the wild passion that was part of her, as if every one of those things were true. And he found himself wishing with everything in him that they were.

But it was hard to accept. Especially after all the years spent punishing himself for not being the man he thought he had to be.

"I don't know if that's true," he said at last, watching little flakes of snow settle on her hair. "I only know that I love you. That I need you. And that sending you away was the stupidest thing I ever did."

A flame burned bright in her eyes and her mouth curved.

They were skating and it was snowing, and there were flakes in her black hair and everywhere, and she was smiling. She was fucking *smiling,* that wonderful, joyous, challenging smile. The one he'd seen that day on Shadow Peak, when she'd raced him home.

"Why did you bring me here, Van?"

He found his own mouth curving, giving her back that smile. "You really want to know? Because of that damn snow globe." He began to slow down, bringing them to a stop in the center of the ice. "Because I thought you needed some better memories of this ice rink than as a reminder of Dad and all his empty promises." Gently, he let her go, watching as her eyes widened. "You asked me if there was no footage, if there was no company, if it was just you and me, whether I would marry you. Well, I can't get rid of the company and I can't stop that footage from going up, but I can make sure it's just you and me out here so . . ." He dropped down on one knee, ignoring the cold wetness of the ice soaking through the denim of his jeans. "Will you marry me, pretty?"

Her mouth opened, her eyes widening even further, and a flush had crept into her cheeks.

The snow fell around them, thick and heavy, blocking out all sound, enclosing them in a snow globe of their own.

"Yes," she said, her voice clear and steady. "Yes, I damn well will."

She was so beautiful. She was everything he'd ever wanted.

Van came to his feet in a surge, pulling her into his arms, kissing her, tasting the bite of snow and the sweet flavor that was all her.

That pain in his heart was still there and it probably always would be. But it was a good pain, he knew that now. It was a pain he could accept.

Because that pain was love.

EPILOGUE

Chloe stared at the envelope sitting next to the plate of eggs and bacon that Van had made her for breakfast. They were going to eat then head out to the airport, take the corporate jet to Wyoming since she was needed back at the ranch. Plus, laying low out there seemed like a good idea since the media had been all up in their grille after the footage of their kiss had been leaked. And of course the news that they'd gotten engaged had only added fuel to the fire.

In fact, they'd been pretty much forced to stay in the Tate mansion by the cameras that kept being shoved in their faces every time they stepped outside. Not that Chloe minded being inside for once, not when she and Van were getting plenty of exercise. The kind of exercise you could do in bed. Or on the floor, or in the shower, or . . . anywhere really.

She shifted on her chair, wondering if he was still in the gym, and whether he'd like a visitor.

You're stalling.

Yeah, okay. She was.

She looked down at the envelope. It had arrived that morning from the Tate family lawyers and she already knew what it was about. Van had told her. Apparently her father had left a letter for her after all. He'd given the lawyers instructions that it was to be sent to her a month after his death, but Van had argued that she needed it ASAP. Chloe herself hadn't been sure she needed it ASAP, though she didn't tell Van that. He'd managed to deal with one of Noah's bombshells and so would she.

Reaching out, Chloe picked up the envelope and tore it open, extracting the letter inside it.

It wasn't long.

> *My dearest Chloe, you may be wondering why you're getting this fully a month after my death. Well, I thought you'd need time to grieve and to process everything. No doubt you've found out the truth about a great many things, none of which will be easy for you to hear.*
>
> *Firstly, I couldn't leave you a thing, sweetheart. Not given who your father is. I couldn't let him use you and so I made sure you would be of no value to him. I've left instructions that the Tate ranch is to go to you should the de Santis threat be successfully neutralized. You always did like the horses.*
>
> *Secondly, I'm sorry. I have done so many things in my life that I'm not proud of, but you should know that keeping you was never one of them. I know I lied to you, told you that I was your real father, but in my defense, I did have a very good reason. It's actually very simple. It was because I very much wanted to be.*
>
> *Except I'm afraid that, even though I tried, I wasn't a very good father, not to you or to the boys. But please know that I loved all of you very, very much.*
>
> *I can't say more. There's too much and none of it is good.*
>
> *You and the boys were the family I didn't deserve.*
> *All my love, Dad.*

A tear slipped down her cheek, then another, then another.

Then warm arms were sliding around her waist and she was being drawn back against the hot, hard wall of a very male chest.

"Damn you, Noah Tate," Van said, his voice rumbling in her ear.

Chloe relaxed into him, letting the tears fall, her heart aching. But it was a good ache, simply grief this time, nothing more. "That'll teach you to read over people's shoulders."

His arms tightened around her. "That sounded an awful lot like a man ashamed of what he'd done."

"He probably was. It was probably why he kept all of us at a distance." She sniffed, brushing away the tears. "Shall we tell Wolf and Lucas?"

Van's short laugh vibrated against her back. "Let's wait until they don't want to kill me for getting engaged to you."

She grinned, blinking away the last of her tears, and turned around, looking up into his beautiful face. He was freshly showered, smelling of soap and shampoo, and home. "That might take a while." His brothers had made their thoughts on her and Van's engagement pretty clear, and it didn't look like they were going to change their minds any time soon.

"True." Van's eyes gleamed gold. "In that case, let's go back to bed."

"But what about my breakfast?"

He gave her a look. "Seriously? What's more important? Me or your damn breakfast?"

Chloe laughed and lifted her arms, winding them around his neck and bringing his mouth down on hers for an answer.

It was him. It was always him.

Looking for more hot billionaires?

Don't miss the next novel in the brand-new
Tate Brothers series

THE WICKED BILLIONAIRE

Coming soon from St. Martin's Paperbacks

Detachment. Distance. Control. That was how he'd lived his life after what had happened at the stables and he was happier for it. The wild swings of inexplicable emotion dampened, rage and pain and guilt blunted, muted. He didn't need those emotions anyway, and as for joy and happiness, well, they were overrated. Desire though, that was different. That was harder to get a handle on, but he was trying.

He had no time to be distracted from his mission and especially not after what had happened today, when he and Van and Wolf had dealt with the board at Tate Oil, and then afterwards, the unexpected arrival of Van and their foster sister Chloe, at Leo's Alehouse. Lucas hadn't even known Chloe was in New York, but it turned out that Van had brought her here from the ranch in Wyoming. Apparently their father's enemy, Cesare de Santis, was after her for some reason and the Tate mansion on the Upper East Side was compromised, which meant Van needed to take her somewhere to hide her. The situation was serious so Lucas had offered them his own Soho apartment since he was here with Grace. Van had been grateful, which in turn had reminded him of the seriousness of his own situation too. Of the danger to Grace and how he really needed to get a handle on it. Deal with it and fast, because the longer it went on, the longer he was going to have to remain here with her. The longer he was going to have to manage the intensity of the chemistry between them.

"You're an arrogant son of a bitch," Grace said, her lovely mouth flattening.

He ignored that, ignored the way his body was hardening in response to her nearness and that delicious, faintly apple scent of hers. "And you're a liar."

Her gaze flickered and she straightened, drawing away from him. The movement pulled the silky fabric of her tunic tightly across her breasts, outlining the hard points of her nipples. Another giveaway.

"Not that it matters" he added. "I simply want you to be clear."

She stared at him for a long moment, then her gaze dropped to the open neck of his shirt. Slowly she leaned over him again, more deliberate this time, her hair suddenly a scented curtain around them. Christ, what did she wash her hair with? It smelled of apples too.

You're thinking about the way her hair smells? What the fuck is wrong with you?

"Thanks for telling all of that." She lifted those long, cool fingers of hers, taking the cotton of his shirt between them. "And I'm sorry about your family. That must have been terrible, and I'm sorry about your foster father too." She slid the button out and he felt the electricity of her touch as her finger grazed lightly against the bare skin of his throat. It was the merest brush, yet he felt it move like lightning through him.

Her breath caught, the delicate flush in her cheeks deepening, making her freckles stand out. She hadn't meant to touch him, it was clear, yet when her gaze lifted to his, there was nothing but challenge in her amber eyes. "But all of that doesn't give you the right to assume you know jack shit about me or what I want."

There was a roaring in his ears, his heart rate beginning to climb. She was leaning against his knees, her long, willowy body stretched out over his and all it would take would be a small nudge and he'd have her over his lap. Then he'd take her down onto her back on the couch, crush her beneath him . . .

Jesus Christ, he was cold. And she was so fucking *hot*.

He stared back at her, unmoving, looking into her eyes because he couldn't bring himself to look away, reading challenge in them loud and clear.

Ah, yes. Like he'd challenged her to undo his tie, now she was giving that same challenge back to him. Fuck, what did she think he was going to do? Run away? Didn't she know that a man like him would *always* answer a challenge like that? And he'd fucking win, too.

Yeah and you should stop fucking panicking too. This is a test, remember? You're a goddamn SEAL. If the test isn't hard, maybe you should join the army instead.

That was true. Also, he wasn't thirteen anymore, battling a rage that seemed to have no end, a rage that really didn't have anything to do with the gun he'd been denied, but something else. Something he didn't understand and didn't have a name for.

He was stronger now. He'd been in perfect control of himself for years. He'd been on missions that had broken lesser men, and this woman, the widow of his best friend, wasn't going to make him lose it no matter how warm and elegant, no matter how smart or fascinating or downright desirable she'd become to him.

He'd never been a weak man and he wasn't about to start now.

A test . . . . Time to make this test harder.

Lucas didn't say anything. Instead, keeping his gaze

on hers, he lifted his hand, moving slowly so she could see what he was doing. With extreme deliberation, he pushed his fingers into her hair, curling them around the back of her fragile, beautifully shaped skull. The red-gold locks were as soft and silky as he'd imagined they'd be, softer even, and warm against his palm.

Her mouth opened soundlessly, her eyes going wide in shock.

She hadn't expected this, clearly.

Excellent. This would be a test for her too.

Keeping one hand on the back of her head, Lucas gently skimmed one finger across her cheekbone. She didn't speak, her breathing getting faster and faster, her small gasps audible in the dense silence of the apartment. Her eyes had gone black, only a thin rim of gold around the outside of them.

She looked . . . exposed almost, the vivid, compelling planes and angles of her face vulnerable.

Who else got to see her like this? Griffin had, obviously, but he was betting no one else ever saw her like this. Only him. The thought was vaguely satisfying.

He held her darkened gaze with his as he tightened his fingers on the back of her neck, drawing her down with aching slowness until at last - *at last* - her mouth was on his.

Electricity ran the entire length of his body, looking for a place to ground itself and finding nowhere, and it as only through sheer force of will that he managed to hold into his control. To resist the urge to ravage that soft, vulnerable mouth, pull her to the floor and get inside her any way he could.

His heart was racing and refused to slow, none of his usual exercises were working, the beat of it loud and insistent in his head. But he didn't stop what he was doing. He'd had harder tests than this in his training. One soft mouth wasn't going to get the better of him.,

And it *was* soft. So fucking soft. And trembling slightly.

He began to explore the seam of her lips with his tongue. Gently, with care. Coaxing her to open to him.

She shook, a husky noise escaping the back of her throat as her mouth opened gradually to him.

So much *heat.* She tasted like coffee and something else, something sweet, and that heat was suddenly roaring up inside him, like a smoldering fire bursting into life with a breath of wind. No, scratch that. This was like someone had poured gasoline directly onto an open flame, turning it white hot, bright and consuming.

If this is a test, you're failing it.

No, he fucking wasn't. He could control this and he would.

Lucas made himself go very still, every muscle in his body tight, trying to force his heartbeat to slow the fuck down. At the same time, he began to kiss her with deliberate slowness, pushing his tongue into her mouth and exploring deeper, letting the flavor of her go straight to his head.

Testing himself. Testing her.

She trembled again, one hand coming down on the back of the couch near his shoulder while she put the other on the arm, as if she needed to lean against something for balance. But she didn't pull away, her mouth open and so damn sweet, and her hair was like the softest silk thread. She was leaning into him now, her body pressing against his legs, and the warm musky smell of her was making his head swim. Then she touched her tongue to his, tentatively, as if she had no idea how to kiss, and he knew if this went on any longer, he *was* going to fail this test and spectacularly.

He began to pull away, gripping the back of her head when she tried to follow, holding her still until there was space between them and he was staring up into her eyes.

They were smoky and dark, her cheeks deeply flushed, and she looked half-dazed. Her mouth was was full and red and he all he could think about was pulling her back down and kissing her again, harder, deeper.